BEWARE THE MALINA!

The man lay sprawled at Nikolai Butkova's feet. Lifeless. His neck snapped like a chicken's.

"Take this traitor back to the drums," Butkova ordered. They followed him, dragging the dead man by gripping him under the shoulders.

The 55-gallon drum they opened contained hydrochloric acid, a highly corrosive, fuming liquid that hissed faintly when the air hit it.

"Head first," he said. "Shoes last. Let him slide in. Don't touch."

First the dead man's head and face disappeared, then his shoulders, chest, stomach, waist, hips, and thighs, finally his legs, ankles and feet. The hissing turned into an audible sizzle as the dead man became one with the acid—flesh, blood, bones, clothes, and all.

Three minutes later it was over.

Butkova raised his leg and kicked the 55-gallon drum on its side. They watched the acid drain into the dirt, melting the snow in an ever-widening circle.

"KGB," Butkova hissed. He glared at the three men. "You tell your people what you saw tonight. You tell them the next KGB informer I catch, I put him in the drum." He paused for effect. Then he screamed, *"Next time I put him in alive!"*

BLOCKBUSTER FICTION FROM PINNACLE BOOKS!

THE FINAL VOYAGE OF THE S.S.N. SKATE (17-157, $3.95)
by Stephen Cassell
The "leper" of the U.S. Pacific Fleet, SSN 578 nuclear attack sub SKATE, has one final mission to perform—an impossible act of piracy that will pit the underwater deathtrap and its inexperienced crew against the combined might of the Soviet Navy's finest!

QUEENS GATE RECKONING (17-164, $3.95)
by Lewis Purdue
Only a wounded CIA operative and a defecting Soviet ballerina stand in the way of a vast consortium of treason that speeds toward the hour of mankind's ultimate reckoning! From the best-selling author of THE LINZ TESTAMENT.

FAREWELL TO RUSSIA (17-165, $4.50)
by Richard Hugo
A KGB agent must race against time to infiltrate the confines of U.S. nuclear technology after a terrifying accident threatens to unleash unmitigated devastation!

THE NICODEMUS CODE (17-133, $3.95)
by Graham N. Smith and Donna Smith
A two-thousand-year-old parchment has been unearthed, unleashing a terrifying conspiracy unlike any the world has previously known, one that threatens the life of the Pope himself, and the ultimate destruction of Christianity!

Available wherever paperbacks are sold, or order direct from the Publisher. Send cover price plus 50¢ per copy for mailing and handling to Pinnacle Books, Dept.17-201, 475 Park Avenue South, New York, N.Y. 10016. Residents of New York, New Jersey and Pennsylvania must include sales tax. DO NOT SEND CASH.

THE MEATMAN

MIKE MALLOWE

PINNACLE BOOKS
WINDSOR PUBLISHING CORP.

PINNACLE BOOKS

are published by

Windsor Publishing Corp.
475 Park Avenue South
New York, NY 10016

First Pinnnacle Books printing: April, 1989

Printed in the United States of America

To Mary Beth, who loves me;
to my father, who believed in me,
and to my mother, who was there
every day, every page,
every minute with this book.

ACKNOWLEDGMENTS

This book has been every person I have ever known. A few, however, deserve special mention. Linda Brookman Vizi first told me about the Russian Mob. Then, she showed me where it lived. Mike Chitwood, the greatest detective of them all, was there every time I needed him. In his book, *Interpol,* Michael Fooner provided a splendid description of how that organization works. I admire his reporting and writing. His book is the definitive study. Alan Halpern, my old editor at *Philadelphia Magazine,* taught me how to write. And think. Adrian Zackheim is a creative partner in the same magnificent mold. Finally, my gratitude to Theron Raines, a wise, kind, tireless mentor, knows no bounds.

ONE

FLETCHER STREET,
GIRARD ESTATE,
SOUTH PHILADELPHIA
FRIDAY NIGHT,
ONE WEEK BEFORE CHRISTMAS

The air was as still as the breath in a dead man's lungs.

Whitey drank in the damp, bitter taste of the cold. He checked his watch. Almost 9:00 p.m. Inside a battered green van, rusted with body cancer near the wheel line, he waited. Muffled night sounds drifted through the open window on the driver's side where he sat, hunched forward over the steering wheel.

Every few minutes the half-heard noises and the low, soft moan of the wind broke the winter stillness. Alert, he listened.

Tonight, parked across the street from the Meatman's house, he kept a vigil in the van. High above him, a canopy of bare brown trees reached out from the edge of a frozen-turfed park where old men played bocce on warm summer afternoons. The sparse covering of the trees gave Whitey a sense of shelter and seclusion. It helped him concentrate.

Whitey's job was to make sure that the Meatman would never get the chance to become one of those grinning old bocce players. He had been planning what he had to do tonight for over a month, since before Thanksgiving, and now he was ready.

His nickname came from his white-blond hair, cut very close to his head. Fair skin with dry, thin lips and large, pinkish hands, chafed from exposure to the cold, exaggerated his pallor. So did his clothes. Whitey dressed almost entirely in black. A flat, bony face and high cheekbones made him appear gaunt and elongated his profile.

Whitey's eyes were brown and wide-set, placed a little too close to his forehead, and his whole face had a top-heavy appearance, as though the geography of it were somehow off. All the parts were there, but the arrangement was haphazard. Even when he smiled, his mouth tilted to the side. Self-conscious about this, he rarely smiled. His eyes, sheltered under steady, slightly hooded lids, betrayed a calm, detached cruelty.

Except for the clipped white-blond hair on his head, Whitey's body was almost totally hairless. Smooth, hard, muscled. His complexion had a waxy quality to it. Where the skin should have been soft, it felt, instead, slightly lacquered to the touch, like the slippery leaves of some enormous plant. The doctors attributed this to a rare vitamin deficiency that dated back to his childhood in Pittsburgh. To compensate Whitey covered every inch of his body, winter and summer, with warm, heavy clothing. He seldom sweated and he always felt cold. His flesh simply refused to absorb heat.

As a teenager, he had taught himself to be ambidextrous. His left-hand signature was almost identical to his right. At six-five and 175 pounds, he sometimes appeared almost spectral, thought he was only twenty-eight years old.

However, Whitey could be deceptively charming. He had a gentle, soothing way with people. That's usually how he caught them off-guard. He ate red meat sparingly and hardly ever touched liquor. His habits were monkish, his demeanor ascetic. Sometimes Whitey thought of himself as the only pure professional left in the world. He saw himself as a blinding gleam of light in a black, endless void. He believed in himself, nothing else.

Fixing his practiced eyes on objects far in the distance—a window box, an auto hubcap, a porch railing—he made certain that his night vision was sharp enough to identify each one. A shadow with a gun in its hand was the last thing Whitey needed tonight.

He was used to interpreting the messages that the darkness sent him, staring hard for any sign; but tonight, the blackness refused to surrender its mysteries and stared right back at him. He had a feeling that it was going to be like this—a long, cold waiting game. But he had a job to do, and Whitey was a professional.

He had always believed that a quiet street had its advantages. People and traffic and noises and movement were normally a good cover, too, but an empty street, in the bowels of the night, when most people were sleeping or thinking about it, offered an element of surprise that was hard to duplicate. All things considered, Whitey preferred working at night.

Suddenly he shivered as a random gust of wind hit the side of the van. The sleeping street seemed to sigh; the wind twirled neat mounds of trash and dead leaves at the curb. Whitey had been in the van for nearly an hour, since 8:00 p.m., memorizing the way the street looked in the dark, deciding the best place to plant the bomb, lining up his route of escape, plotting each detail, over and over again, mentally preparing himself for what had to be done.

Against his cheek, through the open window, he felt the first wet flurries beginning to fall. He hoped he would be able to finish the job before the snow slowed him down.

Whitey's eyes were focused on the Meatman's red brick rowhouse near the middle of the block. Tiny Christmas lights twinkled through his frosted windows. A huge, fresh evergreen wreath hung on his front door, cinched with a red satin bow.

He had never given a thought to the time of year, to Christmas, until tonight, until this job at the Meatman's house. But the whole block, located deep in South Philadelphia, in the section known as Girard Estate, was like a tinseled reminder that Christmas waited patiently behind each decorated door.

Here and there, in dormer peaks or doorways, fat plastic Santa Clauses smiled blankly, their cheeks rouged and round. Some of the houses had elaborate manger scenes in the bayed living room windows. Plaster of Paris wise men, their paint chipping after generations of use, stood poised to welcome the Virgin Birth once again.

The glow of a full moon, heavy and creamy, broke against the winter sky and transformed the street into a ghostly still life. Whitey took no peace from the scene. He was edgy. There was an element of risk in this job that bothered him. He had planned each detail very carefully, stalking the Meatman for nearly five weeks, but the flurries, silently swirling into a steady, gentle snowfall, suddenly seemed to Whitey to be threatening rather than fragile. He didn't have snow tires on the van. That was the one thing he had overlooked. Keyed up and nervous, he checked the side and rearview mirrors again, twisting around awkwardly to make certain that no one was approaching.

Glancing at the rooftops, he watched as their sharp right angles melted into a single, seamless line from his point of perspective near the park.

Whitey had been killing by contract ever since he left Special Ops. He couldn't keep count of all the jobs he had done, all the people he had tracked. But never had he killed a man this close to Christmas. Every situation was so different—unique. He had learned his craft in the army, in Beirut, mostly, but he had perfected it on dark, wind-swept streets like this one, pursuing the quarry, then striking.

The Meatman had been especially challenging, because he had no set routine; his movements varied too much. Eventually, though, Whitey learned enough to anticipate the Meatman's pre-Christmas ritual.

Still studying the top floors, he scanned the boxy roof directly above the Meatman's house, alert for the slightest sign of activity or any unexpected visitor. The eerie glow from a tall streetlamp cast the Meatman's house in a long shadow. Whitey could see only the falling snow, nothing else. No one was there. Blinking rapidly, he shook his head. He couldn't afford to have his eyes play tricks on him now, not after he had come this far.

Once again, Whitey surveyed the sleeping block of three-story porch-fronts. Night lights were on, doors bolted and locked. The street was tucked in for the night, tranquil. In the stillness Whitey could hear himself breathing—breathing a little too quickly. His ears were ringing, too—the kind of high-pitched persistent sound that usually bothered him only if he was forced to spend any length of time in a closed, stuffy room. The cramped front seat of the old van was beginning to make him feel claustrophobic, and by now his feet were numb. Resting his chin on the rolled-down window, he sucked deeply, gulping the raw December air to fill his lungs and clear his head.

Then, for the first time, Whitey spoke to the man who shared the front seat of the van with him.

Ever since they had parked across from the Meatman's house, Vinnie had been careful not to violate the unseen buffer of space that separated him from Whitey. With his body pressed closely against the door on the passenger's side, he had sat there in silence, waiting for Whitey to say something to him. Whitey had done his best to tune out Vinnie's presence, preferring the insulation of his own thoughts about the Meatman and the job they were there to do. But now, Whitey needed the young man.

Without ever shifting his brown-marble eyes from the street, Whitey suddenly ordered, "Get it now."

Instantly, the younger man reached behind the seat, stretched his body across the rippled metal floor, and felt around for a small round object that had been wrapped securely in a dark woolen army blanket. The blanket was soiled and damp and had a strong musty odor.

Slowly shifting back to his seat, he gently placed the bomb on his lap. He stared at it, and the feel of its solid weight resting across his thighs excited him.

"Do it," Whitey commanded again, his tone leaving no doubt as to who was in charge. "Put it exactly where I told you." As he spoke, he continued to look straight ahead, his eyes riveted on the front door of the Meatman's house.

Now. With Whitey, timing was everything. Plant the bomb too far in advance and the chance that someone might discover it by accident shot up alarmingly. He pictured what had to happen in his mind's eye with an engineer's precision, like chart lines intersecting on graph paper. Too soon was just as dangerous as too late. Now was the time, the moment; Whitey's point of no return. The kid had to do it now. The Meatman was headed home any minute. Whitey's calculations were unerring. He could feel everything beginning to mesh, each gear sliding smoothly into place. *Now*. Plant the bomb *now*.

The door on the passenger side opened and the younger man slipped out. Vinnie was twenty years old, and he worked as a cutter in a fur store during the day. He wore a ski cap, an army surplus jacket, and new designer jeans, purchased on sale only the day before. He was a careful shopper. His shirt was silk, his necklace gold.

Earlier that night he'd gone dancing with a girl named Tina. Tina was incredible. Long legs, black hair, hazel eyes. Unless he was working, like tonight, he was always thinking about Tina, remembering her scent and the down on her cheeks. He had hugged her against him on the dance floor of the after-hours club, felt her nipples pressing through the thin material of her dress, nuzzling against his chest. Then he had leaned down and kissed her on the neck—on the place just below her ear, the place that always made her sigh. When she left to go to the ladies' room, he had stared at her all the way across the dance floor. Vinnie had never seen another girl who moved like Tina.

Later, after he had dropped her off at her parents' house and kissed her again as they stood in the doorway shivering, he told her that he had to go to work. Work was the dented green van and the Meatman's house on Fletcher Street. Tina nodded and didn't say a word. She pulled the curtain back from the window and watched as Vinnie disappeared.

Now the kid, Vinnie, ran quickly and quietly through the park, crouching now and then near a bench. Once he rested his head against the cold wooden slats, shut his eyes tightly, and concentrated. He avoided the streetlights. He almost skated over the brittle, frozen ground. By the time he emerged from the park, just across Fletcher Street, just across from the Meatman's house, the swirling snow had turned his blue Sixers cap nearly white. Some of the flakes had attached themselves to the new dark mustache that didn't quite cover his upper lip yet. He'd started growing it because Tina had told him that guys with mustaches turned her on. All the way across the park Vinnie was rehearsing what he had to do, thinking hard about exactly where he would place the bomb, watching for any movement on the porch.

The bomb was wrapped thickly with adhesive tape, the dynamite completely covered. The rest of the package felt like a hard lumpy canister. Vinnie had no idea what was inside. Whitey had made the bomb; Vinnie's job was to deliver it.

The bomb is a very delicate instrument, Whitey had told him. Keep it dry; keep it level. The level Vinnie knew in his heart he couldn't do anything about, not running, not at night. The dry, though, he could handle.

He had used a razor from the fur store where he worked to cut a neat hole in the fabric of his heavy army jacket. First he had widened the fat pocket on the outside enough to accept the bomb. Then he had cut a hole in the lining of the jacket and sewn it up expertly to fashion a cool, dry pouch for the bomb. Now the device lay snug against his side.

All he had to do was plant the bomb just inside the aluminum storm door at the front of the Meatman's house. Fletcher Street. The middle of the block. 2117 Fletcher Street. He had memorized the address—not that he needed to; the house was hard to miss.

The Meatman's wreath was bigger than anyone else's. His lights went all the way up to the window peak of the second floor, and an almost life-size Santa was lashed onto the gray tiled roof. What a showoff prick, the kid thought. Typical. If you ever want to see where the mob guys live, a cop had once told Vinnie, drive down the street, look at who has the best Christmas lights or the biggest Easter bunny or the nicest pumpkin at Halloween. The cop knew his shit; he was 100 percent right.

If the Meatman or his bodyguard—if he had any with him or if any were hiding inside the house—suspected a setup, the planting of the bomb would instantly draw fire. The plan was dangerous, but Vinnie didn't care. Working with Whitey was a way in, a way up.

"If anything goes wrong," Whitey had instructed Vinnie, "just throw the bomb up on the Meatman's porch and get out of sight. I'll cover you and take it from there." Vinnie wasn't quite sure what that meant, but he trusted Whitey and wanted the older man to see that he knew how to follow orders.

From their first day together, the Friday after Thanksgiving, Whitey had developed a good reading on the kid and his motives. He knew that as long as he kept the instructions simple, Vinnie would do fine. Whitey seldom used an accomplice, and never a fellow professional, whom he might have to spend too much time watching to make sure he hadn't decided to go into business for himself.

South Philadelphia, though, where both the kid and the Meatman lived, was unfamiliar territory to Whitey. He really did need a second guy on this one. He had made up his mind quickly to go with Vinnie. The kid had been raised on these streets, and he seemed to know every one of the Meatman's people by sight. Whitey liked that.

At twenty, Vinnie was also too young and too green to have built up many binding loyalties. He was eager and hungry, and just bright enough—exactly the kind of second man that Whitey wanted on a job like this.

From the van, Whitey watched Vinnie's progress intently. If anything happened before the Meatman got home, anything at all, Whitey would floor the gas pedal, the van would screech away, and the bomb, cradled in the young man's jacket lining, would be radio-detonated from half a block away. Bye-bye, Vinnie.

It would have been better to blow up the kid and the Meatman at precisely the same moment with a flick of the little switch in his hand, but Whitey realized he would never be lucky enough to get both of them on the porch together. It was just as well, actually. Two bodies would have given the cops too much to go on. He could deal with the kid another way. No witnesses. Never any witnesses.

In the army, Whitey had been credited with killing fourteen of the enemy during one twelve-month reconnaissance tour in the field as a 97B, an army counterintelligence agent, airborne, a Ranger, on detached duty from a Special Operations force. After the first eighteen-week basic training course at Fort Huachuca, Arizona, Whitey had never once worn a uniform. No shoulder patches or medals or salutes. Just results. His had been a war of getting even—a kill for a kill.

That far back, Whitey had worked mostly on his own, selecting his targets, tracking them and killing them. The officers he reported to never asked how or why. The confirmation of a kill was sufficient. Whitey had experienced such a rush of excitement and satisfaction after his first kill that he knew he had found the one thing he had been made for.

Whitey could feel the small square detonator on the seat between his legs. His left hand was on the steering wheel; his right was wrapped around a .45 automatic. He felt that funny chill that always came over him when something good was about to happen. He blocked out every sight, every sound, every thought, and concentrated on Vinnie. So far, the kid was living up to his expectations.

He could have taken the Meatman out with one shot, but that wasn't the plan. This time it had to be a bomb. The plan was complicated, but he knew it could work. If not tonight, then some other night. Whitey would wait. Patiently.

Watching the kid loping through the falling snow, Whitey felt a tranquility that only the night could afford. No traffic, no people, no city noises. Hit the target, then escape into the darkness, barreling down some black, deserted street. Escape. Whitey was a night fighter. That was when his juices started churning, like tonight.

Vinnie took a deep breath, patted the bomb snug against his ribs, and hurried across the street. He knew that Whitey was following his every step.

His sneakers left rippled footprints in the snow. Could that be a problem? But Vinnie made it to the storm door so quickly that he even surprised himself. He had zigzagged almost up to the corner so that his footprints wouldn't lead directly to the house in the middle of the block. He hoped that Whitey would notice and approve.

He placed the bomb on the sill against the inner wooden door, made sure that it fit without pushing on the storm door, and then gently closed the storm door, careful that the handle latch caught. Perfect.

The snow was just starting to blow up onto the porch and drift a little. Vinnie was still concerned about his footprints. The Meatman wasn't stupid, and if he saw fresh tracks . . .

He decided then to hop over the porch railing and cut

through the tiny garden in front of the house. The grass would absorb the outline of his sneakers.

The kid headed for the park and the dark green van. His heart was pumping so fast, he felt almost light-headed. He had never been happier; had never sensed such exhilaration. He hoped Whitey would talk to him, tell him he had done a good job. Most of all, Vinnie wished that Tina could see him at work.

DOWNTOWN PHILADELPHIA

Paul "Meatman" Presto was fifty-six years old and in the prime of his life. He still carried his 230 pounds like a heavyweight, and his hair, although it was graying, was still thick and full. Even now he could break a man's arm with his fist, and he was remarkably quick on his feet for a man of his size. In a fight, the Meatman would be one tough son of a bitch to bring down.

As he drove his baby-blue Lincoln through the streets of downtown Philadelphia, Presto listened to the radio and hummed.

"Have yourself a merry little Christmas," sang the radio, and the Meatman almost started following along. "Don't worry," he said to the radio, "I will."

Presto had spent most of the day collecting money that was owed to him. Earlier that night, in the back-room office of a real estate company that he owned through two of his lawyers, the Meatman had also gotten laid on a lumpy couch, and he had loved it. It had made him feel like a young kid again.

The girl, about twenty-three, he guessed, was a secretary in the real estate office. Her name was Arlene. Presto had had his eye on her ever since the warm weather when she had come to work one day in a skimpy little sundress. After that, he always brought her coffee and buns from one of his bakeries or water-ice on hot days. The way she used to sit there and work her tongue over the water-ice, he knew that she was getting used to the idea.

He could have forced the issue a lot sooner, of course. He had done it dozens of times before. But he didn't want to; disciplined himself not to. Presto decided to wait her out. He wanted the girl to come on to him; wanted to know that he could still do it. Deep down he knew it was a game, but Paul Presto needed his hobbies.

Finally, just a few hours earlier, it had happened, there in the office as he was getting ready to leave. She had lingered behind, telling the others that she would lock up. Presto had understood. She'd taken him by the hand and led him into the small, cramped inner office. There she dropped to her knees in front of him, pulled the dress from her shoulders, and cupped her dark breasts in offering. *Padrone,* she called him as he reached toward her. Master. Then she started to undo his belt. Presto had to lean back against the wall to steady himself.

As Presto headed home, leaving tire marks in the snow, he felt as content as he usually did only after a delicious meal and a glass of fine wine. But *that* wasn't the appetite he had satisfied tonight. Savoring the memory, he smiled to himself, his big cheeks inflating like those of a grizzled old squirrel.

The Meatman's thick peasant lips and slightly puffy eyes bloated his face into a weary-looking mask this late at night. Beneath his eyes, on either side of his wide, prominent nose, the soft flesh was crisscrossed by thin red broken capillaries. Presto had led a hard life, and it showed. But still, his was a strong, square, confident face that had once been very handsome.

He grinned again, trying to recall each detail, every sensation, the faintest scent.

The girl had moaned under him, clawing at his shoulder, at the thick muscles across his back, squirming, shifting and twisting to accommodate him, breathing in short, rapid bursts, wrapping her long legs around him, arching, panting, just as excited as he was. Then, when she knew he was ready to explode, she had slipped out from beneath him and taken Presto into her mouth hungrily. He could still see her face, a damp mask of passion and sweat. When he came, his big body felt as if it were floating.

Later, as they lay pressed together in the darkness on the old couch, with her auburn hair a tangle of dark, wet strands across her forehead, Presto gently stroked her breasts, bringing the rigid nipples to life. When he made a motion to get up, she kissed him again, laid her head against him, and rubbed her cheek on the matted hair of his chest, begging him to stay just a little longer.

The Meatman considered the prospect of becoming her lover. He was amazed by her strength, her almost violent passion. *Padrone,* he thought approvingly.

Presto hadn't had a woman like that in a long, long time. He just hadn't cared. But now that he had done it, proved himself once again, he felt elated, young again.

The girl was still getting dressed as he got up to leave. "Merry Christmas," she whispered, then kissed him goodbye. As he left, Presto touched her cheek. *Padrone.*

A STOREFRONT ON BUSTLETON AVENUE, NORTHEAST PHILADELPHIA

A silk shirt—white-on-white, French cuffs, gold-knot cufflinks—covered Nikolai Butkova's upper right biceps, obscuring the bluish-purple tattoo. The tattoo depicted a cobra, its coils tight and vibrating, poised to strike, the big hood behind its head flared out and erect. A deadly cobra.

Only the women who slept with Butkova ever got to see the snake. They liked to trace its outline with the pointed tips of their polished nails. He always let them. Then he would roll over, use his bearish strength as he mounted them, and the slithering cobra on his biceps would bulge to life.

He was a businessman now, a prosperous emigré in Russian Bustleton, in Northeast Philadelphia, and tattoos were bad for business. They frightened people. Besides, when Butkova wanted to scare someone, he didn't rely on tattooed serpents.

He had been expecting several men, and the last of them, Boris, had just walked in, snow clinging to his boots. No one knocked. They knew by the light over his desk that he would be there. He greeted this last man with a warm, rough hug and a brusque kiss on each cheek. He was the one Butkova would depend on tonight. As long as Boris was strong, the others would be strong.

Crossing the room, he checked the street outside and reassured himself that the avenue was deserted. Then Butkova locked the door, turned to his men, and croaked orders to them in his hoarse, harsh voice.

FLETCHER STREET

Whitey had gambled that Presto wouldn't have any bodyguards with him tonight. Nobody in his organization had fired a shot in six months, and everyone's guard was down—exactly the set of circumstances that the man paying Whitey had been counting on.

They were across the street and down the block. Whitey had made sure to park in a spot where other cars were also parked. He had arrived at the Meatman's house with plenty of lead time—over an hour—and now snow had accumulated on the roof and hood of the van, making it appear as though it had been left there for the night. That's why he couldn't keep the motor running and the heater on. The Meatman would have instantly noticed a van clear of snow with the motor going and the exhaust smoking.

Angry that his body had chilled to numbness, Whitey had covered his long thighs with one khaki-colored army blanket and wrapped another around his shoulders, shawl-like. He hated the cold, but he could endure it for the job.

Before he had started out that night, Whitey had treated the van's windshield with a spray-on silicone substance that optometrists sometimes use to keep eyeglasses from fogging up in cold weather. The results were amazing. The windshield remained clear and unfrosted.

Pulling the blanket snug across his shoulders, he smiled a crooked, slanting smile. So far, so good. Presto was an important job, worth the waiting. Even in the cold. Almost instantly, Whitey's smile gave way to his usual darkening scowl.

Back when the Meatman really had been a meatman—a hustling butcher with a tiny, falling-down stall on 9th Street, along Philadelphia's teeming Italian market—the Christmases hadn't always been so good. But those were the bad old days.

Beginning the first time he had helped one of the old guys cut up the carcasses from a truckload of hijacked beef, the Meatman had realized that he would never again be content to struggle and sweat out a living like the other merchants along 9th Street. For himself and his family, Presto demanded more, much more.

Manny Goldberg, then his closest friend, had arranged the deal. The guys had given him a box of steaks and a crisp $100 bill for his trouble.

That was twenty-five years ago. Since then, Manny Goldberg had become Emmanuel Gallen and claimed to be legit. Manny was still Manny, though. The brightest crook Presto had ever known. He thought about that night—the night the Old One, *Il Vecchio,* had placed the $100 bill in his hand. They had eaten good that Christmas. That was the same year that his Honoria had been born.

After that, one deal led to the next and the next, until the Meatman had found himself doing so well that he was in a position to begin lending money to other people at a profit. That's how he got into loan-sharking. *Il Vecchio* had conferred his blessing, of course, and Manny Goldberg never ran short of "clients for referral," as he called them.

But Paul Presto had taken to it naturally. A federal prosecutor had once referred to him in front of a grand jury as a "born usurer."

When his "clients" wouldn't pay up, Presto would have them brought down into his cellar, where he kept an old butcher's block in the middle of the floor, next to the walk-in freezer. First he would line up the boning knives, sharp as razors. Then he would get out a couple of saws, with blood and gristle still on them. Finally he would pick up a cleaver and begin sharpening it. This little morality play always proceeded with two or three of the Meatman's associates hoisting the poor guy up onto one of the giant meat-hooks on the wall next to the freezer.

Then, while the guy twisted and cried in agony, the Meatman would move in with a very dull boning knife. Rarely would he do more than scratch a person on the arm or leg, or maybe the face if the guy had been fresh or brazen about the money he owed. Most times, just drawing blood would be enough. Sometimes the deadbeats screamed themselves hoarse. Presto would look at them in disgust and shake his head.

Finally, Presto's hoods would haul the guy down, and the Meatman, in a threatrical flourish of magnanimity, would give him one last chance to pay up. He always emphasized the word "last," with the cleaver in his hand. In most cases, the "beat" would be back with the money in a matter of hours. But if he wasn't, or if he tried to run away, leave town or whatever, he would be caught and brought back down into the cellar. That's when the Meatman would get mean. That's how he had earned his nickname.

Presto would begin by slicing off the tip of the little finger of the left hand, neatly and professionally, just like the master butcher that he was. That usually made the guy pass out.

By the time the deadbeat came to, the Meatman would have stopped the bleeding. He would give the "client" one final chance to pay up. They *always* came up with the bread after that. They might be in pain and missing part of a finger, but they were glad to be alive. That's how the Meatman had built up his reputation.

Once, at a wedding reception, someone stupid had asked

the Meatman what he did with the fingers. Presto glared at him, not quite sure how to retaliate against such a breach of etiquette, and finally growled through clenched teeth, "I fucking eat them."

The Meatman had just bulled his way through "The Twelve Days of Christmas," really booming out the eight maids a-milking, when he turned the Lincoln onto Fletcher Street. "Silent Night" came on the radio, but he ignored it. Lately the Meatman had been very angry with God.

Relic-kissing was okay, and he liked the little girls in their frilly white dresses walking like little angels in First Holy Communion processions, but the Meatman could live without the rest of it. Males of his generation and background joked that three times inside a church was enough for a lifetime—just as long as they were carried two of those times, at the christening and at the funeral.

He did make sure that the cops on his payroll blocked traffic off Broad Street for the May Processions when the schoolchildren lined up under banners of the Blessed Virgin. They marched behind an old monsignor who carried his crucifix mounted on the same pole that they used to open the high stained-glass windows on Sunday. That kind of tradition the Meatman could understand.

What he really hated were these young, interfering priests who refused to celebrate funeral masses for men like Presto and denied them burial in consecrated ground. *That* was when a man really needed his God. They had done that to his friend, Big Paul Castellano, in New York.

Recently, while kneeling in a darkened confessional in St. Bibiana's Church, in a parish that produced half of the Presto Family's income from numbers, loan-sharking, and sports betting, the Meatman had laid it on the line for a young priest who was so new that the scent of the seminary still clung to him like incense. The priest had balked at conducting a funeral for one of Presto's men. The Meatman exploded when he heard that, threatening to hold the priest personally responsible should his man be condemned to hell.

"You got no right not to bury my people in holy ground," he angrily told the silent cleric in the confessional, who was cringing on the other side of the thick canvas screen. "All we do is take care of our own business. We don't break none of God's laws. We never eat meat on Friday and we don't kill nobody who don't deserve it." Then the Meatman stood up, made a hurried sign of the cross, like a bashful little boy, and stomped out.

A few days later, after a discreet consultation with his bishop, a small, clear-thinking Irish pragmatist who pored over the *Wall Street Journal* following Mass each morning, the priest informed the family of the deceased, and Paul Presto that the Requiem Mass of Christian Burial would be scheduled.

An hour-long, Latin-rite Mass for the Dead was celebrated with the Meatman and several of his men occupying the first pew, half kneeling, half sitting, their big haunches resting against the smooth, polished wood. In remembrance of the deceased, the Meatman donated seven sets of silk vestments, hand-embroidered—one for each day of the week—and a gleaming platinum chalice, adorned with seven brilliant red rubies—one for each of the dead man's grandchildren.

On the ride back from the Holy Cross Cemetery, the Meatman winked and asked the young priest, "Does that church of yours still need a new roof?"

By the time Presto parked his car, the snow had filled in the kid's rippled footprints. Presto never even glanced at them. In the old green van, Whitey and Vinnie didn't exchange a word. The kid was dying to talk, but he knew better. Whitey had his ways. The kid waited.

Through the frozen tree limbs, glistening with ice, they watched as Presto carefully navigated the snowy front steps of his house.

"Maybe he'll fall and fucking break his neck," the kid blurted out. Whitey gave him a glance. The kid flushed and became even more engrossed in his thoughts about the bomb. And the Meatman. Whitey would see that he had done it right.

Knotting thick, ashen-white eyebrows together tightly, Whitey thrust forward his long, crooked face in deep concentration. As cold as he felt, his dead brown eyes burned hot.

The wait was nearly over. Snow blew fiercely, but Whitey could see the Meatman just fine—doing exactly what Whitey wanted him to do.

Walking carefully on the slippery surface, the Meatman mounted the five steps that led to his porch. He removed one glove and fumbled around in his overcoat pocket for his keys.

Just one week until Christmas. The days, and now even the years, went by so quickly. Honoria had been a child for so short a time. He hated to admit that she was all grown up, a woman now, a beauty with a woman's perceptions and a woman's needs. So much like her mother, so knowing and intuitive. Instantly, Paul Presto banished his dead wife's image from his mind. It was akin to a sharp pain slowly ebbing away. He tried never to think of her. That was all behind him. He still had his Honoria, and that was all that mattered . . . only a week until Christmas. He had so much to accomplish in seven days. What kind of Christmas present should he buy his daughter? He had been worrying about that, just as he did every year. She loved surprises and had refused to give him even a hint about what she wanted. Russian sable? Presto had been looking at some samples. That might be a good idea. But was that too old for her? Too matronly? He felt as though he were still dressing a child. What did he know about cuts or styles or fashion? Or what young girls were wearing? And he refused to trust some salesman. That wasn't the Meatman's way. Maybe somebody in the business? He knew a man . . . Presto considered the possibilities. He had already made some calls. He'd have to make more. Dammit, as much as he tried to deny it, he did need a woman in his life. Especially for Honoria. Not to take her mother's place; just to help. His daughter was still a child in so many ways. . . .

His hand was almost on the doorknob when the girl, Arlene, suddenly flowed irresistibly back into his mind. How could he forget her? Especially after tonight? He'd have to get something for her now, too—something very special befitting her new position as his lover. Maybe she was what had been missing from his life for so long. There were only a few days left, but he would take care of it. Take care of everything. Give everyone a Merry Christmas.

The handle of the heavy storm door was cold to his touch.

The girl had said it herself—*Padrone.* God, how Meatman Presto loved the sound of that. He *was* the *padrone* now, finally.

He owed it all to the Atlantic City war. Now there was a truce. Presto had survived. He hadn't won everything, but enough. The Commission, *commissione,* had declared Atlantic City an open city for anybody with the smarts and the guts to make money. With the cease-fire in effect, he felt good for the first time in years. He even felt safe—at least in Philadelphia. Safe enough to screw around in back rooms.

Moving almost in slow motion, Presto appeared to be opening the storm door. But then he hesitated, quickly turned around, and started to kick his snow-covered shoes against the porch railing.

Whitey felt his throat beginning to contract. Jesus, nothing could go wrong now.

In the van, the kid didn't even breathe. Whitey's spirits lifted and he felt the moment coming when it would have to happen. He would be quick and use both hands. He glanced at Vinnie and saw that the kid was leaning forward on the dashboard, transfixed by what was about to happen.

Across the street, Presto had again turned back to the storm door. He was beginning to open it, his gloved fingers gripping the handle.

Whitey's left cheek twitched faintly. That always happened before a kill shot; feeling the twitch helped him grow calm and precise.

"Do it," the kid murmured, almost to himself.

Whitey took in Presto and the kid and the wide expanse of Fletcher Street in one sweeping glance. Then, with his left hand, he began to press the radio detonator switch between his legs, under the blanket. And with his right, he jammed the .45 into Vinnie's side.

One last time he looked at Meatman Presto. Then at Vinnie. The kid never even had a chance to turn around.

Whitey squeezed off three quick shots just as the front porch of Paul Presto's house exploded. The vibration rocked the van, then drained away into the snowy night.

The noise of the gunshots was completely masked by the explosion. Timed perfectly. The smell of the powder and the singed fabric of the kid's jacket filled the van. Meatman Presto had disappeared. So had his lights, his wreath, and his jolly fat Santa. Smoke poured from the house like the breath of an angry dragon.

Satisfied, Whitey turned his attention to Vinnie. The kid had been useful tonight. Useful, but dumb.

He shoved the body down on the floor, next to the front seat, careful to keep the spot where the blood was seeping through the jacket elevated and level. Whitey was meticulous about such things. The first bullet had probably gotten him in the heart. The other two, also clean shots, had neatly missed the ribs. All three cartridges were low-impact, with most of the gunpowder removed; otherwise, the shattering power of the .45 would have taken the door of the van right off.

Whitey had a spot already picked out in the Tinicum marsh, behind Philadelphia International Airport. He had scouted it while pretending to be hunting ducks.

After he dumped the kid's body, he would double back to the airport, park the van on the middle level of the long-term garage, change his clothes in the back of the van, and exit, looking like a weary businessman. Then he would lose himself in the terminal crowd.

Before his next job, Whitey would spend several days in the sun somewhere, probably a resort, burning away the white pallor and turning his hair almost silver. Yet no matter how many hours he spent in the sun, he would still feel cold.

As Whitey pulled away from the shelter of the park, about thirty seconds after the blast, the Meatman's house was in flames. He had been parked there for just over an hour and a quarter. The time was 9:17 p.m. He glanced at Vinnie, and a look of annoyance clouded his face. He had been forced to do the kid for free, and Whitey hated to squander his talents.

Soon the fire engines and the police would arrive. Over and over he had calculated their responding time—somewhere between three and seven minutes. Considering the snow and the dangerous driving conditions, he felt confident that he still had five to six minutes head start. Even without the damn snow tires. He hoped Passyunk Avenue would be clear.

Whitey didn't even hurry as he pulled the van out into the freezing blackness of the icy street. Meatman Presto's house was blazing behind him. Whitey never looked back.

TWO

A STOREFRONT NEAR PASSYUNK AVENUE, SOUTH PHILADELPHIA

Phillip Driscoll's eyes were already beginning to change color—from gray to almost blue. That was a bad sign. Driscoll was like a cat, a big, sleek predator, and by the time his eyes hit blue, he would really be crazy. Lida James had been torturing him all night, and she could see that she was finally getting to him. In a way, though, she didn't mind. She had a crush on him, and the way he worked himself up before finally detonating, restraining himself to the last possible second, then *really* exploding, was kind of cute. Sexy. "I have to pee," she said sweetly. He ignored her. She *did* have to go and kept squeezing her thighs together.

Driscoll was a homicide detective and Lida was a short, good-natured, randy sort of girl whose tits had been the talk of whatever division she happened to work in. Now she was in Organized Crime. Her partner was Joe Pepe, Spanish Joe, a Cuban cop who specialized in the Italian Mafia. He was handsome, with a Pancho Villa mustache and the fastest hands in the Roundhouse. Doing it with Spanish Joe wasn't even a challenge; all you had to do was say hello to the guy and he figured his Latin charm, which was considerable, had done the trick. Lida had tried it with him once after a Christmas party; no rockets' red glare, as she liked to say.

Now, all Lida could see was Phillip Driscoll. She had been trying to sleep with him since the first day they had worked together. "Must be the coffee," she said. She knew he hated to be pestered like this on a stakeout; that's why she kept it up. At least it got him talking and looking at her sometimes.

Driscoll was different from any other cop she had ever known. He could be funny and profane and profound—and all at the same time. He was smart enough to read books, but still cop enough to trust no one, to take nothing for granted, and to see a low motive in every high-minded statement he had ever heard. But what really set him apart was the fact that Driscoll was the only cop she had ever met who scared *other* cops. That was sexy, too.

The two of them were sitting high up in the front cab of a big yellow Streets Department trash truck with a hydraulic snowplow attached to the front of it. The truck was supposed to look like part of the convoy that would start clearing the twelve miles of Broad Street as soon as the snowfall hit four inches. The trash trucks were perfect for stakeouts. Driscoll didn't mind them, because the front cabs had real leather seats and enough legroom for him to cross his legs without banging his knees against the dashboard.

Spanish Joe was parked a block away in a standard-issue Ford LTD. They used walkie-talkies to keep in touch. Organized Crime had borrowed Driscoll for the night. They were sitting on the Presto Family's biggest sports betting bank in South Philly. They expected a guy to show up who was wanted for three murders. If he showed, Driscoll, the homicide man, would get the paperwork with the credit going to the OC unit. Driscoll wasn't exactly crazy about the setup, but he had no choice.

So far, he hadn't showed, and Driscoll was getting cold and tired and impatient. He and Lida were dressed like trashmen, in overalls, heavy jackets, and anything else they could pile on to keep warm.

Driscoll was thirty-six years old, with prematurely gray hair and a well-put-together 180 pounds on a six-foot frame. He'd been a cop for fourteen years—two in Highway Patrol and the last twelve as a detective, mainly in Homicide. He was still a young man, but a very old cop. On the outside, it was hardly noticeable; on the inside, though, the transformation had been almost complete. The years had bled the juices from him, and all that remained was a tangy bitterness. Driscoll had seen too much.

Moonlight streaked through the dirty window of the trash truck. There was a thermos of coffee, almost empty, on the seat between them. Lida was working the walkie-talkie. Every few minutes, Spanish Joe would check in. The last time, Driscoll had grabbed the box away from Lida and growled at Spanish Joe, demanding to know where the hell this murderer was supposed to be. Driscoll had never been overly impressed with the OC unit and its intelligence capabilities, and he didn't give a shit if they knew it.

Lida was looking at him, dying to touch his face. She wanted to trace out the furrows of his forehead with her fingers, linger at the tiny crevices at the corner of his mouth, feel Driscoll's hairy fingers all over her body. *God,* he had hairy hands. She was also beginning to believe that he was right. The stakeout was a bust.

A bust. *A bust!* Suddenly, Lida had a terrific idea, and a wicked smile parted her lips. Except for the lookout posted outside the Presto Family bank, there wasn't a sound in the street. Nobody could see them way up there in the big trash truck. Lida knew what she had to do. She had to get Driscoll to start thinking about her instead of the damn stakeout.

While Driscoll stared in disgust at the lookout, she began feeling inside around her coveralls, loosening the bib front, then her bra. Sideways, she glanced across the seat at Driscoll, but he was busy ignoring her. Lida's breath fogged the window on her side of the truck.

If this didn't get him to notice her, then he didn't have a damn pulse. She was fumbling with the hook on her bra, reaching behind her to unsnap it. Lida didn't want Driscoll to realize what she was doing until she was ready. She had considered reaching over and unzipping his pants—she had done that once to a guy on an elevator—but she had a feeling that Driscoll would just look down at her in that weary way he had and act like women unzipped his pants all the time. Be cool, she told herself.

Except for a muffled explosion that had rocked the street about twenty minutes before, not a thing had happened all night. Driscoll had wondered out loud what that strange boom in the dark distance had been, but then he just as quickly dismissed it. He was pretending to be mad again. "I can't believe this," Driscoll said, still staring at the Presto lookout across the highway. Lida had been suspiciously quiet for the last few minutes. "You drag me out here on a night like this because some junkie thought he heard something. This guy you're looking for is never going to show here tonight. He *knows* you're looking for him. My people said he left town. But no, that's not good enough for you. If the damn OC unit says so, then it has to be true. You know that, Lida? You guys are a pain in my ass."

Just a few hours before, Driscoll had been dozing, stretched out in a strange bed on a cold night, with a scented comforter bunched up under his head as he lay back studying the perfect contours of the small pink breast opposite him. The breast belonged to an assistant D.A. named Cynthia O'Neill, who had prosecuted Driscoll's last case. Each time she had exhaled, the breast had deflated appealingly, giving him an excellent view of her dark nipple. Sitting here with Lida, freezing his ass off on a wild goose chase, Driscoll kept thinking back to Cynthia's breast. When she inhaled, it had risen gently, forming a firm, flawless sphere. As soon as she awakened, they would make love again.

But not now.

They had called him right out of bed. When the telephone rang, it nearly scared Cynthia to death. "Meet a trash truck downstairs" was the only message the dispatcher had given him.

Moments before the telephone had summoned him, Cynthia's thigh had rubbed up against his. Remembering that, Driscoll touched the diastema, the space between his two front teeth, and resigned himself to the fact that tonight was going to be a waste of time—thanks to these two, randy Lida and Spanish Joe. It wasn't that he didn't like them.

He did. Especially Lida. She was just about the only partner he could work with. And Spanish Joe had been a stand-up guy since the first day Driscoll had met him. Hell, it was just that he didn't need a stakeout on a night like this. Especially a bullshit stakeout.

Trying to make himself more comfortable, Driscoll relaxed and tensed rigid again, stretching tight muscles as he cupped both hands behind his head. Maybe he had been too hard on Lida. Now he felt like he had to go himself. It was the damn coffee. Too much. She couldn't hold it in forever. He was trying to think where she could find a bathroom.

His square cheeks tapered to a sturdy chin; his face was a little too lean for that muscular body. People always noticed Driscoll. Sometimes he made them feel uncomfortable. Other times he had this way of walking into a room and cocking his head to one side, as though he were waiting for the applause to begin. Lida had seen him make entrances like that; it always made her hot.

He was just about to speak to her—civilly, for the first time all night—when she interrupted him.

"Phil," Lida said innocently, "check this out."

In the dim half-light of the truck cab, he looked at her.

"Yo, Phil, like this?"

"What the hell. . . ?" Driscoll couldn't believe what he was seeing.

"Like that one, Phil? There's another one where that came from."

Lida was flashing him. Her left tit. It had to be twice the size of Cynthia's. Enormous. Lush. With a nipple already tingling erect in the chilly air.

Lida, laughing, giggling, her face red from excitement and just a little embarrassment, kept flipping the front bib of her coveralls open and closed, giving him a peck every time.

"Ever hear the guys talk about this?"

Driscoll was speechless, dumbfounded. He wanted to act cool, but Lida had gotten the drop on him. How in hell had she practically undressed herself in the truck?

"All yours, Phil. This is just a sample." She flipped the coverall bib closed again. "All you have to do is say when and where." Slyly, Lida glanced down at his crotch. She smiled to herself. Phillip Driscoll had a pulse, all right.

"That's going to freeze right off," Driscoll said, never having addressed a breast in a truck cab before. And he *was* addressing the tit. He couldn't keep his eyes away from it. Lida was in her glory.

"Want a little feel, Phil? Just one squeeze before I put it away?"

What the hell, he might as well. But just as he started to reach across the steering wheel, Lida squealed and stuffed the tit back inside her coveralls.

"Not so fast, sucker," she teased. "We have some—"

Crackling static from the walkie-talkie interrupted them.

"Three cars. Bad guys. That's what I make them. Maybe our man is about to show after all."

It was Spanish Joe contacting them. "What the hell are you two doing in that truck? I haven't heard from you for the last half hour," he said.

"I make them, too," Driscoll answered. "Three sharks. It looks like our man brought some company with him."

Three cars had just pulled around the corner and were making their way slowly, like a funeral procession, to the Presto Family bank.

Driscoll couldn't recognize any faces in the dark. He glanced at Lida questioningly. She shook her head and began frantically straightening her clothes. Whatever was about to go down, Driscoll suddenly realized that this wasn't what they had been waiting for.

"Let's hold on a minute," Driscoll said into the box. "This doesn't look like a guy coming to place a bet. You know any of those cars or drivers?"

"Negative."

"Sit on it for a minute. See what happens. This whole thing looks a little bent to me." Driscoll had the distinct feeling that the cars were some kind of war party. Now he was fascinated, intent on the scene unfolding. The three cars ignored the yellow trash truck; so did the Presto lookout. But all at once, the lookout seemed agitated.

"Check out that lookout, Phil. Is he spooked or what?" Spanish Joe had picked it up, too.

"You buttoned up, Lida?" Driscoll said, without looking at her or waiting for an answer. He didn't take his eyes off the three cars. "Something tells me these guys are here to make a withdrawal,'' Driscoll said. Then he locked himself into a tight, constricting crouch on the floor of the truck so the men in the cars couldn't see him.

They came in a three-car convoy. Three men each in the first and third car; Butkova and Boris in the middle car.

They circled the block once.

A lookout, a kid about twenty, with slick hair, wearing a leather jacket, was posted on the corner outside. At first he thought the cars must have flat tires, they were moving so slowly. But when they came around the corner the second time, he broke for the storefront at a run to warn Joe-Joey.

Boris slowed the middle car to line up a good shot. He meant to kill the kid right there on the pavement, but Butkova stopped him. ''Inside,'' he told Boris.

The store had once been a supply house of some kind. Now it functioned as the neighborhood bank and clearinghouse for the Presto Family's biggest sports betting operation in South Philly. The '76ers were playing the Lakers in L.A. and the Flyers were in Vancouver. West Coast games started late and bets came in up till the last minute. The guys who ran the bank, like Joe-Joey, had to pull plenty of night work.

The Meatman had already stopped by earlier that night. He'd had the damnedest smile on his face—as if he'd just gotten laid or something. Joe-Joey, the most trusted soldier in the Presto Family, was relaxed; the boss wouldn't be back. He'd even cracked open a bottle of bourbon and poured himself a strong one. The Sixers were hot again and the money was coming in faster than he could count it.

Long tables, covered with rice paper to record the bets, took up most of the space in the back room. Under each of the tables, big round tubs of water remained permanently. In case of a police or FBI raid, the rice paper would be dumped into the water, where it would dissolve instantly.

A bank of telephones, on smaller tables, filled the rest of the space in the big back room. The phones were manned twenty-four hours a day, seven days a week. Code words were used, each word representing a number from zero to nine. The bets were placed in three digits. When the Phillies or Eagles were playing, they used the pay phones in the tunnels of Veterans Stadium, too.

The front of the store was jammed with low-level Family members and neighborhood people who had come in to place bets, collect their winnings, or settle old bills. Some of them wanted to see Tony Bonaventura, the underboss, who was also the Meatman's brother-in-law. But Tony wasn't around tonight. That left Joe-Joey in charge. Lizardlike, his small tongue dipped into the amber liquor just before he gulped it down. He was all dolled up for the occasion—a $600 brown mocha suit, open-necked tan shirt, cocoa-brown open-weave shoes and socks to match, two heavy gold medallions around his neck, a gold lion's head ring on his finger, and designer sunglasses.

A vintage M-16 lay across Boris's fat thighs on the driver's side. Extra ammo clips were shoved into the pockets of his overcoat. Butkova, however, was unarmed. The men in the other two cars carried M-16s too.

At a signal from Butkova, the three cars stopped in the middle of the street in front of the store. The drivers kept the motors running, and thick clouds of exhaust smoke blew up over the trunks of the cars before evaporating into the darkness. Butkova and his band seemed to come out of some deadly fog as they stormed into Joe-Joey's store, amid a deafening barrage of gunfire, the hot shell casings ejecting in burning arcs, scorching trails of sparks and acrid blue flame. Shrieking and screaming, everybody ran for cover or dropped to the floor. The place was bedlam. A fat bookie, chewing on the stump of a cigar, took a bullet in the cheek; he gurgled blood, his tongue torn.

All of them, except Butkova, wore ski masks. Butkova wanted them to see him. Remember his face. Feel the cold cruelty in his eyes.

Joe-Joey dropped down behind the desk and tried to reach the shotgun that was strapped to the bottom of the desk drawer. Behind him, stuffed into Maxwell House coffee cans, all in a neat row, was about $80,000 in cash.

There was so much shooting, uproar, and bloodshed, Butkova had a hard time taking it all in. Bodies kept hitting the floor—some shot, some trampled by others scampering for safety, some just sinking into the spot where they stood.

The lookout kid now lay in a bloody mess at Boris's feet. Boris stepped right on top of him, crushing his shoulder blades with his heavy boots. Another guy in the corner had been momentarily pinned against the wall by an exploding burst of automatic fire. As he slid down, a crimson smear stained the wall.

Suddenly Butkova raised his hand, and the shooting ceased instantly. Enough. Butkova wanted some of them dead, but not all. This time was a lesson. He needed survivors to spread the word.

Butkova pointed to Joe-Joey, glaring at him from behind the desk. He had never made it to the shotgun. Boris yanked Joe-Joey to his feet. The rest of the ski-masked invaders were emptying the cash from the coffee cans into sacks. The tip of Boris's rifle was inside Joe-Joey's mouth, tearing his palate.

Butkova figured that he was the one in charge. But it really didn't matter—any of Presto's men would do. They would listen, remember, remember good.

Butkova croaked in his usual manner. "You pay Butkova now. Butkova collect. You tell *all* Presto people—now, you pay Butkova."

Butkova and Boris were the last to leave. They backed out of the store slowly, deliberately. The others were already loaded into the cars with their loot.

Joe-Joey's palate was bleedly badly. He was tasting the sharp tang of the blood dripping down his throat.

Just before he walked out the door, still moving like a man in no hurry, Butkova took one final look around. He wanted every man there to get a good look at him and to understand that now Nikolai Butkova was the man with the gun.

The entire attack had taken less than five minutes. The only sounds in the room after the raiders left were coughing and crying and moaning. Joe-Joey, in excruciating pain from the savage wound in his palate, hoped that he could still talk. He looked at the overturned tables, the empty coffee cans, the sprawled, bleeding bodies and the dead ones.

Still spitting blood, his hands shaking, he saw the telephone lying upside down on the floor. He lunged for it desperately and dialed Tony Bonaventura's number. Marie Presto, the Meatman's sister and Tony's wife, answered it on the first ring. She sounded annoyed.

"I gotta talk to Tony," Joe-Joey muttered through thick, bloody saliva.

Marie gave him some smart-ass answer. The whole front of his shirt was soaked and dripping with blood. He didn't need her shit.

"Tony," he screamed painfully into the phone. "*Gimme Tony.* They fuckin' hit the bank."

THREE

NEAR PASSYUNK AVENUE

Driscoll didn't realize that something resembling a massacre had taken place until the shooters were already piling into their cars. He'd heard the automatic weapons fire, but it had taken half a minute for that to even register. It wasn't every day that he heard M-16 clips being emptied on city streets.

"Let's move," he hollered into the box.

Lida already had her gun out.

"I don't believe this," he said to Lida, "but those guys, whoever the hell they are, just stuck up the Meatman's bank."

"It sounded more like they took it apart."

"Joe," he called on the walkie-talkie, "you'd better get an ambulance here, too."

"Done," was Spanish Joe's reply.

"You take the top of the street. I'll move up from here with the plow. Just try to block them."

"Sounds good." Joe was saying something else in Spanish, but it faded.

"Ready?" he asked Lida.

She nodded.

Gunning the big trash truck's motor to life, Driscoll simultaneously started elevating the hydraulic snowplow. He'd use the truck like a tank, with the plow a battering ram. All he needed was some traction on the slick surface.

As the three cars pulled away from the storefront, screeching their tires on the wet street, Driscoll began rumbling the snowplow in their direction. It was slow going and everything depended on speed.

Five miles an hour, ten, fifteen. He kept pushing the old yellow monster, double-clutching and beating against the steering wheel.

Lida was leaning out the window on her side, her knees up on the seat, her chest shoved against the cab door, attempting to get a good shot off. But it was no good. The truck was bumping so badly she couldn't even hold the weapon steady. He slammed on the breaks to avoid something on the street and almost lost her.

"Forget it," Driscoll said. "When I get in close enough, I'll ram the last car." He had the weight and height in the plow, if only he had some traction.

Almost two blocks away, Driscoll could just make out Spanish Joe as he positioned his car in the middle of the street as a barricade and then ran for cover. The headlights were still on, slicing through the misting snow.

Suddenly a red flame pierced the darkness, and Driscoll knew that Joe was firing. Again, three more times, the orange-red muzzle flash leaped out.

As the big truck gobbled up more and more of the street, Driscoll and Lida passed by the Presto bank. He could hear screaming and yelling and saw several men run out onto the pavement and start following in the direction of the cars and the trash truck. There were a couple more red flashes from that sector, too.

"This is like a goddam war," he said to Lida. "If the guys in the car don't kill us, the Prestos will." Driscoll crouched over the steering wheel.

Twenty-five miles an hour. Thirty. Thirty-five. Forty. He scraped parked cars, dented doors.

Now he had nearly reached the last of the three cars. Aiming the plow a notch higher, he pushed the big truck faster.

"Hold on, Lida!" He careened off a curbstone, taking trash cans with him.

BANG! It was metal-on-metal, ripping and crunching, the plow unstoppable.

Driscoll's plow had caught the rear fender of the last car. Driscoll rammed the snowplow right into the trunk area. The auto lifted up slightly, its rear wheels spinning.

"That slowed the bastard down."

Lida was already halfway out of the cab, scampering down the side of the truck. Wind and snow blasted in as the cab's doors swung open.

Driscoll followed. Lida was in front of the plow, bent low, looking for cover.

Just in front of them, the doors to the car that had been harpooned by the snowplow opened and three men, one of them limping from an injury he must have suffered in the crash, began running.

Lida fired at the limper and missed.

Slipping on the glaze of snow that now covered the street, Driscoll ran after the guy closest to him. He was carrying something long and black.

Oh, Jesus! Driscoll thought. It looked like a damn cannon.

The man spun around on Driscoll and opened fire. The cop ducked.

More gunshots were coming from up ahead. Spanish Joe was pinned down and his makeshift barricade wasn't doing the job. The two cars in the front just crunched past his police LTD, shattering some chrome and glass, but easily making an escape. Momentarily, they slowed down. The guy with the limp was being helped into the auto closest to them. They were getting away.

Lida kept blasting away in that direction. Shots were whizzing over their heads, too, from the rear, from the direction of the running Prestos.

But Driscoll still had his man. He sized up the large adversary.

The guy's big rifle had jammed. Driscoll saw him jerking the lever on the side back and forth, desperately attempting to eject a shell that had become caught in the firing mechanism. He looked up, panic in his eyes.

That was just the edge, the second of hesitation, Driscoll needed.

Propelling himself from his defensive crouch, he attacked, tackling the shooter's midsection, knocking him backward, then he reached, jumped up to grab for the man's throat. All Driscoll could do was hang on.

He dropped his weapon just as Driscoll cemented both hands around his neck. Whirling madly, he momentarily swept the detective off his feet. Driscoll looked for something to grab; he needed leverage to knock the larger man down. But the guy ducked and moved as fast as a man half his size. Fighting on the slippery street, all bundled up in heavy clothes, with the wind blowing fiercely, was agonizingly difficult. But both men kept tearing away at each other. The cop banged the other man with nasty, choppy body punches.

They were on their feet. The guy was taller than Driscoll and much heavier—a real brute, swinging away wildly. Driscoll took a short, hard smash to the jaw.

Then Driscoll saw his opening. He landed a loud right-hand smack against the guy's front teeth. When the detective pulled back, his knuckles were covered with blood. But, finally, that had taken the fight out of the shooter. He slumped down in a heap, raised himself to one knee, then went down again.

Driscoll himself was dazed and woozy. Gulping savagely for air, he kept trying to get up, but he couldn't.

"Relax, Phil," he heard Spanish Joe say. Someone—it turned out to be Lida—was reaching under his armpits, helping him to his feet. Joe had a pistol aimed right at the shooter's forehead.

Just then an ambulance came screeching around the corner, sirens wailing, followed by a sea of red and blue flashing lights that appeared to roll on in bright waves that washed out of the darkness.

Driscoll gave Spanish Joe a dirty look, then turned his attention to the man at his feet.

"Who do you work for?" Driscoll demanded. *"Who?"* There was mad fury in his eyes.

"Phil, I have to tell you something," Joe interrupted, putting a strong arm around the detective's shoulders, restraining him. "Listen to me, Phil. This is *important.*"

"I want one more shot at this guy," Driscoll screamed. "I said, *who do you work for? Who's your boss?*" There was no reply.

"Phil, that can wait," Joe said. "You'd better listen to this."

But Driscoll was puzzled. It was almost as though the man on the ground didn't understand what he was saying; didn't speak English. Every once in a while, Driscoll ran into a guy from Sicily like that, but Sicilians had a look which this guy didn't have.

"We'll take care of him," Joe said firmly. "Whatever the hell he is, and whoever he works for, we'll find out. But listen to me."

Driscoll, his rage abated, listened.

"Phil, do you remember that boom we heard?"

"Sure, why?"

"Hey, Phil, that was the fuckin' Meatman. They blew him up. Right on his own front porch. The Meatman's *dead.*"

Spanish Joe let that sink in. He saw Driscoll's stunned disbelief.

The Meatman was dead?

It didn't even sound right saying it.

"Who?"

Spanish Joe pointed to the man on the ground. "If he ever opens his mouth, maybe he can tell us." The suspect's eyes darted from side to side, suspicious, wary.

The fight had taken them to the front of the snowplow. Driscoll hadn't realized that they had tumbled through the snow that far. Leaning down to get a good look at the man he had just beaten, Driscoll grabbed a handful of greasy black hair and yanked the man's face in front of the truck's headlight.

Driscoll didn't recognize him. The guy just stared at him belligerently.

That's when Driscoll's eyes went to almost blue.

With one quick motion, Driscoll banged the man's head and face into the front fender of the big yellow truck. Then he did it again. Blood spurted out from the gash he had opened on the man's scalp. He banged him a third time.

Lida stepped in. She held on tightly to the crook of Driscoll's arm.

"That's it, Phil. You got him. Enough. Don't go crazy here." She indicated the small crowd of Presto's soldiers and hangers-on who were watching in fascination as Phillip Driscoll continued to work over the man who had just tried to kill him.

Driscoll let go, and the man plopped down into the snow again.

"Talk!" Driscoll screamed. *"Talk!"*

But the man refused to open his mouth. This time, a blind rage consuming him, the detective picked the larger man up bodily and hurled him into the scoop front of the snow plow, as if he were tossing a bag of garbage. A small cheer arose from the knot of Presto people as Driscoll just left him there.

"That's *it,* Phil. I mean it," Spanish Joe yelled. "You wanta kill him, don't do it in front of a crowd."

Driscoll spotted Joe-Joey and walked over to him. Joe-Joey was holding some sort of cloth up to his face. His $600 mocha suit and tan shirt were splattered with blood dripping from his torn palate. He was hurting.

"You hear?" Driscoll asked him. He figured if the cops knew about the Meatman, so did Joe-Joey.

"On the phone," Joe-Joey mumbled. "They just told us." It was hard for him to talk.

The two men held each other in a steady gaze. "What about all this?" Driscoll asked, knowing full well that Joe-Joey would tell him nothing.

"You tell me."

Driscoll pressed him. "The Meatman? You got any ideas?"

"It wasn't us, Driscoll. It wasn't the Family. We got no war." Then Joe-Joey hesitated. "At least, not till tonight." Reacting to a sudden, stinging surge of pain, Joe-Joey took in a deep breath, sucking hard. He pointed to the man in custody. "Nice job, Driscoll." Then Joe-Joey walked away, leading the rest of the Presto gang back to the ruins of their storefront.

All Driscoll could think about now was Honoria Presto, Honey Presto, the Meatman's daughter. Was she all right? Safe? Hurt? He had to find out.

"Lida," Driscoll asked, "can I have a lift back to my car?"

"Sure, Phil. Just tell me one thing. Where the hell is your

gun? You mean to tell me you walked into this without that damn gun again?''

Driscoll grinned impishly. ''It's in the trunk of my car. I hate the damn things, you know that. Besides, I'm a lousy shot.''

That was true enough. Guns had always given Driscoll the creeps. He thought of them in the same way as he did the sterile, antiseptically ghoulish stainless-steel instruments that always gave him a sinking feeling in a doctor's office. Or maybe it was just that Driscoll had covered one too many homicides, showing up shortly after the deceased had bought it, while the blood was still fresh. Whatever the reason, Driscoll had never had any use for cops who were gun faggots.

Exasperated, Lida sighed. ''Let's go. We'll grab a blue-and-white.''

OREGON AVENUE

Sitting in front of Presto's house, waiting, Whitey had imagined what it must be like to freeze to death, the body temperature plunging, the extremities losing all sensation. The brain went last, he supposed, after the body had been paralyzed by the cold.

Whitey had always been afraid that he would die like that, freezing to death, blackness gradually taking the place of the cold.

He was aching and angry. Furious, as he pushed the old green van as hard as he dared on the slippery snow. He had to get to the airport; had to get rid of Vinnie.

The momentary satisfaction of the perfectly executed bombing had left him. His mood always changed this way—with rage sweeping down suddenly and fixing itself upon him, upon the world, and finally upon his target. On Meatman Presto. That's how Whitey got even. Tonight, Presto had paid—for the cold, for Whitey's pallid, hairless flesh, for Whitey's having never known the comfortable feeling of warmth.

THE KREMLIN, MOSCOW

The December sky over Moscow was a brittle, porcelain blue on the night of Paul Presto's assassination. The great gray city had been spared. The puffy white clouds of the previous day had retreated, draining the damp, snow-laden moisture out of the air and replacing it with a robust, windless cold.

But Mikhail Zhukov, forty-nine years old, a raven-haired, beak-nosed intellectual and possessor of the finest wine cellar in Moscow, had no idea how the sky looked. In the windowless labyrinth of his interrogation chamber, the atmosphere was that of perpetual night.

Zhukov always thought of his detainees as guests. It seemed so much more civilized that way. A husband and wife were waiting for him—each in a separate room with a soundproof ceiling, several floors below the office levels in the underground passageways beneath the Kremlin's Arsenal Tower. From ancient times, the Arsenal Tower had been blessed with an ever-flowing stream of spring water. During sieges this had been a godsend, but to the men of Zhukov's era, all it meant was that the place was always damp.

He used the subterranean rooms for questioning. Frequently, the sessions became ugly. Zhukov wouldn't admit it, but he looked forward to them. He was especially anxious for today's session to get under way.

As a career KGB man, Zhukov had spent much of his professional life playing cat-and-mouse with the vast Russian underworld. It was an almost impenetrable mosaic of sophisticated black marketeers, common thugs, petty thieves like the roaming bands of gypsies, and highly disciplined, ruthless felons who controlled the network from the Black Sea to Siberia.

From what Zhukov knew about the case, the wife was the brains in this family. He wouldn't even bother talking to the husband. Their file was on a little clipboard that Zhukov always carried around the building. He glanced down at it, then opened the door to the small room.

It was like walking into a cellar, dank and cool. There was a bare wooden table against one wall with leather straps dangling over the sides; a metal chair was attached to the floor in the center of the room, and a single light hung down from the ceiling. There were small holes punched through the seat of the chair so that while a guest sat in the chair, under the light, handcuffs could secure his wrists to the seat of the chair.

The sordidness offended Zhukov's refined sense of comfort, but the stark terror that the squalor of the chamber generated was very effective. He sniffed the air. The odor of sweat.

"What have we here?" he asked one of the two guards in the room, a female matron who usually accompanied women guests.

"A smuggler," she answered. "We found uncut industrial diamonds in a small pouch during a routine strip search at the airport."

The other guard was male, slow and lumbering; Zhukov had used him on many other interrogations. The woman sitting in front of them was a Jew; her husband was a Russian citizen. They had applied for emigration permits and had received them after an unusually short waiting period. That was no mystery to Zhukov. They had simply bribed the right civil servant. But the diamonds bothered him. Diamonds were big money on the black market.

"Strip," he said quietly.

She looked at him, not comprehending.

"I said, take off your clothes."

The woman, fear freezing her face, refused to move. Zhukov nodded to the matron. She grabbed the woman by the shoulders, yanked her to her feet, and began roughly pulling off her clothes.

"Where was the contraband?" Zhukov demanded.

"We found it secreted in an internal crevice."

Zhukov grinned wickedly and shook his head. "You should have swallowed them, then taken a laxative," he told the woman. "That's what most of them do now, you know. I'm having special toilets installed at the airport for just that purpose. A pity. You could probably have gotten away with it this time."

"Please . . ." the woman began, but Zhukov was going to make an example of her.

"Where did the diamonds come from?" he asked. She was about thirty, attractive.

She looked at the floor. He was annoyed that she didn't try to cover herself. "Where?"

"My husband has friends," she said finally, tiny beads of sweat forming on her upper lip. "We sold everything we own in exchange for them."

"You know the rules for taking hard currency or the equivalent out of the country on an emigré pass," Zhukov informed her. "I would certainly call diamonds 'the equivalent,' wouldn't you?"

She said nothing. Zhukov was furious because she had not gone through any of the black-market thieves he worked with. Circumventing the law was one thing, but circumventing Zhukov's own operation was unforgivable.

"Which internal crevice?" he asked the matron, already knowing the answer.

"The vagina."

"Put her up on the table and let's have a look."

The prisoner bolted for the door, but the matron and the big guard easily subdued her. Pushing her down across the low table, they fastened her legs and chest with straps. Her breasts were smashed and reddening.

Carefully, precisely fitting each finger, Zhukov pulled on light-colored plastic gloves that he used for such inspections. The woman on the table was crying and moaning. He motioned the guards over to the table.

Positioning themselves on either side of her, they forced her legs apart. Zhukov thrust a gloved finger into her vagina, then a second and a third.

She screamed in agony. The pain contorting her face, she

begged Zhukov to stop. She swore that she would tell them anything they wanted to know.

He withdrew his hand. "All the contraband appears to be gone," he said. "But one can never be too sure."

Based on her file, she was simply an enterprising Jewess who had found a way to beat the system. She wasn't a dissident. No Zionist activities. He doubted that there was anything of value she could tell them, but there was always a chance.

"Victor," he said to the male guard, "why don't you search the internal crevice more thoroughly, then find out who she paid off for the exit visa and the name of the man who provided the diamonds."

Victor understood. He unbuckled his belt and dropped his uniform trousers. The matron stood by passively. She had been through this before with Comrade Zhukov. Victor performed like a robot.

As Zhukov moved toward the door, he hesitated for one last look.

The screams had died down and the woman on the table lay limp. She wasn't even fighting back as Victor climbed on top of her and began raping her, forcing her legs apart like the two halves of some hideous wishbone. Her eyes were dead.

Whenever Victor did this, it always made Zhukov think of his Tanya.

FOUR

THE BENJAMIN FRANKLIN PARKWAY, PHILADELPHIA

The Meatman dead.

Driscoll still couldn't believe it. If anybody was ever going to be immortal, he would have put his money on that ornery old bastard.

He knew how much Honey had loved the old man. The pain would come spilling out like her father's gushing blood. Honey could never be halfway about anything, happy or sad. Driscoll didn't get off on anguish like that, Mafia or not. He felt sorry for Honey, as much as he despised her father.

The Meatman had raised her like some purebred little bitch terrier. All she had every known was the cockeyed view of the world that the Meatman had given her. For them, there were no laws or rules or ordinary patterns of living that normal people followed—only Families. La Cosa Nostra.

Phillip Driscoll understood that only too well. Once he had come so close to sharing it with her that just thinking about those old days again gave him the shakes. He had done plenty of dangerous things in his life, plenty of stupid things, too. Driscoll knew what it was like to walk the edge, to hold on for dear life to an almost invisible line, separating the cop's world from Honey's world. He knew, too, what it was like to fall off. Driscoll had done that—fallen right into Honey's arms, and then her bed. That first time, he had gotten over her. At least as much as anyone could get over Honey. But a second time? Even Driscoll didn't trust himself *that* far.

Cynthia O'Neill lived in a two-bedroom apartment in an old high-rise on the Benjamin Franklin Parkway. Lida let him off in the parking lot, then said she was heading down to the Roundhouse at 8th and Race streets, police headquarters, to check on their prisoner. Driscoll would handle the Presto business, but first he had to pick up his car. Every time he had gone to bed with a woman after Honey he had told himself that this time it would be different, this time he would feel something. But he never did. Honey had gotten too far inside of him.

Every night that he couldn't sleep, he'd relived every second of that last night they had had together. They were in New York. It was crowded. The holidays, just like now. They figured that was the one city big enough for a cop and the Meatman's daughter to lose themselves. But now he knew better. No place could ever be that big.

That first time they had both gotten off on the danger, as well as on each other. It had been crazy, reckless, dangerous, and irresistible for both of them. A cop and the Meatman's daughter. Each was the other's forbidden fruit. All they had then was each other and a fatal attraction, so compelling that it had knocked the sense right out of both of them.

He had met her when he was supposed to be following her, working on a tip from Intelligence—which turned out to be wrong, naturally—that Honey was out making pickups for the old man. Money-laundering. She was supposed to have a suitcase of hot cash. So he tailed her.

Honey, being Honey, had spotted the tail as effortlessly as her old man. Driscoll had made himself a cop, but Honey had it in her blood. He hadn't caught her in anything dirty. Presto would never have taken a chance like that with her. Driscoll didn't realize that then, but he did now. Before Honey he had just been another flatfoot, fresh, cocky, full of his own bullshit. Honey had changed everything, including Driscoll.

As soon as she made his tail, she panicked and called for help. She thought he was trying to kidnap her, hold her for ransom. And who did Honey call? *Honey called the cops.* That was the one thing Driscoll had never expected her to do. But indignant, she declared herself and told them that she was a citizen, a taxpayer, entitled to just as much protection as anyone else. And how the hell did she know who he was? He didn't look like a cop, he looked like a thug. He could still hear her screaming.

Later, they laughed about it. Driscoll ended up apologizing to her and meaning it. And that had been the start of it. Soon after, hesitantly, positive she'd spit in his face, Driscoll called Honey Presto and asked her out to dinner. A quiet place. Someplace where neither of them would run into anybody they knew. He just wanted to make it up to her, that's all. That's what he said.

Honey listened—he could *hear* her listening and thinking—and finally she said, "What time?" He hadn't even known how to answer her, he was so stunned. It happened so fast for both of them that neither one could think about tomorrow, only now. He never really asked her how she felt about him—Driscoll didn't want to hear her answer if it was the wrong one.

The Meatman must have gotten suspicious. That's what Driscoll surmised. He had them followed one weekend, had pictures taken, and the following Monday a plain brown envelope appeared on the desk of the inspector who ran Internal Affairs.

They tried to take his badge and his gun and hoped to make a case that he was on the Presto payroll. But the commissioner, Alfred E. Smith Lawlor, intervened. He saved Driscoll's career and advised him to flush the girl. Driscoll thought it over. He also thought about the fact that now he owed Lawlor one; he knew that someday, somehow, Lawlor would collect. It was like living with a time bomb in his gut.

That last time it had started out really badly with Honey. Driscoll accused her old man of trying to ruin both their lives. She was barely twenty then. She cried and yelled and hit him; hit him again and again. But in the end there was nothing she could say.

Then Driscoll put it to her. Lawlor had ordered him to choose, and now he was telling her to do the same thing. He could live without being a cop if she could live without the Prestos. That was how much he loved her. There, he said it. He spit it out. She was quiet for a long time after that.

It had been selfish on his part, screaming at Honey, but she had to make a choice. He was mad and scared and hadn't given a damn, but he had forgotten one thing. Being a cop was only what he did; being a Presto was who Honey was.

That night, after the fight, after all the fireworks and electricity with all the juices flowing, they made love as no two people had ever made love before—as if the world could end that night and it wouldn't make any difference. She had been on fire that night, giving him every part of herself. Just before he drifted off to sleep, she promised him that even though it was crazy and hopeless, they could stay together. She would work it out. Driscoll fell asleep with Honey in his arms.

And then she left.

When he woke up in the morning, she was gone. The bill at the hotel was paid and no message had been left. Just like that. Honey shut it down. No calls. No letters. No goodbyes.

Driscoll had ordered her to make a choice, and he figured she'd made it.

He tried to get in touch with her, but she never talked to him again, never saw him again; she stayed away from Philadelphia as much as she could.

Five years had passed. And then, as soon as he heard what had happened to her father, he *knew*. Not a damn thing had changed. He still loved Honey Presto.

Outside Cynthia's building, Driscoll walked through the still-falling snow to his parked car. He opened the trunk and unwrapped his gun—an old single-action .38 Colt Army Special with a smooth wooden handle and extra-long barrel. Slow, but accurate. A museum piece by modern standards, but so was Driscoll. He started to load the gun, then stopped.

He kept the gun, unloaded, in the trunk, and six bullets in his coat pocket. He didn't believe in warning shots, either.

Suddenly he was angry with himself for letting Presto get to him, tempt him to violate his own carved-in-granite rules. Hell, he didn't plan on killing anybody tonight. Driscoll wrapped the gun back up in the towel again. He'd leave the damn thing right where it was.

Driscoll had a quick decision to make: check out the crime scene or visit the morgue. Normally, he would go for the scene, but by this time he was pretty certain that they would have Presto's body bagged and removed. Knowing Honey, she would probably stick with her father's body.

Cynthia's apartment was just on the other bank of the Schuylkill River across from the morgue. He made a sloppy U-turn on the deserted parkway. Driscoll wanted one last look at the Meatman.

He drove west along the expressway, exiting at South Street, near the Penn campus, then headed for the morgue at 321 University Avenue.

Driscoll pulled into one of the diagonal parking spaces that were protected from the snow by a low overhanging roof. None of the medical examiners' meat wagons were around. That meant they were all out on jobs—pickups. A busy night.

He got out of his car and walked up the steep, slippery incline, next to the outdoor scale where they weighed the stiffs. A few minutes later, Driscoll stood in the house of the dead.

It was a long, dark room. Stretching out along either wall there were neat rows of wheeled examination tables, dented and used-looking. On top of each table was a metal tray about six feet long, six inches deep, and coffin-wide.

A body lay on each tray. There were more than a dozen—men and women, black and white, old and young. In death, penises hung limp and exposed; the breasts of women flopped hideously against hollow chest walls. Only a few of the torsoes were covered by sheets. In death, there was no dignity. Driscoll had learned that early. An identification tag dangled from each right big toe. The corpses in front of him were rigid and looked bleached white. The only sign of color was the hair, especially the curly pubic mounds.

Corpses like Presto's arrived at the morgue in thick rubber body bags. They were transported by the police in paddy wagons or by the medical examiners themselves in their black vans. Two men carried a corpse. Driscoll himself had hefted more than he could count.

On arrival, the vehicles backed up onto a concrete loading dock outside the ground-level entrance, partially hidden from the nearby street behind a cinder-block wall. Each corpse was weighted outside and sprayed for lice. In summer, swarms of flies hovered around the dock.

Sensing movement around him, Driscoll suddenly realized that there were other people in the morgue with him. Another body was coming in. It had to be the Meatman.

A silent procession of husky assistant medical examiners, their investigators—glorified clerks in the civil service bureaucracy of the morgue—and big, stone-faced "technicians" walked past the detective. They were huge black men, dressed in starched green smocks, who hauled and warehoused the corpses like sides of beef in a slaughterhouse, stockpiling them before each autopsy and readying them for the undertakers afterward.

Driscoll often wondered how these technicians could rid themselves of the stench of death after their workday ended. Hours after he himself left the morgue, the foul odor would remain in his nostrils. And how about their wives and girlfriends? What was it like to make love with and be fondled by someone who had been touching corpses just a few hours before?

He listened as they began to converse among themselves in the casual manner of professionals servicing their clients. After a few minutes, they left and Driscoll was alone again.

Over the years he had learned that only the best bodies were stored in the main room—or the special ones, like Paul Presto's. The really bad ones, the corpses that had already begun to decompose, were first hosed down to get rid of the maggots and other vermin, then treated by hardened civil service lifters at the morgue in a smaller, grislier adjoining room. Even Driscoll rarely went in there.

The next of kin called upon to identify bodies at the morgue were spared the macabre task of entering the room where Driscoll now stood. They were ushered into a comfortable waiting room upstairs, much like the waiting room of a doctor's office. There they would identify the deceased on a small closed-circuit TV screen, connected to a camera suspended from the ceiling in the morgue downstairs.

It was hoped that such a procedure would reduce the whole ghastly process of identification to a brief TV image and impose an unreality on the stark reality of death.

After the medical examiners and technicians had left, Driscoll went over to the wheeled dolly they had left in the middle of the room and checked the toe tag. It read "Paul Presto." Driscoll snapped the sheet back. The strong smell of smoke and charred wood still clung to the body. The facial features had been almost completely destroyed, the melted layers of skin revealing the teeth and gum line along the right side. Half flesh and half skull. Driscoll had to turn away from the gruesome sight.

Then he heard a commotion behind him. Screaming. A woman screaming. Shrieking. Demanding to be let in. Driscoll moved into the dark shadows far to the rear of the cavernous room and ducked down behind a corpse.

"This is *my father.* Do you understand that? *My father!* I don't want to see him on television. Now let me in. Damn you!"

Suddenly, Honey Presto, the Meatman's daughter, was standing in front of the collapsible metal dolly on which her father's broken body lay.

Driscoll, still in the shadows, could once again feel something hypnotic in her dangerous, compelling beauty. Honey had never been pretty in the usual, cosmetic way—she looked too much like the Meatman for that—but there was a sensuality about her, an appetite that Driscoll had been unable to resist.

Honey's hair was a mass of loose, soft chestnut-brown curls that fell to her shoulders. It was longer now than he remembered it. As she gestured and talked, the curls bounced and framed that petulant oval face. Chipmunk cheeks, full lips with a small pouting mouth, skillfully outlined in color and lip gloss and those raccoon eyes. They could never change—eyes so large and ravenous that Honey looked as if she were ready to bite. Driscoll knew that look.

Dr. Troy, the chief medical examiner, and several of his flustered assistants were with her. An older man, whom Driscoll didn't recognize, hovered at Honey's elbow. He was leaning on a very expensive-looking cane, listening. Every mob lawyer Driscoll had ever seen listened like that, dour and distant. That's who this guy had to be—a mouthpiece.

Honey refused to be still. Her eyes were brimming with tears, but she would not give in. She had battled her way down from the viewing room.

"I want to see what you people have done to my father. Don't try to stop me."

The mouthpiece leaned over and whispered in Honey's ear. "That won't be necessary, Mr. Littlejohn," she snapped. "I don't need any court order to handle these jerks!" Driscoll loved it. Honey could really take care of herself.

"You're only making it harder on yourself," Nick Troy interrupted her. Driscoll could tell by his tone of voice that his patience was wearing thin.

"You let *me* be the judge of that," she replied haughtily.

Troy was fuming now. "Young woman, you're not even permitted to be down here. I'm going to have to insist that you return to the viewing room upstairs."

Then Troy attempted to take her elbow and lead her to the door. But Honey wouldn't budge. She turned quickly, back to where her father lay, tossing her brown curls defiantly.

"This is illegal," Troy shouted angrily.

"So is a bomb on your front porch," Honey retorted.

This girl *still* has balls, Driscoll thought to himself.

"I want to see my father's face. I want to take him out of this place. *Right now.* And I want *all* of the personal effects you took from him." Each word snapped out commandingly like the crack of a riding crop.

Driscoll had almost forgotten how small Honey was. Five feet, if she was lucky—a tiny Borgia princess. How the hell could the Meatman have produced anyone who looked like this?"

Gold glittered and diamonds sparkled on her wrists and fingers. She was wearing the kind of dress, low-cut and snug against her body, that invited guys to take a better look. He guessed that she had gotten the news about her father while she was partying. Honey loved to party.

Her breasts seemed large for her small frame, falling to a soft, full, natural angle. Shivering, she pulled a velvet cape around her. He liked hips that were just a fraction too wide, like hers, and standing there in the halflight of the house of the dead, Honey looked as ripe as a Raphael cherub.

Cross this girl, Driscoll had learned, and you might not live to repeat your mistake. He could see that somewhere in the little dark caves behind her eyes, something wild was stirring to life.

"Will you remove that sheet or do I have to do it myself?" she demanded of Troy, zapping him with a frigid stare.

"Grief is one thing," Troy answered, "stupidity is something else."

"Damn you!"

With that, Honey ripped back the sheet. She gasped. The mouthpiece reached out to steady her.

"We tried to warn you," Troy stammered weakly.

But Honey didn't say a word. She waved the lawyer aside, nudging him with her gloved hand. From his vantage point on the other side of the room, Driscoll could smell Presto's remains and see the skull poking through the flesh. A sight like that would have to knock any woman on her ass, even Honey Presto.

But instead of fainting, she reached out toward the body, carefully removed her glove, placed her fingers on her father's gnarled hand. "I love you, Daddy," Driscoll heard her say. Then she leaned right down across the body and kissed what was left of those burned, mangled lips. As Honey backed away from the dolly, tenderly drawing the sheet back over the Meatman's face, Driscoll noticed that some of the blood from Presto's face had smeared across his daughter's cheek. Honey made no attempt to wipe it away. The room was absolutely still.

Not just balls, Driscoll complimented her, brass balls.

"Whoever killed him is going to die too," she said acidly, calmly, addressing no one, everyone. "A vendetta."

Nick Troy and the mouthpiece didn't utter a word.

"I'll kill whoever did this myself, I promise you, Daddy. . . . and eye for an eye . . . the Meatman's way."

Driscoll was just about to make an unseen exit when he spotted a big, burly black man, Ed Bellows, heading in Honey's direction. He'd burst into the room through the same door that the technicians had used to bring Presto's body in. Bellows was the director of the U.S. Justice Department's Organized Crime Strike Force in Philadelphia. What the hell was Bellows doing here? the detective wondered.

Bellows was bald-headed, six feet eight, with curly black muttonchops curving up from his cheeks like a ram's horns, then stopping abruptly just below his ears.

"I'm so sorry, Miss Presto," Bellows began, his deep voice booming off the echoing morgue wall. "I understand that you and your attorney wanted to see me. . . . We'll get whoever did this."

Honey looked as if she could fit inside one of Big Ed's gloves, but she didn't back off. "You people did this." She gestured in the Meatman's direction. "Don't lie to me. I'm in no mood for your phony sympathy."

"If you know more about this than we do," Bellows said, "why don't you tell *us* what happened? I didn't kill anybody or give any orders to have anybody killed. We're not in that business. That was your father's business."

"How would you know anything about my father?" she said coldly.

Bellows didn't answer. It was dawning on Phillip Driscoll that these two really knew each other.

"I *told* my father he was crazy to trust you," Honey screamed at Bellows. "Now, he's dead. It's your fault—all your fault. And the rest of them. But believe me, you'll all pay for this."

Ed Bellows shot her a withering look. Driscoll could sense the sudden alarm in the huge black prosecutor. The mouthpiece was doing his best to quiet Honey. "Not here, Miss

Presto, please,'' Littlejohn entreated. ''We can discuss this later. *Please.*''

Honey was angry at Littlejohn for butting in. But for the moment, at least, she kept her mouth shut.

''I don't know what your father told you,'' Bellows growled at the raging girl, ''but you are getting into a very sensitive area.'' Bellow's look was a warning to Nick Troy and the other morgue assistants. ''We won't go into anything here. We'll handle it in my office.'' Then Bellows added something that he thought would calm Honey. *''He* has been informed.''

But that was all she needed to hear. *''Been informed!* Is that what you call it now when a man's been murdered? Informed?''

''That's all we can do for now.''

''Well, that's not all *I* can do.''

''Miss Presto, I'm warning you,'' Bellows admonished her.

Honey and the Strike Force chief stood glaring at each other. Driscoll wanted to know what the hell was going on. He couldn't believe what he was hearing. It sounded as if the Meatman had cut a deal with the feds, with Bellows, of all people. And *who* had been informed?

''Move!'' Honey screamed suddenly. ''Get out of my way!'' She motioned to Littlejohn, and together they started pushing the dolly with her father's body on it past the protesting Dr. Troy. Honey practically ran over him.

Bellows stood immobile. Driscoll knew that it was up to him to make a move.

''One more step and I take you in,'' he ordered from the darkness. Every head in the room spun around in the direction of the voice. Driscoll had the edge. Even Bellows was startled. He looked at Driscoll as though he were one of the corpses suddenly come to life.

''What are *you* doing here?'' Honey yelled at him, stunned, dumbfounded, to see him again after all this time. She looked suspiciously at Bellows, then at Driscoll again. He couldn't be sure, but he wanted to believe that Honey, surprised as she was, was also just a little pleased to see him there.

"Where the hell did you come from?" Bellows demanded.

Driscoll ignored him. Then he turned to Honey. "Touch your father's body and you are under arrest."

Driscoll was in full view by now, and he flashed his detective's badge in Honey's stormy face—the number 710 over the City of Philadelphia's official seal. "As of this minute," he informed her, "your father's body constitutes evidence in an ongoing homicide investigation and you are tampering with it."

The mouthpiece started to speak. Driscoll interrupted him. "We have to have an autopsy. We want to know who killed him, too. After that, you can send the undertaker."

"And what if we say no? You can't stop me from claiming my own father's body." She was challenging him. Again. "My attorney . . ." Honey began, pointing to Littlejohn, who was nervously tapping his cane.

"He goes, too," Driscoll said. He knew that she knew he meant it.

Honey was infuriated. "Who the hell do you think you are?" she demanded, ready for a battle, refusing to back off.

Driscoll didn't say a word. He just reached into his pocket, pulled out a clean white handkerchief, and dabbed at the smear of blood on Honey's cheek.

FIVE

MCLEAN, VIRGINIA

James X. Carney was alone with the dream when he found out about the Meatman.

Carney slept in an ornate four-poster bed with a blue-and-white canopy above his head. The frame was so high off the floor that he needed a two-step stool to climb into it. His entire house, a twelve-bedroom turn-of-the-century planter's estate in McLean, Virginia, set on 150 soft, fruitful acres, had a pleasing Victorian busyness to it. The canopied bed was an indulgence Carney had permitted himself many years before. When he had first begun sleeping in it, the lush down had made him feel as regal as a Plantagenet. Over the years, though, that feeling had slowly worn off. Still, he treasured it—outsized, antique, and as comfortable as it was ostentatious.

The dream had been the same as always. The hooded man had stalked him, hunted him, and finally cornered him high up in an ancient deserted building. Pigeons flapped crazily in and out of gaping windows that were improbably tall.

A gray sky, as always. The hooded man's weapon was a revolver, black and shiny. Gripping it with both hands, raising it in a slow dream cadence that seemed to take forever, he leveled it at Carney's head.

Then, suddenly, just as in so many dreams before, a face unexpectedly appeared beneath the hood—a round, boyish, unlined face, as Carney's had once been. Just as it came into view, just as the hooded man opened fire, Jim Carney recognized the face in the dream. It was his own.

Each bullet hit its mark unerringly, but Carney felt nothing. No pain. No blood. The face, his mirror image, stared at him mockingly.

The dream had become so much a part of his consciousness, as well as his subconscious, that he sometimes believed it had moved in with him like an unwelcome guest. He hated sharing his home and his head with an interloper. He was afraid to fall asleep, certain that the dream would be there, waiting, tormenting him. Every morning the dark circles under his eyes were proof that the dream had sought him out and found him, persistent as pain. Carney had come to the conclusion that the dream meant to kill him.

He wasn't ready to die. He would fight back.

Carney was a trim sixty-one, with white wavy hair, perfect teeth, and a slightly patronizing bearing, softened somewhat by a rakishly engaging smile. Carney loved horses, and he rode every weekend. At squash, he was a deadly serious competitor. He adhered religiously to a low-sodium diet and battled resolutely against the encroachments of age. His reward was the fit, well-exercised body of a Potomac patrician.

Born to wealth among the Hyde Park aristocracy of New York, Carney had run unsuccessfully for the U.S. Senate when he was thirty-nine years old—a committed New Dealer whose era had passed. He had abandoned active politics after that, embittered by what he considered a demeaning experience. From there, Carney had served as counsel to the director of the Central Intelligence Agency for nine years, outlasting four appointed superiors in the process. Eventually he tired of that, too, and turned his back on government service for good, preferring instead the considerable creature comforts to be found within the old-boy network of Washington's moneyed law firms. Because Carney had made that transition fully a generation earlier than most men of his age, abandoning public service while still in his prime, he quickly became a mentor of tremendous influence to ambitious men just a few years his junior. Not yet fifty then, he was routinely and respectfully mentioned whenever the Capitol's ten most powerful men were listed. He thrived on his importance. His patronage was viewed as a certain ticket to the Senate, at least—the same Senate that had eluded him.

Never married, he worked diligently at his reputation as a lady's man of renown in some of the most discreetly curtained bedrooms of Georgetown. Carney preferred married women. He found them financially secure, mature enough to realize that nothing was forever, and, on the whole, even hornier than he was. It wasn't unusual for him to conduct business with some cuckolded husband over cocktails the evening after bedding his wife. Rarely did he have regrets and seldom did he spend a lonely night.

His true passion, however, his fatal addiction—Carney sometimes warned himself—was young men. Every time he had sex with a pretty young man under that gorgeous canopy, Jim Carney was playing an outrageous gamble, placing his career and wealth at risk, but the long odds merely enhanced his excitement.

Sex was Carney's theology, the one unalterable absolute in his universe. Because he cultivated his reputation as a stud with assiduous care, he would never admit, particularly to himself, that he was bisexual. That term seemed to him so banal, so clinical, trivializing a situation that he rationalized as simply a full menu of sexual preferences. Women were boring and predictable to the point of tedium—lacking in the ingenuity manifested by his young men.

In any case, Carney had been celibate for two months now, and much too busy to search for any kind of body to share the long hours and the whispering silk of his platform bed.

Consecutively, beginning even before Carney had left the employ of the CIA, three occupants of the White House had paid handsomely for his advice and his services—not sexual, of course, but covert. Think tanks from Stanford to Harvard had sought his cachet. Carney possessed power, the power of extremely high intelligence, and he knew precisely where to apply it. In exchange, he demanded absolute autonomy. His clients were only too willing to accommodate him—even Presidents. His terms were firm—a blank check and complete secrecy about the nature of his assignments.

His closest friend, a man with whom Carney had shared power, secrets, and women, just happened to be the current President of the United States. Only three months before, Jim Carney—"James Xavier Carney, dashing Washington power broker," as the press referred to him—had turned down the job of national security adviser, providing enough conversational fodder for much of the winter among the regulars at Washington's toniest clubs and wainscoted dining rooms.

Carney didn't care. He was beginning to grow weary of Washington and its trappings. But not weary enough to turn down his best friend's urgent request.

The President had asked him to handle some particularly sensitive negotiations, and he had been doing just that for the past few weeks. This unusual portfolio had consumed him so completely that the results had been first a bout of insomnia, and then the recurring nightmare that he had been experiencing almost nightly, including tonight.

The ringing telephone summoned Carney from his troubled sleep. He picked up the phone on the second shot.

"We just lost Philadelphia," a voice, which Carney immediately recognized, informed him. The voice sounded apologetic for disturbing him at such a late hour on the cold night of Paul Presto's assassination.

DOWNTOWN PHILADELPHIA

Driscoll left the morgue, knowing that now he had to find out everything he could about Honey and Bellows and their heated conversation. She had pulled away from him after he had wiped the blood from her cheek. He had wanted to say something to her, but Honey hadn't given him the chance.

Normally, the drive to Presto's house would take about twenty minutes through downtown Philadelphia. Driscoll pulled out into the deserted street, made an illegal left, and picked up the icy South Street Bridge.

There was one more thing Driscoll wanted to do before going to the crime scene. He pulled into the first pay phone he saw and dialed Spanish Joe's number at the Roundhouse. Lida answered.

"Do we have anything at all on the guy in custody?" Driscoll asked. "Any way to connect him to the bombing?"

"Yo, Phil, you're getting ahead of yourself," Lida said. "This guy must be a mute. Not a word, so far. Either that—"

"Or he doesn't speak English," Driscoll said with growing certainty.

"You took the words right out of my mouth. So I guess we'll have to find an interpreter to interrogate him. Got any ideas about where we should start? He's white, we know that. That leaves out Africa."

"I'd like to interrogate him," Driscoll said viciously. "I've never known a cigarette on the balls to fail."

"Sounds interesting."

Driscoll had to make something happen on this. "See if we have somebody there who knows how to contact Interpol. They're overseas someplace. If he really is a squarehead, they ought to have a jacket on him. It's worth a try."

"Interpol?" Lida said sarcastically. "Aren't we continental! I'll bet you've been waiting all you life to tell somebody to do that." She laughed.

"Just you," he said.

She thought for a moment. "It would probably be quicker if we asked the FBI to do it. They have all that information at their fingertips."

"No," Driscoll said sharply. "I don't want any feds in on this. Not yet. The minute we talk to them, somebody's sure to tell Bellows. Then he'll have everything we have. I have no idea where he's coming from on the Meatman thing. We do it all ourselves. You and Joe get the stuff you need. Interpol takes fingerprints or a telefax copy of a mug shot. Get either one and you're all set."

"He's in fingerprints now," she said.

"How come that took so long?" Fingerprinting a suspect was routine.

"I don't know, Phil. It didn't take or something, so we sent him down again."

"I don't understand that," he said.

"When did you see Bellows?" Lida was curious.

"A few minutes ago at the morgue."

"What was he doing there?"

Driscoll wished that he knew. "It's a long story, Lida. Tell you later."

"Did his daughter show up?" Lida had heard all the stories about Honey Presto and Driscoll.

"She showed, all right," Driscoll replied. Then he hung up.

FLETCHER STREET

South Philly and the Girard Estate was a grid of row-houses and corner stores. To Driscoll every store was a numbers drop and every other house a hideout where they sat around the kitchen table planning the next job they would pull.

He glanced at his watch as he turned off 22nd Street onto Fletcher. Exactly twelve minutes from the phone booth. Not bad in a snowstorm. Suddenly two big red fire engines cut in front of him—a fat pumper and a hook-and-ladder with thick icicles forming along the gleaming running boards and handrails. He parked near a barricade of yellow sawhorses and got out. Everywhere heads were poking out of open windows. Cold air was seeping into cozy bedrooms. Driscoll couldn't see any faces, but if he could have, he knew what he would find—a blend of curiosity and pride. Mafia murders were events in this neighborhood, and they had been for as long as Driscoll and his fellow cops could remember. While he was alive, Paul Presto had been half outlaw and half saint. But in death, he would become a martyr. They all did—every hood in South Philly. Their personal effects became relics; the time of their death would become the most heavily played number on the streets for the next two weeks. Fans and groupies who never missed a big mob funeral would show up at the wake as though it were a world premiere.

A blue mobile lab from the Roundhouse was up on the curb, close to the front of Presto's house. Dark-colored four-door Plymouths, FBI cars, had transformed the street into a gridlocked parking lot. Lumpy canvas fire hoses criss-crossed everywhere. Driscoll's nostrils picked up the heavy odor of burned and smoldering wood. The front door of the house and most of the porch had been blown away. The bomb had been just powerful enough.

Captain Biaggio Marinari was the first person to approach Driscoll. He was a dark, well-dressed Sicilian who felt threatened by Driscoll, and he never missed a chance to make the detective's life miserable.

"I'm glad you took your time, Driscoll," he said acidly.

Driscoll noticed Marinari's long gray English warmer with two rows of buttons down the front and epaulets. His scarf was yellow silk with tiny black diamonds; his gloves were soft pigskin. His shoes were Italian leather. Marinari looked like a TV cop.

Phillip Driscoll made no attempt to greet his boss. He searched in his pockets for his gloves, then remembered that he had left them at the apartment.

"Where you been, anyway?" Marinari asked. "You think you're too damn good to let me know where the hell you are?"

"How'd you know?" Driscoll answered, looking down at the much shorter Marinari, then glancing around to get the feel of what had happened. He figured that the killers probably had used the park for cover. Whatever they were doing, they hadn't attracted any attention. They had caught Presto with his guard down. Nobody to help him; no chance to fight back. A bomb in just the right spot. Two of them, he guessed. At least one lookout. Well planned. They had to know the Meatman's pattern, too. They'd hit him on his way home. Driscoll wondered where he had been coming from. He had to check that out.

If Captain Marinari had ever known, he had forgotten what to look for at a crime scene. Driscoll felt his eyes on him, waiting for Driscoll to take the lead. His boss didn't want to embarrass himself. But Driscoll kept quiet on purpose.

Finally, he switched tactics. Biaggio was doing his damnedest to sound friendly now. "What've we got here, Phil? What's it look like to you?" The captain knew that before long, an inspector, then a chief inspector, and finally a deputy commissioner would be arriving, wanting to know what Marinari was doing about this case.

"I think we got a dead Dago," Driscoll replied, grinning. He knew Marinari was trying to control himself. "Conventional wisdom tells us that in cases like this, the next Dago in line usually did it. Isn't that how it works, Biaggio?"

The captain's rage surfaced. "I need to come up with somebody real quick, Driscoll. You cut out the bullshit and tell me what we got here."

This time, Driscoll didn't know what they had. Presto was dead. And after the way Honey and Bellows had gone after each other in the morgue, Driscoll didn't know what to think. Bellows had hustled out of the morgue so fast he hadn't even seen him leave. Honey and Littlejohn and a couple of no-neck bodyguards had all driven away in the same car.

The hit had been professional. Who was behind it? Nobody just walked up and dropped a bomb on the front porch of a man like Presto. He was a member of the *commissione*, for God's sake. A murder like that would have to be cleared right to the top—but where was the top on this one? Some sterile government office in Washington or a social club in Little Italy?

Instinct and experience told the detectives to go for some other more ambitious Family—at least as a starting point.

One Family trying to usurp another's turf was not unusual, but that didn't happen overnight. They always sent out signals and would go to any lengths to preserve the rituals and rites. Symbols were everything. Torn $100 bills stuck up a guy's rectum meant that he had been a greedy pig. Firecrackers in the mouth was revenge for a bombing. If a physical beating accompanied a shooting or garroting, that was a sign of great disrespect. So was being dumped on a close relative's doorstep. If they cut off your penis, you had screwed the wrong lady.

But Presto's assassin had failed to keep up with the sacramentals. Something was missing, and that bothered Driscoll. Perhaps no message was the most compelling message of all.

GARNETT STREET, SOUTH PHILADELPHIA

Tony Bonaventura was listening to his wife Marie's conversation with Honey on an extension in their bedroom. Marie was using the beige wall phone over the counter in her kitchen, half sitting, half leaning on a tall padded stool. She was too short and too heavy to make it all the way to the seat.

Marie was furious. The tone of her voice was enough to tell Tony that. Usually a loud, coarse woman, Marie Bonaventura became deadly quiet when she was angry. Her speech became affected, too. It was as though she became too mad to articulate sounds, and the words came out like clipped, harsh barks.

"I said a dozen rosaries already. I'm so worried about you." Aunt Marie's voice assaulted Honey over the telephone. "I got your Uncle Tony out wit' all the udder men lookin' for you," she lied. "You a bad girl, Honey. You go away, you just disappear, and you don't tell us nothin'. We thought you was killed, too, like your daddy, God bless 'im. Where you at now?" The words kept rushing out. She didn't let up for air. "Oh, you went to the morgue . . . by yourself? Tony coulda done that. . . . Honey, what happened? Did he look awful? Ya know, they're tryin' to hurt us, baby; kill us, too. You come right here to me and Tony. We all gotta stay together now."

Honey was sobbing. "I know. I know. I'm so scared, Aunt Marie. But I'm all right now. I just have to see somebody, that's all."

"See who?" Marie demanded.

"Don't worry who."

Marie made a face that said Honey had an obligation to tell her who. "Don't you tell me don't worry. I'm clear outta my mind. You know you're like my own kid." Marie was blubbering into the phone.

Honey felt guilty. "Please, Aunt Marie, I know you're worried, but I can't help it. I have to find out who killed Daddy . . . I have to . . ." And Honey was crying into the phone, too.

Marie's blubbering ceased abruptly. "Now, you listen to me, Honoria. You tell me this minute where you are," Marie screamed. "Uncle Tony and me—we come get you. *You hear me, girl?"*

"No, Aunt Marie. I won't tell you, and I mean it. I have to do this myself."

"Stubborn. Just like your father. So damn stubborn. But I'm tellin' you, and you better listen if you know what's good for you."

"Goodbye, Aunt Marie. I'll call you again. *Please* don't worry."

"Honey! *Honey!* . . ."

Tears were streaming down Marie's olive cheeks now, smearing mascara all over her face.

Tony Bonaventura put the phone down and walked into the kitchen. Marie was hissing like a boiling teapot. "So, Tony, what'd you think?"

"I don't know, Marie. I couldn't pick up no sounds to tell me where she is. But she has to be close. How far could she get?"

"What goes on, Tony?"

"What you mean?"

"Does that little bitch know somethin' she's not tellin' us?"

"Not possible."

"She's a smart girl, Tony."

"Not *that* smart." Tony spat it out. He and Honey had never hit it off.

Marie had always been jealous of her brother, Paul Presto. He was the family success story, while her own husband, Tony, was the lapdog who answered the Meatman's call. Now, with her brother suddenly dead, assassinated, she was concerned for little Honey—and for herself. But Marie's grief was not half as profound as her greed at the opportunity the unexpected hit might offer. Her niece, Honey, was just a girl—not a proper heir.

She had gotten very quiet after the call from Joe-Joey. So much was happening all at once. In the span of a few hours, Tony Bonaventura had been propelled from his role as obedient underboss, slave to the Meatman's every whim, to boss of the whole Presto Family. But now the Family was under attack. What was that name Joe-Joey had mentioned when he called to tell Tony about the bank—Butkova or something like that?

First the Meatman, and then the bank. And now this Butkova pig. She wondered if there was a connection. And on top of all that, that damn brat Honey was out there running around on her own, no bodyguards, instead of leaving it up to the men, like her Uncle Tony.

"Tony," Marie said to her husband, sliding down from the kitchen stool, "this could be our time." Tony had learned to listen when his wife spoke. Attentive now, his nostrils quivered. He could smell a good thing coming.

"We'll just watch what happens at the wake," Marie advised him. "Our flowers *have* to be the best. I want a meat cleaver made out of red roses. And a clock set at the time Paul died. Tell the florist to use red carnations for the numbers. Then we'll see," Marie assured Tony. "Then we'll see," her mouth had taken on the expression of a wolf's that was wearing lipstick. "Next we have to have a Family conference. The way Paul died, somebody's gonna be next. Maybe us. So we have a meet."

"With Honey?" he asked.

"Forget Honey."

Tony looked stunned. "You *can't* do that, Marie," he began to protest. Then he saw the look in her eyes. He shrank down a full size inside his clothing. Marie was already so many steps ahead of him he could never catch up.

"I'll take care of that little whore," Marie promised. "That little *puttana*. You just find out who this pig Butkova is, and *you* take care of him."

SIX

A WAREHOUSE IN BUSTLETON, NORTHEAST PHILADELPHIA

Less than an hour after the raid on the Meatman's bank, Nikolai Butkova was sitting back in his office at his warehouse with four men arrayed before him, nervously awaiting his decision on a breach of loyalty. He'd ordered them, rasping in his rough, forceful way, to stand where they were. In his presence, they all knew they were permitted to speak only Russian, and only the country dialect from the region outside Odessa where his family had lived for generations.

Two of the cars that had been used in the raid were already on their way back to Atlantic City, where they had been stolen earlier in the night. His men would return the vehicles to one of the casino parking lots, and their rightful owners would never be the wiser. The third car, the one that the snowplow had crushed, would merely be reported as stolen.

Butkova wasn't concerned that the police had caught one of his men, Emil Menschikoff. Even if tortured, Menschikoff would never talk. He had been tortured by experts, by the Soviet domestic police, the Militsia, and had never given the bastards anything. In America, the cops were gutless, like eunuchs, pussies. They wouldn't dare torture a suspect. It was so much easier in America.

Butkova had grown up in a village with rolling cultivated

farmland running clear to the horizon on every side. Killing came naturally to farmers like Butkova's people. He admired them for that. The first time he had witnessed a farmer's wife wring a chicken's neck, he had been just seven. It had been quick, painful, noisy. After that, the farmers' wives let him try. The first few times, the birds, tough and fighting for their lives, had nearly gotten away from him. Nearly. He learned to strangle them, breaking a bird's thick, stringy neck as he worked his thumbs to pinch off the air supply. Then young Nikolai would shop off the head with a small, sharp hand ax, standing well back from the chicken to make sure that its guts and blood and excrement didn't splash up on his shirt and overalls. In the beginning, little Nikolai did get dirty; then he got better at it. One of the fat country wives would just give him a gentle shove, then bunch up her apron above her fleshy legs and dab at the mess, roughly wiping it away.

Butkova was nineteen years old the first time he strangled a man. That had been different, of course, but somehow it was the same, too. The technique was the same. Press strong fingers into the soft part of the neck, just below the jawline; squeeze until the oxygen was cut off, then snap the neck hard, using a knee for leverage. As long as a man had what it took to look another man in the eye and use his bare hands to kill him, a weapon was never necessary. Butkova had learned that lesson early.

After his short speech, he uttered one word in English: "Traitor." He nodded to three of the men; they reacted by seizing the fourth.

The man didn't try to escape. He had known Butkova long enough to realize that the attempt would be futile. There was, instead, a dark, dull mask of resignation on his face as Butkova's rippling forearms, as swollen as hams, gripped him around the throat.

Forced to his knees by his powerful adversary, he finally closed his eyes, barely putting up any struggle at all, as Butkova closed in on him. He had spent close to eighteen years with Butkova, even before they had come to America together in 1978, and he had seen, firsthand, the fiendish torture that Butkova was capable of; better it should end this way.

Less than thirty seconds later, he lay sprawled at Nikolai Butkova's feet. Lifeless. His neck snapped like a chicken's.

Butkova motioned for the other three men to pick up his body. Immediately, they obeyed.

"Take this traitor back to the drums," Butkova ordered. They followed him, dragging the dead man by gripping him under his shoulders, his toes scraping along the floor.

Still using the language they understood, Butkova said, "I trusted this man as if he were my own. I loved him. Dressed his wounds, cared for his children. I would have died for this man. But now he betrays me, betrays all of us. A Judas. A goddamn Judas."

Then Butkova spit on the floor, in the direction of the corpse.

"Open that drum lid," he told them.

They were in the rear warehouse behind Butkova's oil-importing complex of crisscrossing rail spur lines and cluttered industrial yards, ringed with fences. The building was ice-cold, unheated and drafty. He stored a wide variety of chemicals in the warehouse, mostly in 55-gallon metal drums. His business in Bustleton, in Northeast Philadelphia on the ragged fringe of a serene porch-front neighborhood there, appeared nondescript. Sometimes the children would break his windows or spray-paint the sides of his tanker trucks. But he put up with such inconveniences patiently. Gladly. He didn't want to attract any attention. Let the damn little brats have their fun.

The warehouse was no more than half a block from the driveway of a line of houses. He could see lights in most of the kitchen windows.

The 55-gallon drum they had just opened contained hydrochloric acid, a highly corrosive, fuming liquid that hissed faintly when the air hit it.

His green-and-gray trucks picked up cargoes of oil and chemicals from the great ships that moored at the port of Philadelphia and delivered them to customers throughout Northeast Philadelphia and the northern suburbs. He supplied builders, in addition to his residential customers, with oil, varnish, and turpentine. Amid all the seemingly harmless drums of finishes and resins, the acid was well hidden.

"Headfirst," he said. "Watch your hands." They had

already pulled on thick rubber gloves, specially treated, insulated, with rough canvas over the palms and fingertips. "Don't let it splash." But the three men he was admonishing didn't have to be warned. They had done this before, and they knew that just a few drops could cut through the flesh of a man's hand like the blue flame of an acetylene torch.

"Shoes last. Let him slide in. Don't touch."

First the dead man's head and face disappeared, then his shoulders, chest, stomach, waist, hips, and thighs, finally his legs, ankles, and feet. His shoes seemed to float, upside down, on top of the fuming acid for a moment before vanishing into the bubbling vat.

No one spoke, except Butkova, offering his advice and warning them incessantly not to let the acid touch their skin or clothing. The hissing turned into an audible sizzle as the dead man became one with the acid—flesh, blood, bones, clothes, and all.

One man blessed himself. Butkova ignored him. After three minutes, the body wastes and chemicals from the corpse had interacted with the acid and the noxious liquid took on a watery yellow tint.

It was over.

The drum was close to a wide double-door side entrance to the warehouse. Butkova shouldered open one of the doors. A couple of inches of snow had drifted up next to it on the outside. The ground under the snow was frozen dirt; it inclined slightly to a field that was covered with weeds in warm weather, then drained away.

Butkova raised his leg and kicked at the 55-gallon drum, knocking it on its side and releasing the small torrent of acid. They watched it drain into the dirt, melting the snow in an ever-widening circle, as the acid ate away at the snow and frozen earth. Draining down the incline, it seared a path to the barren field. Against the dark silhouette, not a hundred yards away, the happy housewives of Bustleton went about their chores, puttering in their kitchens, opening oven doors, and shooing little ones off to bed.

Only after the last of the acid had drained away did Butkova yank the drum back upright and replace the lid.

This time he spoke in English again in his deadly, patient

way. "KGB," he said, pointing to the ugly trail of liquid simmering in the snow. "I hope Moscow learns its lesson." Butkova looked hard at the three men. "You tell our people what you saw tonight. You tell them the next KGB informer I catch—no matter how close he is to me or how close he thinks he is to me—I put him in the drum." He paused for effect. Glaring, he screamed, *"Next time I put him in alive.* That's how Butkova deals with KGB."

MCLEAN

Jim Carney reached for his half-glasses and shifted the telephone receiver from one hand to the other. "When?" he asked.

"About an hour ago," the familiar voice responded.

"Where?" Carney went down the two steps from his bed to the richly carpeted floor. Crossing the room and taking the phone with him, Carney seated himself at an English writing table nearly two centuries old. He glanced at the fireplace, where embers still glowed red.

"Right outside his house. He turned the doorknob and the porch blew up."

"How?"

"IED."

Sometimes Carney thought he would go crazy trying to cut through all this secret-agent bullshit. "And what the hell is IED?"

"Improvised explosive device. Radio-controlled detonator—"

"Spare me the details," Carney snapped impatiently. "What about Presto's family? The daughter?" The disturbing image of Honey Presto sprang into Carney's mind.

"She's acting just like her father's daughter. Screaming, asking question, talking vendetta."

Carney had been afraid of that. They were all in too deep

now for Honey to jeopardize the operation. He took a deep breath before replying. "Then take care of her," Carney ordered, his voice hollow. "Do what you have to do."

The voice on the phone understood.

There was another long silence. Then Carney replaced the telephone in its cradle and switched on a small desk lamp. Its green glass globe lit up.

Opening the narrow, shallow center drawer of the antique writing table, Carney took out a yellow legal pad. A series of numbers was written on it. Every forty-eight hours, the code numbers changed. At precisely 8:00 a.m. every other morning Carney received a hand-delivered, sealed envelope from a young Marine lieutenant assigned to the Cryptography Center at CIA headquarters. At one time Carney would have just memorized the numbers. These days, though, he needed the yellow pad.

There was a second phone, red, on the writing table, with a black plastic cover where the push buttons should have been. He picked up the receiver and repeated the series of numbers from the yellow pad. A security computer from the government's massive underground complex at Hollow Stream, Virginia, listened. In seven seconds, the code number was verified and a high-speed voice analysis was performed, testing the electronic vibrations of Carney's vocal cords against the memory bank of the twelve persons in the United States who possessed a "cosmic clearance" to contact the President of the United States at any hour of the day or night.

"Proceed," a robotic computer voice instructed Jim Carney, as several million electronic circuits, all linked to a single microchip, began securing his connection from McLean to Hollow Stream to Air Force One, where the President was at that moment, en route to a long-awaited Summit conference with the Chairman of the Soviet Union. This would cap a series of NATO-strengthening meetings with the European allies.

Picking up a Mont Blanc fountain pen, Carney screwed off the top and squared the sheets of another yellow legal pad in front of him. He waited. The summit was to take place in Geneva. Ordinarily, Carney would have been aboard Air Force One with the President, prepping him for the rigors of the negotiations to come, but this time Carney had been most useful by staying at home.

Thirty seconds later, a sleepy voice managed a hearty hello to Carney. It was the President. Carney had to tell him about the Meatman.

FLETCHER STREET

Before crossing the Meatman's block on Fletcher Street, Driscoll detoured to the little park where Whitey had waited. The detective was a firm believer in tire marks, especially indentations in new-fallen snow. The snow would melt too fast to allow plaster castings to harden, but you couldn't beat it for quick visual observation.

The park had a sidewalk on three sides. The fourth side, directly across from the Meatman's house, was grass right down to the street. No curb. That's where Driscoll figured they'd waited. That's where he would have waited had Driscoll been planning to assassinate Presto on his front porch.

The fire engines had turned most of the block into slush, but where the grass met the asphalt on the side of the park, Driscoll found what he was looking for—tire tracks blurred by more recent snow. He brought a flashlight from his car, and trained its beam on the ridges in the darkness, judging the depth and width of the powdery white outline. With his hand he gently brushed the surface snow from the packed treadmarks. Lousy tread, no snow tires or chains or studs. Just big bald tires. Too big for a car, too small for a truck. It had to be a van.

The snow was swirling into his face, but he could see that these treadmarks, the ones that started from rest, the ones that looked as though they came from a vehicle that had been there for a while, waiting, led away southwest toward

Oregon Avenue. Then they disappeared under the mess made by the fire engines.

Standing up, Driscoll brushed the wet snow from the knees of his trousers and switched off the flashlight. Oregon Avenue, with its McDonald's and supermarkets, was closed for the night. The only thing down that way, far beyond the edge of South Philly, was the airport and the Tinicum marsh. And he sure as hell wasn't going to the marsh tonight.

Hit the Meatman and catch a flight out. It was so professional, Driscoll couldn't stand it. This was a big-time hit. He couldn't conceive of a job like this having come from within the ranks of the bungling Prestos.

Just to test his theory, he slowly turned around for 360 degrees, putting himself in the killer's place. North meant going back through center-city Philadelphia, maybe picking up the Schuylkill Expressway. From there to the Pennsylvania Turnpike and upstate. But if Philadelphia was getting a bad snowstorm, they'd be having a blizzard up there. North was out.

West was the counties, the suburbs, the Main Line. Small-town cops poking into everybody's business. And west didn't go anywhere, just deeper into Pennsylvania. That made even less sense.

Normally, he would have liked the east. Pick up the Walt Whitman Bridge into south Jersey, then either head for Atlantic City to spend the money he'd earned for the hit or veer north into New York, where the order for the hit might have come down from. But in this weather, it would be a bitch driving to New York.

The airport felt right, but he knew it was already too late. Except for one thing. Even birds weren't flying in this kind of weather. The hit man probably hadn't figured on his flight being canceled. If they got lucky, they might still be able to catch him in the city.

Searching the crowd of shivering lawmen for Marinari, Driscoll spotted him and grabbed him. "Call South detectives," he said, practically ordering the captain, "and Highway Patrol. We want one, possible two men, in a small truck or a van. Probably a van. It's gonna be traveling real slow. No snow tires, slipping all over the highway, somewhere near the airport. That's who we want. That's our man."

"How the hell do you know all this?" Marinari asked, shocked.

"I'm a fucking psychic."

Marinari didn't say a word.

Picking his way carefully over the hose lines, he reached what was left of the front steps. One uniform on the door and a couple of lab technicians on the porch. Bright lights everywhere. Biaggio was keeping everybody else down on the street. Driscoll decided to break in. No time for a search warrant.

He recognized the uniform by his face, not his name. "Get loud if anybody tries to come in," he whispered to the cop, who nodded knowingly.

Driscoll stood on the porch and surveyed Fletcher Street. He'd never seen so many feds on a mob hit. He knew that had to have something to do with the conversation he had overheard at the morgue. This time, Bellows and the Strike Force were really taking over. But Driscoll had to find out what they knew—had to find out about the deal they had cut with the Meatman.

Maybe once he got inside, he'd find something that would tell him what the Meatman had been up to—an address book, a phone number, a canceled check, something. All the time he'd known Honey Presto he had never set foot inside her father's house. Driscoll couldn't wait.

He made his way back down the steps, avoiding the chunks of stone and marble that had been loosened by the blast. Down on the ground, near the little garden, lay the melted red plastic of Santa Claus's head.

SEVEN

NEAR PHILADELPHIA INTERNATIONAL AIRPORT

Skidding badly, the van's worn tires glazed over the slick surface of the asphalt and made Whitey feel as though the van and everything in it had lost all center of gravity. Vinnie's body shifted slightly.

Keeping the dented green van on the slippery road was almost impossible. Whitey was driving southwest along Lindbergh Boulevard, where he planned to pick up an unmarked back road into the Tinicum marsh. Everything had been set, everything but the snow.

He took his eyes off the road for a moment and glanced down at Vinnie's body. The bleeding had stopped, but not before it had puddled on the floor of the van. Brown ooze was seeping from the bullet holes in Vinnie's side; the rest of his body fluids were evacuating. The odor was making Whitey sick. He felt like vomiting. He rolled down the side window and let in the night air. Better to put up with the cold.

Lindbergh Boulevard was a wide, fairly new road that connected the garden apartments and tract houses of western South Philadelphia with the suburbs. The Tinicum marsh, hard by the airport, was a bird sanctuary in decent weather and an impenetrable natural barrier once the temperature fell to thirty-two degrees. Add the snow and wind, and the area became so rugged that it seemed oddly out of place in an urban setting. It was all totally unfamiliar to Whitey. Vinnie had guided him around here the day they posed as duck hunters and surveyed the marsh. The kid had taken the lead, eager to prove himself, while Whitey followed behind, cautious and watchful. He told Vinnie that in case anything went wrong they might have to make a quick getaway through the marsh. Together, they selected a secluded spot with a soft, vine-covered, liquidy floor as a rendezvous location. Whitey marked it. Vinnie never realized that he was picking out his own grave.

For the first time since he'd gotten into the van, Whitey switched on the radio. He was always anxious to hear what the newscasters had to say about one of his jobs. So close to the airport towers, the reception was poor, but he kept tuning the dial until he picked up the static-filled all-news station that he wanted.

"1060 on your dial . . . This just in. An explosive device of unknown origin was detonated on Fletcher Street in South Philadelphia outside the home of reputed mob boss Paul 'Meatman' Presto. Presto, identified by the Pennsylvania Crime Commission as the leader of La Cosa Nostra in the tristate area . . . Death ends an apparent truce following the bloodiest underworld war in Philadelphia history. . . . KYW News time. . ."

Satisfied, Whitey turned off the radio. He enjoyed hearing about himself. Now he had to look for that damn access road. . . .

Whitey never bought plane tickets in advance. They were too easy to trace. He waited until he was in the terminal near a ticket counter. Then he would make up his mind at the last minute and decide where he would fly. Even when he had a specific destination in mind, Whitey believed in taking a circuitous route. He had tracked enough people himself to know the panicky feeling of being hunted and followed. The best defense, the only really effective defense, was never to know where he was going himself.

He was usually more relaxed just at the point of pulling a job and executing a contract than he was immediately afterward. Tonight was no different.

The Meatman was dead. He had to dump the kid. Had to get away.

But the damn road wasn't where it was supposed to be.

Whitey had pulled off Lindbergh Boulevard and taken a hard left. The next thing he should have seen was the low ridge of scrub bush and barren midget pine trees that marked the beginning of the marsh. The road he was looking for would allow him to cut right through those squat pine trunks.

But he kept driving parallel to the ridge. *He couldn't get through.* Under the bald tires of the van—goddam bald tires—Whitey was almost sure there was still some sort of paved road. He should have felt the change from paving to dirt by now.

Something had gone wrong with his sense of direction. Vinnie wasn't there giving Whitey directions this time, and not a damn thing looked familiar.

He must have taken the wrong street off the boulevard. The only thing he could do now was double back the way he had come and look for the access road again. Unless he used that road he knew he'd have to pass through at least one airport security check, and he couldn't risk that tonight. He had already given some smart cop more than enough time to get a fix on the van.

Christ, he had to find that road. Had to dump the kid. Had to get away.

Whitey was somewhere between the airport and the Tinicum marsh. He could figure out that much. But the road he was traveling, which should have been taking him to the marsh, kept pulling him farther away, toward the main entrances of the airport.

If he could just find that opening between the trees . . .

Suddenly there was an abrupt change in the road surface, and Whitey realized that he was headed straight for the darkness. He slowed almost to a stop, attempting to get his bearings. But all he could see was the distant, twinkling needlepoint lights of the runway signals near the massive outline of the air traffic control tower. There was blackness all around them.

Maybe he should get out and take a look. But it was so damn dark—what would he be able to see?

Red lights and blue lights. Flashers. Red and blue flashing lights. A siren. Lights and a siren out of nowhere. Out of the blackness.

A blue-and-white Philadelphia police car was closing in on him, closing in fast. Its rotating dome lights were nearly blinding him. Impossible to outrun it. Whitey would have to take his chances.

As the flashing lights came to within a car length of the van, Whitey skidded his tires to a wet, uneven stop. Remembering Vinnie's corpse on the floor, he tossed the army blanket that had been around his shoulders over the dead kid.

Whitey reached under the seat, shivering, and felt for the reassuring hardness of the .45 automatic—the same .45 he had used on Vinnie.

FLETCHER STREET

The driveway behind Presto's house was more like an alley, with the fences of the backyards hemming it in as tightly as the walls of a tunnel. Driscoll took a breath and scrambled up and over the slippery fence. Once inside the yard, he was hidden from view.

If there was any kind of a burglar alarm or motion beams or trip wires—which all the mob guys had—the bomb blast would have taken them out. Driscoll wasn't worried. He tried the window on a shed that led into the kitchen. The storm window was down all the way, but there was a chance that the inside window might be unlocked.

Reaching inside his coat pocket, Driscoll took out the cold, shiny locksmith's pick he always carried and worked the thin, flat edge under a corner of the storm window. All he needed was a little leverage.

He pressed his weight against the window and gave it a little nudge, and the spring gave way with a *ping!* He reached inside and up under the window and pushed the pick along the metal frame. Then he tried the inside wooden window. It was unlocked. Driscoll smiled to himself and climbed in.

All the rooms were connected in a straight line. Moving from back to front, he cut through the kitchen, a breakfast nook with a small pantry off to the side, and a large dining room, and then he found himself in the living room at the foot of the staircase.

The gaping crater where the front door had been was sealed with a thick plastic tarp to preserve the evidence. The broad blue back of the uniform standing guard on the porch was visible. Muffled conversation drifted into the room. A car motor sputtered in the cold. The sound of spinning tires digging their way out of the snow.

As Driscoll's eyes became accustomed to the darkness, he sensed a comfortable easy grace about the whole house. It was crowded with overstuffed chairs, Mediterranean-style lamps and tables with lion's-claw legs. Brocaded drapes. The mantelpiece was cluttered with Christmas decorations and framed pictures. It was a mixture of tacky Victorian and South Philly Twelve Caesars. It *looked* like Presto.

The bomb had taken out the vestibule that Presto had had especially installed as a security measure years before. Still a heavy odor of burning wood. He started up the carpeted stairs.

Pitch-black.

Driscoll carried a flashlight, but he was afraid to use it. He didn't need some trigger-happy cop mistaking him for the hit man and shooting him by accident. He'd seen that happen before, too.

Nothing in any of the extra bedrooms. He hadn't yet found the Meatman's or Honey's. Hers turned out to be in the middle of the second floor. The door opened into the hallway. He walked in and looked around.

The furniture was white and small. A wraparound wall unit dominated one corner. Petite princess furniture. Group photos of teenage girls. Triangular pennants. A bright blue-and-silver rug served as a wall hanging. A mountain of stuffed animals and toys spilled out onto the floor, staring at him with blank glass eyes.

The Meatman had preserved Honey's room like a museum exhibit—a monument to his schoolgirl princess. He felt like an intruder. Driscoll had never known *this* Honey.

He reached up and lifted down a picture of Honey from a shelf. It was a seashore shot, with the ocean in the background and the hazy outline of beachfront decks in the foreground. He knew that Presto had a big place right on the beach in Stone Harbor, down the coast from Atlantic City.

Honey, tanned brown as melted caramel, posed in front of it, laughing, touching her hair. Beautiful dark hair. Vain. Her mouth was open just a little. God, she looked tight, firm. Those enormous tits. An ass that rode high. She was wearing a black string bikini and her waist seemed to disappear right into her thighs. *Honey Presto.* Driscoll remembered how she had looked at him back at the morgue with the blood still smeared across her cheek. That had been the first time he had seen her in close to five years.

Glancing over at her teddy bears, he grinned. Honey sure as hell hadn't been sleeping with teddy bears when he knew her. He looked at her picture again, put his fingers to his lips, and blew her a kiss. Then he resumed his search.

Where the hell was the good stuff? There had to be a vault or a safe somewhere, or at least a wad of cash. He hadn't even found a phone number. The place was clean, but there had to be *something.*

MCLEAN

Shaved, dressed, and preoccupied, Carney now knew that he had to go to Philadelphia. His conversation with the President had convinced him of that. Combing his thick white hair and fastening his gold tie bar, he revised his plans.

He had called Andrews Air Force Base and ordered a plane. But with the snow walloping the entire East Coast and no let-up forecast, an officious-sounding major had explained that it was impossible to get anything into the air for several hours at least. No helicopters, either. Amtrak's Washington-to-Philadelphia line had also been knocked out.

Frustrated, Carney cursed the major and the snow and slammed down the receiver. He felt trapped, unable to maneuver and to get to the bottom of whatever the hell was going on with Presto. And he knew he would never be able to do that in Washington. He had to get to Philadelphia, and if he couldn't fly, then he could damn well drive.

FLETCHER STREET

Driscoll was in another bedroom, the flashlight clenched between his teeth. He had to risk it. The noises outside were louder now, more distinct. Maybe some big shot had arrived. He raised his head and peered around the room. This one looked lived-in. The master bedroom, the Meatman's room. The bed covers were rumpled. Worn, scruffy-looking slippers stuck out from under a night table. The closet door was open just a crack. But no phone pads, no date book, not a scrap of paper anywhere.

On his knees, Driscoll quickly rummaged through a bureau drawer and scanned the top of the night table. A tie clip, cuff links, a fading photo. Nothing like Honey in her bikini.

He opened another drawer. Presto's underwear. Driscoll felt two automatics and a sawed-off shotgun, wrapped in white jockey shorts. Finally. He might be on to something.

He crawled over to the closet. The beam of the flashlight caught a long, gleaming automatic rifle propped against the wall, partially hidden by one of the Meatman's suits. A full clip was in the weapon, all ready to go. Maybe Presto had been expecting trouble.

Jesus, the bedroom was an arsenal. So *this* was where the Meatman lived—in one room of his house. There had to be a hiding place somewhere. Wall, floor, ceiling? Driscoll glanced up at the pictures on the wall to see if they might be on hinges. Nothing suspicious.

Then he stood up to check the shelf in the closet, gambling that his movement wouldn't be visible from the street. Several round hat boxes. Driscoll reached up to grab one.

"Hold on," a loud voice practically screamed. Startled, Driscoll held his breath.

"I can't let you in until I see some ID."

Driscoll shoved the hat box back on the shelf and dropped to the floor. The cop at the door was stalling them. It was a signal. Somebody was coming in.

"Okay, captain, as long as you stay with them." The voice was louder. The detective could just imagine what was going on downstairs. Marinari was probably shitting himself, knowing that Driscoll might already be in there. Whoever they were, they insisted on getting inside.

Driscoll hurtled down the steps two at a time and hit the living room floor with a dull thud. There were others on the porch now, but they didn't seem to be coming in. He might have a few minutes.

Driscoll had found unusual hiding places before, and Presto's house bothered him. It looked too clean. He had lightly tapped floorboards all over the house, but nothing sounded hollow. In the two bathrooms upstairs, he had felt around the toilet tanks for any waterproof bags. Nothing. Occasionally, clever carpenters would install kitchen cabinets and wall units to swing up and away on hinges to stash things away. But in this house nothing was hinged that shouldn't have been hinged. He had even checked the trash cans. Sometimes they were fixed right into the ground to be used as storage bins. But the Meatman's trash was real trash.

How the hell could Driscoll crawl inside the Meatman's head? He was running out of time and patience. Any minute, those people would be inside.

The Meatman. What would he do? Driscoll had to outthink him.

The Meatman. A butcher turned loan shark. Meatman Presto. Butcher! Butcher! That was it! The Meatman was a butcher, and every butcher Driscoll had ever known had kept the day's receipts and anything worth stealing hidden somewhere in the walk-in cold box. *The freezer.* The goddam freezer. A butcher considered his freezer his office. There had to be a freezer in the cellar. Maybe even a walk-in box. So what in hell was he doing up here?

The door to the basement was just off the dining room. Driscoll tried it. *Locked.* He took the pick out of his pocket again and slid the pointy end inside the keyhole. He forced it up inside the mechanism. It wasn't working. The tumblers were too high.

Playing against time, he examined the hinges. Ordinary butt hinges, but the top one was so tight it must have been painted over. He knelt down and began working on the middle and bottom hinges, trying to twist the pin upward. The bottom pin was loose under the pressure of his probing finger. He pushed it up, removed it, and dropped it into his pocket. He flipped the middle pin out with the flat end of the pick and forced the door open, attached now by only the top hinge.

Sucking in his stomach and chest and rounding his shoulders, Driscoll squeezed himself between the door and the frame. Once he was on the top step of the basement stairs, he pulled the door back onto its hinges.

The cellar smelled musty. Damp. He hit the floor with the beam of his flashlight and noticed that the concrete was broken in several places, with the dirt showing through the sawdust. Sawdust—just like a real butcher shop. A worn, smooth butcher's block stood in the middle of the floor, with a spotlight, attached to the ceiling beams, directly over it. Driscoll fixed the light on the butcher's block and on a row of various-sized knives, connected to the block by a wooden apron. The Meatman's legendary knives.

Then, there it was. Presto's cold room. Iron shackles with leather straps were mounted on the outside wall. Driscoll couldn't believe it. He had heard stories about Presto and about how he had earned his nickname, but he had always dismissed them as so much South Philly bullshit. But now here he was, standing in the Meatman's torture chamber with one of the knives in his hand. Everything was right there. So this is where he cut off their fingers.

Presto's cold room took up most of the cellar. The handle

that opened the door was so heavy, Driscoll had to use both hands. Opening it, he looked around; then he let it close behind him without catching. A round, hard pressure device opened the door from the inside. Otherwise, the vacuum seal on the heavy door could keep you locked inside forever. The gaskets were as thick as Driscoll's wrist.

Putting aside the flashlight, Driscoll pulled on an overhead chain lamp. Two compartments—the refrigeration room, in front, about as big as an oversized bathroom, and behind that, the freezer compartment. It was stainless-steel with double doors and seemed to be about ten feet deep. Massive.

The refrigerator motors vibrated and droned. Driscoll could see his breath escaping in short, whitish puffs. He could actually see how hard he was breathing. The puffs disappeared immediately in the unnaturally chilled air. He smelled a heavy, ripe, sour odor. Sawdust covered the floor to soak up the blood that dripped from some hanging, curing carcasses in the refrigeration room.

Driscoll almost bumped into an enormous side of beef that hung from a hook, aging, crimson, with deep milky-white marbling running throughout the meat. It was the finest hunk of beef Driscoll had ever seen.

All four walls were lined with built-in wooden shelves, dark brown and stained even deeper from years of dripping blood. Presto had hoarded enough meat to feed half of South Philadelphia. Every shelf was lined with expertly wrapped cuts of beef. The paper was white and waxed, with heavy commercial-grade plastic sheets underneath. A single strip of wide, heavy freezer tape secured each package and labeled its contents. Driscoll read a couple of the labels and realized that the Meatman had been carefully rotating the meat, allowing just so many weeks for aging. He really was a butcher.

The only sound was the humming of the motors, incessant and hypnotic. Driscoll felt as though the cold chamber in which he was standing wasn't much different from the temperature outside. But as soon as he opened one of the big stainless-steel freezer doors, the frigid air inside, where Presto kept beef in cold storage for an indefinite period of time, enveloped him like the breath of an arctic dragon. He glanced at the thermometer mounted on the wall. Minus five degrees.

Blowing on his hands, the cop slammed the freezer door shut and turned to inspect the cold room. The shelve were chock-full, but he knew that here in this underground cold room, Presto, the butcher, had to be hiding his valuables.

Working methodically, left to right, Driscoll examined each bundle of wrapped meat. Every package was meat—beef, steaks, tenderloins, chops, roasts. Each was labeled. Nothing but goddam meat.

Time was running out. He kept ripping, tearing wildly. *Something* had to be here, but he wasn't getting anywhere. Maybe it wasn't in the cold room. Anybody could come down here and get meat. Maybe it wasn't secure enough for Presto.

The freezer. Now *that* was secure—minus five degrees' worth of security.

The cold was already numbing his fingers, but he opened the freezer door and walked inside anyway. In the poor light and thinning air, his head was becoming heavier and heavier. Determined, Driscoll started the whole process over again—yanking at packages of meat until there was almost no feeling at all in his fingers and hands. He went through about a dozen more cold-storage specialties and was close to blacking out when he felt it—a package unlike all the rest. It didn't even feel the same.

This package was triple-wrapped. No label. The Meatman *always* labeled his packages. And it was shoved far back on the top shelf, obviously not meant to be found or opened easily.

Driscoll placed his foot on the bottom shelf and hoisted himself up. There were about ten packages just like this one, in a neat single-file line. Driscoll grabbed the first one, expecting to find cash or dope, and unsheathed layer upon layer of plastic and freezer paper. Finally he came to a brown insulated freeze-dry pouch. It was heavy and rigid, not at all like the packages of meat. The detective was excited. Presto had gone to a lot of trouble to hide whatever was inside.

Slowly, his numbed fingers providing him with practically no sense of touch, he withdrew the contents of the pouch.

He stood there stunned, staring, unbelieving. It was a human hand—white, the right one, frozen solid. It had been severed with surgical precision just below the wrist and apparently drained of blood. The fingernails were ugly—yellow and gnarled, thick as bone.

The fingers of the hand were wrapped around a gun, a .45 automatic. Blued finish. Holding the hand and gun up close to the naked light bulb above his head, Driscoll carefully examined each stiff fingertip, hoping to find that a good set of prints still showed through. But in the dim light, he couldn't be sure. The gun was coated with a delicate, powdery frost.

This was weird. It wasn't the first time Driscoll had encountered dismembered bodies, but he had never seen anything that looked so eerily alive, so visceral, preserved like an ice-age fossil. He touched the top of the hand, the wrinkled knuckles, rubbing the strong, calloused heel above the palm.

Probably one of the Meatman's victims, and a fairly recent one, too, he guessed. A workingman's hand—powerful-looking, even in death, holding a big, dark .45 automatic.

Driscoll carefully placed the hand and gun back into the pouch and pushed it inside his deep trench coat pocket. Presto was a monster—a fucking cannibal. He felt certain that the other packages contained the remainder of the body. He hoped to find the head, look at the face, try to identify just who it was that Presto had slaughtered like an animal. He'd run a check on the gun, too.

Pushing himself up again, he struggled to stretch his arm to the back of the shelf, scraping the buckle on his sleeve as he did so. Suddenly his footing gave way on the slippery edge of the bottom shelf and he hit the sawdust, sprawling flat on his back.

At that precise moment, the overhead light went out and the refrigerator motors stopped. Driscoll lay in the sawdust and cold, his head throbbing and his shoulder aching from the force with which he had hit the floor of the freezer.

In the intense cold, his body and his reflexes were betraying him, but his mind was still alert enough to warn him that he had to get the hell out of the freezer compartment before it was too late. He scrambled to his knees, crawled toward the freezer door, balled his body, and rolled out into the relative warmth of the cold room. As soon as he experienced the change in temperature, he could feel himself coming back. His limbs were losing their heaviness and his head cleared.

In the darkness of the cold room he felt around for the release handle, gulping hard to breathe the acrid atmosphere. Then Driscoll remembered that when the door had closed behind him, he had made sure that the lock hadn't caught. Now it was coming back to him. All he had to do was to push his way out. The thin air and the decreasing oxygen had practically made him forget his own name. In a few seconds, he was standing outside the cold room, in the basement, coaxing his flashlight to work.

Distant voices were talking, nearly screaming, just above him. He knew they were inside the house now, in the dining room probably.

The bomb blast must have shorted out the wiring in the house. The freezer motors had stopped. They had probably been hooked up to an auxiliary unit of some kind, but now that was down too, its battery dead.

Heavy footsteps creaked the rafters directly above his head. Driscoll peered into the blackness as a large, dark silhouette holding a flashlight filled the area at the top of the basement steps.

Cornered, with the severed hand and frozen gun still in his coat pocket, Phillip Driscoll searched desperately for a way out.

NEAR PHILADELPHIA INTERNATIONAL AIRPORT

Whitey had to keep the cops away from the front seat, where Vinnie's body lay heaped on the floor. He opened the door on the driver's side and got out.

There were two of them.

Whitey had studied the patterns of the Philadelphia police while setting up the hit on Paul Presto, and he had learned that two men in a car was unusual. Two men meant they were looking for trouble.

He could feel his flesh turning hard and waxy in the raw night air.

The first cop reached for the microphone on the dashboard. Whitey knew he would be calling in the time and location of the car stop, maybe even his description. He could even be asking for backup or a supervisor. Whitey was already calculating his best angle of fire.

"What the hell are you doing way back here on a night like this?" the first cop asked, as he emerged from his own vehicle. His partner was getting out on the other side. Whitey didn't see any guns yet. Maybe it *was* just a car stop. He might be able to bluff his way through.

The first cop looked very young in the glare of the big double headlights of the patrol car. Not more than thirty. Handsome. Not that big, but well-built. His tone was mock-friendly, insincere. Whitey had heard it from other cops just before they struck. Hell, he put on the same act himself sometimes. No, this was for real. Whitey was sure of it.

The cop's hands were still in his pockets. He wore a black official-issue rubber raincoat over his uniform. Foul-weather gear. The cloth part of his hat above the shiny plastic brim was covered by a water-repellent protector. The hat was stretched back from the peak and cinched tightly along the sides. Highway Patrol. Whitey glanced down and spotted the knee-high black leather boots. Highway cops looked like the Luftwaffe.

The other cop had quickly, professionally moved around to outflank Whitey. Whitey wasn't an expert on the Philadelphia police, but he knew all about their Highway Patrol. They were the elite—no regular sector duties, only special assignments in high-crime areas. They were also used in fugitive searches. Two bad-ass highway patrolmen out looking for him. Some smart cop had guessed the airport, and he had guessed right.

Whitey didn't answer the cop's question.

"Hey, what's with you, buddy? What the hell are you doing back here? This is a snow emergency route. You can't drive here without snow tires or chains. You're not gonna get far in that van."

"Just lost," Whitey answered. "I thought this was the way to the airport."

"You're outta luck. They just closed the airport," the cop answered somberly. "The runways might not be clear till morning."

"It's good you spotted me when you did," Whitey told him, moving away from the headlights. "I think I was headed for the marsh."

"About another fifty feet."

Tall and gaunt, a shadow against the snow, Whitey's body appeared to slowly unravel to its full height, like a snake uncoiling. He was having a hard time keeping them both in sight. Highway patrolmen usually carried magnums—heavy handguns that could penetrate metal much thicker than the sides of the van.

"Let's have a look at your van," the other cop said. He sounded older, steadier. Whitey knew he would have to take him out first. His left cheek was beginning to twitch.

"We need your owner's card and some ID," the older cop ordered. "Why don't you just empty your pockets out on the hood here."

Whitey noticed the cop's elbow bend as he reached inside the slit on the side of his raincoat—the slit that was just even with the bulge of his gun.

Firing the .45 right through his jacket pocket, Whitey hit the older cop in the midsection. He went down, face first. His partner had his pistol out, raking Whitey's general direction with gunfire. But Whitey spun around, still blasting away, and dove for the underside of the van.

He saw the indecision in the younger cop's eyes. Whitey

could have told him to stay put and drop down behind the door of the patrol car and use it as a shield. He could have gotten Whitey from there. Instead, he ran across the open field of fire in an effort to pull his partner to safety.

Whitey aimed one shot for his leg and another for his chest. The bullets found their mark. The good-looking young patrolman collapsed in the snow, his arms and legs folding in on themselves, like a marionette whose strings had suddenly been cut.

EIGHT

NOBLE STREET, NORTHERN LIBERTIES, PHILADELPHIA

"They killed my father," Honey Presto was desperate.

The Fat Man, Manny Goldberg, eyed her warily. Manny could just begin to detect the same look that he had seen in her father's hard eyes. Presto's blind determination seemed reborn in Honey.

"Why do you come to me?" he replied icily, folding the thick pads that were his hands on his lap. Manny and the Meatman had not done business together for many years. Honey had never known why.

"I just came from the morgue, Manny. I had to identify his body. What little was left. . . . What do I do now?"

Honey's face still appeared transfixed by the shock. Her jawline was taut with stress. Manny could tell that she was on the verge of tears, her voice breaking, but she stubbornly refused to give in to her feelings.

"You have to help me, Manny."

"Power attracts enemies. Your father was a very powerful man. I weep for your father, I weep for you, but I can't tell you why or who."

Suddenly she looked hurt and fragile, stunned by what she had just heard. She twisted the hem of her dress in her hand, nervously looking from Manny to the floor.

"But you can find out, Manny. *Uncle Manny.*" Her voice was coaxing, coy. "My father always told me that you were the smartest man he'd ever known. That's why I know you can find out . . . *Uncle Manny.*" Her voice was pleading now. "You *have* to help me."

Her eyes were deep brown and agitated, the impulsive eyes of Paul Presto's princess. Small, double-pierced earlobes, accentuated by a brilliant diamond stud and gold swirl drop, were the perfect complement to those stormy eyes. Her complexion was just olive enough to make her appear permanently tanned.

Honey's face had the subtle implication of innocence—round, open, and slightly fleshy, especially just below her chin, almost a double chin, if she tilted her head a certain way. She detested that single imperfection. Baby fat, her father had called it, touching her there, gently reminding himself of the adorable infant she had been. Expertly, she concealed it with scarves, high necklaces, and other accents. Tonight she wore a wide black velvet ribbon.

She had her mother's husky, low-pitched voice and Presto's sullen stare. But Honey's face was all her own, especially her mouth. It moistened when she parted her lips; full, carnal. Once her gaze dropped, those same sensual lips narrowed into a fierce insolence. Manny noticed that, too.

Honey Presto had never waited in line for anything, except the confessional. She hadn't been spoiled as much as she had been elevated to the most coveted position in Paul Presto's personal collection of sacramentals. To the Meatman, his Honoria was a vestal virgin, and just as long as she hung her rosary beads on the bedpost every night, he could find no fault—even when she demanded a trip to Europe for her sixteenth birthday, narrowly avoided war with another mob family over a jilted romance on her seventeenth, attempted to seduce a boy cousin who had entered St. Charles Seminary by her eighteenth, and nearly sliced off the finger of a boyfriend she found cheating on her by the time she was twenty. Presto had been rather proud about the finger bit. His Honey was a fighter. She'd slash with a blade or shoot with a gun. But her most effective weapon, of course, Honey carried snuggled between her lovely thighs.

Sweating and rumpled-looking, the Fat Man dabbed at

his big face with an enormous plaid handkerchief. He was sitting on a loveseat, and he took up most of it. His pajamas looked like the billowing sails of a ship. Honey had gotten him out of bed. Her father had just been killed and she was beside herself.

Even when Manny slept, he wore rings on the fingers of both hands. Three of the rings were exact duplicates of the diamonds awarded to the winning teams in the NFL Super Bowl. Each ring represented a game in which he had bet big and won big.

Sitting there, staring at her, his breathing seemed generated by some small wheezing mechanism located deep within the layered mountains of fat that enveloped him. For the past month, Manny had been on a diet. He was now down to 423 pounds.

He lived above a delicatessen with a small yellow neon Star of David in the window. The street outside was still paved with cobblestones. He paid an old couple from the neighborhood to run the place for him. The deed to the building and all of the mercantile licenses were in their names.

Perched across from him, Honey could feel his steady gaze. Manny had never seemed so old, so short of breath, so incredibly fat. She could feel goose bumps spreading over her arms and legs, the room was so cold. She had been at a party when she found out about her father. Then from the morgue she had come straight to Manny's place.

She was wearing a low-cut sleeveless sheath. Suddenly she realized her nipples were standing erect in the chill. She quickly pulled her black velvet cape across her bosom. Her face flushed with embarrassment.

"I can pay anything, Manny." She began opening the small beaded purse that lay on her lap. Honey looked at him imploringly.

He cleared his throat loudly, placed the palms of both hands on his knees, and straightened his arms stiffly, attempting to sit up straight on the loveseat.

"Do not insult a friendship that is older than you are, Honoria," Manny said angrily, leaning toward her. "Put that away. Because you are his daughter, I will do it. But," he warned Honey, "*don't* be your father's daughter. Don't even think about revenge. I swear on your mother's memory that you are *not* getting yourself killed with my help. Agreed?''

''Agreed,'' Honoria Maria Presto pledged with a flinty conviction in her tone that even surprised Manny.

''There's more, Uncle Manny. There's something I didn't tell you.'' All of his sleepiness gone now, Manny looked concerned.

''You'd better tell me,'' Manny said, *''tell me everything.''*

''My father left a videotape,'' she confided to Manny, ''with instructions that you and I are to look at it together.''

DOWNTOWN PHILADELPHIA

Arlene, the girl from the real estate office, had been given precise instructions to proceed to the next location and wait. They had counted on her to delay Presto long enough for the next phase of the operation, and she had done it the best way she knew how.

After Presto left, she checked into a downtown hotel, where a room had been reserved under the name Terri Addario. They had taken care of that, too. She couldn't believe how sexy the Meatman had been. She thought it was going to be a simple blow job but she had ended up as turned-on as he was.

Old man Presto had been a real bull. Arlene's jaw and mouth still hurt. Suddenly, thinking about it, she felt hot and dirty. Stepping out of her skirt, and stripping off her blouse, she sniffed at her armpits. Jesus, she thought, can I use a shower. She pulled back the plastic curtain and turned on the faucet. After a blow job, she always liked a cigarette. Naked, she sat on the toilet and lit up a king-sized Kool.

As Driscoll crouched in the darkness, he realized that he had only one chance. Inching his way back toward the cold room, he quietly opened the door. It was solid enough to stop machine-gun fire. Ajar, as it was, the door would be visible to anyone coming down the basement stairs, even in the dark.

Driscoll waited.

The wooden steps groaned under heavy weight. He could just about make out a figure stopped halfway down the steps. The cop held his breath and hoped that this guy would be drawn to the open door. Continuing down to the foot of the stairs, he looked in the direction of the walk-in box. Driscoll knew he had him.

He was carrying a gun. Expertly, he positioned himself on the side of the cold-room door, using the pistol barrel to gingerly open the door just a little wider. Driscoll watched every movement.

After hesitating for just a second, he started to move into the cold box—exactly what the detective wanted him to do.

In an instant, Driscoll was across the basement floor, blind-siding the guy and knocking the gun out of his hand. He spun him around and stunned him with a quick, hard punch, square on his cheek, just below his right eye, snapping his head backward with a vicious-sounding crack. Then Driscoll caught the door with his foot and kicked it hard, right into the guy's face.

Driscoll shoved him inside the walk-in box, slammed the heavy door shut, and made sure that the handle latched. Driscoll could hear him struggling, trying to open the door. He yanked one of Presto's long wooden-handled cleavers out of the apron on the side of the butcher's block and jammed it between the freezer handle and the shiny metal clasp on the wall. Secured by the cleaver, the handle wouldn't work—from the inside or outside. That wouldn't hold the guy for long. Eventually, his pushing against the door would jiggle the cleaver loose and spring the door. But Driscoll wasn't planning to hang around. The banging on the door continued.

Just before he walked up the basement steps, patting the hard freezer package in his pocket, Driscoll called out to the man in the box, "Keep cool." The screaming and pounding drowned him out.

THE KREMLIN

A few hours later, Mikhail Zhukov returned to the interrogation room. The Jewish woman had been taken away, but Victor and the matron were still there. A janitor was with them, washing what appeared to be dried blood from the wooden table. The odor of disinfectant was strong.

"Did she say anything?" Zhukov asked Victor. The big soldier, showing no sign of remorse, replied, "Her final destination was the United States, sir. She claimed to have a sponsor in Philadelphia—a man in business there."

"They were afraid they wouldn't be issued emigration papers, so they turned to the black market for forged passports."

"What about the diamonds? And whom did she bribe?"

"Just a clerk in the office that handles exit-visa applications. Nobody significant." Victor looked at his watch. "He should be in custody by now, Comrade Zhukov."

"Very good, Victor. . . . And the diamonds?"

A knowing smile transported Victor's face into a glowing death's head.

"That was difficult, but in the end she complied." He looked toward the dark stains being scrubbed away by the janitor. Zhukov followed the soldier's eyes.

"Where did the diamonds come from, Victor?"

"The businessman in Philadelphia. She claims that he took care of everything."

"Who is he? What's his name?" Zhukov was insistent. But the big soldier was about to disappoint his superior. He looked up at the ceiling, the thinning hair on the top of his head almost rubbing against the low rafters.

Flustered, Zhukov shouted, "You mean to tell me you didn't get his name out of her?"

"Sir, we can try again. But I don't think . . . what I mean is, I don't think she knows anything more." Victor pointed again to the bloodstains on the table.

Zhukov was dismayed. How could this be happening? And right under his own nose. The issue of false emigration permits for Jews was bad enough, but the diamonds? It was Zhukov's job to be aware of *everything* that was happening on the black market. How could he have been so stupid? So lax? The Kremlin depended on emigré exchanges to get back agents who had been compromised and caught by the Western governments.

He remembered that Victor was still there. At least he could dispose of *this* matter immediately. And finally.

"Where is the Jewess now?" Zhukov asked.

"On her way to the old prison building."

Zhukov pondered Victor's answer, then considered the ramifications of what he was about to say. His mind made up, he dismissed the matron and the janitor and turned to Victor.

"There was another item seized, I believe," he said to the big soldier.

"Yes, sir, I have it right here." Victor reached under the table where the Jewish woman had been spread-eagled and handed his superior a smooth leather case like a doctor's bag.

Zhukov seized it with both hands. "No one else has seen this, you are certain?" A vein in the KGB officer's neck was starting to throb.

"Certain," was the brisk reply.

"Very good. It was the right thing to do, to bring this to my attention . . . my attention alone."

Victor's mouth was perfectly square. When he smiled, as he did now, hearing this accolade from Comrade Zhukov, his teeth showed in a small white rectangle, like a child's drawing of a mechanical man opening his mouth. The first few times, Zhukov had found this disconcerting.

"We keep this between us, yes?"

Victor nodded. He had guessed a long time ago that Comrade Zhukov drew his real power from the outlawed black market. Plenty of men in his position would have been tempted to do it; only Zhukov had the guts for it. But Victor kept quiet—he was always well rewarded for his service.

Zhukov reached inside and took a large pistol out of the bag. It was a large, black American gun—a .45 automatic, military. It was old, but looked to be well oiled and in perfect working condition. He brought the gun level with his nose and stared at the serial number. Zhukov had memorized the first three digits in the numbers that worried him. As soon as he saw the telltale 322, he realized that this was one of them. In the Soviet Union, no less. In the hands of two petty malcontents.

"You discovered this weapon yourself, Victor?"

"After we arrested them at the airport, I searched their quarters. The gun was concealed behind a false wall in a kitchen cabinet. As soon as I saw that it was American, I knew that you would want to know about it."

"Quite right." Zhukov was talking to the gun. He didn't look up.

"It *should* be turned over to the city police . . . it could have been used in the commission of some crime here in Moscow. But, Comrade Zhukov, you know I always take chances for you."

Zhukov was so shaken by the discovery of this weapon that he was finding it difficult to concentrate on the present conversation.

"Of course you do, Victor. And haven't I always shown my gratitude?" You are just making sure that I show it this time, too, aren't you, my Neanderthal friend?

Again, the small square white box flashed in the front of Victor's face.

"Did you question her—or her husband—about the gun?"

"They told us nothing."

"You tried every method?"

"*Every* one." Victor hesitated. "I thought you wanted us to keep them alive."

"Certainly." Zhukov had a serious problem now. The diamonds were a breach of his security, a rupture in the agreement upon which he had based his dealings with the underworld. The gun, *this* gun, this weapon which never should have found its way into the Soviet Union, or anyplace else, for that matter, at least not yet, this gun was a clear message that they were operating completely on their own now. Renegades. Thieves. Bandits. Reverting to type. He was a fool for ever thinking he could trust them even on a business proposition. Their recklessness was now costing him a fortune and putting his life in danger—from the Americans as well as from his own people.

His first order of business would be to keep Victor quiet.

"This Jewess, Victor. I think she will meet with an accident. Her husband, as well." Then he added, "Until then, she is yours—her apartment, too."

Victor stood there, unflappable. Zhukov knew that his orders would be carried out. "You'll see to it, then?"

"Immediately, Comrade Zhukov." The big guard looked pleased.

Zhukov left the interrogation room. He had an appointment within the hour to brief the delegation that would accompany the new Chairman to the summit in Geneva. He expected it to last twenty minutes, no longer. After that, he would have to begin making plans. He would have to call his contact in Singapore and make absolutely certain that the problem had not originated there.

DOWNTOWN PHILADELPHIA

Arlene stayed in the shower until the water had run from hot to tepid to cold. She was tingling all over, her hair wet and matted, her nipples engorged from the cold sensation. Halfway out of the shower, she searched for an orange towel on the wall rack; her eyes were still soapy and blurry. A brisk rubbing brought some feeling back into her body.

A few minutes later, she ordered food from room service,

but she never touched it. A newspaper was on the tray with the food. All she needed to read was the headline above Paul Presto's picture. So that was what this was all about. Presto had been murdered, bombed. Nobody had ever told her it was anything like that. Arlene had suspected blackmail, or something like that. But never murder.

Hours had now gone by, but no call. And this thing in the paper. God, she was afraid. What if the cops started to ask her questions? They might find out where she really lived. She had a record, too. That one time they picked her up for soliciting.

Arlene knew that she couldn't just hang around here anymore. She always sweated when she was scared; the perspiration was dripping from her pits to her rib cage. But what should she do? Play dumb, that was for sure. She might have to get out of town fast now. Real fast. She would really need the rest of the money.

Poking around in her purse, she searched for the phone number they had given her in case anything went wrong.

MCLEAN

A frozen stream that fed into the Potomac was coming up on Jim Carney's far right. In the fall, dressed in riding boots and a stiff derby, he had ridden in fox hunts over this same sloping terrain. Carney believed he knew every inch of it.

Outside the car window, the road, now snow-covered, had almost disappeared. Straining to see through the frosted windshield, Carney coughed into his scarf. He was hours away from Philadelphia.

About twenty yards ahead, his car would pass under a railroad bridge that stretched over the frozen stream. The covered wooden bridge was quiet picturesque and very old.

As far as Carney knew, no train had used the narrow-gauge tracks on it for close to forty years.

Shortly after he had moved in to the estate in McLean, Carney had devoted many spring afternoons to exploring the old bridge and the forsythia-covered gullies and hills around it. Once he had encountered a young man with a backpack and hiking boots there. Carney was infatuated, and the two of them had spent most of that day together, in the romantic shelter of the covered bridge, mellow sunlight streaming in through long windows on either side. Up in the rafters, pigeons flapped their wings noisily.

All at once, Carney remembered his dream. Then he thought back to that afternoon under the bridge. He strained for some connection between the two, for anything to make the dream go away.

He looked at the bridge as the headlights caught it. He had driven under it dozens of times, but today, in the darkness and snow, it looked different. A blur, whitish against the weather-beaten wood of the trestles, filled in one of the long windows that overlooked the road.

The man on the bridge, staring down at Carney's cautiously moving car, was dressed in a white parka and white ski pants. A hood covered his head and face. He blended in perfectly with the wintery scene and the driving snow. Cross-country skis rested on the floor of the bridge behind him. He was carefully estimating the speed of Carney's car.

In the darkness, kneeling against the old wooden guardrail, he was almost invisible from below. Beside him, in a fur-lined case, lay an M-16 combat rifle, fitted with a grenade launcher. This model dated to the early 1970s. He picked it up.

He glanced up and down the tracks, peering through snow goggles, making sure that he was alone. The Vietcong had used this weapon against both tanks and personnel. They had stripped many of them from the bodies of dead American soldiers. In their experience, the M-16 launcher was lighter and more accurate than the widely used Soviet-made RPG-7.

By the time the car had passed beneath him, the man on the bridge had run to the other guardrail. He adjusted his sights on a point a few feet above the retreating taillights.

He was an expert marksman, albeit new to the remarkable capabilities of the M-16.

In firefights, the automatic rifle had occasionally jammed or proved too hot to touch, literally; but with the grenade launcher mounted, in the hands of a terrorist, as a tool of individual assassination, the gun had found a deadly new life.

Used against a moving vehicle, not armor-plated, like the car in which Carney was riding, the grenade would be effective for a reasonable distance. But the man on the bridge would let the car get only a few feet away. He had only this one chance.

The tires of Carney's car were losing traction on the slick road, veering dangerously close to the shoulder on the left. Alarmed, Carney's Marine driver shouted something about not being able to hold the road.

But Carney was so absorbed in thought that he hardly heard the driver. His dream, the recurring nightmare of the hooded man pursuing him, relentlessly obsessed his mind and spirit.

He was still thinking about the dream when the man on the bridge fired. The last thing Carney remembered was a blinding flash of light.

NINE

CAM RANCH BAY, SOCIALIST REPUBLIC OF VIETNAM

Lieutenant Colonel Do Tran Sang was tall for a Vietnamese, almost five feet five. He had just celebrated his fortieth birthday with a quiet family dinner and a round of songs from his three children. His wife had cooked his favorite dish, duck, and had even managed to get some Western wine, a special treat. The wine was courtesy of a big black-market merchant they both knew, a man with important friends and contacts in Singapore.

The wind was from the east, from the warm blue waters of the South China Sea, blowing directly inland, picking up scents as it traversed paddies wet with rice, tall crops of corn, and endless groves of bamboo and mangrove. The tang of salt was the most pungent, and the manufacture of raw salt from the seawater was the most important industry in Sang's village, a small, neat collection of houses and collective farms set well back from the bay.

After the children's songs, Colonel Sang snapped a wooden match against the sole of his boot and lit up his first cigarette of the evening—a short, bitter, dark cigarette that filled his lungs and head with tobacco and the slow-acting narcotic of the poppy plant.

Sang was a compulsive gambler who had lost himself to the seduction of the cards and dice while serving in the army. A discreet man, he had fought to remain as secretive about it as any gambler can. One night, however, he had made the mistake of gambling with the Singapore merchant. Sang lost, but the merchant was very good about it, assuring him that there was no need to rush into paying the gambling debt. This bothered Sang a lot, but he pushed it into the back of his mind and went on with his life.

Sang had spent his eight war years fighting against the Americans and the ARVN forces in South Vietnam, mostly in the Cu Chi district, north of Saigon. Whenever his children asked him about the war, he lied and told them how many Americans he had killed. Sang hadn't killed anyone. He had spent his eight years as a storekeeper, trying to stay alive. During that time he had become proficient in the handling and storage of small arms and munitions. Cu Chi had been the keystone of a far-flung network of underground tunnels that encircled the big American base camp there, on all sides, for over two hundred miles. Burrowing deeply underground, the North Vietnamese had constructed an elaborate city, complete with hospitals, barracks, kitchens, communications headquarters, gun emplacements, and supply caches. Do Tran Sang was in charge of the weapons caches. During one especially fierce series of battles, he went for six entire months without once coming to the surface to breathe the clean air or to see the brilliant sun.

Sang was a good officer. His men worked hard for him, and his supplies were always in mint condition. That was an accomplishment, considering the toll that the humid Asian weather took on the guns and ammunition. During the rainy season, water pouring into the tunnels was an acute concern. But Sang had learned how to keep the ammunition dry and the guns oiled just enough. During his stewardship, not a single battle was lost in the district for lack of guns or bullets.

Do Sang was rewarded, promoted, and decorated as a hero. After the war, with the rank of lieutenant colonel, he was assigned to the massive American base at Cam Ranh Bay—the largest, most modern U.S. supply depot in all of Southeast Asia.

When the last American ambassador left Saigon on April 30, 1975—airlifted by helicopter from the roof of the embassy building amid chaos and fighting in the streets—the greatest weapons booty in the history of the war was left behind, enough to arm the fourth-largest army in the world. The spoils included jet fighters, still in their packing crates, tanks, trucks, other vehicles, and small arms of every description—800,000 M-16 assault rifles, .45 automatic pistols, and assorted rocket launchers, machine guns, and antitank guns.

Many of the weapons had been left behind in the American bunkers at Cam Ranh Bay. Less than a month after the fighting ceased, Sang found himself faced with the awesome task of conducting an inventory of the U.S. weapons and taking responsibility for their safe storage and maintenance. For the next six months, from all over the country, convoys of trucks would come rolling along the American-made roads of Cam Ranh Bay, wet red clay clinging to their tire treads. They came from the hills, the lowlands, and the steaming jungles—from wherever there had been guns and bullets and war. Every truck groaned under its cargo of more guns, more supplies, more items to be stored and catalogued.

In the beginning, Sang had many helpers; later, though, they became fewer and fewer. The North Vietnamese used Russian weapons; the American guns weren't even the same caliber. This stash of weapons was valuable, but a low-priority item in the national affairs of a developing country like North Vietnam.

Before long, he was working almost alone, walking the long, dark, silent aisles in the bunkers, aisles that separated mountains of weapons. Even though he could walk outside the bunkers—long, low, poorly ventilated concrete slabs—and feel the sun and the rain, sometimes he imagined that he was back in the tunnels of Cu Chi. Most people had forgotten about him back then; in his new post at Cam Ranh Bay, they forgot about him again.

Sang was on his own so much that he found time to drink and sleep and dream when he was supposed to be working. His wife complained about the drinking, but he didn't care. Why should he? Nobody else seemed to.

Still, he continued to take a certain amount of pride in his work—he continued to keep his powder dry, as the

Americans said. A small staff helped him keep the guns in good condition; maintaining a low, dry temperature was the hard part. But almost every day, Do Sang was a soldier without a war.

Year after year, he was more amazed at how little the top political cadres in Hanoi knew about or cared about the guns. No one but Sang even knew how many there were—not for certain. They had estimates, of course, but only he had the exact count. Sang had heard rumors that someday the guns would be sold or given away to other people's revolutions or scrapped. But nothing happened. The American weapons of Vietnam just sat there—watched over lovingly by Do Tran Sang, the greatest supply-keeper in Cam Ranh Bay.

During all that time, only one person had expressed any interest in his guns—and he was fascinated with them; in fact, he had come to think of them as his own. That had been the Russian KGB adviser who had visited the bunkers the year before, on the occasion of Sang's thirty-ninth birthday. His name was Colonel Mikhail Zhukov. The big black-market merchant from Singapore had introduced Sang to the KGB man. All that Zhukov had talked about was the weapons—their condition and degree of obsolescence, the quality of security at the bunkers, what interest in the condition of the weapons was displayed by Hanoi. On that last point, Sang had laughed out loud.

Before he left, the KGB man had given Sang and his family many gifts—far too many, in fact, for Sang not to be suspicious. Not long after Zhukov had returned to Moscow, Sang had a visit from the big black-market merchant with the contacts in Singapore. The merchant had carried a briefcase that day. It was filled with money. He had handed it to Sang. Before he even opened his mouth to describe his proposition, Sang understood.

Later, after Sang had decided to go into business with the merchant, the source of the cash in the briefcase was never mentioned, but Sang knew that it had to be Zhukov. Consider the gambling debt paid, the merchant had told Sang.

Once a month, never on the same day, nor at the same time, trucks owned by the merchant would pull into the complex of bunkers at Cam Ranh Bay and unload their cargo of fifty-five-gallon fuel drums. It was Sang's job to store the full drums. When the trucks pulled away from the big loading docks at the underground bunkers, they were supposedly hauling away empty fifty-five-gallon drums. But for almost a year, the drums had not been empty. Each drum was twenty-nine inches high. Broken down, an M-16 was just under twenty inches long. Sang was able to fit five guns to a drum—two hundred drums on each truck; six trucks a month. That first year they moved out over seventy-eight thousand M-16s and .45s. Straining in the tropical heat and the oppressive atmosphere of the bunkers, Sang and the merchant's men worked in three-hour shifts. Unsuspecting, Sang's own soldiers stood guard outside.

Sang thought that the guns went to Singapore, but he wasn't sure. Since he alone kept the records, it was easy to falsify them. He kept half of the money buried near his house outside Cam Ranh Bay—he had tunneled underground as he had been taught to do at Cu Chi. The other half was invested on his behalf at a British Crown bank in Hong Kong by the black-market merchant. Every month, the merchant showed Sang a bank statement. But he didn't worry about being cheated. The merchant was a man of honor, and besides, one word from Sang would have meant the merchant's immediate arrest and execution. Sang often mentioned that possibility to him. The merchant was an enormously fat man who sweated profusely. Sang liked to see him sweat.

On that night of his fortieth birthday, Sang heard an automobile pull up to the dusty patch of ground where his wife had been trying to raise a garden. He went to the door and saw the faraway purple dusk descend like a low-lying layer of heaven on the hills outside Cam Ranh Bay.

The Singapore merchant huffed and puffed his way out of the car—a French Citroën—and removed his hat in greeting.

Sang closed the door behind him and did not invite his visitor into his home.

"I heard from our friend today," the merchant said. "He is concerned about the guns. He wants your reassurance that nothing has changed in our arrangement."

Sang thought this was strange, but he didn't yet become

alarmed. "Nothing at all," he replied. "What could possibly change?"

"Has Hanoi been asking questions—or removing any of the weapons?"

Sang looked at the merchant as though he were speaking nonsense. "Would I be standing here, talking to you like this, if that had happened? That would cost both of us our lives."

"That's what I thought." The merchant sounded relieved, satisfied.

Sang started to walk him to his car. The air was cool; the wind from the sea brought with it the promise of a storm. Three small faces, each a head taller than the next, looked out at Sang through his front door. The little ones are always so curious, he thought.

"Our mutual friend asks for yet another reassurance," the merchant went on.

Sang listened, but he had no intention of allowing this conversation to go on much longer. He had neighbors, and they too would be curious about his visitor and his fancy car. From a rice field in the distance, beyond the houses, both men listened to the lowing of a water buffalo.

"And what might that be?" Sang asked.

"It's best that I be blunt. Are you selling the guns to anyone else?"

Shock contorted Sang's deeply tanned face. Angrily, he retorted, "Of course not. No one else is involved. Never. I gave you my word of honor. This I do not give lightly."

The fat merchant looked as though he wanted to believe Sang.

"Why do you ask that? Has something happened?" Now he was alarmed.

"My trucks deliver the weapons to the docks, and there my ships take them to Singapore," explained the merchant. "From there they are transferred to a second ship, in which they begin the last leg of the voyage. At every point, my own relatives supervise operations. There's not the slightest chance of anyone getting their hands on the guns as long as they are in my possession." He squinted into the dying sun. "After all, who knows?" He shrugged. "I get my money in Singapore. Then the guns become our friend Zhukov's problem. But someone has been diverting the guns—stealing them and reselling them—as fast as Zhukov buys them from us. He is frantic. He doesn't know who in his own operation is betraying him. I know it isn't you, my friend." He patted Sang on the shoulder reassuringly.

Finally, the merchant heaved himself into his car and sat behind the steering wheel. "One of the guns has shown up in Moscow. I think our KGB friend now fears for his own life." Sang's face mirrored disbelief.

"Have no fear," the merchant told Sang, "I think these Russians—they must be stealing from each other." Then he started the car and drove down the darkening road, away from Sang's part of town.

In seconds, Do Tran Sang had composed himself. He returned to his wife and children and his fortieth-birthday celebration.

TEN

NEAR PHILADELPHIA INTERNATIONAL AIRPORT

The bus was a special charter that had been pressed into service by one of the airlines after it had been forced to cancel commuter flights to various points along the East Coast.

The driver, Cornelius Arnold, was a tall, thin black man from the Germantown section of Philadelphia. He didn't know his way around the airport and was sort of lost himself. He normally drove the C bus on Broad Street, but he was at the top of the seniority list of charters to pick up overtime. Keeping warm was a problem, so he had bought a pint of Seagram's and stashed it away in the back flap pocket of his uniform trousers.

He was still a good twenty-five yards away when he noticed the open door of the blue-and-white Highway Patrol car. Even from that distance, it didn't look right. The bus was a new Swedish-made Volvo Articulator, and the driver's seat was unusually high up. Arnold had a better view than from an eighteen-wheeler.

At fifteen yards, he spotted the first body—a white cop in a black leather jacket. No hat. Something brown was leaking from his chest area. The tail of his long foul-weather raincoat had blown up toward his face.

At twelve yards, Arnold began to brake the huge Volvo—it was actually a full bus and three-quarters, joined in the center by a thick black rubber gasket that extended around the frame of the bus, enabling it to better navigate the tight corners of old cities like Philadelphia.

He spied the second body at five yards. It was another white cop with his arm flung out away from his chest. More brown goo in the snow, close to his chest and abdomen. It looked like there was a gun lying beside him.

Arnold stopped the bus, put the transmission in neutral—Volvo gearboxes were as temperamental as pretty women—and left the motor running. Then he yanked the hydraulic handle to open the front doors of the bus. On the second step out in the cold, he stared at the face of the dead white cop nearest him. His eyes were open. Dead open.

Their blood had turned murky brown in the snow. Both were lying face-up, staring at a cobalt-blue dawn, cloudless and purified by a dry arctic wind.

With his hand shaking, Cornelius Arnold reached around into his back pocket and pulled out the Seagram's. He twisted off the cap, put the bottle to his lips, and killed the pint. "Lord God Almighty," he said.

FLETCHER STREET

Phillip Driscoll slipped out of Presto's house the same way he had come in, through a window, then scaled the backyard fence and jumped. His topcoat caught on a loose piece of wood. He yanked at it, ripping the tan fabric as he freed himself. The frozen grass under the window was hard, but it did break his fall. He landed on his hands and knees and rolled over on his stomach. He felt for the hand and gun in his pocket; it was secure.

Then Driscoll ran the length of the narrow space between the Meatman's house and the next-door neighbor's until he reached the driveway. At the top of the block, he rounded a corner.

While he had been in the house a long double-axle trailer had arrived and taken a commanding position in the middle of Fletcher Street. The trailer was mounted on eight wheels and hauled by an olive-drab truck; it had a blue FBI stencil on the side. Driscoll figured it was some kind of field lab. All this couldn't have simply been for Paul Presto. They hadn't even done all that for Angelo Bruno—and Bruno had been a helluva lot more important than the Meatman.

Just then, Driscoll spotted Ed Bellows near the trailer. Angry and tired-looking, the big black man's face was half hidden by a jaunty blue-and-white muffler, Georgetown's colors. Bellows had been a center, backup, on a Final Four team in the NCAA. He could have turned pro; Driscoll didn't know why he hadn't. He had married his tutor down there, a beautiful white girl from an old Catholic Philadelphia family that had been around as long as the Protestants. Driscoll was a Catholic, too; how come Big Ed had all the fucking luck? King Kong and Fay Wray—Big Ed and the missus. Driscoll hated to admit it to himself, but deep down he guessed he was a racist bastard, too, just like every other white cop he had ever met.

Driscoll was freezing his ass off, but Bellows looked well insulated against the cold in a sheepskin greatcoat and gloves the size of catcher's mitts. Big Ed had just knifed his way between a pair of long Mafia limos that had pulled up outside the Meatman's house. They were probably going to go in and secure the place against unlawful searches and seizures like the one Driscoll had just gotten away with. More limos were sliding up to the curb, traveling in schools like killer fish. Driscoll looked for Honey, but he didn't see her anywhere. He was going to have to settle for Big Ed Bellows, who was bearing down on him. "I hear you know the girl," Big Ed said, without bothering to say hello.

Driscoll answered cautiously, "If you mean Honey Presto, that was a long time ago."

"You heard all that stuff back at the morgue. Your girlfriend has a big fucking mouth . . . big." Bellows opened his mouth wide in pantomime, but he sounded ominous.

"So she's got a big mouth," Driscoll said, trying to sound

unconcerned. "What's that got to do with me? Her old man fell down and went boom. That's all I know."

"Fuck that shit," Bellows barked. "You tell that broad to keep her big mouth shut. I got a message for you, too. Lawlor says to get your ass into his office." Then, suppressing a sneer, Bellows added, "The commissioner and I have already discussed this. He may be lending you to me for the Presto investigation."

Driscoll knew that was because of Honey. Considering their past relationship, Lawlor would expect him to squeeze the girl for them.

BUSTLETON, NORTHEAST PHILADELPHIA

The girl's name was Svetlana. She danced in Butkova's small Russian nightclubs—two weeks in Philly, then two weeks in New York on Brighton Beach. She packed them in. Only one problem—opium. The girl was an addict who had brought her addiction with her from Russia, halfway around the world. Her parents, emigrés, had hoped that a new country would mean a new life for their daughter. But in the United States, where drugs were even more easily available than in the Soviet Union, their nightmare had begun anew. Their friends directed them to Butkova. His reputation among his countrymen was that of a man who could solve any problem from red tape with their visas to daughters who were slowly killing themselves.

The first time he saw her, Butkova looked into Svetlana's eyes, then hungrily devoured the soft, supple curves of her body. "Leave the girl with me," he had told her parents. "Go back to work. I promise you your daughter will be reborn. Don't worry."

And so she was, as Butkova's mistress. His own opium

connections were extensive and profitable. It was merely the matter of a phone call for him to supply her with the finest Turkish opium to be had in exchange for her satsifying his desires completely whenever he felt the urge. He controlled her addiction, not as her parents had hoped, but as her supplier, her slave master. He let it be known among the other Russians that anyone who supplied Svetlana with drugs would have Butkova to answer to. A threat, merely a word, from Butkova was enough. Svetlana found herself totally dependent on him. It began with the opium, then, progressively, Butkova took over every aspect of her life.

Svetlana had studied engineering in the Soviet Union, but because there was a trace of Jewish blood in her ancestry—and the Russians were worse than the Nazis about this—the most prestigious jobs and the best departments would forever be denied her. Butkova had arranged for her parents to emigrate. A few months later, Svetlana followed. In the beginning, he had demanded nothing in return for the forged papers he had supplied them, and he had never asked for repayment of the seed money he offered them to establish themselves in business in their new country.

After they came to him about their daughter, and once he had seen that they were beginning to prosper, Butkova collected on his generosity—from that point on, he took half of every dollar Svetlana's parents earned here in the United States and employed their only daughter as his whore. He drove a hard bargain.

But power was the only commodity these people understood. It wasn't Butkova's fault that God had made him strong.

When he came home, Butkova found Svetlana in a small bedroom with the door closed and the windows shut tightly. Nudging the door open, he saw her smoking the antique bong pipe that Butkova had brought with him from Odessa. She was naked. Without disturbing her, he closed the door and waited.

Hours later, after she came out of it, Svetlana had obediently come to his bed. Glassy-eyed from her near stupor, she knew what he would want.

Butkova leaned toward her and kissed her. Then he lay back against the large pillow she had propped up behind him, as her lips and mouth and finally her tongue excitedly sought his penis. Everything in the room had taken on a golden tint; two candles flickered on his night tables. After a few moments, intending to delay his reaction, to stretch out the ecstasy as long as he could, he lifted her oval face, framed by black bangs, toward him. Even in the dim light, he could make out the wonderful contours of her body, the tips of her breasts, dark as flame.

She straddled him, moving slowly, pressing the side of her face into his chest. Her tongue played with his nipples. Moving around behind him, she kneaded his shoulders, working her firm, strong fingers into the muscles of tension and knots of nerves that dissolved in warm, rushing waves. The tips of her nails were sharp as they dug into his flesh. Butkova always preferred her after the pipe when her eyelids were heavy with desire and her body exquisitely responsive.

As her hands explored his armpits, circling around across his shoulders, her soft breasts pressed against his back. The warm bedroom and their own growing excitement had drenched both of them in a light, lubricating moisture.

Butkova turned and took her in his arms. Her tongue sought his. He could feel her falling back against the fur quilt and gently shifting onto her stomach, elevating her hips and buttocks. She sensed what he wanted to do as his fingers, their skin beginning to wrinkle with just the first faint circular age marks showing, probed the soft, moist skin near her anus. Prison had hardened him to prefer sex this way, with men or women; Butkova was almost indifferent to his partner. Her strong haunches moved to accommodate him as he entered her tight opening, burying himself deeply between her yielding buttocks. Moving in powerful, persistent strokes, his heavy hips began rocking the big bed. Instinctively, she guided first his hand, then her own, to the slippery crevice of her vagina. She came sooner than he did, assuming an almost fetal position before Butkova finally withdrew from her anus. Then, breathing hard, he lay on top of her, exhausted, but happy. Once, he could only dream of nights like this.

The first time the Russian police had arrested Butkova, it was on an unspecified charge of "conduct detrimental to the Soviet State." The sentence was six years in a "rehabilitation community" in a gulag in Siberia, where the police assumed that he would die. His first winter there, he almost did die. He finally contracted pneumonia. Of the twenty-eight men who had originally marched into the compound with Butkova—twelve from the streets of Odessa—seventeen had perished, following the first freezing snows. That had been his first prison experience, but he had endured, along with a small group of tough, resilient survivors.

Recovered from his bout with pneumonia, Butkova resigned himself to face his second winter in Siberia. It was during that second frozen eternity of subzero temperatures and endless days and nights of ice-clogged streams and desolate tundras that Nikolai Butkova's life changed forever.

He could vividly recall the black, starless night that it had happened. Nearly driven mad by a vicious hunger that had become starvation, Butkova and his comrades had gathered that night, in rags, freezing, their entire bodies numbed. They stood in eerie silence in a smoky semicircle, around an enormous cooking pot that rested atop a roaring fire. The only sound was the whistling, wailing wind blowing fiercely across the northern Russian wasteland.

They approached the cooking pot stiffly, one by one, shamefacedly avoiding each other's eyes. Like animals picking at a carcass, each man—Nikolai Butkova included—quickly snatched something from the steaming pot, then retired alone to the cold shadows of the communal hut.

That night, Butkova and the others had become cannibals, eating one of their dead comrades so that they themselves might live. Staring into the fire that night, Butkova had experienced none of the revulsion he had expected to feel. Instead, a hot surge of elation shot through him. A malevolence—animalistic and intense—seized him. Butkova and the other strong ones had done what they had to do, triumphing over ego and upbringing and every other human compunction that any of them had ever known. They had tasted human flesh—the last taboo shattered. That night, the men imprisoned with Butkova had become a primeval tribe defying the might of the Soviet state and the unrelenting Siberian winter.

After he had eaten his fill, trudging back to the cooking pot several times, his belly not growling for the first time in months, Butkova curled up on his hard bed of rags and straw and enjoyed the dreamless sleep of a child.

By rejecting his humanity that night, Butkova had soared above it, gaining a superiority that would allow him to ruthlessly consolidate his power back in the underworld of Odessa. That cold, providential night, Nikolai Butkova became the most dangerous man in the Soviet Union, even though it would take the official guardians of the state years to realize it.

By his third winter in Siberia, Butkova was running his sector of the prison. Even the guards were in awe of him. He served three years after that—every day of his six-year term—and was finally set free.

The police followed him back to Odessa, fully intending to murder him and blame it on one of the thugs, the *urkas* of the underworld. But less than seven days after his release, the man known as Nikolai Butkova seemingly vanished from the face of the earth, never again to be seen on the wide promenades of Odessa.

When he surfaced again, it was in America, where he quickly came to study the Paul Prestos of the American underworld, the American Mafia. He even went a step further and adopted Paul Presto as a role model. Butkova believed that he really understood him. The Meatman was a shrewd businessman, a bold leader in his own realm, and a selfless provider who saw to it that each and every member of his Family was taken care of, from the lowliest numbers writer to an avaricious underboss like Tony Bonaventura. But that was not the real secret of Presto's success and power. It had taken Butkova a long time to realize this. He had been searching for some complex series of relationships or some character trait that was Presto's alone; some Mafia secret that had eluded the criminals that Butkova had learned from. But in the end, Butkova understood that the Meatman had remained the Meatman for the most basic of reasons—Paul Presto had been the deadliest animal in his small jungle. And Paul Presto wasn't afraid to prove it again and again.

Given absolutely no other choice, the Meatman would not hesitate to kill. Neither would Nikolai Butkova.

Tonight, at the numbers bank, they had learned that. Tonight Butkova had put to use what he had learned from the great Meatman.

Practically every successful Russian-American businessman in Philadelphia—among the emigrés, that is—was already paying tribute to Butkova. Merchants like Svetlana's father—small, frightened men who had needed Butkova's connections to escape the Soviet system. Some were Jews, some merely Russians—all needed a protector like Butkova. And they paid for that protection. The Meatman had called that kind of protection money a street tax, so that was the term Butkova used as well. He never took enough to break a man or to rob him of all his profits, but enough to keep him hungry. He had learned that from Presto, too.

The Russians in America were becoming fat on their own ambition. Some were actually happy to pay—they were used to operating that way in the old country. Beginning with the corner stores, Butkova had expanded to the diamond merchants downtown, doing battle there with the Israeli gangsters who tried to control the gem trade. He also handled drugs of all kinds, not just the Turkish opium he gave to Svetlana, but anything that would sell. Whatever the Meatman did, Butkova imitated. He attempted to set up an operation that would mirror Presto's. Gradually, Butkova came to control his people the same way that Presto controlled his. And eventually, Presto had become aware of what Butkova was trying to do. The Russian knew that that had to happen.

The police were the least of Butkova's problems. The *Russian* police were another matter. Every group of emigrés that came over included at least one KGB agent. Often they attempted to infiltrate his criminal network, to subvert it, compromise it, use it for their own ends. When Butkova caught them he killed them—and then complained to the sniveling bureaucrat in Moscow who was supposed to alert him to such treachery. The man in Moscow, a powerful government man, was paid handsomely for his efforts. Still, they fell short. Lately, Butkova had been circumventing him altogether. He believed his superiors would approve.

Tonight had been an example of that. Tonight, the real war had begun.

Tonight, Butkova had beaten the great Meatman to the punch. Presto was such a worthy, capable adversary. Through sheer respect, Nikolai Butkova had come to love him like a brother—but a brother who must eventually be defeated.

Tonight, Butkova had given them proof of his manhood. Like Presto, he was not afraid to take what he wanted.

NOBLE STREET

"So where is the tape?" Manny asked.

"I have it right here," Honey answered nervously. She opened her purse and took out a small black rectangular box. Manny recognized it immediately as a VCR tape.

He examined it, held it up to the light of a lamp, and opened it. Carefully, using the fat, stumpy fingers of his left hand, he pulled at the first few inches of the tape and probed them. He indicated an iridescent triangle on the tape.

"That tiny rainbow of color is a holograph. It protects against tampering or duplication. Your father went to a great deal of trouble to make this, to guarantee its authenticity."

Manny hesitated. "There could be something very personal on this tape. Maybe you should look at it first, alone, and then if you still want me to see it, fine."

"No," Honey answered quickly. "That's not what he wanted. We're supposed to look at it together. That's what Milton Littlejohn told me when he gave it to me at the morgue."

The lawyer. Manny recognized his name. He had entered the scene after Manny gradually receded from the Meatman's inner circle.

"He said it was in my father's will that we do it this way. We *must* watch it together."

Manny sighed and scrutinized the tape again. "I suppose there's no harm. The VCR is in the other room." The Fat Man waddled off.

As she followed him, Honey thought back to what Littlejohn had said at the morgue. The conversation had taken place right after her confrontation with Bellows, right after she had seen Phillip. She hadn't expected to see Phillip there—she had hoped she would never see him again. He was still so handsome, those eyes of his were so alive, so mysterious when they turned blue. But Honey knew that tonight of all nights, she couldn't deal with her feelings for Phillip Driscoll. That was why she had practically run away from him at the morgue.

"You're a very wealthy young woman now," Littlejohn had told her, carefully removing his glasses and polishing the thick lenses with a neatly folded handkerchief he had taken from his breast pocket. He was about sixty, very pompous, as far as Honey was concerned, but a confidant of her father's. Littlejohn wasn't a *consigliere* in the traditional sense. But she knew her father respected her abilities. "Remember, I am at your disposal, as I was at your late father's."

Why did he have to put it *that* way? Your *late* father. Just hearing it hurt so much.

He walked with a slight limp and required the aid of a heavy walnut cane with a duck's head, carved in ivory, perched on top of it. The cane had a brass tip that made a slight *bing* sound on the cold tile floor of the morgue. For several long minutes, it was the only sound between them.

"How much money did my father leave me?" Honey asked awkwardly.

"A little over twenty million," the lawyer replied. "But we can go over all of that later. No need to bother you with it now."

She knew the lawyer was assessing her, attempting to handicap her chances of continuing to run the Presto empire. Honey didn't even resent him for that. That was his job; her father would have approved.

Littlejohn reached for his glasses again and leaned his full weight on the cane for support. Choosing each word with care, he went on, fastidiously smoothing down the lapels of his black cashmere coat.

"Your father was not a record-keeper. He never believed in putting things down on paper. . . . But there is the matter of this videocasette." That's when Littlejohn had handed it to her, looking relieved as he placed the flat black box in her hands. By then, they were shaking. His own large hand, on hers, tried to calm her.

"Your father had one more request," he told her. "He wants you to view this tape with your Uncle Manny—Mr. Goldberg in the old days, Mr. Gallen now. 'Make sure they watch it together' were his very words."

Then they had left the morgue, Honey walking unsteadily on her high heels beside Littlejohn, clutching the cassette, gently placing her arm in his, with the old lawyer supporting himself on the duck-headed cane. The *binging* of the shiny brass tip on the hard floor broke the spooky silence as the door closed behind them.

What would her father say to her on the tape? As much as she loved him and pretended to bully him, Honey had always been just a little afraid of the Meatman.

Manny removed the cassette and placed it inside the slot of a sleek VCR, an imposing RCA Dimensia, set above a big Sony TV.

Manny was doing his best to help Honey relax, but she was impatient; uptight. Manny backed his ponderous bulk away from the VCR and sat down next to her. He aimed a remote-control module at the screen and pressed the play button. Slowly the tape began to unreel.

The first few inches of the tape flickered white. The palms of Honey's hands were damp. She scarcely noticed the air conditioning in the room. Manny touched her shoulder gently. "It will be all right," he reassured her. Then he folded his thick arms across his chest and waited.

Honey heard a soft click, and the video image of the Meatman appeared. An aching, painful sob ripped through her body.

"Don't be afraid," Paul Presto's deep voice comforted her from the television screen.

ELEVEN

MOSCOW

Mikhail Zhukov lived across from the Kremlin, atop a small, grassy promontory of the brown Moskva River. On this modest bluff, overlooking the sweeping lowland of modern Moscow, the KGB had long ago commandeered a group of massive mansions, once the choicest abodes of the merchant class. They dated back to a time just before the Revolution. Only the top KGB officers, like Zhukov, lived here. By Moscow's standards, his sitting rooms, den, bathrooms, bedrooms, kitchen, and small servants' quarters approached the palatial. Directly above him, men who were far closer to the Politburo than he had been assigned ten- and twelve-room apartments and limitless luxuries. He envied their space and access to the Chairman.

Zhukov's manner was languid, but his tone of voice had an edge to it that held the promise of imminent retribution. He delighted in frightening his subordinates, and they despised him. But Zhukov didn't mind. He believed that a trace of malice produced the creative tension, the energy that his profession demanded. There was also his unconscious clinging to tradition. For as far back as he could remember, he had always hated his own superiors, beginning with the father he had never met.

The Chairman had first spotted Zhukov when he was in charge of an obscure domestic police section, the antismuggling militia, in one of the unglamorous divisions of the

KGB's Second Chief Directorate. It was responsible for suppressing corruption and economic crimes—Zhukov's job was to contain the very same black market that had supplied his own famous wine cellar. The best part of his work then had been the ease with which he could skim off the cream from any type of confiscated contraband—and all in the name of gathering evidence.

His wine cellar had only been the beginning. Among his accumulated booty were autos, blue jeans, records, stereo equipment, cameras, perfume, shoes, leather goods, lingerie, pornography, and every sort of canned or bottled delicacy imaginable from succulent Polish hams to an incredible American concoction, Campbell's Pork and Beans. To store all this, he had secured a small two-story warehouse twenty kilometers outside Moscow. Once a week he drove along the new Ring Road, the capital's beltway, to inspect his ill-gotten stockpile.

Zhukov shared his home with a young woman, Tanya. She was an interpreter for Aeroflot, the official state airline. Normally, the KGB used Aeroflot as its private charter service, and generations of KGB personnel had been disguised as Aeroflot employees to facilitate their worldwide travels.

Tanya's case was different—she actually was an Aeroflot worker with no KGB responsibilities at all. Yet Tanya was on the KGB payroll with a captain's rank and salary—a deal arranged by Zhukov. He never thought of himself as corrupt, merely inventive, ingenious. He wasn't working against the state, just parallel to it.

On her frequent trips abroad, Tanya deposited cash for Zhukov in a numbered Swiss bank account against the time when he might have to defect. Just the prospect of that eventuality caused Zhukov's blood pressure to elevate precipitously.

Tanya was tall and slender with slightly wide hips and an otherwise boyish figure. Her breasts were compact, pert and pointed. She could be playful when they made love and sometimes teased him to a point of exquisite agony that bordered on the sadistic. He sometimes wondered if that was the real reason they stayed together. For him, sex was unappealing without that erotic mixture of pleasure and pain.

Zhukov entered his building through a barrel-shaped vault that covered a passageway of heavy masonry and compacted earth. On either side of the handsome door, grinning gargoyles perched, mounted on slender Doric columns. On his good days, the small stone monsters seemed to laugh with him; on bad days, though, he could barely tolerate the derision in their granite faces.

On the elevator to the third floor, he noticed that the old woman who usually operated the lift, squatting on a stool near the buttons, had been replaced. A powerfully built young man with a decidedly military bearing pressed number 3 for him before inquiring what his floor was.

"Where's Aelita?" he asked, referring to the old woman.

"Transferred," the young man answered pleasantly. Then he added, almost sternly, "I'll be working here from now on."

He probably wasn't KGB. Zhukov couldn't begin to keep track of their fifty thousand agents, but he knew instinctively that he would have picked that up right away. He'd spent too many years in the service himself to miss it. GRU, he guessed, Military Intelligence, regular army—the only other wing of state in the Soviet Union that could match the KGB gun for gun and man for man. The two agencies were committed and frequently deadly rivals.

Suddenly he felt apprehensive, suspicious. A switch like this, especially in his own building, should have been cleared through his office.

The GRU man, if that's what he was, was dressed in civilian clothes. No indication of rank. He was extremely fit and deeply tanned—the sun had bleached his brown hair to a dry-looking wheat color. He hadn't been in Moscow long. Recalled from the field for a special assignment, most likely. If he had seen any action, it probably would have been in Afghanistan. The GRU was running the whole show there. Now, without a word of warning, overnight, he was in Zhukov's building.

Zhukov instantly conducted a census of the other tenants in the building. All senior party men. But who could be in trouble? Had the Chairman shunned anyone at a recent reception? Then he began matching up names and faces, hoping he could remember some miscalculation one of his neighbors had been guilty of. But he could think of nothing. This was a safe building, a privileged building. Why a GRU agent?

The elevator stopped at his floor. As he approached his door, he heard the young attendant call out, "Good evening, Comrade Zhukov."

Turning around quickly to reply, he noticed the slightest, almost imperceptible look of disdain darken the elevator operator's face. As the door slid closed, Zhukov picked up the thick, telltale bulge on his hip. A gun. He was sure of it. Zhukov didn't say a word.

NOBLE STREET

Honey Presto and the Fat Man listened with rapt attention as her father's mesmerizing voice spoke to them from the slowly streaming videotape.

"Don't be afraid, Honoria," Paul Presto repeated. "It's not so bad, this being dead. No cops. No feds. No more grand juries. I don't even have to listen to your Aunt Marie. It's like I was Florida."

This was the way he had always talked. His usage of the language was his very own. If he wanted to say that he was in Florida, he simply shortened it to "I was Florida."

Honey loved him for that. It was only when she had been very young that she had felt the slightest twinge of shame. But she had learned very soon that Paul Presto, her father, was an original.

"I only wish you were Florida," Honey answered him softly.

He grinned a big, toothy smile. Honey managed to smile back at him.

"How do I look? Like the movies?"

It was as though he were waiting for her to reply.

"Just like the movies, Daddy."

"I worry, Honey. I should be there with you, like when you was a little girl. But that's not possible. I don't even know what happened to me. Did they shoot me? Bomb me? Maybe a heart attack. Hey, that's not so bad, either. We all gotta go, Honey. Your number's up, it's up. Even your daddy's."

Presto gave a short, ironic laugh, then a weary nod of acceptance and resignation. That had been so typical of him in life. Helplessly, Honey reached out toward the screen. She longed to return the gesture. He was still worrying about her, afraid for her. Even in death, he was trying passionately to contact her, to look out for her. She was overcome, seized by the realization of just how much, how deeply he had cared. He was her father. Nothing—not even his dying—could ever change that.

"I made this video—this whatever-you-call-it—because I had the idea that if somebody tries to kill me, they might try to kill you, too. I gotta help you save yourself, Honey. You don't understand about what we do—not all of it, anyway. You was a girl. How could you know? How could I make you a part of all this?"

When Honoria was a child, she had cried because she wasn't a boy. She sensed the rejection that her father tried so hard to hide. Drying her tears, he had hugged her to him, and Honoria promised that she would do more to make him proud than any boy could. And no one tried harder than Honey. No one better appreciated the sacred nature of *the* family, of *his* family. She never questioned what he did or why he did it. She simply accepted the Meatman for what he was, and made her separate peace with his way of life.

"The first thing you gotta do is go your Uncle Manny. You go Manny." The audible rhythm of Manny's labored breathing was hushed as the Fat Man listened, sharing Paul Presto's obstinate refusal to allow even death to stand in the way of what he believed had to be done.

"Listen to Manny," her father's voice urged her. "He loves you, too. And, Honey, your momma loved you. You have to know that. She did. That was part of the trouble we always had . . . but now is not the time for that. She was hard enough on you . . . God forgive her. . . ."

Manny was squirming, and when a man of his size squirmed, the whole couch moved. He looked away from Honey and from the screen.

Honey Presto had enjoyed only a minimal relationship with her mother. Her childhood gropings for warmth and love had been met with a stern toleration, nothing more. Her mother had been jealous of Honey from the moment she had been born. That devastating undercurrent of rejection had never been far from Honey's heart. The Meatman had done his best to make it up to her, but he had been a clumsy man emotionally, particularly with a little girl. His sister, Marie, had been the closest fill-in for a mother that Honey had known. But brother and sister had battled constantly over how Honey should be raised. The bickering intensified when Presto's wife died shortly after Honey's eleventh birthday.

Honey thought briefly of her Aunt Marie, a big-bosomed, chain-smoking tyrant of a woman. By now, Honey guessed, she would be draped in some shapeless black tent, rosary in hand, a black veil draped over her head, covering her face, while she moaned and cried, tears streaking her mascara and the rouge on her cheeks, impatient to begin the ritual of the professional mourners. Still, her Aunt Marie was the matriarch of the family, and Honey believed her aunt loved her. And Honey loved her back. It was just that right now, after everything had happened so quickly, she simply couldn't face her Aunt Marie's cloying kind of family togetherness. Honey wished that she could draw strength from that, but she couldn't. But she knew, too, that her father would understand.

"I hope you stopped your crying, Honoria, because now you have to pay attention. Now, we have a sit-down—you and Manny and me.

Because I don't know why I am dead, I can't begin to explain everything to you now, Honey," Paul Presto's voice told them from the screen. "But no matter. Unless I died of a heart attack or got hit by a bus, I got a good idea who did it." Honey and the Fat Man looked at each other.

"Now we know the *real* reason for the tape," Manny whispered to her.

Her father continued, "A long time ago, right after you

were born, I did business with some men. Just one time. Not a lot of business, but enough. I had to keep it secret from Manny. He never woulda understood. That's what I thought then; now I know better. It isn't that he woulda not understood. He woulda not let me do something so stupid. But I did it."

Honey leaned over to Manny. "Do you remember what he's talking about?" Manny shook his head.

"Not Sicilians, but *contrabbandieri,* smugglers.

"After I finish my business with them, they say, "What about *oppio, eroina, hascisc?'* I tell them never. I fight my own people who deal in that."

"Opium, heroin, hashish," Honey translated for Manny. *"Oppio,"* he repeated knowingly.

"I check around and I find out that these men are *fugitivi.* They escaped from someplace in Russia. I never found out their real names. They set up business, like us, here in America. At first they don't bother us, we don't bother them. They're small potatoes. But I watch them. Every year they get a little stronger; have a few more men. I go to the *commissione,* the Commission. I say, 'We better take care of these guys.'

"The old cigars—they laugh at me. The *commissione* forgets everything I tell them. But I don't forget. I keep my eye on them."

Her father's voice went on. "They start to make moves. I have to protect myself, Honey, and I do. But nobody knows about it. Not even the Family. This I do myself. I send them a message that I know they understand.

"Before he died, I had gone to the Old One, to *Il Vecchio.* I tell him about these foreigners. At first *Il Vecchio,* he don't wanna talk about it. 'I'm old,' he tells me. 'I want to die in peace.' But I see in his tired eyes, he's afraid. Finally, the Old One takes my hand. He's shakin'. He kisses me on both cheeks—like he's about to have me killed. I pull back from him.

"I think he's gone crazy and he's givin' me the evil eye, *malocchi.* But then the Old One raises himself up in bed and grabs my shoulders. He speaks to me in Sicilian.

" 'They are here,' he says.

" 'Who?' I ask him. But he starts to drift off. I think it's the end for him, but he motions me to come nearer. I lean low over him. 'Malina,' he whispers.

"He falls back on his bed and does not speak again. *Il Vecchio* died with the word *Malina,* on his lips."

"Manny, what does this Malina mean?" Honey searched the Fat Man's face.

"Raspberries," he said, without looking at her.

"What?" she asked again impatiently.

"Be still. Explanations later. The tape isn't finished." She had never seen Manny like this—so absorbed in his own thoughts. So detached.

"Who were these fugitives my father's talking about?" she screamed.

Manny made another gesture for silence, but she persisted.

He aimed the remote control and stopped the tape. He turned to Honey.

"There's a legend that once in Russia, when the people were starving, there were only wild raspberries to eat. Outlaws had confiscated all of the raspberries. People were dying of starvation, but these men forced everyone to come to them for the only food available, the raspberries. They sold the raspberries to the desperate people at a great profit. Then other things, until they had set up a black market that spread everywhere. Nothing moved unless they gave the okay. To do business with these thieves, the peasants had to go to a secret place—the place where you could find the raspberries, the place of the Malina. The hiding place was Odessa, on the Black Sea.

"That's a rough translation. I don't know the Russian words, but among themselves, they call it the Malina."

"But what is it doing here?"

"It's the Russian Mafia—like our Mafia, but much older and more deadly. No honor, no Families, no men of respect. It came here with the emigrés. Mostly, I thought they just robbed their own people—protection rackets, arson, shoplifting rings, a few burglaries. Drugs, when they can move them. They've taken over a few businesses, cab companies, restaurants, clubs—things like that.

"They were precisely as your father described them—small potatoes. Until now. Thousands of Russians came out of Russia during the 1970s; maybe close to a million, between here and Israel. And the Malina traveled with them."

Suddenly the Fat Man held her with a look that warned of a cold intelligence. "Your father thinks that the Malina killed him. He's afraid that they might try to kill you too. Honey, we can't ignore a warning like that."

"Manny, how do you know all this—about the Malina?"

"In Russia, many times, Jews must go to the black market, the Malina, to get out of the country or to get set up here. Not all of them, of course, but a few. Enough. It's the most despicable kind of blackmail. Worse than the Nazis.

"I am a Jew. I make it my business to know about such things. Sometimes these Russian Jews have come to me to get away from the Malina. . . ." Manny stopped and shrugged. "I do what little I can for them. But with the Malina—against the Malina—there's not much you can do, except to protect yourself."

"Russians? Here?" Honey was incredulous.

Manny feigned surprise. "America is still the land of opportunity, is it not? The lady in the harbor still holds her torch high. Castro made the United States a dumping ground for all the criminals and misfits in Cuba. You remember that? He emptied the prisons and sent them here. The Russians know a good thing when they see it. If the Malina comes here, they don't have to worry about what they might be doing back in Russia. Every so often, they slip in a KGB agent. Who knows if this agent is a real Jew or Malina or what he is? Very convenient.

"In this country the Malina thinks that it has been turned loose in a candy store. Believe me, our police are nothing like the Russian police. I know. I've dealt with both."

Honey started to interrupt him again.

"No more now. No more questions. Your father may have something else to tell us."

On the video screen in the quiet room, the image of Paul Presto again appeared—impassioned, sweating, almost coming to life over his concern for Honey.

Manny rubbed his forehead, as his thick fingertips slid down to his cheeks, then to the wide spread of his jowls. He was nervous and preoccupied.

Paul Presto's sad, gentle eyes flashed one final time. They listened.

"This isn't the end, Honoria." Presto's tone was one of conviction. "That you haveta believe." He stopped as though waiting for his unseen audience to adjust to his absence.

"That goes for you, too, Manny, my old friend. Somehow, don't ask me how, I'll be there with you. Always. You have your daddy's word on that, Honoria. I swear it as sure as I swear that I'm the Meatman.

"Maybe I'll come back and haunt whoever did this to me. But don't you worry. You just believe. I'll never leave you, never, Honoria. I love you too much to do that. *Believe . . .*"

Presto's body moved forward on the screen toward the unseen camera. The backdrop behind him was sterile white, a standard studio setup. Then the Meatman's image vanished.

Honey Presto's tears flowed hot and bitter.

INTERPOL HEADQUARTERS, RUE ARMENGAUD, SAINT-CLOUD, PARIS

Gaston LeClerc, a wiry, agile man with a peppery way of talking and a black mustache that he had kept meticulously trimmed for the last thirty years, was the ranking inspector on duty at the General Secretariat when the telefax photo came in. He had just returned from a breakfast of sweet rolls and Turkish coffee and had deposited his hat and scarf on a settee in the small waiting area outside his private office when an assistant handed him the photo facsimile on a sheet of computer paper. There was a gentle rain falling outside, and the leaded windows of the old Second Empire mansion next to Interpol's modern office building at number 26, the mansion in which LeClerc's department had been housed since the reorganization in 1980, were already slippery with the traces of the heavy storm that was blowing in somewhere from the choppy waters of the North Sea.

As was LeClerc's custom, he studied the picture for several seconds before deciding exactly what to do with it. LeClerc knew that he recognized the face. Not Corsican; not Italian; not Arabic. For several more seconds he pondered his mental index of every known international terrorist. The face refused to be pigeonholed there, either. But he *knew* that he knew it. The man seemed to be somewhat past thirty; naturally muscular neck; no scars, though he looked to be the type who would wear a scar comfortably; thick hair cut short and unevenly. It looked like an army recruit's haircut. But he was much too old to be a recruit. A mercenary maybe—he had that look.

Summoning the assistant, he asked from which office the request for identification had come.

"Interpol Washington," the aide answered. "The query originated in Philadelphia."

LeClerc noticed that the photo facsimile had been flagged as neither a State Department nor an FBI request. That meant the telefax had come directly from the police in Philadelphia. That was unusual initiative for a local cop. LeClerc decided to do everything he could for this unseen brother-in-arms. A good cop.

LeClerc asked the aide if he had any ideas. He returned a Galic shrug and left the inner office to answer the phone. LeClerk kept examining the photo from different angles. No fingerprints, obviously, but why no prints if they had the suspect in custody, as the accompanying information explained?

LeClerc, his mustache now moving beneath his small nose like an inquisitive squirrel's whiskers, buzzed for two men at once. A few moments later they entered together. The first was from the *portrait parlé* section; he was fat and a little slovenly for LeClerc's tastes, but the best analyst in his department. His job was to take a photo like this, from anywhere in the world, with no other clues as to the subject's identity, and attempt to come up with a name, a criminal record if any existed, and a last-known location. The first step would be to employ the Bertillon system of photo identification, utilizing bone structure, facial characteristics, coloring, etc., and try to ascertain an ethnic type or point of origin. Next came an arduous process of cross-referencing the vast Interpol files—millions of them. There was no quick way; sometimes an analyst got lucky, but usually success depended upon old-fashioned police work—long hours, cigarettes, and plenty of coffee.

As soon as the photo expert left, LeClerc turned to the other man. "Let's assume," he said, "that this suspect had his fingerprints surgically removed. Perhaps acid. The Americans don't tell us this in so many words, but it must be the case." The other man listened. He had fought in Algeria with LeClerc; they were as close as brothers. His name was Marcel de Letan. His department was Group C of the International Criminal Police Cooperation Division. The client list consisted of every police department in the world, outside of the Soviet Union and its spheres of influence. "Marcel," LeClerc asked, "what does that remind you of?" For most of his career, de Letan had concentrated on organized crime groups, from the vicious French underworld to the American Mafia.

Marcel's eyebrows raised, then seemed to melt into his forehead. "I've only seen it once before—and even then, our information had gaps in it." Marcel was loath to offer any theory that he could not completely substantiate. But for his friend Gatson, he would make an exception. "*Malina.*" He uttered the word like a curse, like a man who wished to spit on the floor and cleanse his mouth because of what it had just held. Gaston nodded gravely. As soon as he had seen the telefax LeClerc had also thought of the Malina, the most feared conspiracy that Interpol had ever faced.

TWELVE

THE HARRISON BUILDING, INDEPENDENCE MALL, PHILADELPHIA

The Strike Force occupied the entire eleventh floor of the Harrison Building, a block-long Federalist-era dinosaur. There was also a vaultlike armory in the basement. Sometimes Bellows felt like one of the Untouchables.

He had a corner office with a sweeping view that overlooked Independence Hall and the Liberty Bell, with Carpenter's Hall peeping in from the extreme left. The focal point of his office was a handsome fireplace surrounded by a tiled mantlepiece. Bellows loved the feeling of warmth and security it gave him.

Without any warning, a round blue light, strategically recessed on the uppermost edge of Ed Bellows's desk, began to flicker. It was a silent telephone signal.

He took a key out of the watch pocket of his vest and unlocked the bottom drawer of a cluttered credenza behind his desk.

Reaching inside, he pulled out a large, rectangular metal box. It moved on two tracks, attached to the bottom of the credenza. He flipped up the lid to reveal what looked like a miniature teletype machine. It was a transistorized electromechanical typewriter that transmitted its letters over a fiber-optic wire. The machine was activated by dialing a highly classified combination of random digits, changed on the second Tuesday of each month. The box could send or receive signals.

Bellows watched intently as the tiny typewriter keys reacted to the silent, invisible electrical impulse. At twenty-eight-second intervals, a scanner swept the device as a precaution against bugging.

Each time that blue light on his desk began to glow, Bellows could feel his pulse accelerate. It was happening again, every damn time the typewriter keys touched the paper with their nearly inaudible click.

Right next to the credenza was a paper shredder. After each message, Bellows had been instructed to put the print-out into the shredder. Since he had taken over the Philadelphia office, he had had to use the shredder only six times. The machine's primary limitation was its inability to transmit more than one paragraph at a time. Usually, though, that was enough.

Finally, the clicking stopped. Bellows ripped the small sheet of paper from the carriage of the machine and began to read it.

NOBLE STREET

Manny had been fasting for almost forty-eight hours, but after he had watched the tape with Honey and sent her upstairs to rest, he made up for it. He had a lot of thinking to do, which meant that he had a lot of eating to do.

He closed the deli, locked the door, pulled the cream-colored shades down, turned off the neon Star of David, and began piling jars and trays of food on a large wooden table in the rear.

He arranged everything so that once he sat down, he could reach for it without getting up again—corned beef, roast beef, a cheese board, more cold cuts, condiments, two long loaves of Italian bread, a carton of soda, pretzels, chips, and a box of the deli's famous chocolate-chip cookies. He also added smoked Norwegian salmon, a house specialty, and Russian sturgeon, and a deep dish of cream-style herring. He ate in three-hour stretches, stopping only long enough to relieve himself. And when that became a nuisance, he'd use a bucket under the table.

Manny had planned it all out. He'd start off with hoagies on Italian loaves, then his first dessert, followed by his Jew food, as he called it, the salmon, sturgeon, and herring. Then his second dessert, maybe another sandwich, the rest of the soda and cookies, and a couple bags of chips for a final snack. *Never enough.*

Manny ate to think, but he also ate to forget. And there was so much to forget. A childhood spent as a fat boy, a Jew boy, an outsider in an Italian Catholic ghetto. Every day a fight, tears, humiliation, until finally Manny found a protector—a boy who somehow understood what he was going through, a boy of instinctive sympathy and gentleness, the kindest boy Manny had ever known. They became closer than brothers. Two bodies—one grotesque, the other powerful. Two personalities—one cerebral, the other savage. But only one mind. A single instinct for survival. That's how close Manny Goldberg and his true friend, Paul Presto, had become.

At the table now, stripped down to his boxer shorts and V-neck T-shirt, Manny ate. *Try to forget; try to forget the hurts.*

His binge over, the Fat Man started to feel sick and dizzy. High blood pressure was a constant concern. Surrounded by bags and boxes and gallon containers, Manny had gorged himself, not by the spoonful or handful, but by the jarful, as he plunged his knife into every container, scraping the bottom, consuming the last drop. Meticulously, he ended his meal by brushing the last crumb from the table into the wide hollow of his hand and licking off every morsel.

MOSCOW

Tanya was already home. She had started a fire in the largest sitting room, crumpling newspapers and kindling under two fat logs that now smolderd on the iron gate. Zhukov heard her singing a sweet old peasant song from the nearest bedroom. He felt edgy and exhausted—an odd combination; his body craved sleep but his mind rebelled.

The apartment was hot—Tanya should have been born in the tropics, he was always telling her—so he quickly removed his long fur coat and round mink *shapki,* the trademark of cold-weather Russia.

The cold rarely bothered him. His childhood had been spent in unheated shanties and the spartan dormitories assigned to the families of low-level workers. Zhukov had known few comforts until his KGB career really began. He was as much of a self-made man as the system permitted in the Soviet Union, and he was inordinately proud of that fact. He was prouder still of the fact that he had learned how to use the party, even as it demanded unquestioning loyalty from him.

Filling a delicate china teacup with hearty light-amber *starka,* the strong vodka that he preferred, he sipped slowly and contemplated the day's events.

Soon he was sweating, his face beet-red from the abrupt change in temperature. Loosening his tie and top shirt button, Zhukov propped his feet up on a red-tasseled leather ottoman, settling himself as far away from the now roaring fire as he could get.

Rich Persian carpets, rare booty from Iran, and now utterly unattainable in the East as well as the West, covered most of the sitting-room floor. He stared fixedly, absorbed by the deep, luxuriant colors, the seamless perfection of the weave, the complexity of the impossibly difficult design.

His precarious situation seemed to be mirrored in the inscrutable design of his carpet. He now knew that the guns he had been smuggling out of Vietnam through Singapore for delivery to the Americans were somehow being diverted. He had believed that he could trust his people in Singapore and Vietnam. He thought he could also trust his people in America. It now seemed obvious that he was wrong.

Just then, Tanya appeared, naked except for a damp terry-cloth towel wrapped around her wet blond hair in a turban.

Zhukov glanced at her firm body, at her high, pointed breasts, at her slender hips; but he was too distracted to appreciate her as he normally did.

She was only twenty-nine, many years his junior. Sometimes she was annoyed by the perpetual weariness that enveloped him like a heavy cloak. Tonight his small eyes looked red above the rimless glasses that he wore pushed almost to the tip of his curved, beaklike nose. His whole body slumped, but his eyes, as always, rotated like gun turrets. Ever alert.

"Darling, I didn't hear you come in," she said, sitting opposite him and folding her long legs beneath her, Indian-style. When she did this, only the curly blond band of her pubic hair showed above the soft hollow of her thighs. Although she knew he was tired, Tanya still chose this provocative pose; she needed to be close to someone tonight.

"I had an appointment to brief the Chairman today, just as always," he began, "but when I arrived, the deputy first secretary informed me that our meeting had been canceled—the Chairman was otherwise occupied."

She searched his worried face. He was waiting for her to tell him what she made of that. Frankly, Tanya wasn't sure.

"He is the Chairman, darling. The demands on his time must be incredible. He understands that he has no problem with you, so maybe today you weren't a priority." Why did he worry so? she mused. Then, to him, "Why so concerned?"

"Never, never before," Zhukov replied, beginning one of the orations she had heard so many times before, "did he miss one of my briefings, unless he had someone call ahead of time to reschedule."

"Perhaps some functionary merely overlooked it."

"A *functionary,* as you so aptly put it, who made mistakes like that would not remain a functionary of the Chairman for very long."

Tanya couldn't argue with that. She said nothing, but

picked up a pack of American cigarettes, Virginia Slims, tapped one from the pack, lit it, and sucked in deeply as she inhaled the smoke. The down on her forearms was dark and still moist from her bath.

"A Jewish woman was caught at the airport yesterday. No file as an active dissident. But this woman had a perfect set of exit papers. Flawless. So did her husband. The best forgeries I've ever seen. She also tried to smuggle out a sack of diamonds."

"Diamonds? How?"

"In her vagina. Tied and knotted in a prophylactic."

Tanya, smiling and appreciating the woman's ingenuity, glanced down at herself.

"The whole operation was so professionally executed, it frightens me."

"Did she tell you anything?"

"America. A contact in America. That hardly narrows it down. Except for one thing. She said he was a businessman in Philadelphia."

"Philadelphia?" Tanya, too, was surprised. The word had a special meaning for both of them. A black-market entrepreneur with whom Zhukov had been dealing for years, and who he thought he could trust, had emigrated to America and had made Philadelphia his headquarters. But now all that Zhukov could think about was treachery. His mind couldn't get away from that American gun that had been found in Moscow.

He finished off the *starka,* then offered some to Tanya.

"What are you going to do?" She could now discern the direction of his forceful logic, and it unnerved her. Tanya crushed out the cigarette and pulled the turban from her head, shaking her hair vigorously. Then she used the towel to dab at a line of perspiration that had formed beneath her breast. Zhukov's eyes followed her every movement. She opened her legs and crossed them. The fire had transformed the sitting room into an oven, but she was irresistibly drawn to the heat. She got up and threw another log on the metal grate. He continued.

"There's more. I came home today and the old woman who operates the lift is gone. Replaced. A young man whom I never laid eyes on has taken her place—he knows my name and floor before I even speak to him. You saw him, too?''

Tanya had; a change in personnel might have been harmless enough, but Zhukov chose to see it as the culmination of the day's unusual happenings.

''I saw him, yes,'' she answered. ''A very handsome man to be working a lift.''

''Not the type.''

''What do you suspect?''

He was about to answer her, then he caught himself, walked over to an antique half-table and pushed a Barry Manilow cassette into the opening of the stereo on the table. On purpose, he nudged the volume up a little too high.

Suddenly, Zhukov's eyes were tracing every inch of the familiar sitting room, searching for unfamiliar wires or outlets. Anything that looked out of place. He had bugged plenty of rooms himself. He placed a finger on Tanya's lips for silence, then guided her to the couch closest to the fire. They sat down together.

''All of this may be nothing,'' he whispered, drawing his face close to hers. ''Or it could be the beginning of the end. I have a feeling they're trying to work *around* me. See where, if anyplace, I lead them. If they were sure themselves, I wouldn't be here now.''

Tanya leaned into his shoulder and snuggled up close to him.

''When is your next flight?'' he asked, still speaking in a barely audible whisper. She reached for another cigarette, clutching the pack in her hand.

''Not for almost a week.''

''Switch with someone. I don't care how you do it, but *do* it. Promise to take the Gorki run for a month. Anything. Just make certain that you are on the next flight to New York. The *next* flight . . . that's imperative.''

''I'm sure I can take care of that,'' she replied, touching his face with a tenderness and concern that had been missing from their relationship for a long time.

''You know who to contact, what to do.''

Tanya nodded. Then he looked at her in a way that told her they might not be together again for a very long time.

"If anything goes wrong, don't be a fool. *Don't* come back. I'll understand. I'll meet you. Somehow."

She said nothing.

At least they would have tonight. Suddenly she felt guilty for all the pain she had caused him, all the time they had wasted fencing with each other.

"We'll speak no more of this. It's not safe."

Tanya removed his glasses and kissed him, her tongue, rough and urgent, probing for his, hungering. Next to the fireplace was a television with a VCR on the top. She left him momentarily to press a cassette inside. A few seconds later, the TV screen was filled with the image of a man and a woman, both naked, engaged in sex. The woman on the screen was Tanya. Zhukov had never before seen the man. He watched as Tanya knelt down, then dropped to her knees to allow the man to enter her from the rear. "I made the film just for you," she whispered. Zhukov had seen tapes like this one before. Tanya looked eager and proud to see herself on the screen. "I love you, Mikhail," she told him. "I need you, darling . . . now . . . please."

He felt a wild response that banished his exhaustion. Taking his eyes off the screen, he reached out for Tanya, aroused now, as excited as she.

First he tasted her nipples. Tanya was already removing his clothes, tugging and coaxing. As she slid between his legs, her hand lingered near his penis, teasing, inflicting her delicious agony. Her mouth was hot.

On the floor, in front of the fire, the carpet of many colors beneath them, Tanya eased herself down as Mikhail reached his hands toward her swelling body. The cassette soundtrack spoke to them like another presence in the room. Zhukov could hear her coaxing her lover on the screen, using the same tone she used with him.

In an instant, Tanya reversed positions and sat with her thighs on either side of Zhukov's middle, her strong legs bent at the knee, her back toward him. As he entered her, she began moving quickly, almost spasmodically, bringing both of them to the edge again and again, then expertly slowing her motion at the last possible second.

Zhukov felt strangely light-headed. It was as though there were two Tanyas. The one he could feel and touch, and another on the TV screen. A bluish vein on the side of his neck that became engorged and prominent only when he found himself terrified or sexually aroused began to throb and pulse against his skin as his face glistened.

"Watch now," she said. "Just a moment, it's coming up now . . . this is the best part, isn't it wonderful? *There, see* them." Zhukov felt his throat go dry, his hands tremble as a burning desire inflamed him. They both stared at the images on the screen. A second man was now entering the picture, approaching Tanya. Mikhail gasped, too excited to speak, as he watched her practically disappear beneath the men on the screen, sandwiched between them.

His slim hips thrust up to meet Tanya's while his small hand kneaded her breast. Totally absorbed, they were lost in their lovemaking and the film.

As she moved up and down against him, riding Zhukov to an exquisitely delayed climax, Tanya's buttocks brushed against his stomach and abdomen again and again, drawing him deeper inside her each time. Tonight he filled her with a power and force she had never known in him before. As she cried out his name, desperate that he might stop, she wondered why it had not always been like this between them.

A few minutes later, Mikhail was asleep on the floor in front of the fireplace. Tanya had covered him with a blanket she had thoughtfully taken from the bedroom. A big towel was thrown around her shoulders. She shivered. But Tanya wasn't cold; she was scared. She turned the television off and knelt next to Mikhail to make sure that he was still sleeping. A low snore convinced her.

Tanya tapped out the third and last cigarette from the Virginia Slims pack and lit it, grateful for the rush of the nicotine. It cleared her head. He hated her smoking and nagged her about it. He wouldn't even touch a cigarette. That's what she had told her superior. It had been a relatively simple matter to fit the miniature tape recorder inside the Virginia Slims pack, still leaving room enough for a few cigarettes. It recorded soundlessly, was voice-activated, and was equipped with a tiny directional microphone that was good for up to twenty feet. She really hadn't been able to get him to say that much tonight, but she hoped it would be all that they would need. Taping their conversation secretly like this frightened her.

He was still snoring as she drew the towel around her as modestly as she could and went to the door of the apartment.

The handsome young elevator operator was waiting across the hallway. She motioned to him. His shoulder was propped up against the open lift door. He looked very surprised to be seeing Tanya like this, but his smile told her that he liked what he saw. Tanya made sure that the loosened towel revealed most of her breasts as she motioned him over and pressed the cigarette pack into his eager hands.

"So good-looking," she sighed, as he disappeared inside the elevator door. What a pity she would have to leave for New York so soon.

THE HARRISON BUILDING

Ed Bellows kept reading and rereading the decoded message. He wanted desperately for it to be a mistake.

> TOP SECRET UMBRA. GREEN BADGE. HANDLE VIA COMINT CHANNELS ONLY. REPORT IMMEDIATELY OCS ROYAL TERMINAL.

Umbra was the Justice Department's highest security classification. Green badge meant that Bellows was to report to Washington—he was to bring his green badge. It was actually a color-coded IBM card, keypunched so that once it was inserted into a cipher machine, the computer brain could instantly determine the holder's clearance status. OCS stood for the Organized Crime Section in the Justice Department. Bobby Kennedy had originated it himself, with a single dented file cabinet in 1961.

Comint was the code for a top-secret intelligence communication.

Royal designated James X. Carney.

Bellows and a handful of other Strike Force chiefs knew about the designation.

Terminal. In any language or code, its meaning was clear. Jim Carney was either dead or dying. The last time Bellows had spoken to him, he had been in perfect health.

THE ROUNDHOUSE CENTER CITY, PHILADELPHIA

The Homicide squad room was deserted except for a cop who had his face buried in a dog-eared copy of *Hustler.* Driscoll checked the box on the secretary's desk where the pink message slips were pigeonholed. Nobody had called.

Then he went to the sour-smelling cubicle that he shared with three other detectives and finished off a meatball sandwich he had picked up on the way over. His hand felt hot against the container of bitter black tea. Sipping the tea, he leaned back in an old desk chair with stiff springs that groaned for mercy. Feet up on the edge of his desk, Driscoll inspected a beat-up old map of the United States with a big inset for Philadelphia, then an even bigger inset of Philadelphia's police districts. The map was covered with blue and red pushpins. He stood up, walked to the map, and withdrew the blue pin that had signified Paul Presto's house on Fletcher Street. Then he replaced it with a red one. Stepping back a few feet, he was able to take in the dimensions of the wide U.S. map; there were pushpins there, too—blue and red. He reached up and plucked a blue one from southeastern Pennsylvania, Philadelphia—that identified Presto on Driscoll's national map. He stuck a red one in there too.

Altogether, there were twenty-four pushpins on the U.S.

map, each one representing the boss of a *borgata* or traditional Mafia Family. The pins were congregated heavily in the northeastern United States, where the mob had the five New York Families, Presto in Philadelphia, the North Jersey crime bosses, and the heirs of the old Patriarca gang in New England. The remaining pins were scattered over Chicago, Las Vegas, Florida, Detroit, Cleveland, New Orleans, Kansas City, Phoenix, Los Angeles, and the other locations where the mob exercised its territorial imperative.

Less than a year before, every one of Driscoll's twenty-four national pushpins had been blue, which meant a living, active boss. Gradually, almost without him or anyone else noticing it, here and there, the blue pins had been replaced by red ones. Red stood for death, incarceration, or terminal inactivity. At first, Driscoll had written off the gradual change as little more than natural attrition, the shrinkage of the mob as it entered its third and fourth American generations with fewer and fewer "made members" and more and more semilegitimate associates. The FBI and the federal Strike Force had also been getting better at applying their broad RICO antiracketeering legislation with increasing creativity.

In a strange way, the Meatman himself had been a direct beneficiary of all that ruthless Mafia-hunting. Presto had been one of the survivors who came to power, along with men like John Gotti in New York and Nicodemo Scarfo in Atlantic City, following the relentless federal war on organized crime that had peaked in the 1980s. Eventually, the feds took out Scarfo, almost nailed Gotti, and did manage to sentence the old-time bosses of the Lucchese, Genovese, and Columbo Families in New York. New, younger, shrewder men had taken their places. Prominent among them had been Meatman Presto, who, not only because of his age but also because of his courtly reverence for all things traditional, had managed to bridge the generation gap between the old Mustache Petes and the high-tech hoods who had emerged as the inheritors of the Apalachin era. This new wave of organized-crime bosses was characterized, Driscoll knew, by tough, unemotional businessmen, more influenced by the ledger than by vendetta. They were as apt to embezzle as to extort, and more in love with controlling companies and commerce than with merely infiltrating trade unions. Presto had run successfully on that fast track, but had also succeeded in embodying enough of the old world to awe the young Turks with his experience and earthy sense of history.

Driscoll hated to admit it, but in some ways he had admired Presto. Hell, how could you *not* admire a guy who had grown up butchering chickens at a stall on 9th Street and then made a successful transition to learning to play the commodities market? When it came to the Mafia, Meatman Presto had represented the establishment.

But now, after one brutal act of assassination, he had to replace Presto's blue pushpin with a red one. He glanced at the U.S. map again. Presto's made the fifth red pushpin in less than twelve months. Something was definitely happening, but Driscoll couldn't put his finger on it. He had checked with his contacts all over the country and no one knew of any major mob wars; just the normal bickering within the Families, which usually amounted to little more than a few low-level hoods left in the trunks of Buicks. Yet the American Mafia was under fire from the feds, from its own success and its inability to inculcate the unquestioning loyalty of the Mustache Petes, and especially from rival Mafias all over the country. These were the embryonic little crime cartels that had come in with the persistent immigrant influx of the 1970s. Everybody had a mob now—the Vietnamese, the Koreans, the Haitians, the Cubans, the Jamaicans, the Greeks, the Puerto Ricans, the Mexicans, even the Russians.

Driscoll kept his Meatman file in the locked bottom drawer of a metal cabinet. He took out the file and dumped its contents on his desk and began rereading notes, newspaper clippings, police reports—anything that could give him a clue.

He finished his tea, ate the lemon slice, and threw away the rind. He was developing a headache and he wasn't getting anywhere. There had to be a connection between Presto and the other red pushpins, but the problem was that Presto's profile was lower than whale shit. The only time he even came into contact with other Family bosses was at meetings of the *commissione,* and who the hell knew when they took place? Apalachin had been the only one the cops had ever stumbled on, back in 1957, in upstate New York, and that had been entirely by accident. Meatman Presto had been there, riding shotgun for an old hood named Joe Ida. Presto had escaped that day by gunning a car at two state troopers, then jumping into the bushes and running for miles through a forest until the cops gave him up for lost. They still talked about that narrow escape when the old men sat around on crates at the 9th Street Market.

Driscoll kept the names, dates, vital statistics, and historical highlights of every Mafia boss on five-by-eight index cards. He went over them again and again, like a good hitter who maintained a file on every pitcher he had to face. The file cards that corresponded to the red pushpins were separated from the rest. Flipping Presto's like a baseball card, he added it to the red or "dead" pile.

Driscoll started reading: Nunzio Falatico, Boston, fifty-six, shot by an unknown assailant as he opened the door of his Mercedes in front of a girlfriend's brownstone on Beacon Hill, February, unsolved.

Mark "the Shark" Lucinda, Chicago, seventy-two. Died of a massive heart attack brought on by an electrical shock in the men's room of a fancy restaurant in the Loop. Witnesses said his bladder started to bother him between the second and third courses, so he hit the head, turned on the lights, and sizzled. The coroner ruled it an accidental death. Faulty wiring. April.

Driscoll turned the next card: Fabrizio Pipalla, aka Frankie Pips, aka the Butcher of Kansas City. Frankie was a hit-and-run victim. Twenty minutes after he opened a new nightclub in the plush Country Club Plaza in the outskirts of K.C., witnesses reported that a dark sedan came out of nowhere and smeared Frankie all over the parking garage. No suspects, no license number. The Kansas City cops decided to call it a hit-and-run instead of a hit. July. Frankie had been the baby. He was only forty-eight.

Gabriel Michael Scalpato was number four. New Orleans, fifty-two. He ran the waterfront. A fifty-ton containerized cargo box decided to break loose and fall on the exact spot where Scalpato had been standing, shaping up a shift of stevedores. No one else injured. That was remarkable in itself, Driscoll thought. A box that size should have wiped out half the people on the dock. That death was ruled as accidental, too. September.

And Meatman Presto made it number five. December, Philadelphia. Death by bombing. It looked like they were varying the pattern again. Everybody couldn't die by some half-ass phony accident. Guys in Presto's line of work did get killed sometimes, so this time they whacked him out with a bomb. Made it look legitimate in a perverse kind of way. Just like the guy in Boston. It was a nice mixture. Questionable accidents and murders that the cops knew they didn't have a prayer of ever solving.

What was the pattern? Driscoll couldn't answer that question. No dramatic takeover had followed any of the hits. Something else was at work—something subtle, and sinister and patient. Driscoll slammed the file drawer shut and left.

THIRTEEN

PHILADELPHIA INTERNATIONAL AIRPORT

Killing the two highway patrolmen near the airport was just what Whitey needed. It made him level-headed again, allowed him to focus in that detached way of his with an unhurried concentration on what had to be done. Next was Vinnie. He had found the spot in the Tinicum marsh and dumped the kid there in a shallow depression beneath some undergrowth. He had neither the time nor the tools to do much else. They probably wouldn't find the body until the spring, and by then it wouldn't matter.

After the marsh, Whitey had backtracked to the airport, avoiding the stretch of highway where the two cops lay dead. The only vehicle that passed him was a slow-moving bus. He had been forced to make so many adjustments already, it was imperative that he get back to his original plan. He was thinking about that as he parked the van on the middle level of the long-term garage, locked it, and took an elevator to the terminal level of Philadelphia International Airport. Maybe he could wait it out.

Whitey checked to see if there were any outgoing flights, but the runways were still too slick. Before leaving the van he had changed into a black three-piece suit with thin pin-stripes. His shirt was white and his tie black silk. The clothes contrasted magnificently with his white hair.

When he saw two cops walking down a corridor in his direction, eyeing the stragglers who had been stranded there, he didn't think much of it, but when he rounded a corner and saw two more cops doing exactly the same thing, Whitey knew that he wasn't out of the woods yet. The same guesswork that brought the highway patrolmen out on the icy airport road had filled the airport itself with cops.

He looked around him, and the first thing he saw was the square red sign above a terminal lounge. He walked right in, sat down, and ordered coffee without looking at a menu. In the dim light, his skin looked close to normal, but he could do little to conceal that crooked smile. Turning around, Whitey glanced out the door of the terminal and saw the two cops pass by. For a moment it looked as though they might come in, but they changed their minds and kept walking. He wondered if anyone had discovered the two highway patrolmen yet.

As the bartender put the coffee down in front of him, Whitey asked, "Is anything leaving the airport—anything at all?"

"Try the train," the bartender advised. "That should still be okay."

"The train?" Whitey replied questioningly.

"It's a new high-speed line that goes back downtown," he explained, as he reached up to hang a wineglass upside down from an overhead rack. "You miss your flight?"

Whitey nodded, aware for the first time that unlike practically everyone else at the airport, he was not hauling much luggage with him. A good cop, an observant cop, would pick that up right away. Whitey knew he had no choice, as he looked down at his single small overnight bag.

"Yeah." The bartender laughed. "You and the rest of the world, but it might be tough to get a room downtown."

"I'll manage," Whitey said as he slid off the barstool.

The train took him to Suburban Station in a surprisingly smooth twenty-five minutes. Whitey got off. Stalking the Meatman, he had gotten to know the city fairly well—at least the Center City area.

Presto had conducted many of his business meetings at the Barclay Hotel on the east side of Rittenhouse Square. It was only a five-minute walk. Presto had taken his lunches in a dark rear booth in the main dining room, the plush Le Beau Lieu. When he needed privacy, the Meatman had used an upstairs suite. Whitey decided to follow Presto's example. He hoped the Barclay would have a room for him.

SOUTH PHILADELPHIA
SATURDAY

Vinnie never showed up for his job at the fur store on Saturday morning. The manager called his apartment, but there was no answer. No one had heard from him since the day before. The manager called his relatives, and they naturally thought the worst and began visiting one another to talk about it and console each other.

One of his aunts went to the police station, but at first they didn't even want to listen to her. "We'll file a report," a cop said, "but I'll bet he's missing because he wants to be missing. Maybe he got lucky with a girl."

"A buck says he'll show," a rat-faced detective yelled to one of his men just after Vinnie's aunt left. But in the deliberate, methodical way of the police department, the report of a missing person was duly filed and logged, with the time, date, and location noted. The piece of paper then began its circuitous journey from desk to desk.

Frantic and weeping, Vinnie's mother called Tina Conti, the pretty little thing he had taken dancing. Tina was trying her new eyeliner when the phone rang. "Dammit," she cursed. The ringing had startled her and made her line crooked. Vinnie's mother stammered to her in Italian, laced with a few English phrases, that her son was missing.

Tina had been wondering why she hadn't heard from Vinnie herself. He tried to call her every day. Listening on the phone, Tina could just picture the older woman becoming more and more hysterical. "Call the cops," Tina told her.

"They won't help," she answered between sobs. "Something awful's happened to my Vinnie. I know. I feel."

By this time, Tina was experiencing the same sick sensation. She just didn't want to admit it to herself, but she hadn't liked the way Vinnie had kissed her goodnight. He was in such a hurry, sort of preoccupied. Usually he had his hands all over her.

Tina knew he was doing something wrong when he told her he had to work that night. Some work, she thought suspiciously, but he didn't seem to want to tell her about it and she hadn't pressed him. All she worried about was that maybe he was going to see another girl. Now she felt guilty for her silence. She was angry with herself for not making him tell her what he was doing.

Tina held the receiver away from her ear, thinking back to that last cold kiss on the doorstep. She realized she would have to go to Vinnie's mother. Tina shoved the new eyeliner in her vanity drawer.

"I'll be right over," she said, attempting to calm her. "I'll stop at St. Bibiana's and burn a candle for Vinnie that we hear something soon."

GREEN STREET, FAIRMOUNT, PHILADELPHIA

In the old days, when he was a rookie, Driscoll had worked with Harry Capri. Harry's breakfast menu never varied. Every morning he poured himself a bowl of all-bran flakes and a six-ounce glass of prune juice. Then he uncorked a bottle of bourbon and sloshed it over the all-bran. Harry claimed that it kept him regular.

"Right, Harry," Driscoll used to tell him. "Regularly drunk."

Harry was still a good cop. He was a lousy homicide

man. Most cops were. The routine trips to the morgue spooked them. But when it came to burglary and major theft, larceny of any kind, there was nobody better than Harry Capri, including Driscoll.

Driscoll preferred strong tea for breakfast. He hated coffee. Ordinarily he wouldn't have been bothering to think about Harry Capri or breakfast, but today was different. Today Driscoll had a problem; in fact, he had several of them, and they all started with Honey Presto. Sooner or later, he was going to have to face her again.

He'd worked through Friday night and into Saturday and wasn't sure what time it was now, but he had a feeling that it was dark out again. But his body told him it was breakfast time. In Homicide, you just went where the bodies were, which meant that you were constantly losing days. A cop like Driscoll had to develop his own internal rhythm.

He had been thinking about Honey a lot. He could always put events out of his mind, but never people. With her father dead, he had a good idea where she would turn for help. The only person her father had ever really trusted was the Fat Man. Noble Street. Noble Street meant Fat Manny, Presto's old-time partner. That was like pressing all of Driscoll's buttons in precisely the correct order. A long time ago Manny had almost cost Driscoll everything.

Driscoll had gone home—an apartment on Green Street, near the park—to grab a quick shower, a change of clothes, and a little time to plan his next move. But the last thing he remembered before waking up about half an hour ago was sitting on the edge of his bed to untie his shoes.

He shaved with a straight razor and a soap mug. Leaning over the sink, lathering his face, he decided that Harry Capri would have to help him on this one. If anybody knew what the hell was going on, Harry would. Harry had opened a pawnshop after they pensioned him, and the guys he used to arrest had become his best customers. He knew about every important job that went down north of Miami and south of New York. Cops always made the best crooks. Retired cops were even better.

He thought about the hand with the gun in it that he had taken from the Meatman's walk-in box. It was in safekeeping for the time being. He could check on it on his way. He had the serial number; that was all he would need for the computer at the Roundhouse. Determining the make and origin of a weapon had become little more than a matter of calling up the pertinent data base. Driscoll could handle that himself; he wasn't proficient with computers, but he could type in a few numbers.

Driscoll finished shaving and splashed some water on his face. Then he poked a comb at his wavy silver hair and hoped he would find a clean shirt in the closet.

THE ROUNDHOUSE

They brought the bus driver down to the Roundhouse to question him. He was still dressed in his blue Septa uniform; his peaked hat lay on a table beside him. He was sipping coffee out of a chipped mug that they always gave to visitors. God only knew what you might catch.

Driscoll looked into the driver's eyes and discovered that the Seagram's had gotten there ahead of him. "What did you see out there?" Driscoll asked him as he turned a chair around backward and straddled it, leaning his chin on the backrest.

"Nothin', man, just them bodies."

"Think about it."

Cornelius Arnold didn't like cops, and he particularly didn't like to be questioned by them. He was very nervous about how all the other cops deferred to Driscoll as if he were the main man.

"You see anybody drive away?" Driscoll pressed him.

"I don't want no trouble with no cops, man. I put in eighteen years on this job."

Driscoll was losing his patience. "You wanta sit here for another eighteen?" he asked the driver.

"I said I'm thinkin', man." The bus driver looked from

the ceiling to the door that Driscoll had just come in and then back to Driscoll again.

Driscoll was still wearing his topcoat. It flared out like a wrinkled tan tent around the legs of the chair. He was positive that whoever had killed the Meatman had also killed the two highway patrolmen, and Cornelius Arnold was his only witness. They had taken .45-caliber slugs out of the bodies of the two cops. The gun held by the dead hand in Presto's freezer was a .45, too. The guns had to be the connection.

"I'm waiting," Driscoll said threateningly.

"Listen, all I saw was one thing, and that don't make me no accomplice."

"That's right," Driscoll answered. "You're just an upstanding citizen helping us out on a homicide investigation. And if you help enough, we might not even tell your boss about the Seagram's."

"Nothin' on the road but a van—a beat-up van, that's all I saw." He stuck his finger in between the collar of his shirt and his neck and pulled the shirt out as though he were trying to make a little breathing space. He should have just driven that goddam bus back to the depot and never said a word about those two dead white boys.

"When?" Driscoll asked. "What time was it when you saw the van?"

"Just a few minutes before I saw them cops. Just before first light."

All along Driscoll had guessed a van. "What did it look like?"

Cornelius Arnold shrugged. "Just a van. Green, I remember that. All rusty and beat-up. Real old."

"How about the driver?"

"Some white dude, that's all I saw. He was all bundled up. Only thing I know is that he had white hair."

Driscoll didn't know anybody with white hair. It didn't sound like anybody associated with the Prestos. "Which way was it going?"

"Couldn't tell, man. He was going slow, like he was lost."

Lost or looking for something, Driscoll mused. But *what?* Back *there?* Just before they were killed, the highway patrolmen had logged their car stop—that was SOP—and called in a good description of the van, along with a license number, although he wasn't counting on that to tell them too much. Probably a rental. The dispatcher had a tape recording of their description of the driver, too. Driscoll had listened to it about ten times; he had it memorized—"White male; tall; slender; dark coat, dark or black pants; white hair . . ." Then the recording had stopped.

White hair? Driscoll didn't know if he was looking for an albino or somebody's grandfather. And this boozed-up bus driver was no help at all. Every instinct told Driscoll that the same killer had assassinated Presto and also murdered the two cops. He had seen plenty of things change—always for the worse—during his career. But a cop killer was still a very rare bird; and a man with the balls to walk up to Meatman Presto and clip *him* was one in a million. And both on the same night. It had to be the same guy, and that guy had to be one crazy whacked-out son of a bitch.

"I'm real sorry about them cops," the bus driver blurted out. "I truly am. There was no reason. Nobody had to go and kill them." He sounded like he meant it.

Distracted, Driscoll looked at the bus driver as though he were seeing him for the first time. Cornelius Arnold shook his head. "No reason at all, man."

"I wouldn't bet on that," Driscoll said.

"Whoever killed Presto did the two highway cops, too," Driscoll said. "It had to be the same guy."

There was a glass of orange juice on top of Captain Marinari's desk. He opened a drawer and took out a bottle of aspirin.

"Three bodies in one night. That's hot stuff, even for these guys." Marinari gulped down three aspirins at a time. "I don't know about the soldier part. Just because he used a .45."

Driscoll hated to think what the lining of Marinari's stomach must look like. "Or an ex-soldier," Driscoll corrected him.

"Where does that leave us, if the .45 and the soldier stuff is all bullshit?"

"Exactly where we are now—nowhere."

Finally, Marinari made a face and belched. "Tastes like lye," he said, putting the glass down on his desk. "So, okay, have it your way. Catch me a soldier who moonlights as a hit man. You got somebody in mind?"

"Just a guy with white hair," Driscoll said.

RITTENHOUSE SQUARE, PHILADELPHIA

Even with the storm and the Christmas crowd, the Barclay had had a suite. Whitey had selected the best accommodations they had—three rooms, $800 a night. He had made a careful notation of the cost. He lived well and charged his expenses, all of his expenses, to his clients.

He made contact with a client by leaving his telephone number with a call-forwarding service. That way he never even had to lay eyes on a client if he considered it too risky. Under those circumstances, he had the money wired to him by Western Union and deposited into one of several bank accounts he maintained, under false identity, around the country. This time, however, Whitey had made contact with his client as soon as he had checked into the Barclay, leaving a number where he could be reached. He had explained his delay, said he awaited further orders. He had wanted a woman but knew he'd have to wait. He had slept for some hours. When he awoke he made a second call.

Now he felt restless and keyed-up again. He hoped a shower would relax him. The water, steaming hot, tingled his flesh but didn't warm it. Turning around slowly in the tiled shower stall, he leaned his tall frame against the wall and shut his eyes tightly as he looked directly into the jets of the nozzle.

Afterward, he walked into the bedroom and tried his client again. If there was no answer this time, he planned to wait out the bad weather and take the next available flight out of Philadelphia. He dialed a number in Pittsburgh. It was his parents' home. Both of them had been dead for ten years. The house was closed up and musty-smelling; the furniture was shrouded under graying sheets. But tucked away on a shelf in the pantry was a telephone-answering machine.

As soon as the phone rang in the pantry, the electronic call-forwarding mechanism began transferring the message through a series of relays connected to other answering machines and call-forwarders. At all times, three separate area codes were utilized. With these elaborate precautions, it was almost impossible to trace Whitey's calls.

He was getting dressed when the phone rang.

"Room 410 . . . we have a message for you," the desk clerk told him.

"I'm listening."

"The message reads, 'We want to place another order.' "

"Thank you."

Whitey depressed the button on the phone cradle and immediately called his parents' home. The message would be waiting for him on the machine there. He dialed, then listened. "Like father, like daughter," the cold voice of his client informed him.

Just then he heard a gentle knock on his hotel door. "Who is it?" Whitey asked, just before opening it. He was expecting someone.

FOURTEEN

SOUTH PHILADELPHIA

It was evening by the time Driscoll was on the street again. He drove back downtown, to 11th and Ritner in South Philly, to see an ex-fighter, Augie Marranzano.

Augie was also an ex-junkie. His late wife was a dead junkie. She had OD'd on some very bad stuff. Augie had nearly died, too, but he recovered and then went searching for the dealer who had sold them the drugs. Augie found him, and junkie or not, he was still damn good with his hands. The dealer died two days later—multiple contusions and a fractured skull.

Driscoll had arrested him and made a good case, but then he had made an even better witness for Marranzano. Driscoll convinced the jury that the little fighter had performed a valuable service for humanity. Augie got six months probation on a miracle verdict of justifiable homicide. After that, Augie—Mad Dog Marranzano in the ring—got this demonic look in his eyes every time he heard that someone had given Driscoll a bad time.

He lived in an "office" behind a garage. The office consisted of a wooden desk, a toilet with a plastic shower curtain around it, and a telephone. Everything in the place, even the air, felt sticky. Driscoll could never figure out where Augie slept, and he didn't want to ask.

After his trial, Augie had found Jesus. For the past two years, he had been selling hot dogs and sausages from a cart outside City Hall. Bundled up against the cold, Augie looked like one of the hall's gargoyles.

If you bought a hot dog from him, he said a prayer for you. If you bought a sausage and a soda, which cost more, Augie wrapped the bun in a little piece of paper with a verse from the Psalms written on it. In the summer, he sold Italian water-ice, a South Philly concoction of crushed ice, artificial food coloring, and sugar, all squeezed into a cone-shaped cup.

Augie came out of the shadows wearing an apron and drying his hands on a towel. He had been splitting open packages of rolls, getting ready for the next morning's rush. His two three-wheeled, yellow, and stainless-steel pushcarts were parked on the side of the garage under a naked hundred-watt light bulb.

"Praise the Lord," Augie said, as he saw the big cop approaching. "You look awful, Phil."

Driscoll nodded in agreement.

"God have mercy on the Meatman's soul." The vendor was small and wiry—barely even a true lightweight. He hopped around from side to side like an organ grinder's monkey.

"The bastard didn't have a soul," Driscoll answered. His gray eyes intense, he was radiating a firm sense of control, and Augie was impressed.

The vendor was checking his big jars of yellow mustard and wiping the jars with the bottom of his dirty apron. Driscoll frowned deeply and poked with his toe at a mound of something wet and black sticking to the middle of the garage floor. All the while, the little fighter's legs kept pumping up and down against the bitter cold of the garage. He was almost dancing, circling around the stainless-steel bay that held his hot dogs and sausages.

"You got it?" Driscoll asked him.

"Sure, Phil, sure. I did just what you told me to do."

"Let's see."

Augie walked to the rear of the garage and bent over a small refrigerated cooler that was propped on two bald tires.

"Safe and sound, Phil," he said.

Then Augie opened the lid of the cooler and began lifting out a few frozen packages of hot dogs. The fourth package he lifted out was the hand. The night before, when Driscoll had given him the hand, he had told Augie to keep it on ice.

"How the hell can you keep that thing in there with stuff people are going to eat?" Driscoll asked him.

Augie ignored him and began carefully unwrapping the hand.

"How about the gun, Aug?"

"I had a small problem with that."

Driscoll knew that Augie never had *small* problems. "Where the hell's the gun? You didn't lose it, did you?"

"Come on, Phil. How could I lose a gun?" Augie was offended.

This time Augie reached into a huge jar that looked as if it was filled with grease. "I ain't no surgeon, Phil, and I had a helluva time gettin' the piece loose from the fingers . . . so I had to saw a little. No damage. I got this knife that cuts through frozen food. I had to nick off a couple, three of the fingers. The knife worked great." Then he held up the hand—missing three fingers—and gave it to Driscoll.

"That's okay," he said, pushing it back toward the fighter. "Put it back on ice for me."

"Hey, Phil, where's the rest of this guy?" Augie asked.

"Cold," Driscoll replied.

"I kept the gun in grease. Guns love grease."

Driscoll found a grimy rag on the garage floor and wrapped it around the slippery .45.

"Praise the Lord," Augie called after the big cop.

FISHTOWN, PHILADELPHIA

Harry Capri was wearing a blue surcoat, sleeveless and tied in the middle, over a white shirt. He had a big stomach and pink, meaty hands. About five years before he retired from the police department, his eyes had given out on him and he had taken to wearing glasses. They hung on a cord around his neck and bounced on his chest, near his diaphragm, every time he moved. He was almost bald, except for a few black-and-white wisps that he vainly combed back flat on his head. His pawnshop was near Front and Girard, behind the El tracks, in the no-man's-land between white Fishtown and Spanish Kensington.

"How're the bowels?" Driscoll greeted him, as he extended his big hand to the other man.

"Lubricated," Capri answered. "What the hell's so important? Something tells me you're still running your own investigations."

"They're the best kind." Harry was one of the few people Driscoll respected. The pawnshop looked like the cave of some very untidy bears. Items for sale or trade were piled from floor to ceiling. Each one was tagged and numbered. There were stuffed animal heads near the ceiling, forty or fifty guitars and banjos stacked side by side, and shelves and shelves of beat-up small appliances. The doors and windows were covered by iron gratings, and at this late hour the shades were drawn. The only display case in the shop—small and glass-topped—was directly in front of the cash register. In it were more watches than Driscoll had ever seen. There was a centerfold of a naked girl pasted up on the wall, just over the cash register. Eye-level.

"Let's see it," Harry said. "You said you needed my expert opinion."

"No bullshit, either, Harry." Driscoll's eyes were irresistibly drawn to the picture of the girl; she had huge tits that looked a little like Lida James's—two pointed, pumped-up footballs. On the paper poster, her crotch hair appeared as scratchy as a Brillo pad. But Driscoll couldn't help staring.

"You'll always be a hard-ass, Driscoll. The only thing harder than your ass is your head."

Harry turned on a small lamp on top of the glass display case. Then he fitted a jeweler's loupe into his eye. His skin was flabby, like unbaked dough, and oozed around and over the black edges of the magnifier. A small hedgerow of nose hairs and unshaven lip whiskers joined the opening of his nostrils.

Driscoll unwrapped the gun and laid it on top of the case. The .45 was gleaming from the grease Augie had pampered it with.

"While I look at this, Phil, you look right at that broad's pussy behind me and say 'cheese.' "

"You're a dirty old man, Harry."

"Gotcha."

"Where's the camera?"

"Right in the old manhole. Pretty nice, huh?"

"Closed-circuit?"

"The best. I never did deal in junk, Phil. Works every time. Every guy who comes in here checks out her cunt, first thing. Talk about eye contact. I got a pedal down here. . . ." Harry was sitting on a wooden stool, but he moved off to show Driscoll the device that operated the hidden camera. "The lens is right in her vagina. Even the fuckin' Japs don't have that yet."

"You're beautiful, Harry."

"I have a complete photo record of every punk, junkie, yahoo, or upstanding burglar who comes in here and tries to sell me anything. I might even have a picture you can use. Old Harry Capri takes care of his own."

"You always did," Driscoll said, almost stubbing his toe on emotion, but swerving away from it just in time. He hoped that Harry understood how much he missed working with him. After Harry had spent several minutes examining the weapon, Driscoll said, "I need where it came from, who stole it, and why I found it in a dead guy's hand in the Meatman's cellar."

"Last part's easy," Harry said. "Presto was part fuckin' cannibal. A long time back, back when he was makin' his bones in the mob, he chopped up a couple guys. Then he got class and just took off the little fingers. But you say the guy was chopped up pretty good?"

Driscoll nodded.

"Hell, that's a tradition with the Meatman. It's like I say, fuckin' part cannibal."

"What about the other stuff?"

Harry removed his eyepiece and smiled indulgently at the detective. "I hope to hell you go a little slower than this with a broad. You come when she's still takin' down her drawers, or what? Take it the fuck easy, okay? You came in here, you had ants in your pants; what's your hurry?''

Driscoll *was* in a hurry. He had no secrets from Harry. ''Honey,'' he answered. ''I don't want to stand around talking in case she's on the list to get popped next.''

Harry had never approved of Driscoll's liaison with Honey Presto, but he also didn't believe in telling a man whom he should or should not screw. Especially Driscoll. There had been a time when Phillip Driscoll was a very bad—and very young—boozer. Alcoholism was as much an occupational hazard for Irish cops as getting shot; maybe more. Driscoll's poison had always been his customized Silver Bullets-lethal mixtures of martinis with a long shot of scotch. Harry had lectured Driscoll about them. But back when he first started fooling around with Honey, back before the old man had broken them up, Driscoll had weaned himself off the Silver Bullets because he had fallen so hard for Honey. Harry had seen that happen before—a good woman doing that for a good man. That convinced him that there had to be some good somewhere in Honey. Harry could tell that this Presto business had really gotten to Driscoll; the last thing he wanted to see him do was get really jumpy and reach for a Silver Bullet.

''This is a heavy little mother,'' Harry said, weighing the gun in his hand. He blew on it and polished it on the sleeve of his shirt. ''I see .45s in here every so often, usually a vet who's down on his luck, or his widow. But I never see them in this condition.'' He polished the gun again. ''This is mint, Phil.''

'So where's a piece like that come from? Who wants you to fence it?''

''First tell me about the job on the Meatman. Anybody leave a signature?''

''It looks like it's from out of town, all the way,'' Driscoll said. ''I got a guy in a van, that's all. I think he might have also done the two highway cops down at the airport. But I'm not positive. If he did, then he's probably still in town, because nothing flew out. And if he *is* still here, then somebody might want to end the dynasty all at once.''

''And there goes your old girlfriend,'' Harry said, appreciating Driscoll's concern.

"There she goes," Driscoll said with a dull resignation in his voice.

"Guys like the Meatman don't get mugged, they don't get robbed, they don't have the fucking rain fall on top of their heads unless it gets okayed from somewhere. They especially don't get killed."

"Wrong!" Driscoll said, picking up one of Harry's banjos and strumming it. "The Meatman *did* get robbed. Same night it happened. They hit the biggest bank he had downtown. And guess what? They used M-16s. Mint condition, too."

Driscoll handed the instrument to Harry, and he replaced it on the shelf. "It gets better," the detective said. "I got inside Presto's place, and his bedroom was decorated early armory. There was even a brand-new M-16 with a full clip stashed away in the back of his closet. It was like a showroom for guns."

Harry was at the gun again, searching for a serial number. But as he found it and scribbled it on a pad of paper, Driscoll said, "Don't bother. I already checked."

"What do you mean?" Harry asked.

" 'Access denied' is what I mean," Driscoll said. "I punched in that serial number on the computer and I got 'Access denied' on the screen. Then I figured I'd get cute and I punched in the serial number from the M-16 we took off the holdup guy. They were both military weapons, so I figured what the hell. And guess what happened again?"

" 'Access denied.' "

"Bingo!"

"Two different kinds of guns that had to come from two factories, most likely," Harry said. "Maybe different shipments. But when you try to get the provenance or the history of these particular weapons—a nosy cop like you, that is—you can't get to first fucking base."

"And *that* ain't any accident," Driscoll said with conviction.

"Somebody went to a helluva lot of trouble to cover this up," Harry agreed.

"That's right," Driscoll said. "And I was using a computer that hooks right into the FBI's data banks. So if they don't have it, nobody has it. I've been a cop for fourteen years, Harry, and this is the first time it ever took me more than a couple of hours to get a complete rundown on a gun. I can't understand it."

Harry laughed the weary cackle of a man who had just seen the impossible happen yet again. "Oh, I can understand it, all right," he said. "You ever hear of the expression 'Your tax dollars at work'?"

Driscoll nodded.

"Here we have a prime example. Exactly who the hell do you think put a blackout on those serial numbers?"

"I think it's the same people you think it is."

"Alphabet soup," Harry said as he hiked up his drooping pants over his paunch. "Take your pick—CIA, FBI, NSA—who the hell knows?"

"I bet the Meatman knew, and that's the reason—or at least part of the reason—he's dead."

"That could be."

And now they must figure that Honey might know, too, Driscoll thought to himself.

"Where's the M-16 now?" Harry asked, pulling Driscoll out of his thoughts. "This is really funny, you know, you bringin' me a piece—your only clue—the way you hate guns and all. This is like a teetotaler lookin' for a nickel in a bottle of hootch."

"I got more against the assholes who use the guns than I have against the guns," Driscoll said. "But I still can't believe some of these cops who won't take a crap unless they have a piece with them."

"Ah, the fraternity of the gun faggots," Harry said knowingly.

Driscoll made a face that showed his absolute revulsion. Then he answered Harry's question. "The M-16's in our lab at the Roundhouse. Looks real clean."

"Anything special about it? Not that a weapons expert like you would notice."

"It's a big, ugly gun—what can I tell you?" Driscoll said. "It's in the same shape as this one. Vintage, but well preserved. Like it's been sitting in a packing crate for years and years, all greased up and ready to go."

"You know how long I been lookin' for a broad like that?" Harry smirked. Then said, "Even if it was legal to buy and sell M-16s, it wouldn't do me any good,. That's a very expensive weapon. The people I sell to have to go out and rob somebody to come up with fifty bucks.''

''What do they go for?''

''Around three thousand; twenty-five hundred is a bargain. Like I say, they're illegal. Some collectors might take the chance, but most can't afford one anyway.''

''I'm arriving at an inescapable conclusion here, Harry,'' Driscoll said.

''The Meatman was running guns—and in a big way, too.''

''You got it.''

Driscoll looked beat, like a tired cop who had pulled one too many all-nighters. Suddenly, Harry felt very nostalgic. He really missed being a cop. ''Leave the gun with me, Phil. I'll try to find out what I can. You come back in a few days. Somebody heisted it from somewhere. I'll see if I can put a face with it.''

Harry took off his glasses and rubbed his eyes. ''Two, three days,'' he said, ''no more. I know I'll have something for you.''

''I don't even know if I have that much time, Harry.''

Just before he left, Harry asked, ''Is Honey okay, Phil? This has to be really tough on her.''

''So far, so good,'' Driscoll said.

Going to Harry for help had gotten Driscoll thinking about the old days—about Honey and Fat Manny and the bribery frame that had almost destroyed him. He could still recall every minute of every hour of the day it had all begun. Manny had set Driscoll up seven years before at the precise moment in his career when his capacity for Silver Bullets had turned him into a very sloppy cop.

Driscoll had been working Major Crimes then, long before he got on Homicide. They had a solid case against the Fat Man; had him cold on receiving stolen goods and fencing. He had master-minded a burglary ring that performed like the General Motors of burglary rings, specializing in oriental rugs. None of it was sexy, but the district attorney had enough to go on for a warrant.

Driscoll drove to the Fat Man's house to make the arrest personally. He should have taken another cop with him as a witness, but he knew that the Fat Man wouldn't put up a fight. Besides, he liked the idea of reading in the newspapers the next morning that the arrest had been made by Detective Phillip Driscoll. Who needed a costar?

The Fat Man must have been reading his mind, anticipating him. Back then, he lived in a big split-level with a swimming pool, in Cheltenham, just outside the city limits. The proper procedure would have been to contact the Cheltenham police to coordinate with the Philadelphia police, but Driscoll figured that he didn't need them either. Just a simple arrest. Bag the Fat man and take him downtown.

Manny opened the door on the first knock. He grinned and invited the detective to come inside. The Fat Man's smile was lost in the folds of his round face as his lips curled back toward a thick, flickering tongue. He reminded Driscoll of a fat snake.

Driscoll placed him under arrest and read him his rights. Manny was unflustered, as though he had been expecting him. He even offered Driscoll a cup of coffee.

"Cut the bullshit," Driscoll ordered, and he took out the handcuffs.

Manny obligingly extended his arms as far as he could, but his stomach was so huge he had trouble putting his wrists together. He pushed up the sleeves of his shirt.

Driscoll opened the cuffs to their full extension and tried them. He knew they would never fit. The Fat Man's wrists were as thick as a large man's ankles. It wouldn't have bothered Driscoll if he drew blood jamming them on, but he knew it was hopeless.

"I'm supposed to cuff you," he told Manny, "but you're too goddam fat. I wish to Christ I had leg irons."

"You try that and you'll hear from my doctors," Manny replied. "I'm a very sick man. I can't stand all this exertion. My heart . . ."

"I think you'll make it," Driscoll said. "We're going downtown."

"Wait, I need my medication."

"Go get it."

Manny waddled into his kitchen and returned with a small

brown envelope stuffed with what appeared to be prescriptions and a few small pill bottles. The flap of the envelope was folded over and secured with two red rubber bands. Manny placed it inside his jacket pocket. "I'm ready," he announced.

Once in the police car, Driscoll should have radioed in that he was en route with a prisoner, but he didn't bother.

Sloppy.

He shoved Manny into the backseat of the car and headed for Philadelphia. Twenty minutes into the ride, Manny started.

"I'm going to be sick," he said. "I always get carsick."

"Shut up," Driscoll answered.

"I vomit when I get carsick."

"What the hell do you want me to do?"

"Pull into a gas station. I'll throw up in the toilet. You keep this up and I won't even try to hold it in."

Driscoll made a left into an Amoco station on Cheltenham Avenue, a busy ten-pump station, sandwiched between a McDonald's and a twenty-four-hour Korean dry-cleaning service.

"Help me up," Manny said. "I feel faint."

Driscoll pulled at his arm. Manny smelled awful. The whole backseat of the car smelled. Now Driscoll felt like vomiting. He couldn't budge Manny. He considered calling an ambulance but figured the hell with it.

Sloppy.

"Push," he yelled at Manny.

There were tears in Manny's eyes.

"Knock it off, Manny. Just pull yourself up."

"I'm trying, believe me. And I'm gettin' sicker." Manny was really getting loud.

"Push, you son of a bitch."

Manny was beginning to attract a crowd. Two customers and a kid pumping gas walked over.

"What's wrong with him?" the kid asked.

"He's too damn fat to get out of the car," Driscoll said.

"You wanta use my jack?" the kid volunteered.

"Yeah," Driscoll replied. "I'd like to shove it right under his fat ass."

"Oh, God!" Manny screamed. "I feel a tingling in my left arm."

"He's having a *heart attack,*" a woman shrieked. "This poor man is having a heart attack."

"I'll call the cops," the kid said excitedly.

"I *am* the cops," Driscoll yelled at him. "Help me get him out of this car."

Together with the kid and the woman who had shrieked, Driscoll tugged and shoved and pulled Manny out of the backseat. He stood swaying on wobbly legs, resting his hand against the open door of the car. Driscoll was sweating now, and he had his jacket off and his tie loosened.

"Bathroom," Manny whispered. "Have to throw up.,"

Driscoll turned to the kid. "You got the key to the men's room?"

"It's out of order. No toilet."

Manny was starting to moan. "How about the ladies' room?" Driscoll asked. "You got a ladies' room?"

"I don't know," the kid said, scratching his greasy hair. "The guy who owns this station don't want nobody gettin' raped or anything, you know?"

"Does *this* thing look like he could rape anybody?" Driscoll barked at the kid. "Go get the damn key."

"Here, hold my medicine," Manny told Driscoll, whispering again. "Keep it safe for me."

He thrust the brown envelope into Driscoll's hand. "Here." Manny made sure everybody at the gas station heard him say, "Put it in your pocket." Then he made his way to the bathroom. Driscoll reached inside the car and threw the envelope up onto the dashboard. The kid went back to pumping gas, and the other customers started up their cars. Driscoll followed Manny to the ladies' room. The envelope was still lying on the dashboard. He had forgotten about it.

Without too much trouble, Manny got back into the car. The rest of the trip was uneventful.

"Did you or did you not accept an envelope from my client?" Manny's lawyer screamed at Driscoll two months later.

The courtroom was an ancient, high-ceilinged chamber that dominated the northwest corner of the fifth floor of Philadelphia's grim City Hall. Years of human odor had been trapped in the stale air. It reeked of guilt and innocence and fear.

Throughout the five-day trial, Driscoll's eyes had kept straying to the ceiling of the courtroom. Its circular murals of truth, law, fidelity, and blind justice seemed to plunge down from its great height on the heads of the spectators, judge, jury, and defendant. Gold-leaf calligraphy identified each mural—*Veritas, Lex, Fides,* and *Iustitia.*

"I did."

"Was this witnessed by other people at the gas station?" the lawyer pressed.

"Of course, it was, but—"

"No further questions, Your Honor."

"What was inside the envelope, Mr. Goldberg . . . er . . . I mean, Mr. Gallen?"

"Money, Mr. District Attorney . . . five thousand dollars that Detective Driscoll had demanded to suppress evidence against me and to make sure that I received special treatment while in his custody." Manny had never sounded more convincing.

"Special treatment? What exactly does that mean?"

The D.A. was a small, stiff man with a fine, wispy mustache and dandruff on his shoulders.

"Drugs," Manny answered innocently. "A straight business proposition. A bribe. I gave it to him. There *are* witnesses. The envelope he returned to me contained drugs."

"That's correct. Drugs that can be found on the proscribed-substances list," the district attorney informed the jury.

The undercurrent of tittering that had been making the courtroom so noisy that testimony was difficult to be heard in the back, near the door, suddenly erupted into one deep, full-bodied gasp.

"No further questions, Your Honor."

Driscoll was lucky. The jury found him not guilty. But the trial itself became his leper's mark. After that, everybody he knew, except for Harry Capri, started to look at

Driscoll as if he were walking around with a third eye in the middle of his forehead.

Even after the trial, after the not-guilty verdict, the questions never stopped. Why hadn't he taken another cop with him? Why hadn't he called in to report that he was en route with a prisoner? If the Fat man really had faked a heart attack, why hadn't Driscoll called for the rescue squad? What the hell was wrong with Driscoll, anyway? Too many Silver Bullets? Too many press clippings? Sloppy. Very sloppy.

It was almost funny the way Manny had pulled it off—faking the heart attack, pretending to be sick, conning Driscoll into accepting and holding the brown envelope. Almost.

It didn't take long for Driscoll to be lateraled out of the flow of Roundhouse politics. He wanted to kill the Fat man, but Harry had talked him out of it. Then Harry persuaded him to dig in and wait it out. His career, command, promotion—things like that—were shot to hell. But at least he was still a cop.

During one four-month stretch in 1983, Driscoll didn't receive a single phone call. Not one pink message slip. They sent him on errands. He picked up bullet fragments at the morgue. That's where he'd met Nick Troy. Then, every afternoon, as soon as he knew that nobody would be looking for him anymore, he'd find a bar, where nobody looked up from his drink, and begin to order Silver Bullets.

He went on binges; never drunk on duty, Driscoll was seldom sober off duty. He started brawls and even finished some of them.

He screwed up on the petty jobs they did assign him. He became a permanent member of the "Brigade," the departmental foreign legion of lost cops—cops about to be indicted, cops who couldn't be trusted around guns, cops who had ceased being real cops. Driscoll volunteered for *anything,* but one unit after another said no.

The turning point came the day the Organized Crime unit ran out of bodies—too many vacations and sick days. There was a big push on against the Prestos then, and any warm body would do. Somebody remembered that Phillip Driscoll had once been a helluva stakeout man; he never fell asleep on the job. They grabbed him to sit on a bookie, and that led to the next one and the next one. Nothing dramatic, just a gradual easing back into handling responsibilities again. Driscoll was still firing the Silver Bullets at himself then, but he made sure that enough of them missed.

Finally, his big chance came when they assigned him to follow Honey Presto, just lurk around and see what the hell she was doing for the old man. Driscoll did such a bang-up job that Honey thought he was setting her up to be kidnapped. He could still laugh remembering that. At first he was flattered that she knew who he was—she remembered his name from the bribery trial. It got too crazy for either one of them to handle after that, but in the beginning they were like two black sheep looking for a meadow somewhere.

Now it had all gone haywire again. Her father was dead, Driscoll was working the case, and Honey, he knew, had gone to the Fat Man for help.

Almost from the moment the thing with Honey had started, Driscoll had left the Silver Bullets in their glasses. That was almost five years ago. Five years straight.

He was thinking of how good a Silver Bullet would taste right now when he inadvertently ran a red light. Harry would have kicked him right in the balls for that. He could hear the other cars peeling rubber to avoid hitting him. That was *too* damn close. Here he was, after all these years, getting sloppy again.

FIFTEEN

THE ROUNDHOUSE SATURDAY NIGHT

Driscoll watched a rivulet of sweat begin at Tony Bonaventura's hairline, drip down his forehead, then dissolve into a little pool of perspiration that broke across the bridge of his nose. Tony strained against the handcuffs. Driscoll smiled.

The cops still had no idea who had knocked off the Presto sports bank, but Tony, the underboss, sure as hell was an interested party.

The body count had been impressive—two DOAs, another one critical, four more injured. There had been thirty people inside the store and another hundred outside on either side of Passyunk Avenue, but no one had seen a thing. Typical.

"Tony, the underboss," Driscoll began. "Tony, the dumb brother-in-law, Tony, the dumb fuck, but you're in good shape now, Tony. You used to scrape the shit off the Meatman's shoes when he stepped in crap, but now you're in charge. That puts you at the top of the hit parade, Tony. The Meatman's dead and you're the primary beneficiary."

"I didn't kill him," Tony growled. Massive sweat rings were spreading out from his armpits.

"So how come you got so smart all of a sudden?" Driscoll asked. "You're the Meatman's driver, and you didn't drive him that night. You're supposed to be his faithful fuckin' Indian companion, Tonto. So what happened the other night? Where were you?" In a Family like Presto's only a trusted senior man was ever given a job as important as being the boss's driver. Men like Joe-Joey had angled for that position for years, but out of love for his sister, the Meatman had given it to Tony. And on the most important night of his life, Tony was missing.

The stuffy interrogation room became absolutely still. Driscoll poured himself a cup of scalding black tea. Tony was manacled to the floor, his wrists pulled down behind him through the open back of a metal folding chair and attached to giant eyehooks and screwed into the floor. Tony's spine arched backward but he stared straight ahead, trying to avoid Driscoll.

He'd have to let Tony go in a couple of hours. This was probably the only shot he would get at him. He was a hard case, the same as every career wise guy Driscoll had ever met. There was little the cops could do to wise guys that would compare with what the Presto Family would do if they talked. Still, Driscoll had a few tricks.

The tea was so hot he could hardly hold it. "Thirsty?" he asked Tony, hovering over him menacingly with the tea, almost pressing the hot mug against Tony's forehead. Tony nearly tipped the chair over backward trying to avoid the hot liquid, but the more he struggled, the more painfully his back arched.

Driscoll leaned down closer to his ear. "Why?" he whispered. Tony didn't answer. His small eyed flickered like a caged bird's.

"Why?" Much louder.

Still nothing.

"Why was Presto killed?"

Nothing.

"Whyyyy?" Driscoll screamed himself hoarse this time, savagely kicking at the chair.

Tony jolted forward, as if he'd been hit by an electrical shock. Suddenly, without saying a word, Driscoll loosened his cuffs. They fell from Tony's wrists.

"Where's my lawyer?" Tony hissed.

Driscoll sipped the tea. "Sit down," he ordered, indicating the collapsed chair.

Tony refused to move.

"I said, pick it up." This time Tony complied.

"Why'd you kill the Meatman?" Driscoll asked.

"Fuck you."

"You killed Presto."

"You're a liar, Driscoll. You got nothin' on me."

"You were his driver, Tony."

Silence.

"Who hit the bank, Tony?"

Again, the flicker of the tiny birds eyes. Merely asking that question appeared to frighten Tony. Driscoll liked that, except if Tony was really *this* scared, then he wasn't going to say a damn thing, no matter what.

Driscoll suddenly leaped across the floor and was on top of Tony in a second. He grabbed the underboss's jaw with one big hand, and with the other he came down hard on the top of his head.

Tony was fighting to get away from Driscoll's grip, muttering some obscenity even though his mouth was clamped shut. Driscoll didn't let up on the pressure until he saw the pain shooting through Tony's cheek and into his jaw.

Enraged, Driscoll yanked Tony to his feet and heaved him across ten feet of floor space, bouncing the startled underboss right off a wall. Then he came up behind him and pressed his face into the wall. Tony couldn't speak; he could scarcely breathe. Driscoll didn't give a damn.

"Who?" he screamed. "Why? Who set up the Meatman? Who hit the bank? Was it you, Tony? Was it you?"

Coughing and half choking, Tony tried to answer. "No . . . what I gotta tell ya? I didn't kill Paul. Fuck you, Driscoll. It wasn't any of us, and you knew that before you dragged me in here. You got nothin' on this one."

Driscoll jammed Tony's cheek into the wall again. Harder. But Tony wasn't giving in.

"How come you weren't driving that night?" the detective pressed, finally releasing his iron grip. There was a thin line of blood under Tony's nostrils. "I asked you, creep, how come you were conveniently missing? You know how that looks? Tell me how it looks to you. Okay, that's the way it looks to us, too. And you know what? That's how it looks to Honey, too. That little broad has a temper. She'd cut your balls right off."

Bonaventura kept squirming. Driscoll could tell he'd hit a nerve. "How's that look, Tony?" he asked again, poking Tony repeatedly in the chest.

Tony was thinking fast now, deciding just how much to tell Driscoll. He knew the cops could make it look as if he really did set up the Meatman. He was worried about Honey, too, about what she might do.

"I told you he gave me the afternoon off. Told me to go buy some Christmas presents. Handed me a hundred-dollar bill." For the first time, the driver sounded almost cooperative. "I swear, Driscoll, that's the *truth.*"

"Like hell it is."

"How many times do I have to go over this? . . . He told me to take the rest of the day off. It was quiet. Real quiet. He wasn't lookin' for anything to happen. Besides . . ." Tony caught himself and stopped.

"Besides *what,* Tony?" Driscoll's ears perked right up.

"Nothin'. Forget it. I changed my mind."

"Change it back, fast—you fuck. You'd better talk while you still can," Driscoll barked at him.

"Hey, I said all I'm gonna say."

"That's what you think. You haven't even started yet. You got a book to write on this thing."

Driscoll was sitting behind a dented, scratched government-issue desk now. He yanked open one of the drawers, pulled it all the way out, and put it on top of the desk. Tony's small, sharp eyes never left him. His nostrils wrinkled as though he were trying to pick up some threatening scent.

"Notice, Tony," Driscoll began again, loosening his tie and opening his shirt collar and rolling up his shirt sleeves, "we have to check our blackjacks and guns outside. No more rubber hoses. Just bear with me a minute while I fix this drawer." Then he reached into the empty space where the drawer fit and took out a metal runner about a foot long and an inch thick. The bottom was flat. "Solid steel," Driscoll said, smacking the runner against the palm of his hand as he stood up and walked toward Tony.

"Nice heft to it. Didya ever hear how I fractured a guy's skull with one of these? And you know what the best part is? I checked my gun and blackjack outside. I was unarmed. Now, who's the judge gonna believe?"

Tony grimaced. His thick eyebrows arched in mock surprise. "Fuck you, Driscoll," he said, looking right at him. He kept putting his hands up to his face, over his eyes.

Driscoll looked at his watch. The second hand made its revolution, sixty seconds, then it started again. Driscoll was exhausted. He just hoped Tony felt as bad as he did. But Tony just sat there, searching the pale green walls or glancing up at the soundproof ceiling. Every once in a while he stole a look at Driscoll. "You're all bullshit," he finally said to the cop. "You got nobody on this one. You got nothin'. You're bullshit, Driscoll."

Without a word Driscoll walked back behind the desk and sat down. He picked up the telephone receiver and dialed. He held it out for Tony to hear. The voice on the other end came crackling into the room.

"Yeah, what is it?"

"Driscoll. 222. Interrogation. In about five minutes, I'll need an ambulance. I'll have a prisoner who will need medical attention. Can you take care of that?"

"Ten minutes," the disembodied voice repeated. "Room 222."

"Bullshit!" Tony screamed defiantly. *"You can't touch me!"*

Driscoll leaped to his feet and crashed the metal runner on top of the desk with all his might. Tony ran to the nearest corner, cowering, but Driscoll was right behind him, the runner raised like a hammer. Driscoll could see Bonaventura wondering just how crazy this bastard really was.

"Don't talk, Tony," he said. "That just gives me an excuse."

"Oh, what the hell," Tony said abruptly, startling Driscoll, some debate in his own mind apparently resolved. "You'll find out anyway."

Driscoll was intent now. "Find out what?"

"About the broad."

"What broad?"

"How the fuck do I know?" Tony shrugged. "Some young broad, that's all I know. She worked at the real estate place. Paul was dying to take a shot at her but he didn't want anybody to know, so he sends me home early. I knew, though. Had it figured all along."

"Who was she?"

"Beats me."

"What's her name?"

"Arlene. I never heard her last name."

"Where is she now?" Driscoll demanded.

"Gone."

"How do you know?"

"Hey, Driscoll, don't you think we figured it out too? She had to be part of the setup," Tony said sarcastically. "We went looking for her, too."

"When?"

"You guys didn't even have him at the morgue yet."

"Who went looking for her?"

"Me."

"Who else?"

"Forget it, Driscoll."

"WHO *else?*" Driscoll screamed. He punctuated his question by banging the runner down on the desk again. It made a noisy thud.

"She's gone, Driscoll. Gone. The place is empty. It was a fuckin' mail drop."

"Who'd she work for?" Driscoll yelled again, stunned by what he was hearing.

"What're you, stupid, Driscoll? What'd I just say? The Meatman. Didn't I just tell you that? She worked at the real estate office."

"Who paid her to set Presto up?"

"Tell us when you find out," Tony said. Then he snarled, "Where the hell is my lawyer?"

Driscoll knew he wasn't going to get any more out of Tony. He gave his chair one last vicious kick.

SIXTEEN

BRIGHTON BEACH, BROOKLYN

The lights dimmed, a single spotlight framing Svetlana in a golden glow. She began.

Moving slowly around the perimeter of the small, raised wooden platform that served as a dance floor, teasing, beckoning, trailing her veils, undulating her smooth, flat stomach ever so slightly, snapping the tiny finger cymbals on each hand, she focused her dark, liquid eyes on one male face after another, commanding, holding each one in her power. Her tongue darted out to moisten crimson lips, her own slender fingers caressed strong, willing thighs. Every movement assured every man in the room that her dance was for him alone.

Abruptly, with no warning for the audience or Butkova, the throbbing rhythm quickened as Svetlana became a whirling temptress. Even Butkova, who had watched her perform many times, was captivated.

Her long raven hair thrashing madly in time to the music, her whole body glistening with perspiration, Svetlana seemed possessed. Her navel, fixed with a large round ruby, reflected the spotlight's beam like a prism, refracting its glow into an explosion of color.

Her breasts vibrated; her hips churned and swayed in a continual forward-backward, forward-backward, forward-backward invitation. Her dark, thick triangle, a wicked shadow beneath the sheerest silk, kept threatening to burst free.

Turning, spinning, reeling, twisting, reaching wildly toward the ceiling, then plunging down, down, ever lower toward the floor, the dancer's hips and breasts in motion, defying gravity, straining against the garments that covered them, she promised ecstasy with each bold movement—writhing, hurtling toward a climax.

Then, suddenly, just as magically as she had begun, Svetlana slowed the frenzy of her dance; her undulations became suggestive, hypnotic. She seemed lost within herself, transfixed, as her hands, her long, slender fingers cut through the air . . .

Then she was gone, the stage empty.

The house lights came on amid long, loud, sustained applause. Scanning the room and clapping politely, Butkova nodded in approval.

Earlier that night, Butkova had driven from his home in Bustleton in Northeast Philadelphia, first picking up the Pennsylvania Turnpike, then exiting into New Jersey and heading north to Brooklyn. He made the trip at least once a week. Now, ever the businessman, Nikolai Butkova sat in his smoky restaurant on Brighton Avenue in Brooklyn and thought about the past, about Odessa.

It reminded him of other nights like this, spent in the sidewalk café on Primorsky Boulevard that overlooked the great, brooding Odessa Bay. The noisy elevated tracks and open-air vendors had the smells and dialects and good-natured bartering of Odessa's Deribasovskaya Street, where he had often done business.

His appearance, particularly his complexion, ruddy and unblemished, helped Butkova project a surprisingly youthful glow. He always wore open-necked shirts with starched collars and full, brightly colored ascots. The effect was dashing and decidedly continental. His heavily accented English complemented the emigré persona. Carefully pouring a vodka into a tall tea glass in a tin holder, Butkova thought back over all the years, over his many lifetimes. He sighed deeply and closed his eyes.

Once again he was back in the port city of Odessa on the Black Sea, where hundreds of miles of dripping, musty-smelling catacombs—never captured by the Germans—extended deep beneath the city, into the outskirts of the town. It was a brick-and-mortar labyrinth of secret passages, whitened skeletons, and mazes of subterranean hiding places.

During the war, the Resistance had used the catacombs as a base from which they stole out, by night, to murder the unsuspecting Nazi occupiers as they lay sleeping.

For centuries before that, and directly following the Communist Revolution, the catacombs of Odessa served as the underground refuge of the brotherhood of professional criminals—a brotherhood older than Russia itself that had grown up around the old port city on the Black Sea, the Pearl of the Black Sea, the brotherhood of the Malina.

Butkova had become a member of that timeless brotherhood—a desperate, soulless company bound by blood and mutual need. It was within these catacombs, among these thieves, that Butkova discovered his destiny.

Over thirty years later, that destiny had taken him to his fuel-oil business in Philadelphia, to his restaurant on Brighton Avenue in Brooklyn, and eventually to the emigré underworld in America.

All of the waiters in Butkova's restaurant were Russian men. So were the chefs, the bartenders, and the manager.

Tonight the restaurant was packed. Besides the tourists who poured into Brighton Beach to sample its exotic food and entertainment, his customers represented a cross section of the large, bustling emigré community that surrounded his place. Families were celebrating, young people cruising, and couples, cemented in whispered conversations, had eyes only for each other.

In his stiff, almost aristocratic manner, Butkova greeted each of his patrons, gallantly kissing the right hand of each woman and bowing slightly to the men.

Most of his dinner guests were drinking vodka, like himself, or a thick black tea, *chai,* flavored with lumps of bran sugar. The bar was crowded with men, who all seemed anxious to speak to Butkova. Granting a brief audience to one after another, he listened to some, waved others away, and jotted down notes on a napkin in reference to a few.

Butkova's suit was cut in the square, ill-fitting Russian

style. He still didn't like the flimsiness of American clothing.

Like most of the emigré restaurants, Butkova's stressed entertainment—Russian entertainment. That usually meant a small combo, a female vocalist, and an exotic dancer—a "belly dancer," he learned they called it in his new country.

Butkova had gotten the idea for the belly dancer from a club in the Russian neighborhood of Northeast Philadelphia. Belly dancers or their equivalents had also been popular in the Turkish quarter of Odessa where Butkova had operated. Also, upstairs opium rooms. Butkova had reproduced it all in the grimy narrow streets of Brooklyn.

Just then the lights began to dim again, allowing Svetlana to make her second appearance of the evening.

As he looked up, he noticed the tall, strong, leather-clad youngsters who lined the walls of the restaurant, slouching, shifting their weight, smoking and talking. Be patient, he thought. There'll be plenty of work soon.

When it served his purpose, he could play the unctuous emigré, and tonight that was exactly what Butkova was pretending to be.

The keen internal radar that had kept him alive for so many dangerous years was alerting Butkova again. He was distracted by a table where three attractive American women, tourists, had seated themselves. Some of the more aggressive Russian men had begun to hover around them. Butkova was suddenly concerned about how they would take all this attention. The last thing he needed was a problem with them, or the police.

The three women had heard about this Russian emigré bistro and longed to be a part of its beckoning atmosphere. Tonight had begun as an adventure: the ride to Brighton Beach; chatter about work, about clothes, about men and sex, whispered among themselves in the fast, unmistakable dialect of midtown Manhattan. Then the rush of anticipation as they opened the door and finally the intoxicating feeling of being in some foreign place—the Russian soil of Brooklyn.

The women had gotten up to dance, and a hulking Russian kid had singled out the prettiest one. Butkova saw her trying to free herself, pushing him away, but he kept pressing against her, his arms encircling her waist and back. Grabbing at her hair, he pulled it back and kissed her. Suddenly she was backing away from him across the dance floor, not looking where she was going, screaming and bumping into the other dancers and customers.

"No! Get away from me. No! Stop it! Stop it! Get the hell away from me!"

Her girlfriends cowered behind her. They looked terrified. Several drinks had spilled. A chair was knocked over. Bright house lights came on. Svetlana had fled.

The manager motioned to the musicians to keep on playing. One of the women had begun crying. The other two were shrieking.

Butkova grabbed the Russian kid, eighteen or nineteen, by his shoulder and rammed him against the wall. The kid was stunned by the vicious attack, but Butkova wasn't even breathing hard. Continuing to hold the kid trapped against the wall, Butkova shouted a few words in Russian—a harsh, cold command. Then he jammed a thick finger in the kid's chest and called two burly waiters. They seized him roughly and hustled him out to the street. Butkova shouted after them, in Russian.

Then Butkova turned to the American girl. "My pardon, miss, our humble apologies. The young man will be taken care of. He won't bother you again. How can we atone for this unfortunate incident? . . . The young men . . . when they see such beauty . . . what can a humble Russian tell you?"

"Can we just leave?" she hissed.

"Of course, anything you want," Butkova oozed. "Your bill, forget it. I hope you enjoyed your dinner and drinks. I'll have you driven home. I am truly sorry . . ."

"Look, we just want to get outta here. We don't want a ride."

Butkova bowed low and kissed her hand. Then he ushered them to the door.

"Creeps," one of them said. "Fucking Russians," her girlfriend concurred.

Just then the front door opened and another small party of wide-eyed Americans came in, brushing the snow from their shoulders. For the first time all night, Nikolai Butkova relaxed. Rushing forward, he greeted the newcomers, pumping the first man's hand furiously.

"Welcome, welcome," he gushed. "My English is not so good, but welcome, my American friends. Eat, drink, and see how the good Russians live, the White Russians. Here, a table . . . but first, vodka, on the house."

The Americans were enchanted.

CHURCH OF ST. BIBIANA, VIRGIN AND MARTYR, GIRARD ESTATE

An hour after the cops let him go, Tony Bonaventura was sitting in church. Marie was very nervous about bugs and wiretaps. She figured that St. Bibiana's had to be clean, especially tonight during the Novena Mass.

Tony, exhausted from his session with Driscoll, had slept through the Introit and the Kyrie Eleison. The Offertory was beginning, as the good-looking young priest repeated the ancient prayers. *"Dominus vobiscum . . ."* Most of the Masses were said in English now, but for certain services, like this one, they were permitted to return to the beloved Latin rite. The Meatman had considered any Mass said in English to be sacrilegious. Tonight, all three concelebrants of the special Mass were attired in vestments he had donated. At the Consecration, they would raise solid-gold chalices, worked with rubies and emeralds, that Marie had just given to the church in memory of her brother's passing.

She rested against the pew, her big behind spilling over the seat and providing as much natural padding as a comfortable chair. Tony was still nodding off next to her, a red carnation in his buttonhole. Marie and Honey often went to Mass on Sundays, but for Tony, Christmas Eve was usually it. And the bum couldn't even stay awake for a couple of hours then.

She jolted Tony in the ribs with her elbow. His head bobbed to life, his small ferret eyes blinking into recognition.

"Quit it, Marie, I'm awake," he mumbled.

"I'm worried about Honey," she said. "It's Christmas. She should be here. How does it look?"

Tony shrugged. Maybe it didn't look right, but Honey was hiding and there wasn't a damn thing he could do about it, unless he wanted to let the world know that a serious schism was developing in the Presto Family. And being the underboss, Tony wasn't doing that—not even to please Marie.

"Sanctus, Sanctus, Sanctus.

"Dominus Deus Sabaoth . . ."

"Holy, Holy, Holy," the priest intoned solemnly. "Lord God of Hosts . . ." He raised his arms, the white chasuble unfolding.

Marie was trying to talk out of the side of her mouth so the other worshipers wouldn't give her dirty looks. "Tony, what're we going to do? This whole thing, it takes too long. You're slow like an old man."

"Who's slow? Don't call me an old man." He tried to whisper.

"Mary, Mother of God," Marie implored. "They hit our bank, dammit, the best bank my brother ever had—and you just sit on your ass. How much did we lose?"

"Too much."

"Sssssshhhhhhh!" An old woman behind Tony was chastising him. He tried to slump down and disappear into the pew.

The priest had moved on to the Commemoration of the Saints. "In the unity of the holy fellowship, we observe the memory . . ."

"You're a lazy bum, Tony," Marie murmured low. "We take care of this business now. No more waiting. You take care of that goddamn bastard."

For the first time, Tony looked as though he were about to protest, but he thought better of it and swallowed his words without a gulp. Marie was silent until the beginning of the Consecration, the most sacred part of the Mass, the changing of the bread and wine into the body and blood of Christ.

The priest genuflected after pronouncing the words of the Consecration, rose and elevated the sacred host, placed it upon the gleaming corporal, then genuflected again. After each act of adoration, two small altar boys, dressed in red cassocks, rang the small bells at their sides.

"Hoc est enim corpus meum . . ."

"*What're* we gonna do about the bank?" Marie asked in a voice so vicious-sounding it frightened Tony.

"We know who did it," he answered. "We take care of him."

"What's with this guy, this Russian? He thinks he's big enough to take over Paul's territory? It's not bad enough we have to put up with the Spics and niggers and the Chinks; now this Russian. This dirty pig bastard. You better take care of him, Tony."

The old lady behind them leaned forward, patted both of them on the shoulders, and put her hands up to her lips for silence. Marie smiled at her over her shoulder and blessed herself demurely, as she whispered to Tony, "You *kill* that motherfucker."

"Soon," Tony said with a small look of triumph momentarily brightening the dark angles of his face. "Soon he gets a Christmas present early."

With that, Marie hoisted herself up from the seat and stepped out of the pew. She was going to the altar to receive Holy Communion. Even Tony Bonaventura looked aghast.

THE ROUNDHOUSE

Tina Conti was a member of the steno pool. That's how she described her occupation. They sat in a dreary, chilly conference room and she answered Driscoll's questions.

Tina was sweet. Driscoll liked her immediately, even though she had acted terrified in the beginning and had responded to most of his questions like a schoolgirl who had been summoned to the principal's office. What he didn't like was the things he had been hearing about her boyfriend.

He had been struggling to reconstruct everything that had happened the night of the Meatman's murder—reviewing activity reports, arrests, stolen cars, domestic disturbances, everything. Not a single piece of useful information had popped up, with the exception of a missing-person report that had been making the rounds.

Some punk in South Philly, a kid named Vinnie, had disappeared at almost exactly the same time that Presto had been hit. Same neighborhood. On this case, Driscoll wasn't buying coincidences.

The report had been filed by the kid's aunt on behalf of Vinnie's mother, who spoke only Italian. Tina had come into the police station to see if anything had turned up on Vinnie. Driscoll thought it would be worth his while to talk to her.

"This Vinnie," he said to Tina, "he was an Italian kid? That's what you're telling me."

She nodded. She was twisting a small silk scarf in her right hand. Her left hand drummed the tabletop. Under the table Driscoll could see that she'd kicked off one shoe. Her toes were digging into the carpet, nervously probing its fibers.

"Tina, did Vinnie ever talk about the 'wise guys'?" He could tell by her expression that he had. "You know who I mean, don't you, Tina?" She nodded again, not answering in words. "And you're thinking that maybe Vinnie got mixed up with them and you're frightened, aren't you? Don't be. Just tell me who Vinnie hung with."

Tina said that she wasn't really sure. Driscoll patiently went on with the questioning. "When was the last time you saw Vinnie?"

She answered, "It must have been around seven or eight, that night."

"Did Vinnie take you out that night?"

"Yes, we went to a club, an after-hours club. We like to dance there. We always have a good time."

"Did you have a good time that night?"

"It was okay, not as great as usual. Vinnie said we had to leave early, right after we'd eaten, and he acted funny, kind of nervous, I thought."

Driscoll felt encouraged that she had told him this much, but he had a feeling she was holding back. He could sense it in her little agitated gestures. She couldn't keep her hands still.

"Tina, you haven't told me everything," he said sternly. "If I thought that's all there was to it, I wouldn't be here talking to you like this right now. Do you think it's just a coincidence or some accident that all of a sudden I'm so interested in a missing-person report? You couldn't begin to guess how many of those we get every single day. The thing is, your boyfriend disappeared the same night that Paul Presto was murdered. He could be a suspect.

"How do I know that you two didn't have a fight or that he isn't shacked up with some other girl somewhere? Maybe he took a trip. Maybe he went down to the shore. All this must have gone through your mind, too. But you really think something's happened to him, don't you?"

He reached across the table, put his hand on hers, and with the other hand gently raised her face until her eyes were directly on his.

"Come on now, Tina. You saw on television what happened to Presto. You know who he was. He lived in your neighborhood for years. And that's really why I'm here. The last time you saw your Vinnie was just an hour or so before he was killed. And in almost the same location. This is very serious business, little girl."

Tina's eyes were filling with tears. Then, looking over his shoulder at some invisible spot on the wall, Tina began talking. The words came out quickly, tumbling, filling the room with tension and expectancy. Driscoll felt like Tina's father.

"I don't know what all this means," she began, "but I just know it has *something* to do with Vinnie. I just feel it." She was dabbing at her eyes with a tissue. "He told me that he had to go to work that night. That's why we left the club early. But he *never* worked at the store at night. When I tried to ask him about it, he didn't want to talk about it, so I dropped it. But now I wish I had made him tell me."

Tina was sobbing, and all Driscoll could do was sit there and watch her helplessly. But he had to get her to keep talking. "Tina, tell me about the store that Vinnie worked in. You said it was a fur store in the Northeast. What was Vinnie's job exactly?"

Trying to compose herself, she told him what Vinnie did, explaining that he cut the patterns and sewed them and that he was really good at it.

"What was the name of the store?"

"Arctic Furs."

Driscoll knew there were a lot of Russian emigrés up there. Northeast detectives had received several complaints from some of the store owners about being shaken down for protection money, like a Russian Black Hand. But because there had been no reports of homicide, there hadn't been any reason for him to get involved until now.

"Did he talk about the people he worked with?" Driscoll asked.

Tina hesitated. "Well, not really—Vinnie's half-Russian, you know. I should have told you that."

"Yeah," Driscoll said, "that would've been nice."

"His father was like really Russian, really old-country. Vinnie hasn't seen him since he was a little boy. Vinnie said that somebody told him that they thought he'd gone back over there to Russia, but his mother won't talk about it at all."

"Did Vinnie speak Russian?" Driscoll asked.

"Not to me," Tina said.

"I know that."

"Maybe a little, I guess." She looked like she was trying to remember. "You know, I think he did say that his boss wanted him to talk Russian . . . yeah, he did say that. But he couldn't stand his boss. He hated him. So I don't know whether he did or not. He always put Vinnie down like he was a jerk. But I know how hard Vinnie worked." Tina's tears had given way to indignation. "They act dumb, you know, these foreigners, but they're not. They have more than he did."

"Tina, what was his boss's name?"

"Mr. B," she said. "He had another name, a Russian name. Vinnie said it a couple of times but I could never remember it. He used to say that Mr. B. was a pain in his butt.''

But you're absolutely sure that this guy was a *Russian,* the guy he worked for, this businessman, Mr. B?''

''I'm sure,'' Tina said.

''Thanks,'' Driscoll told her as he assessed this unexpected piece of information. Russian. Like the holdup man from the Presto bank seemed to be, Driscoll was suddenly willing to bet.

SEVENTEEN

RITTENHOUSE SQUARE

Arlene, who had been knocking on his hotel door, had her coat off and her blouse halfway unbuttoned before Whitey had said a word. She stared at him apprehensively. This was certainly the guy they had described to her. No doubt about that. She looked up at his white head and disjointed face.

"They told me you'd take care of everything," Arlene began. The morose brown eyes she was peering into, Whitey's eyes, came alive as they penetrated her. She spoke slowly. "You know, the money. That's what they said." Then, to make it perfectly clear, she continued, hoping that this big, odd-looking man, hairless except for the tuft of white on the top of his head, would understand how the game worked. "I'm what you call an out-call girl, an escort. I go where they send me. I fuck and you pay."

"You have it right," Whitey answered, taking her in from head to toe. "I pay. I handle everything."

Relieved, she sighed, and started undoing the rest of the buttons on her blouse. Glancing at him in surprise, she stopped. "Is this okay? Some guys like to undress me."

"You go right ahead."

"You're not gonna keep your clothes on, are you?" she asked Whitey in a voice that had been trained to sound like an invitation. Arlene snapped on a synthetic smile.

Whitey managed a benign nod of his large head. His

client had told him about Arlene and explained the part that she could play in providing them with information about the Meatman's movements and his schedule. Many months before, the client had infiltrated her into Presto's operation, although she wasn't exactly sure what she was being paid for. It had been at Whitey's suggestion that she delayed Presto long enough for him to get into position for the hit. The client had taken care of all of it on his end. This was the first time Whitey had seen Arlene. He felt confident that she assumed he was just another customer. Just another part of this unusual gig.

After a job, Whitey always needed a woman. He had mentioned that to the client when he first reported from the Barclay and asked him to arrange for it. The client had agreed to send Arlene sometime on Saturday. Now, looking at her, he had an idea he would enjoy himself.

"Relax, honey," Arlene said, walking around Whitey in a small circle, sizing up his lanky, muscular form with little sounds of approval. "Straight sex is one-twenty an hour; anything kinky, I get a tip. If you're a big tipper, I can make you feel real, real special."

He sat in a big overstuffed hotel chair across from her, letting the excitement of the moment sink in. She was naked from the waist up now and beginning to play with her breasts. She licked her nipple. "Hey, honey, I thought you wanted to party," she said.

"I'm in no hurry," Whitey answered. "But you do precisely what I tell you to do and you'll walk out of here with more money than you've ever seen for a job like this."

Arlene thought that over. Whitey had still made no move to undress. She removed the barrette from her pretty, soft hair and let it fall to her shoulders. "You always dress like that?" she asked. "All in black?"

"Always." His rigid brown eyes were flickering in anticipation.

"No blood. Okay? No rough stuff. I don't do that. You want to go up my ass, that's gonna cost you a lot extra. Now, can we get friendly?" She walked over to where Whitey was sitting, leaned toward him, and gently pushed her breast to within an inch of his face.

Whitey didn't move, didn't react at all. Arlene sniffed,

spun around, and continued to strip. "Boy, this'll be a challenge," she said haughtily.

Her shoulder-length hair was red and thick and her legs long and powerful-looking. He noticed muscles in the calves.

"When did you stop dancing?" he said.

"How did you know . . . ?" Arlene regarded Whitey with renewed interest. He returned an all-knowing smile.

"Are you sure you're not a cop or something?"

"Cross my heart."

Arlene loved to talk about her dancing. "I had to stop when I found out how much money I could make in this business. Do you know how tough it is to make a living as a dancer if you're not a stripper?" She smiled demurely. "And I *never* stripped. I was strictly exotic. I even went to school to study for it. Hey, how *did* you know I was a dancer? I'll bet you saw me dance sometime, didn't you? I worked some real nice clubs in Jersey; even had a tryout for Atlantic City."

Whitey was pleased with what he saw. He stood up, walked toward her, and began to take his shirt off.

"That's more like it." Arlene was getting into it herself now, and walked over to the night table, and turned on the radio. "How about a little music?" Arlene was fascinated by his white hair and the chalky cast to his skin. He looked weird, but very virile. Arlene reached out to touch him, but Whitey nervously withdrew. "That's okay, honey, we'll take it real slow. But you oughtta try to get some sun somewhere. You're awful pale and tall. I'll bet you're long all over." She uttered a low, lewd laugh.

"I want you to shave and shower," Whitey told her. "You'll find everything you need in there." He gestured to the bathroom.

Arlene looked surprised, then amused. "You wanta take a shower with me, is that it? But you're a little shy. You just come in with me." She took Whitey's hand in hers; his skin was smooth and waxy.

"No, that's not it," he said patiently, letting go of her hand. "I want *you* to take a shower, alone, and wash very thoroughly." He sounded clinical.

"You're a real creep," she began angrily. But Whitey just kept on talking. "Then I want you to shave every inch of your body. I don't want to see any hair when you've finished. Particularly there." He pointed to the rich red curls between her thighs. "After you've finished, it's my turn."

Arlene stroked her pubic hair before answering. "I can't believe you," she said. "You must think this is some damn freak show. You can shove your money, lover. Call another girl."

She had stepped out of her skirt and panties. Bending down, she gathered up her clothes and started moving toward the door. Her eyes, frightened now, were on Whitey. "What's wrong with you? You have some kinda skin condition?" she spat out, fumbling with her bra. Her hands were shaking.

In a single long stride, Whitey cut her off. She trembled as he touched her shoulders. Squirming, she spun away from him, and he released her. Reaching into his wallet, he withdrew five crisp $100 bills and fanned them like a poker hand. "Sure I can't change your mind?" There was a slight pulsation in Whitey's left cheek.

Grabbing the money, Arlene counted it and put it in the toe of her shoe. "Looks like you win," she said. Her tone had changed. Strictly business now. "What's your name, anyway? Your real name. I know it's not Mr. Smith like you told the escort service."

Whitey could see her struggling with herself, forcing her better judgment into the background. Five bills was a lot of money. But Whitey would make damn sure that she earned every penny. "You can call me anything you like," Whitey told her. "Pick your favorite name."

"God, you're strange," Arlene said, dropping her skirt to the floor once again. "What's with this hair thing, anyway? That's a turn-on for most guys. You don't mean my head too, do you? You're not that freaky."

"Of course not," Whitey said. "Your hair is beautiful and you're a very attractive woman. You're making me very excited."

She opened the bathroom door, went in, and switched on the light. She saw the shaving gear on the sink. "Now, after I shave, then what? You're just fulla surprises." Arlene leaned against the sink, turned, and spread her legs apart.

She didn't realize that Whitey had walked into the bathroom behind her, and now he too was naked. Creeping up on her like that, he startled her, but Arlene stared at him hungrily.

"Then this," he said, pointing down at himself. Arlene was looking at the biggest erection she had ever seen.

WALTER REED HOSPITAL, WASHINGTON, D.C.

Jim Carney stared up at a blinding circular light; the persistent electronic pulse of life-support systems, located somewhere behind him, disturbed his rest. The odd, sharp odors of the sickroom assaulted his nostrils. He couldn't move. The bandages were too confining. Gradually, his blurred vision was becoming clear. His neck felt stiff, but still mobile enough to move, carefully. The pain was intense. He searched the room for the hooded man from his dream.

Slowly, Carney managed to blink away the false halo of the overhead light. Two faces appeared. The first was sleek and beautiful, a gorgeous young man's smooth, unblemished countenance. Precious. He was blond and gentle-looking. Confused, Carney probed his eyes for some signal. Some subtle indication that he was willing. The young man's eyes did betray interest, but not the same kind as Carney had in mind. And blond, too. What a waste. He could give this young man such a glorious night. Just for a few hours.

A voice was calling Carney's name, insistent, deep. He tried to focus in on the second face, a black face. Carney never slept with black men. Suddenly, moving from one plane to another, Carney understood. This wasn't part of the dream. The hooded man was gone.

"He's coming around," the handsome young doctor said, bending low over Carney's elevated bed.

"Jim, do you know who I am?" The black man was speaking again.

"Mr. Bellows, please. Take it easy," the doctor cautioned. "He's still in shock . . . the concussion."

Finally, Jim Carney was waking up.

"Jim, this is Bellows, from Philadelphia . . . *Royal* . . . This is Bellows."

But Carney had lapsed back into unconsciousness. The attending physician noted his reaction to Bellow's voice on a bedside chart. Then he said, "I still can't believe how well he's come through this, all things considered. His driver was killed instantly."

"Our best guess is that the grenade went right through the car into the engine compartment before it exploded," Bellows informed the curious physician. "It blew all the doors open, but the shrapnel never hit the backseat."

"So he was blown clear when the doors opened?" the doctor asked.

"Exactly. There was a lot of snow around, banked up on the side the way the plows had pushed it, and it cushioned his body when he was thrown out the door. The gas tank didn't explode for a few seconds, just long enough for Jim to roll clear, to the other side of the snowbank." Bellows looked down at his friend. "Damn, I never saw anything like it, though, Doc. This man here should be dead right now." He pointed to the bed.

"It's more common than you think," the doctor said. "Since I've been here I've seen three supposed DOAs walked out the door. We just never know. Mr. Carney's in very good shape; he's got the body of a man fifteen years younger than his actual age." The doctor felt Carney's pulse. "Strong," he said approvingly. "The man has an incredible will to live. What can you say?"

Bellows just shook his head."How long will he be here, Doc?"

"He has no temperature, and his pulse is probably better than yours or mine. As long as there's no cerebral irritation or vomiting, it shouldn't be any more than twelve to twenty-four hours once he's fully conscious. His other injuries are mostly bumps, bruises—all light trauma. In a day or so it should be pretty much up to him to leave when he feels like it.''

BRIGHTON BEACH

All night long, Nikolai Butkova had heard the cars of his departing customers getting stuck in the snow, trapped between the high drifts and the unyielding support pillars of the overhead El tracks. That's what he thought the noise was now. Behind the restaurant, in the small room that he used as an office when he was in New York, he sat counting the night's receipts. A single brass desk lamp glowed an amber yellow.

Just before attacking each stack of bills, Butkova would lick the rough skin of his blunt thumb and forefinger, turned currency-green after handling so much cash, then count to himself in a sequence of twenties. He was up to $3,600 when he heard the second noise.

It wasn't a car.

It was the carefully muffled sound of breaking glass, a burglar's sound. To a trained ear like his, it was unmistakable. He himself had forced entry that way plenty of times.

Quickly shoving the money into a cash box, he pressed a hidden button under the right front corner of his desk and moved to the wall panel behind him. It opened to reveal an immense black safe. He spun the cylinder several times, left, right, two more lefts, then right again, tugged on the heavy, vacuum-sealed door, and placed the cash box inside. Then, he picked up a pistol, a .45 automatic, that was lying in the darkness, inside the safe. Silently, he closed the door and turned the cylinder once again.

Remembering the light, he reached back to switch it off, then moved gingerly to the other side of the room. That's when he heard the footsteps. Heavy footsteps; clumsy men.

In the eerie quiet, he thought he could hear them breathing. Two men probably. One still near the front door of the restaurant, he surmised. The other across the dance floor. Ordinarily, Boris, the loyal bear, his bodyguard and companion of a lifetime, would have been with him and the intruders would be easy prey between them. But Boris was on another vital mission tonight. Butkova would have to handle them alone. He'd have to manage.

Chairs were piled on tables, upended, and the tables were shoved into a rough semicircle in the middle of the main room. The waiters hadn't bothered to clean up yet. Not with the holiday. Other chairs had been placed, legs up, on top of the long bar. He cracked open his office door and looked out. The interior of the restaurant was like a forest of upended chair legs—the only light the dull red glow from the two exit signs.

At least he knew the layout of the place better than they did.

Suddenly he heard a rush of movement.

Butkova dropped to his hands and knees, reached behind him, and removed his shoes. Then he began to crawl, silent and light as a cat, toward the bar.

Less than three feet from the brass foot rail, he dropped to his belly, hoping they would take a shot at him—a shot at where they *thought* he would be standing. Pinning down their locations was essential. But he didn't hear the cock of a trigger.

That's when Butkova smelled the strong, acrid odor of gasoline.

With the fumes almost gagging him, he began inching backward, retracing his movements, making a run for the little office again.

A seldom-used rear door connected the office to a driveway in the back—a kitchen delivery dock for food and beverages. They'd have that covered, for sure. But in the darkness, with the snow blowing, they might have overlooked the unlighted rear office entrance. It was his only chance. He had to try.

Hearing more scuffling behind him, he reached the back door, but it was stiff and swollen from the dampness. He had to get it open somehow.

He shoved the big gun under his belt, turned the key in the deadbolt on the door, and began pushing and shoving with all his strength. It wouldn't budge—maybe they had blocked it.

Voices hissed out behind him. Then the sound of shuffling and running feet. Just as the door moved a fraction of an inch, he felt the blast of the gas; almost an explosion, as it ignited in the main room of the restaurant.

Fire was racing toward him, but the door wouldn't give any more.

Butkova couldn't breathe. The flames had reached his office; he could feel the heat on his shoeless feet. With a single bright flash, the office was consumed with fire. The smoke was choking him; the heat was intense.

Panicking, Butkova threw his shoulder against the door so violently he thought his bones were cracking. He could feel himself blacking out; the fire was at his back—*on* his back—his heavy tweed jacket in flames.

One last time he hurtled himself against the door.

He thought his hair was burning. Pain was shooting down his back.

Miraculously, the door finally gave way; harder and harder he pushed until he had squeezed his burning body through.

Then he fell on his face into a big drift of snow that had been blocking the door. He felt the cold wetness against his mouth. Still on fire, he rolled himself into the slush, back and forth, back and forth, pain ripping him with every movement, trying to extinguish the flames.

He heard a deafening, rumbling sound coming from the restaurant—the whole building was about to go up.

He was still too close; he knew he would never survive, but he had to; he had to live to find the men who had done this to him.

With an energy that Butkova didn't realize he could muster, he forced himself to struggle up out of the snow, on his hands and knees at first, then staggering to wobbly legs. The rumbling grew louder. At last he was on his feet. He could feel blood oozing from them, but he began to run, propelling himself across the frozen, slippery driveway, running for his life.

Behind him, what was left of his restaurant on Brighton Avenue burst through the roof of the building into the winter sky all at once, rocketing a thousand spinning pieces of debris upward, the flames making a violent roar that shook the air and transformed the darkness into a fierce dazzling light show.

Bleeding and burned, he was sprawled on his back, slush still in his mouth from where he had rolled out the flames. As Butkova looked up, the sky appeared to be on fire.

But now the snow tasted cold and good and life-giving. Once again, Nikolai Butkova had cheated death.

A RECEPTION CHAMBER IN LENIN'S HALL OF HEROES, THE KREMLIN

Vladik Vladovich Zinijakin, the seventy-five-year-old Marshal of all the Soviet Armies and decorated hero of the Great Patriotic War against the Germans, looked even wearier than usual. He stood perfectly still, staring at the microphone before him. The redness of his fat, full cheeks contrasted with the sallowness of his complexion; with the dryness of his long, thin lips. The stocky, square-faced Zinijakin, with his steel-rimmed glasses, bushy eyebrows, and flat, sloping forehead, was standing at the edge of a precipice, and he knew it. With retirement, obscurity, and eventually that black oblivion ahead of him, and a hungry pack of slightly younger, even more aggressive competitors behind him, Zinijakin realized that his days were numbered.

Over the last few years, he had had to depend more than ever on his fragile hold over the GRU, the Chief Intelligence Directorate of the Military, to remain in power; and that GRU—suspicious, demanding, and increasingly arrogant—had been searching for some sign from him, some guarantee that he recognized their problems, shared their concerns. *They* required some gesture from him that told them that he, Zinijakin, understood. *He* needed some master stroke that would reassure them.

Instinctive politician that he was, Vladik Zinijakin sensed all this. Despite the cold, silent isolation of the Kremlin, he still knew his people. From conscript to general, he had maintained a clear, crisp appreciation of the Russian character. He even understood the new Chairman's obsessive need for consensus. Zinijakin, alone among the old men of his prewar generation, still commanded influence with the new leadership. And respect.

Today, five hundred of Russia's top military personnel were arrayed before him—looking to him, as always, for leadership. They sat, clench-jawed and uncomfortable, upon row after row of ornate antique chairs. Zinijakin had gone to great pains to make sure that the speech he was about to give would be a clear signal to the GRU that he *would* keep faith with them.

The jackals on the Politburo were spread out behind him, seated serenely on a little platform. They were essentially patient men, waiting, observing.

It was under Zinijakin's disciplined, deliberate administration that Russia's military espionage service had become the largest, best-financed, and most active in the world, with its intelligence bureaus in each of the Soviet Union's sixteen military and four naval districts, and its fifty thousand *Spetsnaz*—special-designation soldiers, professional saboteurs and terrorists—strategically positioned around the world. The GRU's impregnable barracks and training facility at Khodinsk Field, just southeast of Moscow's central airport, was Zinijakin's command post. From that secure stronghold, with its electrified fences, motion detectors, guards and guard dogs, and land mines thickly placed around the perimeter of the top-secret complex, Zinijakin had been monitoring the actions of the traitor Zhukov. Zhukov had to be stopped.

Today, in this gilded reception room in the Kremlin, Vladik Zinijakin was fighting for his power, and perhaps his life—fighting against the intrigues of the Politburo members seated in the first row behind him.

As soon as his speech was finished, the old marshal paused

and looked for one long, last moment at the generals and admirals stretching out before him, warmly responding to the words he had spoken.

Then Zinijakin glanced back over his shoulder at the dignitaries assembled there. The first row were already on their feet, beginning a polite, proper round of applause.

MOSCOW

Just before the Aeroflot car, a comfortable black sedan, arrived to pick up Tanya, Zhukov had been called back to his headquarters—some emergency, he told her.

They had said their goodbyes over the telephone. It was easier that way. Nothing else could match their last night together. She didn't even want to think about what would happen to him now.

Her flight had taken off at 10:15 a.m. Moscow time and would arrive at the International Terminal at JFK Airport in New York at 2:00 p.m., Sunday, New York time. That would give her more than enough hours to sleep. And think. She knew she was betraying him, but they had given her no choice. She didn't want to die.

She had been given her orders. Tanya reviewed them in her mind as the cool air from the little nozzle above her seat chilled her. The powerful engines in the big Aeroflot jet droned comfortingly outside. At least she would probably never have to face Mikhail again. By the time she returned, he would have been removed. That was the word they had used—"removed." It sounded harmless, clinical, painless. Like removing a hangnail.

After she landed, Tanya was to proceed to the Soviet Mission in midtown Manhattan. She had made that trip many times before—136 East 67th Street, between Third Avenue and Lexington. It was a modern office building. The plainclothes guards in the lobby would be expecting her. Tanya would be escorted from JFK by two GRU officers. At the mission they would see that she remained in their section of the building, away from the KGB floor and its complex of smaller offices and electronic monitoring rooms. There she would await further orders.

Tanya had worked with the crew on this flight before. One of the stewards had been pursuing her for months, begging her to go to bed with him. She spotted his excited face coming down the aisle in her direction. He was carrying a tray with caviar, a small bottle of wine, and two sparkling glasses. Without a word, he slid into the empty seat beside her.

EIGHTEEN

THE KREMLIN SUNDAY

The ceremonial guard was changing in Red Square, the dying sun reflecting off its polished bayonets. From his window overlooking the permanent parade bleachers in the square, with the State History Museum to his far left, Zhukov enjoyed exquisite sunsets, framed by the onion-domed cupolas of St. Basil the Blessed Cathedral and the soaring red star of Spassky Tower, the clock tower. He thought it ironic that so much of Christianity had been preserved by the stout red-brick fortress walls of the Kremlin, saved from Tartar, from Napoleon, and from the tiger tanks of the Nazis. Now a hundred churches in Moscow alone were the most heavily visited tourist attractions. Zhukov drew a deep inner strength from those ancient spires, reminding him that the cult of Christianity had been as enduring as the cobblestones of the square. Church and state had quietly reached an accommodation. That was the key. Accommodation. Send no one away empty-handed. In his personal philosophy, he could apply that equally to the Americans or to his own people.

As he moved away from his desk and deposited himself on a fabric-covered window seat, Zhukov observed a busload of departing Japanese tourists. He looked hungrily at their cameras. Nikons, mostly, telescopic lenses, leather carrying cases. Then his eyes moved down their bodies to their running shoes. Reeboks and Nikes. And blue jeans—the marvelous, decadent traveling uniform of every capitalist Zhukov had ever seen. He wished he could line them up in the square and strip them, one by one. Nikons and blue jeans brought hard currency—foreign currency—in the little back-alley stores that Zhukov supplied for the black market.

Suddenly, a perfunctory knock on the door interrupted his calculations.

"Enter," Zhukov called out, smoothing a hand-stitched Savile Row tie and checking the polish on his boots. "What is it?" he asked the lieutenant, seating himself behind an oak desk that had once dominated a study in the summer home of Czar Nicholas's first cousin.

"We just intercepted a coded message from Washington to the American ambassador here," the lieutenant said. He was a peasant from a farm near Kiev. Even in his green KGB uniform, he still looked like a farmer. "Apparently, there's been some sort of terrorist attack outside Washington, and the embassy here has been put on a red code alert." The lieutenant was flushed, excited to be the first with the news.

Zhukov had learned to listen to such news with what the Americans called a poker face. "Any details?" he asked with detachment.

"Very few, sir. We know they haven't told their own people about it yet. A news blackout. Possibly because their President is out of the country, to attend the Summit."

"I don't need any geopolitical lessons from you, lieutenant. Just give me the name of the victim. Surely you have that."

"Carney, sir. James X. Carney. He's supposed to be a personal friend of the President's. He was supposed to accompany the President to the Summit, but . . ."

Zhukov closed his eyes, struggling with himself for control. The vein in his neck was beginning to pulsate. "I *know* who he is lieutenant," Zhukov cut him off. "You're telling me he's dead?"

"No confirmation as yet, sir."

Zhukov folded his hands tightly in his lap and willed himself to appear calm. No sense alerting this lieutenant and letting him surmise too much. For all Zhukov knew, he could be GRU, too. He couldn't let them know that the name Carney meant anything to him. He cleared his throat and tried to budge the sand from his vocal cords. "The groups responsible for the attack?" He removed the rimless eyeglasses from the bridge of his nose.

"Our Operations Section claim they know nothing about it."

"Of course they don't," Zhukov retorted angrily, "because we didn't order it. I'm asking you who *did*."

The lieutenant was staring straight ahead, not nervous, merely prepared to absorb the next blow of Zhukov's displeasure. Zhukov glanced out of his window again. The ten thousand bells of Moscow, their tone sounded by the Blood Bell of Ivan the Terrible, were beginning to peal the hour.

"Bring me everything we have on this . . . *everything,* understand?"

"At once, sir." The lieutenant left, closing the door behind him.

Jim Carney couldn't be dead. Zhukov could taste bile invading his throat as his last meal regurgitated. He felt sick, trapped.

Below him, in Red Square, the frost on the cobblestones was returning as the last long shadow from the obelisk faded before the fleeing sun. Soon the stones would be too slippery to navigate. A man running across them, even one as surefooted and resourceful as Mikhail Zhukov, would never be able to escape. Yet that was his only option now. *Escape.*

SHUNK STREET, SOUTH PHILADELPHIA

Joe-Joey had arrived home just in time to watch his children begin decorating their towering Douglas fir Christmas tree. He liked them to wait until Christmas Eve, but they were just too impatient. There was less than a week to go now and the Christmas presents were all they could think about.

He had five, three boys and two girls, eighteen months to eighteen years. Not bad for a funny-looking little Italian guy, he thought to himself. He only stood a shade over five feet five inches tall, but Joe-Joey's upper body was grotesquely well developed, and he hit the barbells, faithfully, five times a week. None of the males in his family had ever been cursed with a single gray hair; his eyes were as inquisitive and animated as his eighteen-month-old's. Joe-Joey still liked to slip his short, strong arm around his wife's hips two or three times almost every night—and "bother" her, as she called it. As far as Joe-Joey was concerned, nobody on the face of the earth "bothered" better than he did.

He was a thug and a thief and, on rare occasion, a killer, but with his kids, Joe-Joey was all parent and all responsibility. He liked to tell the guys that making kids was his hobby. They'd just grunt and wink at him. His kids were all gorgeous, too. And his wife was pregnant again. This one had to be the last; she threatened to tie it in a knot if it wasn't. The way his wife was, Joe-Joey could already feel the pain.

It was not his *family* but his Family that Joe-Joey was worried about. The Presto Family. Marie and Tony were trying to take over now, and neither one could wipe Paul Presto's ass. Especially Tony. Had Tony not existed, Joe-Joey would have been the underboss; Paul had said as much himself. But Tony, pariah that he was, was also blood by marriage, and Joe-Joey just had to respect tradition on that score and go along with Paul.

His oldest girl's boyfriend had come over to help hang the balls and tinsel. Joe-Joey didn't approve; the kid had a weak handshake and he had never heard of him having any kind of a part-time job; he lived off his parents. His daughter could do better, and he would make sure that she did. But he didn't make a scene. His wife was in her seventh month. Joe-Joey didn't need any more grief. But that oldest girl, Lisa, was getting to be a handful. When she thought he wasn't looking, he had even caught her patting her boyfriend's ass, instead of vice versa. Now, while they stretched the lines of reflecting lights around the circumference of the tree, they only had eyes for each other. Too soon, Joe-Joey feared, she might make him a young grandfather.

His wife, enormous with the child, but normally petite, set the three little ones playing among themselves and motioned for Joe-Joey to follow her into the kitchen. She was more familiar with his work than any of the other wives of the Presto soldiers. She too had been troubled since Paul's tragic death. As she spoke, she stirred a large ladle in a bowl.

"So how did it go last night? Was the traffic bad coming back?" Joe-Joey knew she was referring to his secret trip up to Brighton Beach, to Brooklyn.

"It's what Tony wanted. He's the boss now. The place went up like a torch." Joe-Joey didn't tell her that he had accidentally spilled some of the gasoline on himself; it had been close. But this was no time to make her worry. He just hoped that the Russian bastard was dead.

When Joe-Joey's wife thought of Tony Bonaventura and his wife Marie, she was reminded of how she screamed at her kids for forgetting to wipe dog shit off their shoes. The thought of her Joe-Joey taking his orders now from Tony instead of Paul nauseated her.

"Any trouble?" she asked, still stirring.

"Some." He didn't elaborate.

"These Russians, I don't understand. There's so many of them, we have to worry?"

"It only takes a few," Joe-Joey said carefully. "How many were in the gang that decided to kill Angelo Bruno and take over—seven or eight? These Russians are just like we were fifty years ago. Getting organized. When people want to get ahead, they mob up. Protect each other. Paul always said these guys were tough. Their cops are a lot worse than ours. Paul saw all this coming. That's why he did what he did. Maybe he was wrong?" Joe-Joey shrugged.

"I never knew Paul to be wrong about anything," his wife said bravely. This wasn't exactly like talking back, and Joe-Joey would never lay a hand on her, but not every husband in the Presto Family was as interested in his wife's opinion as her Joe-Joey was.

"Was it a mistake to go after the Russian like you did, to burn him out?"

"He robbed the numbers bank; we gotta fight back. I give Tony credit for that at least."

"I don't give him credit for anything."

Joe-Joey still had a painfully sore palate from the rifle one of the gunmen had stuck in his mouth. For that alone Butkova deserved to be burned. But he understood what his wife meant. Tony's next bright idea would be his first.

"Everybody made money with Paul. No trouble, no cops, no wars." She corrected herself. "Maybe just little wars. So, okay. That's business. But Paul made sure that everybody had money in his pocket. You got jealous of somebody, he took care of you. Paul was a leader. He had respect from everybody." She turned away from the stove, wiped her hands on a towel, and said, "You think Tony can do that?"

Back when he was a young boy, Joe-Joey had done hard time—once. Two years at Graterford; 890 blacks and twelve whites. Maximum security. He had to fight every day for almost all of the two years to keep from having some big shine stick his pole up his ass. Joe-Joey didn't know if he could ever face that again; he wasn't getting any younger. When Paul was in charge nobody even *thought* about prison. Joe-Joey wanted to make damn sure that his little boys never had to worry about Graterford. But how could a stupid fuck like Tony keep everybody out of jail and making money?

"Come on, answer me," his wife persisted. "Can Tony do what Paul did?"

"What are you asking me to do?" His wife never told him to do anything, but Joe-Joey always got the message.

"Think about it, that's all. Tony don't even wear the pants in his own family." She made a face that she always made when she imitated Marie. "Maybe you should talk to the other men; talk to Honey . . ."

The telephone ringing interrupted her. Joe-Joey answered. It had to be important if they were calling him at home like this.

Joe-Joey's wife felt the baby kicking, letting her know that he or she had heard the phone ringing, too. She patted the small mountain in front of her, now covered by an apron.

"I'll meet you there," Joe-Joey said as he hung the phone on the kitchen wall.

"Who?"

"You'll never believe it if I tell you," he answered, obviously pleased with himself. It seemed as if he had grown three or four inches taller in front of her eyes.

"*Who?*"

"That was Mr. Milton Littlejohn—can you *believe* that? Paul's personal lawyer, calling *me* at home. On Sunday. The white-bread-and-American-cheese Protestant from Chestnut Hill wants to see Joe-Joey. *Me!* This is the best part, how he put it . . . he wants to see me as the *senior* man."

Joe-Joey's wife looked impressed. "Put on your good suit," she said.

"No time."

"You have to see him now?"

"Right now."

"Is it about Paul . . . Tony?"

"Maybe Honey," Joe-Joey said. "Who knows? Maybe he knows who killed Paul."

"Has anybody seen Honoria?"

Joe-Joey shook his head, "She's been laying low since Paul got it. Scared, I guess." Then Joe-Joey squeaked open the kitchen door and took another look at his kids. His oldest girl was sitting too damn close to the boyfriend. "*Lisa,*" he called sternly. "Come in the kitchen and help your mother." Then to his wife he added, just before kissing her goodbye, "Home for dinner, I promise."

The baby kicked her again.

SOUTH PHILADELPHIA

Milton Littlejohn was waiting for Joe-Joey inside the real estate office. No one had been in the place since the bombing. Littlejohn wasn't alone. He sat behind the main desk where the customers usually leaned across from the other side, poring over the fine print of their mortgages and settlements. Arrayed along two walls, sitting packed together on pews that the Presto Family salvage company had rescued from a church the minister had paid them to torch, were all the ranking *capis* in the Family. It was a major sit-down.

Suddenly, a rogue thought stampeded through Joe-Joey's mind. How come nobody told him about this sit-down? Was he in trouble? The guy getting hit was always the last one to know. Was Tony setting him up, afraid of the competition?

He looked around at the other men, nodded to each one, and tried to get the feel of whatever the hell was going on. Bundled against the cold, the *capis* looked as lumpy and anthracitic as sacks of coal. Their eyes were as red as the belly of a furnace—nobody had been getting much sleep lately.

"So very kind of you to join us," Milton Littlejohn said, tapping his cane, trying hard to sound friendly through the upper-class clip of his Chestnut Hill accent.

Joe-Joey took his place with the rest and prayed that God wouldn't let him be killed without seeing his new baby.

RITTENHOUSE SQUARE

Whitey woke up with Arlene's small hand on his chest. Her touch was light. He shuddered, half rose out of the bed, and remembered where he was. Arlene suppressed a giggle as he pulled the blanket up over his bare chest. "Don't hog the covers," she admonished him, pretending to be angry.

"Oh, I'm sorry," Whitey said quickly. "I didn't realize . . . I get cold easily." He spread the quilt over her exposed thigh.

"Cold! . . . Jesus, you're like an ice cube. You're not sick or anything, are you?" She seemed to be examining the man beside her in a new light.

"No, I'm fine. Just cold, that's all. Just cold-blooded, I guess."

"Where'd you go last night?" she asked.

Whitey had met with his client at a small restaurant in downtown Philadelphia, The Three Threes. It was only a few blocks from the Barclay. By then, he needed another car, more money, a better plan of operation. The restaurant had been crowded, but they had been able to talk undisturbed at a table on the second floor, near the back. When the waiter came to take their order, Whitey's eyes remained on his plate. The client ordered for both of them. After the meal, they left, no handshakes, no goodbyes. It was hours after that before Whitey returned.

Whitey didn't answer. Arlene didn't mind; she was used to that. "So how'd you like it?" she continued. "You zonked right out when you came back."

"Like? Like what?"

"Me! . . . How'd you like *me* . . . with no hair down there." She put Whitey's palm on her crotch, smooth, cool, but starting to stubble already. "God, you're really dense. Remember, you made me shave?"

"Of course," he replied slowly, cupping her with his large hand. "Fantastic."

"That's more like it, lover. So did you see my man last night—the guy who sent me here?" He started to move his hand away, but she squeezed it between her thighs. "It feels funny this way, but it feels *good* . . . know what I mean? I guess I could get into this hair thing." Her head vanished under the covers and Whitey felt Arlene's mouth begin an up-and down, up-and-down, friction. His legs tightened, his hips jerked spasm after spasm, and he came almost as soon as she touched him. The sheet under him began to dampen.

"A little jumpy today, aren't you, baby?" Arlene said as she slid out from under the covers, off the side of the bed.

Whitey's head ached. He needed his vitamins. Each day he consumed dozens of the pills, supplements to make up for the deficiencies that had plagued him since birth. Vitamins were a fetish with him; in every new city he stocked up again, carrying hundreds of pills and capsules in his luggage.

Arlene saw him place several of the tablets in the palm of his hand and swallow them. He was in the bathroom at the sink and washed them down with a glass of water.

"Honey, aren't you gonna share?" she called out to him. "I can't get started in the mornings without my diet pills. Then I do Quaaludes at night when I like to come down. Sometimes I do it the other way around. But 'ludes are a little hard to come by. I could sure use some of whatever you got."

Whitey looked at her sadly, his voice gentle. "These aren't drugs—*dope*—just vitamins."

"Vitamins. *Yuck!*"

"You're welcome to them, but you should be careful about what you put in your body."

She jumped out of bed and reached for his robe. "Do you *mind?*" she said, laughing, as she scooted past him and closed the bathroom door behind her. Whitey heard her turn on the shower. Then he noticed the little food cart at the end of the bed.

"Is this yours?" Whitey called into the bathroom.

"Oh, yeah. I got hungry while you were asleep, so I called room service. That's okay, isn't it? I got a paper for you too. Most of the guys I do like to read their paper."

"That's fine," he answered. She'd left a piece of toast on the plate. He sniffed at it, then took a bite as he scanned the headlines. Presto was all over the paper again. More pages of interviews with the police and FBI and pictures of the house on Fletcher Street. But there was no photo of Presto's daughter. Too bad.

Just then, Arlene came out of the bathroom, dripping on the plush pink carpet. "Why did you ask me if I saw the man who sent you to me last night?" he began.

"No special reason. I just thought that was where you

went maybe. Maybe he had another job for me, that's all. Cool it, baby. Chill out."

"No more jobs," Whitey said distantly. "Just hang around here with me for a while." Then he looked directly at her. "The pay's good, isn't it?"

She was rubbing furiously at her curly red hair; wet, it appeared as richly liquid as wine. Her head was tilted severely to one side as she worked to pull out the curls with her towel. "That's okay by me," she told him.

"Did you read the paper?"

"Not really."

Whitey had noticed that the stories relating to the Presto murder—to his murder—were smudged here and there. Arlene's fingertips must have been moist when she read them.

"I mean the stories about this bombing."

"Why?" Arlene was beginning to feel uneasy again.

"I thought you told me you worked for Presto. Didn't you say that?"

Arlene had never said anything like that. "I . . . guess I don't remember. What's wrong?"

"Who do you think killed him?" Whitey had made no move to get dressed. The distorted lines of his face meshed into a tortured smile.

"I don't get into that Mafia stuff," Arlene said. "Scares me."

"Me too." Whitey gave an exaggerated shudder.

Arlene was about to get dressed when she saw Whitey shaking his head. He said, "Not yet, please." He sounded coaxing. She shrugged and fell back onto the bed, crossing her arms behind her head on the pillow. Then she drew up her knees and crossed them, too. She was totally exposed that way, pink, vulnerable, inviting. Whitey pretended not to notice, but his body, responding once again, was giving him away. He quickly wrapped a towel around his waist.

"He had a daughter, didn't he?"

Arlene's eyes were closed. She had taken her last two Quaaludes in the shower. She was pretending the bed was a huge flower, its petals about to close around her. "Who?" she asked Whitey through thickening tongue and lips.

"Presto. Paul Presto. Remember . . . you were just about

to tell me about when you worked for him before he was killed."

"Did I say that? . . . Oh, yeah. What? Do I have to talk so much? Slide in here with me, will you?"

"The daughter?" Whitey pressed.

"Honey. Everybody knows that little bitch. Yeah, Honey. She's really stuck up. Hot shit—that's what she thinks."

Whitey moved to the side of the bed and sat down. "You didn't like her?"

"Hated her. Guys liked her, though. Not girls. But boy, could she boss her old man around. You never saw anything like it."

"Is she pretty?"

"Are you *kidding?* Honey looks just like her old man. You ever see the Meatman? But there *was* this thing about her. She was always so . . . I don't know . . . *alive*. Know what I mean? Like she glowed or something. But, nah, she's not that pretty at all."

Whitey thought for a moment. "What does she look like?"

"Small. Hey, why all the questions?" Her eyes were still shut and the petals of the flower were beginning to caress her with the sweetest perfume she had ever smelled. "I don't remember we talked about any of this stuff."

"We did," Whitey said. "I'm just curious, that's all. I mean, you knew her so well and all that."

"Hey, can we go somewhere? Eat? I been in this room with you since yesterday."

"Later." Whitey had his hand on her knee. "What else can you tell me about Honey Presto?"

"She's a little hippy. Guys don't mind that, though. Honey lost a few pounds, though nobody would notice, *believe* me. She's real short, nice legs, nice chest—I have to give the devil her due. Everything has to be the best for her, cars, clothes, rings—she really spent the Meatman's money."

"Boyfriend?"

"Tons of them. It was funny . . . I don't know if this was true or not, but I heard people say she went with a cop once, can you *believe* that? Honey Presto went with a damn cop? The old man broke that up."

Whitey was still thinking about the clothes, the cars. "What was the last present Presto gave her? Do you know that, by any chance?"

"The Meatman gave everybody presents. Honey always wore something new. But . . . a . . . *yeah!* This *coat.* Fur, *really* ugly. But Honey wore it all the time to please him. She looked good in fur."

"Describe the coat to me," Whitey said. Arlene told him what she could recall, propped up on the pillow against one arm. Then she fell back on the pillow.

"You've been a big help," Whitey said, as he slowly opened her thighs, knelt between her legs, and lowered his face to trace the fine stubble of her crotch with his tongue. Then his mouth moved a few inches lower as her legs clamped around his head. He could smell the bath oil from her shower, taste her.

"*Do* it!" Arlene begged him. "Make me feel it, *all* of it." Her skin felt wet and soft from the heat of the shower as Whitey probed, his tongue urging her into one gushing climax after another as he stroked her clitoris over and over, his tongue as persistent as a triphammer. She gripped his short white hair with both hands, pulling as hard as she could, then she lifted his face from between her thighs and brought it up to her lips. She pressed his long, cold body on top of hers. "Baby, let me warm you up." Then a small sigh escaped her throat.

"Whatever you want," Whitey said.

"I'll do you now."

He removed the pillow from under her head and started to bunch it up. "This way now, okay?" he said.

Arlene smiled, and closed her eyes again, assuming that Whitey wanted her to put the pillow under her stomach; he'd done it that way the night before.

She turned over, lifted her mid-section, and elevated her buttocks provocatively. "This better?" she cooed. "Where's the pillow?"

"Right here," Whitey said as he leaned halfway out of the bed and opened the night-table drawer. "Just like that. Perfect." He snaked one hand under her hips, lifted her stomach, and entered her. As he did so, he brought the pillow down on top of her head and savagely smashed her face down against the mattress.

"Hey, wait . . . what is this?" Arlene had trouble getting the last few syllables out.

Suddenly he withdrew, bathing her back with wet white splashes of semen. He jammed his left knee into her spine until he heard it crack. He used the bunched-up pillow to muffle the loud bang of the .45 as he fired one bullet into Arlene's brain.

WALTER REED HOSPITAL MONDAY

James Carney's erection would not go away. That had to be a good sign. He felt absolutely tumescent, but tired, too. Considering the circumstances, his fatigue was understandable. He could finally piece it all together now.

Somehow, they had penetrated his security, staked out his place in Virginia, and attempted to kill him the first chance they got. It had to be the Russians. But *which* Russians? That was Carney's dilemma. Their own internal feud was raging so furiously, he didn't feel confident giving credit to either side for his assassination. How bizarre. He was lying in bed recovering from a grenade attack, carefully analyzing what someone now undoubtedly believed was his death.

But that would have to wait. First things first.

He grabbed the buzzer next to his bed and pressed it. A nurse entered, stooped, and checked the chart on his bed. The nurse was pleasant and professional, pretty in a tight white uniform. The skirt broke at the crease of her knees. As she leaned over to adjust his pillow, he caught the scent of her perfume. Carney had been hoping for the lovely young blond doctor. Instead he had gotten the nurse. His disappointment manifested itself and his erection began to fade.

"I'm glad to see you're feeling better, Mr. Carney," the nurse said.

"Much," Carney said.

"There's been a call waiting for you for a long time. We're supposed to put it through as soon as you feel up to it. Shall I tell them it's all right now?"

"By all means," Carney said.

The nurse left the room, and seconds later, one of the two telephones installed next to his bed rang. This one was red with a smooth plastic plate where the pushbuttons should have been.

He picked up the receiver and once again recognized an all-too-familiar voice. "Much better, Mr. President," Carney said. "I'll be up and around in no time."

Having exchanged their mutual greetings formally, as they always did initially in a conversation, Carney and his friend got down to business. "I'd better tell you where we stand on this thing," Carney said. "I have a feeling you might not like it."

The President of the United States listened.

NINETEEN

NOBLE STREET
MONDAY NIGHT

The drunks were already on the streets, screaming and shoving, off-balance, and greedily pulling at each other's cheap wine, wrapped in brown paper bags. Whitey loathed the neighborhood. Suddenly two drunks bumped into him, started to mutter and panhandle, but then, as soon as they saw the evil in Whitey's lopsided face and took in his full height, they made a drunken display of clearing the sidewalk for him.

It hadn't taken him that long to find out where she was—Presto's daughter was hiding out in this rambling old warehouse with a delicatessen on the first floor. She hadn't come out, he was sure about that. He'd taken up a position in a loft directly across the street and checked the entrances to the building. No one could go in or out without his noticing. A car moving slowly along the street caught his attention. It pulled up to the the curb in front of the deli, rounded the corner, then stopped. The driver had a cop look—big, alert, eyes sweeping the street like the needles on a sonar screen. Whitey had seen enough cops to be able to spot one.

He'd been holed up in the loft since he had left the Barclay, surviving on his vitamins and willpower; his fingers were so numb he could barely feel them. Just then, Whitey saw the guy he had guessed to be a cop get out of his car, give the exterior of the building a professional once-over, checking rooftops and alleys, then start in the direction of the deli.

Whitey accelerated his pace to make sure to reach the deli ahead of the cop. It was crowded with last-minute patrons and the food smelled delicious.

Driscoll counted four customers and the night counterman. They didn't know it, but the place was about to close early. He was positive Honey was with Manny.

"We're closed," Driscoll said, as he walked in, reached behind him, and flipped over the cardboard sign on the door that said "Closed." Then he pulled down the shade and hooked it on a small peg at the bottom of the door. The startled customers looked at Driscoll as if he might be there to pull a stickup, started to say something, then stopped themselves when they saw his eyes. The counterman was quiet—Driscoll had locked him up before, plenty of times; he was one of Manny's little coterie of old-time goons.

"I'm not even finished with my meal yet," a woman said to Driscoll, pointing to a half-eaten corn beef on rye, sloppy with coleslaw. Driscoll picked up her plate and handed it to her. "Board of Health," he said, grinning. "Somebody smelled a rat." Clutching her plate and handbag, she backed out the front door. Another customer started to open his wallet to put some money down on the table. "Forget it," Driscoll said. "It's on the house."

They all left except one guy—a tall, thin white-haired creep. Driscoll had never before seen him in the neighborhood. He had a nose that came down straight like the hard slab on a statue, and a face that was almost scrambled. He didn't say a word, just glared at the cop. There wasn't even any food in front of him yet. That white hair bothered Driscoll; the bus driver who had found the dead highway patrolmen had mentioned white hair. *Who was this guy?*"

"I said we're closed," Driscoll told him, then added, "Move it."

Whitey had never experienced such instant antipathy toward anyone. Now he *knew* this guy was a cop. A real badass. "I haven't eaten yet," he told Driscoll.

"I guess you lost your appetite all of a sudden," was the cop's reply. Driscoll felt like arresting this creep just for having the white hair, but he knew he could never get away with that. He hadn't seen any van outside, either.

The two men measured each other; tense knights before the joust. Neither blinked. Suddenly the counterman interrupted them. "Hey, Driscoll," he screamed, "what're you doing? If you got a beef with the Fat Man, I better see some papers. Where's the warrant?" The guy's tongue worked itself frothy over each word.

For the moment, Driscoll ignored Whitey, as he saw the counterman reach for something. Springing at him quickly, Driscoll yanked on the strings of his apron, grabbed him by the back of his neck, and slammed his head down hard on the smooth surface of the counter. *"There's* the warrant," Driscoll said. *"Read it!* It's right under your nose." Then Driscoll produced a revolver from the cold-cuts counter behind the register. The guy said something about the Fat Man, but a husky voice interrupted him. Driscoll reacted to the sound.

"Go on, Al. It's all right. See you tomorrow." The voice belonged to Manny. Driscoll turned to face the Fat Man, and as he did so, Whitey unfurled his long body from the table where he was sitting. He took another look at Driscoll and the Fat Man, then left without a word. This was one cop Whitey would remember.

Driscoll reached up and pulled the string on the big ceiling light that provided the illumination for most of the room. "Let's go," he said to Manny threateningly. "I want to see Honey. Right now."

Manny used a tight freight elevator to move himself from one floor to the next. Driscoll squeezed in with him and pressed the button for the living quarters on the fourth floor. The expression on Manny's face deflated like a wrinkled balloon; his dark-rimmed eyes were miserable.

"She'd better be here," Driscoll said. Manny looked as though Driscoll had just ripped a scalpel across his swollen belly. He snatched at himself, attempting to close an imaginary incision. The detective nudged him along in front of him after the straining hydraulic pulleys stopped and the heavy metal door clanged open. Manny half turned, started to mumble something under his breath, then stopped. He wheezed as he walked along the hall, holding on to the wall every few feet for balance.

Driscoll saw a stream of light from under one of the doors. "Knock on that door," Driscoll ordered, as he shoved a knotted towel from the deli into Manny's mouth as a gag. "Knock, I said. Don't talk." Manny looked at the detective the way a condemned man stares at a jury foreman.

"Yeah, I know. I hope you drop dead, too," Driscoll said, mocking the thoughts that he knew Manny was directing his way. "Knock." he repeated. "Hard."

Thump! Thump!

Wrapping a robe snugly around her, Honey placed a small .22 revolver in the large, deep pocket near her waist. She ran barefoot across the room when she heard the knocking and made her way almost soundlessly to the door.

Thump! Thump!

Driscoll, on the other side of the door, was glowering, annoyed. He was convinced that Honey was in there. Through the makeshift gag, the Fat Man was coughing, trying to warn Honey.

Her hands shaking, Honey peered through the small round peephole in the door. Bending the image on the other side into a grotesque fish-eye shape, the peephole revealed the familiar muscular figure of Phillip Driscoll. What was he doing here? She didn't want to talk to him. Where was Manny? Why had he let him in?

"What do you want?" Honey called through the door.

"Will you please open the door? I'm here about your father. Honey, I have to talk to you. If you don't open the door, I'll break it down."

Honey knew he meant what he said. "Where's Manny?" she asked. She felt trapped.

Driscoll loosened the gag and yanked it out of the Fat Man's mouth.

"It's all right, Honoria," he said. "I'm here." He was gulping hard for air again. Driscoll had pushed him down into a chair in the hall. Now he was struggling to heave his bulk up, but the detective shoved his shoulder roughly and he fell back down.

"You stay put." Helpless, Manny obeyed.

"Just a minute," Honey called, trying to sound calm. Just seeing him at the morgue had been bad enough. She would never be able to talk to him without falling apart. With the revolver in her hand, she carefully opened the locks, then crouched to one side and yanked it open. The gun was pointed at Driscoll. *"Leave me alone!"* she screamed.

Driscoll saw the shiny pistol coming directly at his beltline from behind the door. Leaping to one side, he grabbed toward the tiny wrist that was holding the gun.

Before she had had a chance to say anything else, his rough hands were dragging her forward, almost making her lose her balance.

"Take your hands off me!" she shrieked as Driscoll spun her around in front of him, careful to bend her gun hand toward the floor. He forced the .22 out of her strong grip—surprisingly strong, just the way he remembered it.

"I don't believe you . . . what do you mean, coming in here like this? Scaring me half to death . . ." Honey's eyes were flaming, her chin tilted up defiantly as she stood her ground, daring the big detective to move her.

"That's a helluva way to say hello to an old boyfriend." Driscoll smiled. Then he added, "You know I'm afraid of guns. Remember?"

"You didn't have to try to break the door down," she snapped.

"Before we go any further," Driscoll said, "tell me if you have any other guns in here, and don't lie." His tone was almost threatening.

"No!" Honey's round cheeks, tinged now with rage, were even more prominent. She looked like an angry stuffed animal.

"You sure?"

"Of course I'm sure. . . . You'd better tell me why you're harassing me. Who the hell do you cops think you are, anyway?"

"I'm here," Driscoll replied, seating himself heavily in a chair and beginning to unzip his jacket, "because somebody blew up your father." Honey recoiled when he said that. "What happened between us isn't important. What happened to your father is—at least it is to me. So you'd better sit and listen."

Honey sat down across from him, making sure that the long robe covered her knees and legs. But Driscoll's eyes never left her face. He was searching for that look—the one she used to have whenever she saw him, the one that made her toast-brown eyes melt his.

"Why can't this wait until morning?" Her voice was sullen.

"If some bastard had murdered my father," he said with just the right inflection on "my," "there's no way I'd let anything wait. I'm sorry I frightened you, but I couldn't trust the Fat Man here. He would have sent you out the back door." Driscoll was in the bedroom, but Manny had remained in the hall; he didn't have the energy to fight Driscoll. "You were crazy to even come here," Driscoll said. "You need all the protection you can get now."

Again, Manny fought to push himself out of the chair, but he couldn't. He made a loud groaning sound. Honey ran out of the bedroom to him, ignoring Driscoll. She knelt at his side and buried her head in the great cavern of his lap.

"I was afraid something had happened to you," she said. "He didn't hurt you, did he?" Honey turned in Driscoll's direction.

"No," Manny began, gently raising her head and stroking her soft hair, "but he practically broke in here. I couldn't keep him out."

Honey was worried. Manny's face had paled from its normal splotchy red to a deadly gray. His eyes were submerged in twin seas of small ugly red veins. The agitated noise of his breathing filled the room. She knew he was trying hard to pull himself together for her sake.

"I'm fine," Manny told her. "Just answer his questions so we can get rid of him." Manny watched her as she returned to the bedroom. She was pacing again, using those lovely slender hands as eloquent, emphatic decorations for her body. Nervously, she played with the ring on her middle finger, turning the small stone in toward her palm. She wanted to hide it.

Driscoll caught the ring action. Five years ago he had given her that ring. Honey was still wearing it. He began to question her. "Now tell me, why the gun? Has somebody threatened you, too?" That was exactly what he had been afraid of. That's why he had come.

But Honey was still being obstinate. "I always sleep with a gun," she said sulkily. "I didn't kill my father. Why aren't you out there trying to catch whoever did do it? What's all this about, anyway?"

"That's what I want you to tell me," Driscoll replied, reaching into his shirt pocket for a small notebook and pen.

Infuriated, Honey Presto sighed and resigned herself to the interrogation that she knew was coming.

"Can we discuss this alone?" Driscoll pointed to Manny, still stuck in the chair.

Honey went over to him and pulled his arms forcefully, but not roughly. Finally, he got to his feet. "I'll be here if you need me," he said, and he kissed her cheek. Annoyed, pretending he wasn't noticing what was going on, Driscoll glanced up from the notebook. "How about making a pot of tea," he said. "It's been a long day. No cream or sugar. You remember?" He went back to scribbling on the notepad.

"Tea? I don't believe this." Her hands were on her hips. "Forget it. I don't want to play house with you anymore. *Never.*"

But Driscoll knew that she was remembering.

Then Honey, her shoulders trembling, stomped angrily out of the bedroom and headed for Manny's kitchen.

Phillip Driscoll smiled to himself. The same old Honey. Coming at him with a .22. It was just like she had never left him.

HOLLOW STREAM, VIRGINIA

A smug look was beginning to spread across Ed Bellows's wide brown face. That expression always gave him away whenever he was on the verge of solving some particularly complex problem.

Shortly before he had lapsed back into unconsciousness, with the attending nurses and physicians imploring Bellows to leave the hospital room, Carney had revealed most of his dealings with the Meatman. Bellows was picking up the rest on his own.

It hadn't all come together yet, but Bellows knew that he was on the right track. Working with Carney's outline, he was determined to fill in the details himself. Bellows had been at it for nearly two hours, crouching his huge frame over the green screen of one of Hollow Stream's most sophisticated computers. Bellows was balanced precariously on a swiveling desk chair normally used by a computer programmer. Every time he moved, the springs and ball bearings complained under his weight. In the microprocessing, instantaneously decoding world of this hardware that was used to conduct white-collar criminal investigations, two hours was like an eternity.

Bellows knew that for the last year, a significant amount of money had moved between Paul Presto's offshore accounts, including the ones that were in other people's names, and an institution called Bank Handlowy. All of this had made Carney extremely curious when it had first been brought to his attention and had been the impetus for the initial investigation.

Following Carney's instructions, Bellows programmed the big computers to scan the most active trading partners on both sides of the Iron Curtain. No more than ten minutes into its run, the machine began hammering out data on the green glass screen. Bank Handlowy: corporate identity of the National Bank of Poland in the West. Its assets were staggering, close to $300 billion. There were addresses in New York, Chicago, Philadelphia, and several other American cities. Handlowy also had big operations in Vietnam, Singapore, and the Soviet Union.

Bank Handlowy had been set up in the United States in 1947 for trading purposes, then reincarnated every time financial conditions in Europe demanded reorganization. It was an international clearinghouse for Warsaw Pact nations with strong ties in Zurich, transmitting their hard currency abroad in exchange for consumer items and vice versa. Everything was done via electronic bank drafts. It was like a private bank for the best-connected, most influential members of the government and the party from Berlin to Moscow. Bellows could grasp the principle behind the operations even though he had never investigated a Hydra with this many heads.

Paul Presto or one of his surrogates must have been doing one hell of a lot of business with Handlowy or one of its unlisted client banks in eastern Europe.

The payments received by Handlowy from Presto always went for "special consignments." No other description. The funds were deposited into Bank Handlowy, where they conveniently disappeared. Handlowy did not hold any money. It merely acted as a middleman, taking a hefty commission for processing. Bellows guessed that that cash—the cash from the Mafia—was sitting in someone's account in Zurich right now. But whose account?

Back in the hospital, Carney had revealed to Bellows what those "special consignments" consisted of—at least as much as he knew. Apparently, the CIA had become aware of this pattern, too, at about the same time that Carney had picked it up. The CIA had been attempting to figure it out without tipping off Bank Handlowy about its suspicions, and it was at that point that Carney had made contact with Paul Presto on a one-to-one, man-to-man basis.

Bellows already knew what the Meatman's response to Carney had been. Gangster or not, he was still a flag-waver, and that was the reason he was dead. Carney had needed Presto, reached out to him, and used him. Carney was the best. Almost casually ruthless. Now Carney had to depend on Bellows to see it through with an equal degree of remorseless efficiency.

The computer Bellows was using was voice-activated. Unaccustomed to conversing with a machine, he spoke slowly, exaggerating each word.

"I understand the big picture," Bellows said, feeling like an ass for talking to a metal box. "What I need now are some predictions based on available data."

"Restate your question, please," the computer instructed.

"Who the hell has the guns now?" Bellows boomed out. "You're the know-it-all."

"Please restate . . ."

"Oh, just shut the hell up!" Bellows shouted at the machine, scowling.

INTERPOL HEADQUARTERS, SAINT-CLOUD

Marcel de Letan smelled of nicotine and sleeplessness, but he had a triumphant expression on his handsome face—not unlike Ed Bellows's, half a world away.

Gaston LeClerc had cut short a staff meeting when he heard that Marcel wanted to see him. The last people were just leaving the conference room as Marcel walked in, a thick file tucked under his arm.

"Do we have something for Philadelphia?" LeClerc asked, his tone upbeat.

"Yes and no," Marcel said. "The only thing I have for them is an apparent ghost. But this ghost is *very* much Malina."

Then Marcel explained. The telefax was a photo of a man called Emil Menschikoff, a cashiered Red Army noncom who had made quite a reputation for himself among criminals from Odessa to Marseilles. Interpol's last contact with him had been as a bodyguard on board a ship that regularly made smuggling runs from one Black Sea port to another. They had no direct confirmation from the Soviet authorities, of course, but unofficially, Marcel had been assured

that Menschikoff had not been seen in the Soviet Union for several years and was presumed dead.

"By whom?" LeClerc demanded, suddenly aware that Interpol's detailed intelligence on every known criminal organization on the globe was spotty, at best, when it came to this damnable Malina.

"KGB," Marcel answered. "They should know. My informant was under the impression that the KGB had killed this Menschikoff themselves."

"Or thought they had," LeClerc corrected.

"But how could a man like this—a gun for hire in Odessa—be living in the United States? In Philadelphia?" The professional concern in Marcel's strained expression was evident. Now that he had secured the information that his friend and superior, Gaston, had wanted, he saw that his problems were only beginning.

"Evidently, the KGB has enemies, too," LeClerc said. "Powerful enemies. The enmity between the KGB and the Malina is bitter. This time, the Malina won. It looks as though Menschikoff—or someone else controlling him—outwitted the Russians as well as the Americans, and I'm afraid, my friend, Interpol, too."

RITTENHOUSE SQUARE

First the day maid, then the night maid had obeyed the "Do Not Disturb" sign on the suite that Whitey had used. The door was locked, and knocking had brought no response. Finally, the assistant manager was called, but he was busy booking Christmas parties at the time, so he sent the house detective, a recently retired cop who had never worked anything more significant than traffic duty at the Mummer's Parade.

Two maids were just behind him, hovering and speaking in rapid Spanish. One was attempting to describe the man

she had seen go in there—Whitey—to the other; the best she could do was twist her face in imitation of his and reach her hand up as far above her head as it would go.

"Fuck!" the house detective said as he fumbled nervously with the passkey.

Arlene was on her stomach when they found her, naked, the top of her head a clotted brown hole where the .45 had opened a grotesque cavity. The maids began shrieking in Spanish and crossing themselves, pointing and gesturing and screaming half-English questions at the unnerved house detective.

He could see where the dried blood had soaked through the pillow and run down the side of the bed, gushing into the carpet beside the night table. There was already a blue tint to her flesh, except around her buttocks—they were still chalk-white, with very light bruises on each cheek, fingertip bruises, where Whitey had gripped her hard, just before he had come.

The detective couldn't figure out if it was rape or not, but he had seen gunshot wounds before. Homicide, for sure.

A maid, blessing her bosom as if her arm and hand were robotic, approached the bed and pulled tentatively at a sheet, feeling that they should cover Arlene's body, at least.

"Leave it!" the house detective ordered. "Don't you people know nothin'? You can't disturb a thing at a crime scene. That sheet could have prints all over it. Now just leave it."

They backed away from him, cowed, hoping that they weren't in any trouble now.

He dropped to his hands and knees to look at her from different angles. Then he peeked at her face, pressed against her shoulder, most of it hidden by the bloodstained pillow. Just what the detective was afraid of—*her eyes were open!*

The room looked as though no one had even been in there. No signs of a struggle. By this time the maids were gone and he could hear a growing commotion out in the hall; he recognized the assistant manager's shrill voice, spitting out the few Spanish words he knew, trying to shape them into questions.

Using his handkerchief, the detective dialed the police

number, 911. "I need the desk man in Homicide," he told the dispatcher.

TICONDEROGA ROD AND GUN CLUB, QUEENS, NEW YORK

Don Antonio Coia, seventy-three, with a body as stout as a wood-burning stove and a jowl-encircled face that fluctuated between the passive features of a sleeping bulldog and the angry twitches of an aroused gargoyle, appeared to be dozing in his barber's chair. The chair was in the center of the largest room in the Ticonderoga Rod and Gun Club, a short, fat red-brick building that aped the massive architecture of its owner. The club was on the corner of a busy street in Queens—the two buildings on either side were vacant. Don Antonio's men manned the windows and rooftops in those buildings around the clock; theirs was the safest neighborhood in all of New York, perhaps all of America. Little children could play in the street at midnight; young virgins could walk the darkest alleys unmolested; burglars who were dumb enough to steal in the neighborhood gave back the items they had taken as soon as they discovered that they had violated the great Don's personal fiefdom. Coia was the boss of all bosses, the chairman of the *commissione,* the *capo di tutti capi* of organized crime in the United States. He also happened to have been the best man at Paul "Meatman" Presto's wedding; he had paid for the dress that little Honoria had worn at her christening, and as soon as he learned of the Meatman's assassination, Coia had entered a self-imposed period of introspection and mourning. His was the largest Cosa Nostra army outside Italy; the Five Families of New York responded to his every whim; seven Atlantic City casinos had named suites in his honor. All

this, and Coia had been unable to save the life of his friend Paul Presto. At the news of the murder, Coia had wept. Now he wanted nothing more than to make other people weep for that crime. Only the *commissione* could sanction the taking of a life as valuable, as revered, as that of Presto. And the *commissione* had given no one permission.

"How many does this make?" Coia had asked one of his sons when the word came in about Presto.

"Five," the son said. "Gabe Scalpato in New Orleans was the last one before Presto. Then, before him, Frankie Pips in Kansas City and—"

"Enough!" Coia had roared. "You say that list so many times and maybe next time your old man's name will be on it."

The son was silent. Then he said, "Pop, we got guys with machine guns all over you, twenty-four hours. I don't care who this is—they can't get near you."

Coia looked at his son fondly. But he had known that his son was wrong. Anybody could get to anybody. The trouble was, Antonio Coia wasn't ready to go yet.

Coia had been a barber, which was why he spent all of his important thinking time in a barber's chair. It was like his desk and his shrink's couch. And his command post.

Almost asleep, as he usually was during periods of deep concentration, he could feel the girl lifting his foot to the padded footrest, red leather, cracking from use and age. Moments later, he sighed as the warm, soapy water from her bowl began to bathe his toes in a small fragrant pool of cleanliness. His twice-weekly pedicure was about to begin. Her touch was light and sure.

No one spoke during his pedicure. The men in the club, which had never once functioned as a club for hunting or fishing or anything else, sat in various stages of tension against the walls and near the rear. There was only the smallest, most functional of windows opening onto the busy street. But no one sat close to that. Too many people like Presto had been killed lately. They all knew the Meatman here; most of them had even liked him. The ones who had seen him with Honey had all experienced the same electrifying hard-on as soon as they were near her.

Every man in the club, especially Coia's two middle-aged

sons, was worried about the same thing. No one, however, would express that worry or act on it until Don Antonio spoke his mind. Protocol had to be observed.

"The big toe . . . more . . . the nail feels rough," Coia said to the pedicure girl, without opening his veiny eyelids. "That's better."

She was finished in twenty minutes, carefully replacing his shoes and cleaning away any sign that she had been there. Coia was fastidiously neat. As soon as she was let out the back door, with a crisp $100 bill in her apron pocket, the Don's council of war commenced.

As he lay back listening, thinking of what he would say, he heard much uncomfortable shifting of buttocks and seats, some shuffling of feet, a glass of water being poured—at a moment like this there was bound to be more than one dry throat in the room—and the inevitable standing and pulling at crotches as starchy shirt tails cut into the sensitive skin of scrotums. Only when there was absolute, utter, impenetrable silence did Don Antonio speak.

"I got a decision to make," Coia announced to his men under his hooded lids. As he continued, he cleared his throat of wet phlegm, then raised a handkerchief to his lips, nearly pursing them. "All of a sudden, I have a problem in Philadelphia, and it's not the only problem. Just the latest problem. You follow me so far?"

His eldest son spoke first. "We follow you, Pop," he said, "but I see no reason for you to bail out the Prestos. They got a fight with the Russians, they take care of it themselves. Why get involved?"

Coia hated for either of his sons to sound stupid or inept in the art of leadership in front of the other men. Now this son was doing both. Coia, his red eyes open now, leaned over from the height of the barber's chair and drove a small, tight fist into the chest of the man nearest him. He was hopeful that his sons would get the message without his actually embarrassing them. *"So?"* Coia thundered. "None of you have told me what I need to know yet!"

All of Coia's men were concerned because he was demanding answers about Paul Presto. They had none to offer the old Don. His anger was apparent. They studied the floor or the ceiling, or traced the intricate scrollwork on the yellowing wallpaper. No one had the courage to make eye contact with Don Antonio.

"Like I say," Coia continued, "I got this problem in Philadelphia. Now, just last night I get the word that a certain person—let's say he was as close to the Meatman as a *consigliere*—he suggests that we have a major sit-down and thrash this thing out as soon as possible. He thinks this is a matter the *commissione* should rule on."

Coia's eldest son was waiting for a break, an out. He saw none. "Go on," he said to his father.

"Well," Coia said, twisting in his chair to face him, "do we go for the sit-down or not?"

"We stay home, Pop!" both sons shouted together.

"We fight where we know the lay of the land if we have to fight at all," said the eldest.

Coia had anticipated this. All the luxuries he had provided for his children had made them cautious conservatives before any of them reached the age of twenty-one. Not for a day, not for an hour, not for a moment of their lives had they ever felt the hunger that had made Don Antonio what he was. It followed, therefore, that when threatened, they could never be expected to realize how much they stood to lose. But Coia realized it. He remembered what it had been like before they were born, when he had nothing, when he was just a soldier in another man's army.

"What happened to the Prestos," he said quietly, "could happen to us all. A long time ago, the Meatman tried to tell me about these Russians, but I thought at the time that it was none of our business. I ignored his warning. He let it go at that, but I knew he always resented it. Now Paul's dead, and now he's convinced me that he was right and I was wrong the only way he could." Coia hoped this was plain enough to penetrate them all.

"So, are you tellin' us to kill all the fuckin' Russian bastards now, before they get a chance to do anything else?" the oldest son asked.

Coia rubbed his index finger and thumb together, as if he were giving the sign for hush money. He did it without even thinking. "Maybe we get the Prestos to kill them for us," Coia said, inflecting his suggestion into a statement. He heard grunts of approval.

"Maybe we give the Russians what they want—the Presto territory?" his son suggested, trying to sound as wise and clever as his father.

Coia glared at his middle-aged child. "We pay tribute to no one," he said sternly. Then he added, "Besides, if anyone takes over Paul's Family, *we* do, and we do it quick, before somebody else gets the same idea. The Meatman had a nice little thing going for himself down in Philly. You wanta give that to the Russians? We got enough problems with them here in New York on Brighton Beach. You can't make a deal with people like that. You give them money, they take your house; you give them your house, they fuck your wife; you give them your wife, they steal your children. All you can do is kill them. Or, better yet, get somebody else to kill them for you."

"So what about Honey Presto?" the eldest son asked.

Don Antonio allowed himself a look of regal disdain. "You afraid of a woman now?" he demanded. "All Honey needs is a man to keep her in line."

Coia shut his eyes again and replayed the words of the Presto emissary in his mind. "Where did they say they wanted to have the meet?" he asked his son.

"Someplace in Philly. Some restaurant I never heard of," his eldest son explained, addressing the full war council. "Out in the suburbs. They said to just come in like it was a private party. Leave the same night. Short and sweet. As many of the *commissione* as can make it. They'll provide the security. No problem with the cops. In fact, if we need the local cops that night for something, we got some friends there, too."

"Where in the suburbs?" Coia asked again.

"Willows Hills, near the Schuylkill Expressway."

"So, if we get there and don't like the way it looks, we can turn right around and come home?"

"I guess so, Pop."

"So, where's the problem?"

"Pop! Somebody else is getting killed every week! That's the problem. Let's lay low. See what happens."

"We're like rats all of a sudden? We aren't men who can come out and take the streets back if we have to?"

They knew better than to answer.

"I like this sit-down in Philly. Nobody would ever suspect it would be there. Too damn cold. They think we go Florida or someplace like that. We get in and out in a few hours. Maybe they can tell us some things we don't know, too. Maybe some people in the other cities know more than they tell us, too. If we see them face to face, man to man, that can't hurt."

It was no use arguing. They would bring as much firepower as they could fit in the cars. "Pop," the oldest said, "I hope we won't have to fight our way out of this fuckin' sit-down. I don't like it."

"Maybe we will," Coia said, touched that his grown sons still cared for him. "And maybe it's just as well we do it now. Get it over with. You can't fight a shadow. And right now, that's what these damn Russians are. Shadows."

TWENTY

NOBLE STREET

"You *have* to have some idea who killed him," Driscoll said, counting on the fact that over the course of the last five years Honey had learned more about her father's business than she knew when he had first met her.

"You're just as bad as the rest of them," Honey said. "You're just a lousy cop, too. How do *I* know who killed my father? If I did, do you think I'd be sitting here talking to you?" Honey sounded as if there were a firing squad lining up, locking and loading somewhere in her heart. "I don't need *you* to kill whoever did it. I can do that myself," she added.

"I bet you can."

"Driscoll," she said, "why don't you get up off your ass and go out and do your job. Whoever killed my father isn't in here with me and Manny."

"Don't be so sure about that."

"Me?" Honey asked quizzically. "Manny?" She sneered at him. "If that's the best you can do, boy, Phil, you're really washed up."

"Still a bitch," he answered.

"So you're no better!" she screamed. "Go do your job! You probably let him get killed. You cops always know when somebody's supposed to get it. You used to tell me that yourself, Phil. You *know* you did."

"Not this time, Honey. Nobody knew."

"Bullshit!" she screamed again.

"Who hit the bank where Joe-Joey was sitting collecting that night?" he asked. "You got any ideas about that, smart mouth?"

"What bank?"

"You mean you don't know?" Driscoll asked, surprised, but certain that Honey wasn't lying to him. She had never lied about things like this, only about how she felt about him. As he talked and gestured, he almost knocked over the cup of tea she had poured for him.

Honey was trying hard to conceal the fact that she really *didn't* know about the bank. Why hadn't someone—Aunt Marie, Uncle Tony, Joe-Joey—told her? Or Manny? Manny knew about *everything* that happened.

"Clumsy," she spat out, remembering that Phillip had done practically the same thing with a glass of wine that first night they had been together.

"Of course I know about the bank—what do you think I am? I just forgot, that's all," she lied.

"Bullshit," he said, mimicking her small, husky voice. "You don't know a thing about it. They didn't tell you. Nice family, Honey. You can *really* trust them, can't you? Great people—especially Uncle Tony."

"Shut up!" she yelled. *"Just shut up!"*

"Make me."

Honey took a swing at him; not a slap such as most women would have tried, but the sort of neat, economic jab that she had to have learned from the old man. It was a nice punch for a small woman like Honey. Actually, it was a *great* punch, landing solidly on Driscoll's breastbone.

"Nice move," he said, as she started to hit him again. "You're really a class act. Can't deny those genes, can you? Just like your old man." He was fading a little under her blows—they *were* beginning to hurt—backpedaling and bobbing from side to side.

Finally, she was exhausted and just collapsed into a chair. She had never felt so frustrated, so tired. Phillip felt sorry for her. She hid her face in her hands, determined that he wouldn't see her cry. She had too much pride for that. "Go away, please. Now."

But Driscoll wasn't about to leave. "Not this time. No

rerun." He had to know, had to ask—*why?* Just saying it was like showing a passport at the border. The tension dissolved. "Why did you leave that night? We said we could work it out."

"Go!" Honey screamed again, five years of longing and denial surging out of her with that single syllable. "I don't want you anymore. I never wanted you. I never needed you. You were nothing but a dare—I wanted to show my father how grown-up I was. I *used* you, Phillip. Don't you know that?" As much as she wanted to, Honey couldn't find the words. "I couldn't admit that I needed *them.* My father's people, his Family. But I was wrong. I learned that too late. Blood is blood."

"It isn't too late for us." He moved closer to her and could feel the heat burning through her small body.

"It was too late for us before we started," she said. "It always will be."

"Don't be afraid of a goddamn ghost," he said. "Your father's dead. Everything's changed now. Are you gonna let him reach back from the grave and keep using you? That's all this is. You don't have to be loyal anymore. There's nobody left to be loyal to. You aren't his *son*—nobody expects you to do a thing. Let it alone."

Honey was seething. "Nobody but me." Then she added, "And the Meatman. This is the last thing I can do for my father. Don't try to stop me."

He wanted to shake some sense into her, but that approach would never work with Honey. "Save yourself," he said. "Use your head. You can't handle this alone."

"You're the one who told me I had to make a choice, remember?"

Driscoll remembered, all right. If he had to pick an exact moment in time when he lost Honey, that was it. Now he could see this chance slipping away, too. He touched her shoulder. It was nothing more than a gesture of friendship, concern, but Honey was too afraid of her own feelings to even accept that. She jumped up and began hitting him again, pounding with both small, balled fists.

"I'll give you the shorthand version," she snapped. "Get lost!" Her deep brown chestnut hair curled around her shoulders, nuzzling the tops of her breasts, the way he used to; she was really flying around now, and all the physical activity had opened her robe just enough for him to glimpse the smooth bareness inside.

At the same instant, they both noticed that he was staring. Honey reddened, quickly pulled the robe tight around her waist, and saw that he was looking away now, almost embarrassed. She thought that was sweet. Suddenly, Honey could feel her body swelling, just from being this near him again. The moisture was spreading from her thighs to her stomach to the lush undersides of her breasts.

It was an awkward moment for both of them as she attempted to conceal what was happening inside her. Driscoll, seldom at a loss for words, especially with a woman, could only fumble for all the things he shouldn't say.

Finally, Honey tried to recover; her tone was normal now, all the forced anger drained out of her. "You look great," she said, somehow noticing him, really seeing him again for the very first time. "Different than I remembered you, but still great. You're a lot grayer, Phillip."

Momentarily, he touched his hair, then shrugged it off. "You, too," he said, practically whispering. "Different, too. I mean . . . better."

Honey's smile was luminous. "You mean older?" she said, as she sat on the edge of the bed, her face tilted up at him on an angle.

Driscoll shook his head back and forth as if there were a debate raging inside of him. "I remembered a girl; now I'm looking at a woman. All I know is, it's better. Can't you leave it at that?" Honey never could.

Driscoll closed the bedroom door and locked it. Then he moved toward Honey. He expected her to put up more of a fight, but she just sagged against the quilt, then curled up and began sobbing into his shoulder. Driscoll couldn't be sure whether she was crying for them and for what they had lost, or for her father. He held her tightly, her hot tears dampening his shirt and jacket. He wanted to kiss her but didn't. A few minutes later, he finally got her to stop, but her dark eyes were red and her face a mess of running mascara and streaked makeup. He still thought she looked beautiful. Maybe it was because he was convinced that she had never needed him more. When he put his arm around her, she didn't make the slightest effort to move away from him, but instead moved into him so that her nipples crushed against his chest.

"Nobody's playing by the rules on this one," Driscoll said, smoothing her hair, his rough fingers responding to the silkiness, "and that includes me. All I want is to find out who killed your father and to make sure that nothing happens to you. I know how much you loved him."

"I still love him."

This time he saw a renewed interest in her. She was thinking now, not merely feeling. "All I ask," Driscoll said tentatively, "is that we do it together. Whatever happens, we catch the killer and save your life."

"And what if my Family beats you to it? You expect me to turn whoever did it over to you?"

That's exactly what Driscoll expected. In fact, he would insist on it. He might be a lot of things, but he wasn't a bad cop. But she didn't want to hear that now. So he said, "If your people get there first, I'll walk away from it. No questions asked." She wanted him to lie, so he did.

"How do I even know I can trust you?"

"You know," he said, leaving the intense feelings they still felt for each other unspoken.

"He was mixed up with the government," Honey said, then, catching herself, she added, "That's all I can tell you. I don't even know that much more myself."

"With Bellows?"

Honey nodded.

"Was it some kind of a deal? Was he getting ready to go into the Witness Protection Program? If he saw the hit coming, maybe he wanted to get the jump on whoever ordered it."

"No, no," Honey began, exasperated. "The Meatman would never do anything like that. That went against everything he ever believed in. But he *did* expect to be killed."

"How do you know?"

"He told me . . . and Manny."

Driscoll was surprised, but he wanted Honey to go on. "What did he say? Tell me exactly what he said."

"I can't." Honey knew what Phillip was thinking. "It's not that I *won't;* I can't. It's the truth. He made a videotape before he died and told us everything that he suspected, but my father wasn't even sure himself.'' Honey was fumbling for the words again as she got up off the side of Manny's big bed and started to pace, walking so near a sliding glass door that dominated one wall of the room that Driscoll thought she was headed for the deck outside. But she stopped, and turned to face him again. ''My father believed in signs, in premonitions. He was superstitious. He didn't always think, sometimes he just *felt.* But he was usually right.'' She went back to the glass wall again. ''I know it's going to sound so crazy when I say this, but it's what he said on the tape, when he was warning us about who might be trying to have him killed.''

Driscoll listened; he immediately recalled his conversation about the fur store where Vinnie worked—the *Russian* fur store. It was starting to make sense to him now. But he still wondered how much Honey really knew.

Honey was still going on, but not looking at him any longer. ''He said there was this thing; it's called the Malina. Manny knows a little about it . . . he said this Malina was trying to take over, but the other Families wouldn't listen to my father when he warned them.''

''Russians!'' Driscoll said, startling Honey, taking her by such total surprise that she spun around to face him, open-mouthed.

''How did you know . . . ?'' Honey started to ask, but she was interrupted by a shattering *crack!* The air around them was transformed into a hurricane of glass particles, and an ear-splitting clatter, as a projectile ripped through one side of the sliding glass door that overlooked the gray pine deck just off the bedroom. Shards of glass exploded against Honey's back and pin-pricked Driscoll's face and forehead like a deadly hail of shrapnel.

Honey gasped, then cried out, as a jagged splinter of glass lodged itself in the thick curls of her hair, just inches above her neck, close to her vital artery. Instinctively reaching around to cover her body with his, swiveling Honey from the point of impact, Driscoll felt for the glass sliver in her neck. Carefully, he brushed it away, but as he drew his hand back, it was wet with Honey's blood.

''Stay low,'' he ordered, flattening her behind a low

velvet-covered chair. "Is it bad?" Gently separating the strands of her hair, he examined the ugly crimson cut. Honey was being tough. "I can't even feel it," she said through clenched teeth.

"The hell you can't."

"What about you? Are you hurt?" She was holding his wrist, pressing something hard into his hand. He looked down and felt the tiny .22. He mouthed the word "no" silently and put his fingers to his lips. The shot had just missed him but had sprayed itself out against the walls of the bedroom in a distorted circle. A shotgun.

They were four flights up. The only way to reach the deck was through the bedroom's glass doors. There was a fire escape outside, too—dull black iron, like an old tenement fire escape, telescoped above the pavement like a huge, narrow accordion. It wouldn't have been that hard to leap from the fire escape to the deck, get off one shot, and jump back. Driscoll figured that's how it had been done.

But where the hell was Manny? As soon as he heard the gunfire, he should have been in the bedroom at Honey's side. But he wasn't. That could only mean that he couldn't respond, perhaps that he was dead. Driscoll didn't particularly care which it was.

"Stay put," he whispered to Honey, but she began to get up, raising herself onto one knee. "Your neck," he said, concerned about the bleeding.

Honey-like, even now, she responded, "I said I'm fine."

"Keep it that way."

He crossed to the bed, crouched, then pressed himself flat against the wall nearest the broken glass. There was a full, milky moon outside, a brilliant dollop of color against the wet, wintry sky. It reflected on the deck, where a single empty shell casing, fat and brass-colored, lay amid the broken glass, much of it pulverized into sharp, crystallized powder by the force of the explosion. A shotgun casing.

Gripping the .22, he held it hand over hand, brought it up level with his eyes, and cautiously moved through the doorframe, crouching on the debris-covered floor. The deck was clear. Driscoll had been holding his breath. When it came, the physical release in his tight throat and heaving chest was welcome. The .22 felt odd, too light, too small, like a toy.

Now the fire escape. He started in that direction.

From her hiding place on the floor, Honey could see Driscoll's unshined wingtips start, then stop, in rapid flashes of movement. She wondered what was happening out there. Her heart was pounding and she couldn't control her trembling.

The outside wall next to the deck was red brick, badly in need of pointing. As Driscoll's back brushed against the rough surface, motes of dust and tiny chucks of dry, frozen mortar rubbed off on the green material of his jacket. Deftly, he inched toward the place where he would have to jump onto the fire escape, hugging the red bricks as he moved cautiously along, all too aware of the easy target he made in the moonglow.

He turned; pushed against the heavy metal steps, heard them begin clanging down as they reached their full length, and looked into the blackness. It was like staring into the pit of a bottomless well. No one was visible. He waited a few seconds, listened and searched the night. And that's when he heard it—the muffled thud of running feet four flights down. The cop stood motionless.

Still in her robe and barefoot, Honey had ventured from her hiding place behind the chair and traced Driscoll's steps to the glass door, unseen by him. She waited, tried to see what he was doing, pressed her nose against the smashed doorframe, and looked in his direction on tiptoes as he jumped from the deck to the fire escape.

Driscoll realized that someone had removed the outside bulbs from the mesh-covered safety lights that marked each floor of the hulking old building. Suddenly he saw the flash of a long double-barrel leveled in his direction. He brought up his .22 and aimed at the spot where he had noticed the flash. The shooter was below him, firing upward.

Just then, up above him, at the rear of the deck, Honey pressed her whole round face through the opening of the door that remained, struggling to make out the scene below her, but as she did so, the damaged door pulled loose from the flat metal track—the *screech* of metal on metal.

Startled by the noise, she let out a small cry just as Driscoll spun around, aiming the gun in her direction. Honey screamed. He looked. He couldn't believe it was her. Everything was happening at once.

At that very instant, a shotgun blast ripped across the red-brick wall, shattering his eardrums with a deafening blast, as fragments, minute chunks of brick, pelted his head and face, like a shower, cutting him badly.

Then he saw Manny, down on the pavement, walking in a dazed, wobbly way, holding his head where he must have been hit. The Fat Man had heard the gunfire and finally come out to see what was happening. But now Manny was in the way.

The force of the massive discharge narrowly missed Driscoll's head. Up on the deck, Honey was screaming in terror. She kept calling his name.

The fire-escape steps rattled and vibrated as Driscoll saw his attacker dash away, shotgun in hand, leaping the last few feet, spinning past Manny.

He aimed the .22, cocked the trigger, but it was no use. There wasn't anything left to shoot at. He wanted to go after whoever had fired at him, but he heard Honey sobbing. Cursing her and his missed shot, Driscoll ran back up the steps to make sure that she was all right.

TWENTY-ONE

KHODINKA BARRACKS, THE OUTSKIRTS OF MOSCOW

Marshal Zinijakin eased his tall, stiff, arthritic body into the soft leather armchair in his barracks sitting room and thoughtfully reappraised each word of the conversation he had held an hour before with the new Chairman. He could have demanded an apartment in Moscow, an elaborate affair that would rival any housing the *apparatchiks* were entitled to, but the marshal still believed that a commander's place was among his troops. The *apparatchiks,* bloodsuckers and political whores, every last one of them, mistrusted Zinijakin for staying at the barracks, but damn their souls—Zinijakin preferred the company of men—of soldiers. His wife had been dead for ten years now; the light of his life. There was no one left to please except himself.

Lately he had been reconstructing most of his important conversations; he wasn't sure if that was a sign of caution or old age. But at this point in his life, he didn't really care.

The new Chairman had welcomed him warmly, deferentially even, bowing slightly as he gauged the vigor and conviction in the marshal's countenance.

The younger man had waited for the older man to set the tone of the meeting. Even Zinijakin could find no fault with that. This new Chairman never kept him waiting, either. But deep down he knew that it was all pretense. This new regime would love nothing better than to replace him. But for the moment, at least, Zinijakin still held the respect of the military and the GRU. The new Chairman could afford to wait—Zinijakin wouldn't live forever. They knew he was loyal; he had shed his blood for the Motherland and he would do so again, eagerly. He was a soldier. He had made his eternal peace with mortality.

"And what do you propose to do?" the Chairman had asked him, after he outlined Zhukov's apparent defection plan, the one that Tanya's secret tape recording had helped firm up.

"Absolutely nothing," had been Zinijakin's startling reply. He knew that the Chairman had expected him to ask permission to arrest Zhukov, at least, if not kill him.

"Why?"

"Because we propose to catch him and his cohorts in the United States and deal with them there," Zinijakin explained, almost telling the Chairman the truth. "If we do anything to him here, in Russia, it will look like one more feud between the KGB and the military, the GRU."

The Chairman had listened intently, reaching across his desk to open a cedar humidor from the back and offer the marshal a Cuban perfecto. Zinijakin declined with a curt nod. "That would put you and your colleagues in a difficult position," Zinijakin said, "appearing as it would that you were sanctioning the GRU to take action against a KGB man as prominent as Zhukov." Then he added sincerely, "Not that I won't miss the opportunity to kill the traitor myself."

The Chairman looked thoughtful, then his mouth—almost a fish's mouth with its wide arc, reaching back to just below his earlobes, ravenous, scooping up smaller fish as it trolled the murky waters—lowered its jaw into the most artificial grin that Zinijakin had ever seen. "Your grasp of politics never ceases to amaze me, Marshal Zinijakin. You truly understand the essence of balance—the party, the military, the KGB. Each must be accommodated and made to feel that it has not been slighted in favor of the other. Such is the genius of our system—each element a watchdog on the others."

"I know," Zinijakin said. "I learned that under Josef

Stalin. No man ever studied with a more demanding mentor."

"Quite."

"I have your permission then?" He waited for a reply.

Pensively, the Chairman continued. "Do you know what it is that Zhukov is selling the American? You haven't given me many specifics."

Zinijakin knew that was quite correct. But he had done so on purpose. "Accuracy, Comrade Chairman. I pride myself on it. So does my GRU. When we are certain—truly certain—I will inform you personally. Until then, I prefer to limit our discussion of those specifics." Another half-lie, but necessary.

"You agree, my request is not unreasonable." The Chairman was expecting some acknowledgment of his position from the older man; his eyes were downcast, condescendingly so.

Zinijakin hated these petty power games. But they too were necessary. "Esteemed Chairman," Zinijakin replied, nearly choking on each word, "the only thing unreasonable is my delay in providing you with the information. But I am sure you will indulge an old warrior on this point. Then, again, I may have grown too careful in my old age."

Now it was the Chairman's turn. "You honor us with your long and courageous service, marshal. I pledge you my support until such time as you decide to step aside." He came around from behind his desk and began to spin an ornate wooden globe of the world that stood on the three carved lion's-claw legs. "I know I can count on your continued support with the loyal troops of the armed forces." He was turning the globe in ever-increasing revolutions. Abruptly, the Chairman stopped and thrust a manicured finger at the light blue outline that identified the United States. The finger remained there.

"I only hope to serve the Motherland for many years to come. I don't mind saying I feel as fit as a recruit."

The Chairman raised an eyebrow visibly at that assertion. They both knew that Zinijakin was ailing and almost certain to be forced into retirement soon. But "forced" by whom and under what circumstances?

"Never fear, my old friend."

Zinijakin was not his old friend; the two men, separated by generations, barely knew each other. The marshal bristled at such familiarity from a young pup.

"The timing," the Chairman continued, "will be up to you. I have no intention of looking over your shoulder. I have a reputation, I am told, for replacing the old with the new—forcing out loyal, long-standing party officials and replacing them with men of my own choosing, *younger* men—"

Zinijakin cut in. "I am not aware of anyone being replaced who did not need replacing," he said diplomatically.

The Chairman smiled that hungry grin again. "Precisely," he said. "You may be an honored grandfather as far as my contemporaries are concerned, but you remain flexible enough to see that what I do I do for the good of all the Russians."

"I'm to stay in my present command, then?" Zinijakin asked.

"For just as long as it benefits both of us—which I'm sure will be a *very* long time."

Zinijakin was ready to leave, but the Chairman had one more question. "Your plan to remove Comrade Zhukov on American soil . . ." He was playing with the globe of the world again. "That's expedient for us, troublesome for them, wouldn't you say? I can't believe they will accept it without protest. The form that their protest will take . . . *that* concerns me."

Zinijakin looked at the Chairman. "Soon, you will be sitting down with the American President in Geneva. Arms control again. The American public demands that he return with something substantial this time. It is, as they say, an election year. You, comrade, are the only person in the world who can give the American President what he has come so far to obtain. You can give him the illusion—the promise, to put a better face on it—of peace. Mention this *other* matter to him—it amounts to nothing more than housecleaning."

The Chairman looked as though he could not give Zinijakin what he wanted. "I can hardly tell him that we are asking his permission to commit murder in his country." He was already anticipating what he would have to tell the American leader at this historic Christmas Arms Control Summit, a publicity coup for both.

"The mechanics are irrelevant," Zinijakin said. "Let the Americans have one of their people do the killing for us. Have someone on your staff broach the subject. As long as they understand, it will be done—regardless." Zinijakin walked to a window and pulled the drape aside. Misty out, a fog was seeping into the capital from the rivers.

The Chairman was behind his desk again. The room had darkened noticeably.

"In his place, wouldn't you agree to it?" Zinijakin asked quietly.

The Chairman reached for one of the cigars, took a sleek lighter, black with tortoise inlay, from his trousers pocket and proceeded to set the tip of the perfecto glowing. Talking with the cigar in his mouth, the Chairman said, "I repeat, my old friend, your grasp of politics is nothing less than uncanny." He emitted an almost perfect circle of gray-brown smoke. "This is a filthy habit, but I picked it up in America. They call this the ultimate status symbol over there."

"Phallic, as well."

That *was* impertinent, but Zinijakin didn't give a damn.

"Perhaps I worry too much. . . . *Of course* the Americans will have to accept our terms at Geneva—*all* of our terms." He held the long, thin cigar like a wand and pointed it in the marshal's direction. "Carry on, my old friend. Deal with the traitor Zhukov as you will, as you must. Leave the KGB, and the Americans, to me." Then he dismissed Zinijakin with a smile and a flick of cigar ash. "Tell my chief of staff what has to be done and he will deliver the message to his opposite number in the U.S. delegation. We'll be firm."

Unsmiling, the old marshal walked out of the new Chairman's office, limping just a little, but still as straight, as soldierly as one of the eighteen-year-olds parading for the tourists in Red Square.

All of it was still vivid, as Zinijakin mused in his barracks. He considered his adversary. Zhukov, you are not merely bold, but march-up-to-the-cannon bold. Damn you! You are an able man gone bad; a man who must be stopped.

Clearing his throat, Zinijakin harrumphed loudly.

No, the old marshal resolved, we will not alter Zhukov's plans. We want him to reach the United States and we want him to reach it safely—for that is part of our plan. Let the traitor make his tracks. Zinijakin will follow.

The marshal harrumphed again and attempted to stretch out a recalcitrant knee, extending it along the length of a small streamer truck at the foot of his bunk. In the Great Patriotic War against the Nazis, he had taken some shrapnel in that knee when he and his men ambushed a German convoy less than five kilometers from Moscow. The knee had healed, but on damp days the pain would be there for the rest of his life to remind him. To the best of the marshal's extensive knowledge about Mikhail Zhukov, that sniveling little KGB mongrel had never seen combat anywhere, never come close to a wound. He was an *apparatchik* like the rest of them, a well-placed party toad. There had not been a generation of *real* men born since the war, since the days when he had been young. The new regime included. *Especially* this new regime, strutting diplomats and pansies always aping the ways of the Americans, like their damn Cuban cigars. They were all so soft.

Zinijakin harrumphed one last time, roaring like some angry old lion.

NOBLE STREET

Pressing his eyesockets against his infrared binoculars, Whitey twisted the small round device between the lenses and focused. The recently unfolding tableau had been as interesting as it was becoming worrisome.

After he had left the deli, Whitey had returned to the loft, hoping that Honey might come out with either the cop or the Fat Man, and that would give him his opportunity for a clear shot. Instead, Whitey had watched in amazement as another car pulled up outside the warehouse, this time with two silhouettes in it. The one who got out was tough-looking and wily, carrying a gun. Whitey recognized him immediately. He went about his job deliberately, first casing the closed deli, then breaking in through a rear service door, like an experienced burglar. After several minutes he re-emerged and scaled the fire escape at the back of the building. Whitey had seen and heard all of it: the first boom of the shotgun, the man racing down from the deck, the cop he had encountered in the deli pursuing the man with the shotgun. Then, lastly, the second volley from the big gun and the disappearance of the cop. Finally, Whitey observed the shooter make good his escape as the getaway car returned, tires peeling rubber and the passenger door flung open. All that mattered to him was that somebody *else* was trying to kill Honey Presto.

He pondered the alarming implications of that discovery. His client would have to be informed at once. Unless . . . unless this other killer had been brought in on *his* job. Whitey was infuriated that someone was trying to cheat him out of a big payday. But it was even more than that. This was a question of principle—of professional pride. It struck at the heart of the brutal ethics of Whitey's trade. The Presto girl was his. No one else's. His contract. His responsibility.

What the hell was going on? Had his client brought in this second man? Whitey had to find out. He wouldn't stand still for an insult like that.

Crouched like an animal in the cold loft, Whitey's mood quickly changed, and his thoughts refocused on Honey Presto. Was she even still alive? What if the first shot had gotten her? What about the cop? He needed some answers fast.

He wished he could be in two places at the same time. As he looked after the speeding car, he could still pick up the taillights. Should he follow it or stay put?'

Reluctantly, Whitey decided that he had to abandon his hiding place, assume that Honey was still alive, and find out why these other people were trying to kill her. He rushed down from his perch in the loft.

BUSTLETON

After the attack on his restaurant at Brighton Beach, Butkova had dressed his own wounds as best he could and driven back to Philadelphia, in agony every mile of the long trip. When he finally slid out of the car and crawled into his house, there were bright red bloodstains in the driver's seat.

He had remained in bed, knowing that his body could not be rushed in its healing process. Only once did he set foot outside, and then he only walked down the six concrete steps that marked the front door, set off to the side, as was the style in his part of Northeast Philadelphia.

He lived in a modest twin house, not unlike the Meatman's. There was a small lawn out front, lumpy with the frozen earth of winter. But in the spring, his garden came alive with the fragrance of hyacinths and trumpet-shaped azalea blooms, red, pink, yellow, and purple. Butkova tended to the garden himself. His block was crowded with driveways. Clotheslines were hung with laundered bed linens; stick-ball was played by screaming children. These neighbors thought of Butkova as an exceedingly gentle, introspective, and harmless man. A good Russian, as he knew they called him.

The restaurant fire had been the counterattack of the vengeful Prestos, who he knew must have set it. The flames had burned the coat right off his back, but he was used to injuries, and after nearly forty-eight hours his back looked badly sunburned, no worse.

He was sitting on a stool in the bathroom, waiting for Svetlana to come in. He had sent her to the drugstore to get ointment for his back. In a little while, he heard the door slam. He tried to turn around, but for some reason, the pain was bad today. Butkova merely leaned forward, his face in his hands. The medicine would soothe him.

He heard her come in, making slight noises on the tile floor of the bathroom as she approached. Butkova said something in Russian, but Svetlana didn't answer. Busy, he supposed.

"Did you get it?" he asked, as she began spreading the

balm across his back with feathery touches. He eased backward as the pain subsided. Most of his people were also in Philadelphia now, called down from Brighton Beach. He was sure that the Prestos weren't done with him yet. They were poised, awaiting his command.

"Feels good," he said, without looking up. "The pain is going."

Suddenly, a small, dry pair of hands, the softest hands he had ever felt—nothing like Svetlana's strong, able peasant hands—covered his eyes. He spun around on the stool, trying to get up.

Tanya stopped him.

"It's all right," she said merrily. "Boris is on guard outside, and Svetlana let me in."

Butkova was so surprised, so shocked to be seeing her here, like *this,* in his own house, in his own bathroom, that he hardly knew what to say. "How?" he began. "When?"

"Just a few hours ago. A flight from Moscow to JFK. I checked in at the mission in midtown and came here as soon as I could." Then she kissed him. "Nikolai, I've missed you so much." Her arms were around him, careful to avoid the places where his flesh had blistered.

Exactly one year before Tanya had met Mikhail Zhukov, her lover and KGB patron, she had been finishing her studies at the ancient University of Kiev. Before that, she had been a foundling, another Malina child, not unlike Butkova himself; only the generations had separated them, not their intertwined fates.

Her mother had been a prostitute who died during childbirth, her father unknown. The only family, the only love, the only world she had ever known had been the secret society of the Malina, mother, father and lifegiver to all those it touched, to all those who swore fidelity to its mystic rites and timeless prohibitions. Tanya had been such a child.

The Malina Headman in Odessa had instantly recognized her talents and intelligence and had selected the university course for her. Other such children found their way into the government, the military, the world of commerce, or even the highest echelons of the Communist Party. To the Malina, they were all the same: mere objects to be used in the pursuit of its goals.

Accordingly, arrangements had been made, the proper bureaucrats had been bribed, and Tanya had been guaranteed the finest education available in the Soviet Union.

Butkova had met her once before he left Russia for good, and many times since during her frequent Aeroflot visits to the United States. It had been through Tanya that Butkova had first learned about the existence of a profoundly corrupt KGB official name Mikhail Zhukov. By then the Malina knew of Zhukov's black-market activities and had placed one of their best and most trusted operatives, Tanya, close to him. Her single failing, of course, was her driving, obsessive sexual appetite. A gift from her mother, no doubt, the Headman believed. As it was, they monitored her lovers closely. Butkova had taken Tanya the second time he ever met her. He had been hard with her, demanding, almost brutal, and had been amazed at how much she seemed to enjoy that. From then on, they had spent as much time together as possible, whenever she was in the United States.

"My darling," Butkova said, "I had no idea, I wasn't even expecting you."

"Don't be concerned. It's just a small errand."

As long as she wasn't volunteering information, it had to be Malina business. Butkova didn't probe further. "I trust our esteemed Headman is well, enjoying life? You saw him recently?"

"A while ago, Nikolai, some time ago, in fact. But when I spoke to him, he was well and hoping the same for you."

"I'm touched." Butkova sounded sarcastic.

"Don't be brazen," she said abruptly. "I know that you and our Headman have been friendly rivals, adversaries, even, for many years."

"Since long before you were born," he told her, smiling.

"And you respect him, as he does you. I refuse to be some messenger for mutual insults."

"Of course, you are correct."

She sat on the toilet opposite his stool and began to undo her coat. Even in such a pedestrian setting, she was breathtakingly beautiful, poised, calm, almost regally detached. A czarina. Reaching into her purse, she drew out a slender, tapered Virginia Slims cigarette, tapped it lightly against the washbasin, and reached for a match, brushing aside a strand of golden hair.

"I see you've met our guest," Svetlana said, peeking into the bathroom. Then she left.

"My replacement?" Tanya asked, just a little acidly.

Butkova walked over to her and held her match, making sure to touch her wrist as he did so. He could just catch the hint of her perfume.

"Thank you," Tanya murmured ever so softly. Then she held his leathery hand in hers. The top of each finger bristled with coarse black hair, but she stroked it and squeezed it gently. Nikolai, she thought, it has been too long, so long. Without warning, she kissed him.

When they moved into the bedroom, Tanya's hands slid across his chest, working the healing balm into the tattooed serpent on his arm; the muscle responded to her touch. "So strong, Nikolai," Tanya said huskily. "Such a lover."

He sensed another person there with them. Perhaps it was only his imagination.

Then he turned around and saw Svetlana. He had never expected to see her standing there, next to Tanya. "You can go," he started to say dismissively, but Tanya stopped him.

Tanya had her arm around Svetlana, balancing herself on the larger woman's shoulder, as she began to step out of her leather skirt. In an instant, Svetlana was doing the same. Tanya caressed the other woman's rich, dark hair. "So lovely," she said. "So beautiful, Nikolai—you have good taste, very good taste."

Svetlana blushed. He was on his feet now, the balm still wet across his back, but the pain almost gone. As he watched, Tanya knelt down and removed a garter belt from Svetlana, carefully rolling down the sheer stocking attached to it, first one leg, then the other.

Tanya's hand lingered near the dancer's powerful, muscular thighs, momentarily playing with the curly mound once her panties had come down.

Then Tanya composed herself and quickly removed the rest of her clothes; she seemed almost boyish compared to the ripe, deep curves that burst from Svetlana's young body. They both started pointing to his hardening erection and laughing. It sounded as though they were sharing some secret girlish joke. Tanya was giggling. Their laughter warmed him more than the balm. "You must tell me how this happened," Tanya said to him, brushing her palm across his back, "but not right now."

Both women approached him, first one dropping to her knees in front of him, then the other.

MOSCOW

He had to know whether or not James X. Carney was dead; but dead or alive, Zhukov had to determine who would try to kill him and why. Especially why. He summoned the lieutenant again. "Any more information on Carney's condition?" he demanded, before the young man had even gotten inside the room. He needed a definitive medical report.

"Nothing yet, sir."

"And what may I ask is the holdup?" The reddish vein in Zhukov's neck was popping again, protruding through his thin flesh, just as it had done earlier when he was making love to Tanya.

"I'll get right on it, sir," the lieutenant answered as he hurried out the door.

Carney's files had arrived on his desk about half an hour after he had ordered them, and had proven to be disap pointingly routine: cosmic security clearance; suspected h mosexual—an alert KGB case officer in Washingt stationed at the embassy there, had been trying to work angle for some time, specifically aiming to seduce C through the use of a male prostitute whom the emba used before. But none of this was new informatio certainly didn't explain the attempt on his life.

An hour went by, then two. Mikhail Zhuko still couldn't come up with any more inform

Carney's condition. He seethed, then screamed, then threatened, but it did no good. The KGB, for all its power, all its personnel and all its resources, was failing him again. How he hated infernal bureaucracy.

Disgusted, he summoned his driver and instructed him to take the long way home. Tanya wouldn't be at the apartment waiting for him, and he missed her.

When he used the phrase "the long way," the driver understood that to mean a stopover at Zhukov's dacha, his country home, forty miles outside Moscow. The roads were clear even though the shoulders were packed with plowed snow. He could make it in less than an hour, using the fast left lane, always reserved for the black Volga sedans, their windows always curtained off, used by important party officials.

To help pass the time on the ride and to anesthetize him against the pressure that was building up, Zhukov had brought along a flask of Jack Daniel's bourbon—black-market, another magnificently decadent Western vice.

Zhukov was into his third tumbler and almost beginning to see double when the mobile telephone, located in the backseat console, began to hum. He picked it up and said, "Zhukov here."

It was his lieutenant. He listened for a few moments as all thoughts of his dacha vanished. "Forget the long way," he snapped, leaning forward and tapping his driver on the shoulder. "Return to Moscow immediately." Then he settled back into his comfortable leather seat, twisted the top of the flask, and poured his fourth tumbler. *Carney was still* Zhukov drank to his health.

TWENTY-TWO

SOUTH PHILADELPHIA
TUESDAY NIGHT

Every year the police department took over the same mob joint, Roberto's, in South Philly, for its annual Christmas party. If you had any political ambitions whatsoever, attendance was mandatory; to see and be seen was the order of the night. Police Commissioner Alfred E. Smith Lawlor presided. Nobody dressed as Santa Claus. The drinks were watered and the pigs-in-blankets cold—very few people knew it, but the club had been one of the Meatman's top-earning investments. On the set of books that Presto's lawyers, like Milton Littlejohn, showed tax people, Roberto's bled red, year after year. Actually, however, it practically coined money, netting the Meatman only slightly less—mostly cash—than the money he put out on the street for loan-sharking. In fact, Roberto's had put Honey through college and had kept her in Corvettes since the day she picked up her driver's permit.

Anyone connected with the bench, the Bar, or the cops came. Guys who were actively making a run at rank, promotion, or advancement spent most of the night trying to wash Lawlor's balls, as old Harry Capri liked to put it. He and Driscoll had annually gotten drunk together at this party. This year, however, the big detective was alone. Driscoll had invited him but Harry had taken a pass.

Driscoll was scrunched into a corner, holding up the wall, nursing a ginger ale and successfully talking himself out of reaching for a Silver Bullet.

He had parked on Catherine Street, close to 7th Street, not far from Palumbo's, to avoid the jam of the big lot. As he walked to the club, along the dark, windswept streets, the refuse of the market—rotten lettuce, other spoiled produce, and the smelly, messy remnants of fresh-killed fowl and pork—steamed in little piles near the sewers, making the gutter run iridescent with grease and animal fluids.

He missed the action in the big parking lot, though. Last year he had caught Spanish Joe and Lida in the backseat of a Civil Affairs car—his pants were down and her dress was up. That's the kind of a party it always was. Enough could happen over the course of a few hours to keep potential blackmailers in business for the next year. This was a brutal week to be a murder victim, Driscoll knew. Just try to find a sober cop.

Himself, Alfred E. Smith Lawlor, as usual, had the best spot at the bar, coffee mug in hand. The mug was filled with an amber liquid. Lawlor's elbow was resting on one of the silver dividers that marked off the narrow space where the waitress stood to put in her orders. Lawlor was really crowding her space on the busiest night of the year, but the ignorant old bastard seemed oblivious to it. His shoe was locked into the brass rail, heel first, as he faced a knot of sweating white-haired judges and defense lawyers who were pushed in close to his flat stomach, their big guts bumping against him. Probably begging him to run for mayor again, Driscoll guessed.

The place held about 250 comfortably for a wedding reception or a First Holy Communion dinner. Honey's sweet-sixteen birthday party had been held in this very room. Harry Capri told great stories about that night, and Driscoll never tired of hearing them. Harry had been sitting stake-out right across the street and a doorman he knew had let him come in and stand in the back to watch Honey making her social debut.

Tonight, though, there had to be four hundred people jammed inside. It was eighteen above on the street, but everybody inside Roberto's was sweating as if in a sauna.

Someone, acting on Lawlor's orders, had just killed the canned rock music that had been dribbling out in the background through scratchy speakers, and now an old man who stood before a microphone on a small raised platform in the center of the room was singing arias from the commissioner's favorite operas. Two older, even more shriveled-up little guys were backing him up with mandolins.

"Hi, Phil," Lida James greeted him, pecking his check and clasping his arm around her waist. She made sure that both big tits pushed into him as she reached. Lida was well on the way to being drunk, but still in control. "Boy, you look good enough to eat tonight," she said.

Driscoll didn't feel especially good. What had happened at the Fat Man's house when someone had almost killed him and Honey with a broadside from a shotgun still had him jumpy. Whoever was trying to kill her also had to know that the Meatman's wake was coming up, too. There was no way Honey wouldn't show. If Driscoll himself had been trying to kill her, that's when he would take his best shot. Out on the street, at the wake. So would *they*.

Driscoll hadn't seen Lida or Spanish Joe since the night they'd run into the fireworks at the Presto numbers bank—the night of the Meatman's assassination.

"Anything else on the guy we caught at the Meatman's bank?" he asked her.

"Oh, you mean the guy you almost beat to death," she asked merrily. Lida had been waiting for this. Finally she had something that Phillip wanted. "Plenty," she said, beginning to curl the tip of his tie up toward his chest.

"I'm waiting. I don't have a lot of time, Lida." She wanted to play games. He didn't.

"So am I." Flickering, Lida's tongue kept dipping into the drink in her hand. She caught Driscoll's eye and her brows arched, as two very obvious, very expensive false eyelashes fluttered. Lida had always envied women—little bitches like Honey—who knew how to wear them.

Driscoll leaned down and whispered something into her ear. Her lips parted, her tongue shot up almost to the bottom of her nose, and her face broke into the lewdest smile he had ever seen. "When?" she asked him.

"Later," he answered. "First, tell me about the guy. What have we got?"

"No fingerprints. That's what's been holding us up. The tips of his fingers were all burned off. Somebody probably dipped his hands into a saucer of acid—just enough to scar them. And the fucker still won't talk.

Driscoll thought back to the hand he had taken from Presto's basement, the hand gripping the .45 automatic. The fingers of that hand had looked strange, too—unnaturally smooth. None of the normal little ridges and indentations. Now he knew why. Acid—to burn away the prints forever. *Damn.* Even La Cosa Nostra didn't do that. *Very* professional people.

"So how did you find out finally?" Driscoll asked.

Just then, Spanish Joe walked up. The detective hadn't even noticed him listening in. He wondered how many other people were eavesdropping in the hot, crowded room. He had intended to use the mob of people to his advantage tonight. But it did have its problems.

"Interpol," Spanish Joe said proudly. "That was a very slick idea you had, Phil. Of course, I'm the guy who got them to tell us everything they know." Joe smoothed down the bushy points of his black bandito mustache. "We sent his picture by telefax to Paris and they just got back to us about an hour ago. Those frogs take their time over there."

Driscoll didn't even notice Lida beginning to play with the hair on the top of his hand. Joe was about to give him the first decent lead he had gotten since the whole thing started. "Nice," Driscoll said.

"We guessed right. According to their records in Saint-Cloud, on the Rue Armengaud, that's their headquarters"—he was really laying it on thick, all this newfound knowledge, going out of his way to impress Lida—" our stickup man is one Emil Menschikoff, thirty-four, born in Odessa in the Ukraine, Red Army Veteran. Infantry. Decorated. Saw action in Angola and on the Chinese border. Tough fucking hombre."

Driscoll looked impressed. Joe went on, "But here it gets weird. He received their equivalent of a dishonorable discharge."

"For what?" Driscoll asked.

"Conduct detrimental to the state." Joe seemed to be repeating word for word what the Interpol people had told him. "That's a garbage charge in Russia. In his case, Interpol believes that he was moonlighting as muscle for their black market. Emil's a real leg-breaker, according to them. Active on three continents."

"Make that four," Driscoll corrected him. "Who does he work for?"

"Interpol says that the Russians have a helluva black market. Very big-time. Makes our Mafiosi look like potato-chip gangsters. It's controlled by a very tight, very secret group. It doesn't even have a name, but if you say 'Malina' to some of these Russian emigrés, they'll know exactly what you're talking about." Spanish Joe was beaming as if he had just delivered an oral report to the teacher. He kept looking at Lida.

"I've been hearing this stuff over and over for the last hour," Lida sniffed.

"How did Emil wind up on Passyunk Avenue with an M-16 in his hands ripping off the Meatman?" Driscoll asked.

Spanish Joe was ready for this one. "Guess fucking what? Interpol wants *us* to tell *them* as soon as we know." Joe took Lida's drink out of her hand and downed it. "Interpol says that about three years ago Emil walked to the edge of the earth and dropped off. They thought he was dead. But he ain't dead, Phil. Not yet. Not that you didn't try."

Honey had mentioned the same thing to him right before they were almost shot. Malina? What the hell was it? Tina Conti said that her boyfriend, Vinnie, had worked for a Russian guy, and Vinnie just happened to walk off the same edge of the earth the night that Presto got dead.

At first, he hadn't wanted to believe it, but he couldn't ignore it any longer. The Russians were moving in on the mob; on Presto. This Malina had to be behind it. If they killed Presto, what about the others? The red pushpins on his map? But who was orchestrating the assassinations?

"How do you think Emil got here?" Lida asked him.

"The guy's probably dog shit over there," Driscoll said. "Russia's got cops just like us. They're happy to be rid of the bastards. Guys like that find a way out, and nobody goes looking for them too hard."

"They could use them as spies," Spanish Joe said hesitantly. "Put their own army over here. Infiltrate. Fifth column. Just like the Japs before Pearl Harbor when they took pictures of everything important they could get their hands on."

Driscoll thought about that. "Maybe," he said. "They could do that with a few, but they're not *all* spies. And you mark my words, this son of a bitch is no spy. Emil is a garden-variety strong-arm man. I've danced with enough to know."

"I gotta go," Joe said. "Whizz. I had a six-pack on the way over."

Lida giggled.

"Now, I gotta talk to you about something else," Driscoll said. "I wanted to do it here because this is going to have to be an unofficial operation. Just you, me, and Joe. We play it like an ordinary surveillance."

"What?" Lida asked intently.

"Somebody tried to kill Honey last night, and we got the wake coming up tomorrow. We don't have much time."

She listened.

As soon as he was finished outlining what he intended to do, smiling all the time as if he were just making small talk with Lida, Driscoll said, "Fill in Spanish Joe when you see him." Lida, now serious, nodded. "See you in the parking lot," he added, then winked. "Bottoms up."

Her full, pretty face turned red. "You bastard," she called after him, still blushing.

Driscoll had been there nearly an hour and he still hadn't seen what he was looking for—not that he even knew what he was looking for. But, he told himself, as soon as he saw it, he would know it. That's how it had been for most of his career as a detective. Instinct, plain and simple. Driscoll wasn't the most deductive cop he had ever met.

Five minutes later, Big Ed Bellows walked in and yanked off his blue-and-white Hoya muffler. Driscoll gave him a half-hearted nod.

Big Ed was beautiful. First he worked the room, pumping the hand of every black cop or lawyer or judge he could reach. The white guys got a wave. Separate, but equal. Bellows didn't slip once. Always politically correct. Somebody handed him a bottle of beer; he politely declined and reached instead for a glass of white wine that was passing under his chin, held aloft by a harried waiter. Driscoll had always known that Bellows was a social-climbing ass.

Lawlor noticed Bellows, too. The old man made eye contact. Big Ed must have been born with the peripheral vision of a panther. He began moving through the dense crowd towards Lawlor; simultaneously, the commissioner began shooing away supplicants who were begging for his attention at the bar.

Lawlor and Bellows were ignoring everyone but each other. This could be what he had been waiting for, Driscoll concluded. He grabbed Lida James, just as she passed by again, patted her on her behind, and started steering her toward Big Ed and Lawlor. Eavesdropping time, his turn. "We're gonna go over to the bar and you're gonna buy me a drink," he informed Lida.

She slurred something. He couldn't make it out, but answered yes anyway. He wanted to get as close to them as he could, using the normal pushing and shoving of the bar for cover. Lida was squeezing his hand as if she were afraid of getting lost.

Bellows, who was taller than everyone else to begin with, towered over Lawlor, but he bent himself down to the commissioner's height. For Driscoll it was like watching them on a movie reel, minus the sound, neither man smiling, Lawlor talking, Bellows listening. From where Driscoll stood, it was all pantomime.

Driscoll felt a drink, wet and slippery, being shoved into his hand. He took it, arching his neck and upper body to listen. The opera tenor was on a break; Christmas carols were blasting over the PA system. To get anywhere tonight, dammit, he would have to be a lip reader.

Lida had her hand inside his pants pocket, but he ignored her. She was saying something else, too, leaning against him now as if ready to fall over. Driscoll did a quick once-over of the room looking for Spanish Joe to take Lida off his hands. Smashed together as they were at the bar, only three people away from Bellows, Lida was acting as if she were in her bedroom, working away on Driscoll through his pocket, almost ripping the material. The girl was hot. He hated like hell to waste a night like this worrying over the goddam Meatman and the rest of it.

Without the slightest warning, abruptly turning, Bellows backed away from the bar and started to scan the room. He had eight inches on Driscoll. His head almost bumped against the foil-covered silver bells that hung from the low ceiling.

Who the hell was he looking for now? Driscoll tried to follow his line of sight.

Bellows spotted somebody and began moving off again in a hurry. Driscoll gently withdrew Lida's sweating hand from his pocket; she could just about stand. He leaned her against the bar. Then he saw Spanish Joe. "She's all yours," Driscoll said, and then he tried to follow Bellows from a safe distance. The crowd parted in the big black athlete's wake like some wavering, inebriated Red Sea.

It looked as though Bellows had made his contact and was waiting for somebody to leave by the dining-room entrance. That door was always roped off between two silver stanchions for the Christmas party. There were so many people in front of the bar that the dining-room door was completely obscured.

Bellows stepped over the velvet rope and went outside. Driscoll was a good ten feet behind him, but he could still feel the difference in temperature from the air seeping in. He followed.

There were two kids outside for valet parking. A traffic cop was on duty and about a dozen cabs were lined up. A couple of very old cops were standing under a streetlight, chatting, wobbling, too bombed to even notice the cold.

Bellows hit Catherine Street at a fast gallop and disappeared around the corner. He had to be going to the parking lot. Driscoll had his collar up and his hands in his coat pockets. Big Ed never looked behind him. Whoever he was going to see, he was in too big a hurry to worry about it much.

The one attendant on the lot was inside the little ticket

house, bent over a newspaper. The orange mouth of a kerosene heater glowed behind him.

Bellows went down the wide double lane in the middle and then turned left and headed for the last line of parked cars. The three-story wall of another restaurant loomed above them.

Driscoll crouched down. He was almost moving on his knees, hopping and stutter-stepping like an oversized toad.

For the first time since he had left Roberto's, Bellows pulled up, waiting. A few seconds passed. A door opened on one of the cars parked against the wall; for just a moment, the overhead interior light blinked on. Big Ed practically folded himself in half and jumped into the passenger side. Still in his crouch, Driscoll headed that way. He was nearly on top of the car when the passenger door swung open and Bellows stuck his long legs out to straighten himself up. Instantly, he was on his feet and barreling out the side entrance to the lot. Whatever had happened had happened fast. Just a quick pickup or a few words exchanged.

Driscoll waited. Finally the driver's door on the same car opened and a much smaller man struggled out into the darkness.

This second man appeared to be coming right for Driscoll. Driscoll had no choice; he hit the cold, dirty asphalt of the parking lot like a rookie going down for a push-up. Then he rolled under the nearest auto.

In the moonless darkness, with just the first freezing drops of an icy drizzle beginning, the second man passed by. Driscoll could see as far as his knees and ankles and shoes. Cuffed pants, a dark suit, most likely. But is was so hard to really make anything out.

He almost stepped on Driscoll's outstretched hand, and the detective quickly pulled it back and folded it under his chest.

Then, suddenly, at precisely the wrong moment as far as Driscoll was concerned, another car pulled into the crowded parking lot—a late arrival, coming too fast, zigzagging, probably a drunken off-duty cop who was afraid the party wouldn't wait.

The beams from the car's headlights caught the man who had met with Ed Bellows in their glare, setting him up perfectly, but the bright lights also blinded Driscoll. He raised a gloved hand to shield his eyes, as his head projected from beneath the car, but it was no good.

The slow-moving figure in the darkness was already gone. So was Ed Bellows. Disgusted, Driscoll crawled out and dusted off his clothes.

BUSTLETON

Nobody knew how old Butkova was. There were no birth certificates where he was born, no doctors and no hospitals. The midwife had cut his cord, opened his eyes, and spanked him into a bellowing cry. His mother had loved him and dreamed that he would grow up to be like his father—a quiet, gentle farmer who seemed to grow ever closer to the black earth as each harvest season passed. All that Butkova could claim from his father, however, were his ears and his love of pigeons. He had watched his father's ears elongate, stretching and lengthening as the tanned skin around his farmer's face lost its elasticity from old age. By the time his father was seventy, his ears had become the dominant aspect of his face, standing out like miniature wings on either side of his thinning white hair.

Nikolai Butkova used to wonder, when he was young, if he would eventually look like that. Now he no longer wondered. Just before he climbed the attic steps to the roof of his warehouse building, treading gingerly in the darkness, climbing to his pigeon coops, he had stared at his reflection in the mirror mounted on the inside door of his office. Like all men, he had become his father. In one way, though, Butkova was very unlike his father—as far as he knew, his father had never killed anybody, not even in war.

Fat and patient and round, the pigeons were on the roof, waiting in the night. The blackness made them look agitated. He had nearly a hundred in his flock now. They cooed a muttering, excited greeting, flapping their wings noisily at his arrival. The cold didn't bother them, although the roof was windblown and freezing.

The flock was segregated into racers, his favorites—they could be vicious, fighting for position and advantage—then carriers, his workhorses, and finally the few young ones he bred for eating. Curried pigeon pie with thick garlic glaze on a bed of brown rice had been a delicacy in his village, and Butkova had never lost his taste for the birds. Unfortunately, he had never found anyone who could prepare a pigeon as deliciously as his mother—pigeons were dry meat; overcooking without enough basting killed the pungent flavor—and his mother had been dead more than thirty years now.

Whenever he thought about them, about his mother and father, Butkova realized that he too was growing older. But he still had time—time to see his ambitions through. In America, anything was possible, even the empire that he envisioned. It would be an empire inspired by the Malina, manned by an army of his own choosing, and dedicated to the same vast criminal enterprises as the Mafia. That was his vision—to take over the Mafia, little by little, city by city, boss by boss, territory by territory. His method was the oldest one known to man—assassination.

Back in his native village, when an important man or a beloved man died, it was the custom to kill two of the finest birds and send them to the widow as a token of respect and hope that the soul of the deceased would fly, as on the wings of birds, to heaven. Butkova supposed that the tradition was at least a thousand years old. He had only met the great Meatman, Paul Presto, once, but had instantly recognized in him the kinship, the brotherhood of hard men who understood that without tradition, there was nothing. Moving left to right along the roof, Butkova inspected the crude wooden coops of the birds that he kept for eating. He had constructed the coops, small, narrow enclosures where the birds would have room enough to spread their wings but not enough to peck each other to death. His father had taught him how to measure a coop and fit in the wooden spindles all around, shaping each piece so tightly that no glue was needed. After a few moments, Butkova selected the birds that he would send to Presto's family. He was careful as he lifted up their short, squat, gray bodies, first one, then the other; he cooed back at them, stroking the tenderest feathers just under their necks. He would kill the birds himself, dress them, and finally have them packed in ice. A fitting tribute to the great Meatman.

SOUTH PHILADELPHIA

Now, for the second time in his career, Ed Bellows was being ordered to kill someone. Even with the authorization coming directly from the White House, Bellows had a hard time not feeling morally bankrupt. A conservative Baptist grandmother had raised him, with Sundays spent in his suit and tie, singing with the choir in the oldest black section of Baltimore. Coming from a background like that, taking a human life was wrong, no matter what. But a long time ago, Bellows had traded the little Baptist church for his career, and rationalizing came easier these days.

It hadn't been easy the first time, either. Bellows had been with the Drug Enforcement Administration only a little over a year when it had happened. As a reward for a spectacular bust, and also to spirit the suddenly hot Bellows out of New York, where his face was becoming too recognizable to the drug underworld, they had posted him to their Far East bureau. The assignment eventually took him to a whorehouse in Bangkok.

Two of the biggest pushers in the South Pacific had succeeded in hooking an admiral's twin teenage daughters on heroin. The scandal was covered up with a great deal of hush money, and the girls were spirited away to a detox center in Manila. However, their father, a tough navy man, had sworn to get even.

The admiral's brother and the girls' uncle was a power in the DEA and a personal friend of Jim Carney's, whom he had asked to expedite the matter. As soon as they came up with a location on the pushers in the tourist district of Bangkok, Bellows received a call from his old teacher. Carney's orders had been direct and to the point—"Terminate with extreme prejudice." Bellows never questioned the order.

He had pried open rickety French doors in the rear of a brothel and had climbed up a winding back staircase to the second-floor hallway. Creeping stealthily, he checked each room. A distinct cackling laugh tipped him off. Then he heard one of the young Thai whores giggling.

Bellows charged into the room, blasting away. He caught the first man sprawled on his back on a bamboo mat, his round white stomach thrust up into the air like a hideous hump. A beautiful Thai girl with waist-length black hair was kneeling beside him, bending low.

Firing one round after another, then jamming in a second clip, Bellows followed the trail of bullets that began at the pusher's forehead and ripped across his chest and abdomen. He barely missed the young prostitute.

Then he turned on the second man, an Australian, who had darted under an old canopied bed in the middle of the room. Bellows picked up the bed frame like a piece of dollhouse furniture and dragged the Australian out to where he could get a good shot at him. He emptied what was left of the clip into the pusher's prone figure, opening a gaping red hole where his pelvis had been. Running back out into the hallway, desperate to get away, he hurtled headlong into Jim Carney, splendid in a white three-piece suit and wide-brimmed Panama hat. He had followed Bellows to assess his capabilities. Without so much as a glance, Bellows brushed past him.

A week later, a nervous Ed Bellows was standing in front of Jim Carney's desk. A police inspector from Melbourne was there to investigate the bloody execution of the Australian drug czar, a well-respected lawyer back in his home city.

Carney performed brilliantly, lying more convincingly than Bellows could ever imagine. Genial and helpful, Carney steered the inspector in the wrong direction and ended up accepting the man's profuse gratitude. Ed Bellows learned how a pro operates at that session.

Carney arranged for Bellows to go to law school and promised him a place in his organization. Subsequently, he mentored his rise in the U.S. Justice Department, eventually installing him in a key command post in Philadelphia with the Organized Crime Strike Force. That was the way Carney did things, constantly expanding his network of contracts, acting in the dual role of benevolent patron and shrewd manipulator—fattening his portfolio of IOUs along the way.

From his hospital bed, Carney had told the black giant that his final chit was being called in.

TWENTY-THREE

A CAFÉ NEAR PRIMORSKY BOULEVARD, ODESSA

Mikhail Zhukov looked unaccustomedly stout. He wasn't a husky man by nature, and the extra girth gave his body a bloated look. Drawn, thin, and colorless, his cheeks had the pasty appearance of wheat that had been harvested before its time. He was dressed down, too. His normal attire was his custom-tailored KGB uniform for formal occasions or one of the best off-the-rack Western suits that he could acquire on his infrequent travels abroad. But today he simply looked like a well-dressed businessman—hardly the appearance he usually projected.

The weight would be easily explainable, if one of the many GRU agents he had thought he had seen noticed it. That wouldn't attract more than a mention—Zhukov is getting fat in his middle age. Let them say what they wanted; the illusion of weight was simply the price he had to pay for wearing not one, not two, but three money belts stuffed with as much foreign currency as he could fasten, tie, or hook to his body. Give or take, in all the denominations, he calculated that he was walking around with just under $250,000. Even in the Soviet Union, that had to buy him a degree of anonymity and the promise of secret passage abroad.

He had taken a military flight from Moscow into the southern city of Odessa, then arranged for his own transportation away from the airport. For an officer of his rank and influence, that wasn't unusual. Even in the glacial cold of late December, the spas near Odessa were favorite vacation destinations for the party and the KGB elite. That was the cover story he had decided to use. With Tanya out of the country, and several days to spend alone and on his own, that seemed natural enough. Several of the best spas also doubled as very discreet, very expensive brothels, so, just in case his movements had attracted too much attention, he would admit, with a sheepish grin, to whoever might ask, that one of those spas—with his lover safely out of the way—was his real destination. There had been the usual inquiries at the office when he requested a seat on the military plane—nothing else was flying into that part of the country—but he had convinced the clerk that he was going down that way to interrogate a prisoner in a local jail.

Before leaving, Zhukov had liquidated as many of his holdings as possible. Still, because everything that he was doing was illegal, he had been forced to leave an enormous amount behind. But he knew that would serve a purpose, too. He had left everything in the dacha near the last exit of the Ring Road that led out of Moscow.

His only thought now was escape. Once he reached the West safely—and quickly, that was imperative—he could retrieve the remainder of his black-market fortune. Zhukov was confident that his bankers in Zurich would oblige him. And there was also Tanya. She would prove extremely useful.

For the moment, all he had to do was wait. Literally.

He was sitting alone at the last table of a café that had once been very grand, even elegant, with his back to the wall, and no one else near him for at least three tables around. Many years before, the black-market thugs he used to arrest, then work deals with, had given him the name of this café and the time of day when he should sit at the last table on the left side. That was all they told him. The rest would be taken care of. Now Zhukov was waiting. Almost thirty minutes had already gone by. They had served him tea and black-bread—he had ordered neither. The waitress, a blond, warmly dressed country girl, he guessed, had also seemed inordinately interested in him, inquiring where he had come from and why. After all of her questions had been asked, he responded as he had been instructed to do years before: "I've come to call on some long-lost brothers," Zhukov said.

The waitress had given nothing away when she heard that, not so much as a knowing smile. *Very* well trained. A few minutes later, a second glass of strong tea had been brought to him. That time, the waitress didn't even bother to peer up from her tray.

Zhukov was more than a little nervous. This was, after all, the first time he had ever sought out the Malina, as such. His previous transactions with the black marketeers had always been done either at a distance or with some harmless middlemen. Everything that he had ever done with his contact in Philadelphia had been conducted long-distance, through messengers.

This would be his first face-to-face meeting, and he was at a disadvantage—they knew who he was, but he could only guess at their identity. Every time a rough-looking man or woman entered the café, he expected to be contacted. But no one came near him. He had promised himself to give it an hour—and forty-five minutes had already passed.

Leaning back, bored, he tipped the glass of tea to his lips. A young boy, no more than ten or twelve, had begun sweeping the floor near the doorway. Cold air puffed in from time to time. Peeking out the window, the child with the broom stopped sweeping and let in a very feeble old man. He appeared to be earnestly talking his way into a free pot of tea or a cup of hot soup. Zhukov watched as the old man leaned his hand on the child's shoulder. Then he noticed that the old man was blind. His sightless eyes, almost all white ball and very little pupil, stared uselessly up at a forty-five-degree angle at the ceiling. The old fellow was shabby, smelly, bearing down too hard on the little boy's shoulder.

They seemed to be leading him into the back of the room, toward the kitchen area. He was mumbling inaudibly as he shuffled along. A moment later, two very tough, rugged-looking men entered the café and sat down opposite Zhukov. Neither moved, nor made any attempt to remove his fur hat. Both seemed anxious to get the blond waitress's attention.

Zhukov decided at once that these two must be his contacts. He looked at them sideways, fearful of making the first move. Just then the little boy with the broom began speaking to him. "You'll have to leave now, sir," the boy said. "This table is reserved."

Shocked, Zhukov looked at him uncomprehendingly.

"Please, sir," the boy persisted. "Right now."

Zhukov made a move to leave, profoundly upset, desperate for someone to make contact with him. As he did so, the waitress came bustling past him, shouting rudely at the two big men across from him. Without a word of protest, they excused themselves, their eyes downcast. Zhukov followed them.

Just as he was about to step outside, he felt a tugging at his elbow. It was the old man, the blind man. Placing his lips so close to Zhukov's ear that he could feel the breath of each word as well as hear it, the old man said, "About your brothers, Comrade Zhukov—we may have word."

Zhukov followed the blind man. The small boy remained at his side.

SHUNK STREET, SOUTH PHILADELPHIA

Joe-Joey's wife had dozed off in front of the television in the living room. She awoke when she heard these strange, sort of muffled sounds coming from downstairs, from the cellar that her husband and his men had transformed into the most elaborate, marble-floored, paneled, track-lighted rec room in all of South Philadelphia. The local paper, the *South Philadelphia Review,* had wanted to do a photo layout on the family room; it was the talk of the neighborhood. But

Joe-Joey had forbidden it. The Meatman would never have forgiven him.

She rubbed her eyes, felt the baby move as she straightened up and pressed the button on her remote control to turn down the sound on the TV.

There it was again. Like a *pop-pop-pop*. But like a *pop-pop-pop* inside a bag of cotton or something. What was it?

All the kids were at her mother's house around the corner, except her oldest. She was out on a date. Joe-Joey had been downstairs for hours. Maybe there was a hockey game or something on the television down there that he had to watch for the point spreads. He worked so hard. She loved him so much—he was the best husband, the best provider, the best lover that a woman could want. But she worried. With Paul Presto gone now, the business was so dangerous. It was the way it had been back during the Atlantic City War, when that miserable little worm Nicky Scarfo had caused so much trouble. So many men had been killed then—Angelo Bruno, Phil Testa, his son Salve Testa, so many. She had been so happy for her Joe-Joey when Paul Presto had beaten them all. Paul had been such a good man, such a gentle Don.

She pulled her robe around her, fastened a little knot over her big stomach—this last pregnancy had gone *so* fast—and tiptoed down the carpeted stairs. All the lights were off in her end of the long, narrow room. The TV *was* on down there. She checked the screen. *The Godfather.* Why was Joe-Joey watching an old movie, all by himself? The sound was turned almost all the way down. He didn't even *like* that movie. He used to sit there and tell her all the things they did wrong. Joe-Joey *knew*..

Her husband was all the way at the other end of the cellar—she *still* called it that—doing something with telephone books. *Telephone books?* She watched. Then, after a moment, after she saw what he was doing, after she heard that deadened *pop-pop-pop,* she started to cry. Quietly—she was afraid to let him see her.

But Joe-Joey did see her. He spun around with a look of genuine alarm on his face. He said, "Donna, you scared me. I wish you hadda stayed asleep upstairs." He noticed her tears. "This is business now. Go on."

Two long, wet tears shone against her tan cheeks. She wiped them away, put her hand on the small of her back to help balance herself, and prayed that the baby she was carrying would be asleep now so she or he would not have to hear her arguing with his or her father. But argue she would.

"You make me ashamed," she said, loud enough so that Joe-Joey would know she was really mad. "In our own house. What if one of the kids came down here and saw this? With a silencer, no less. Mr. Big Shot. Mr. Killer. You always told me you couldn't hit the side of a barn and Paul didn't care if you couldn't!"

Joe-Joey had been practicing with a new silencer on a .22. He was firing into a stack of telephone books he had tied together with some string from the supermarket. The phone books were propped up on the little metal hood over the fake fireplace, an electric heater that hung from the back wall. Joe-Joey had tried to make the cellar look like a subterranean ski chalet.

"That's why I need the practice," he said simply. Donna followed his eyes. Where the bullets neatly penetrated the phone books about one inch deep, you could see little tufts of torn pages, as if the Yellow Pages had blossomed with little paper flowers. But deadly flowers.

"What if you hit the wall?"

Joe-Joey laughed. "I'm not *that* rusty," he said.

"What's happening to us?" She came over and hugged him. "What about the children? They need a father. Now I find you down here with a gun. In *our* house. Joe-Joey, it makes me sick!"

He wasn't sure how much to tell her. He had never lied to her, but sometimes he had left things out. "It's just a precaution," he said. "Tony's the boss now, and I don't know what's gonna happen anymore. If I have to use it . . ." He let his hands tell her that it couldn't be helped.

"But *here?* In our family room?"

"This is the first time in a month that all the kids have been out at the same time, Donna." He was almost pleading with her. "It was the only chance I had."

She backed away from him and sat down. "You better tell me what happened," she said knowingly. "Ever since you had that meeting with Milton Littlejohn, the lawyer, you haven't been yourself. Now I come downstairs and you're practicing to shoot somebody. You're lucky you don't shoot yourself—or me—or one of the kids!"

He looked up at the oak millwork along the walls—he'd selected it himself.

"How come Paul never asked you to practice with a gun—with a silencer?"

"Maybe he should have," Joe-Joey said. "Maybe he'd be alive now." She started crying again. "I wish to God he was."

Joe-Joey came over, put the gun with the silencer on it down on a coffee table, and put his arms around her shoulders. "How's the baby feel tonight?" he asked.

"The baby's afraid, like me."

He put his hand on her stomach. Donna left it there just a second, then demurely moved it up to her breasts. Joe-Joey kissed her behind her ear. All he wanted to do now was to go upstairs before all the kids came home.

Joe-Joey saw a little tear trying to break loose from one of his wife's brown eyes. "The way I hear it," he said, "Littlejohn thinks he's the one running the Family now. I don't know where that's gonna leave Tony and Marie."

"Or Honey," his wife added.

Joe-Joey just looked at her. The lone little tear had given way to a flood of tears now, and Donna didn't care anymore. She was scared for her Joe-Joey.

THE FOUR SEASONS HOTEL, BENJAMIN FRANKLIN PARKWAY, PHILADELPHIA

Whitey was satisfied. He had just dined with his client at one of the small tables for two that overlooked the sweeping circle of Logan Square, with its soaring fountains and endless beds of tulips, covered by a tarp now and protected for the winter. He played with a box of matches that read "The Fountain." It was an ostentatious room, working overtime to achieve an ambience that still eluded it. Whitey studied the graceful neck on the swan fountain in the parkway.

"After-dinner drink?" his client asked. "I'm developing a taste for Sambuca, myself. The company I keep, I suppose." He handed Whitey the tiny liqueur list.

Whitey waved it away. "No more mistakes," he said gravely. "I work alone." He stared out the window at the passing traffic. "Or I don't work at all."

"Perish the thought," the client said, almost patronizing him. "I assure you, it's been taken care of. Merely overzealousness on the part of some very emotional people. Had I known that an attempt was going to be made on Miss Presto's life, before your own, of course, I never would have allowed it." His gesture indicated a desire to wash his hands of the entire matter. "But, of course, I wasn't consulted."

"This conversation should never have been necessary," Whitey persisted. "I hate amateurs. When you're dealing with me, you're dealing with a professional. These are your people. Control them."

His client called a waiter and ordered the Sambuca. "Sure I can't tempt you?" he asked again. Whitey said nothing. After a few tense, silent minutes, his client spoke again. "The woman I sent—was she satisfactory? Personally, I've always found her charming." He attempted to affect a dirty laugh.

"She asked a lot of questions," Whitey said. "That was a problem." By now, he supposed, they had found her body. But it would take time to identify her.

"Oh, that is a shame." He shook his head slowly in a sign of mock condolence.

"Couldn't be helped. She asked questions."

His client sipped the Sambuca and put down the delicate glass. He called the waiter over again and pointed to a spot—microscopic—on the glass. Bowing, the waiter removed the offending glass as if he were cutting out a tumor. Whitey was beginning to feel uncomfortable, and cold. There was a draft coming in through the plate-glass window on his left. He shivered as his client surprised him by asking, "After you take care of the Presto girl, would it be possible to stay in the city for a while? Another job has come up. This time you would be dealing in quantity."

ODESSA

Doing as he was instructed, Zhukov walked up two flights of stairs above the café. The blind man was in front, the small boy behind. Not a word was exchanged; all he could hear was the fitful breathing of the old one.

When at last they reached their destination—a dimly lit corridor with curving Moorish-style arches and impregnated by ripe body smells and the heavy, bittersweet narcotic odor of opium—Zhukov saw one door after another running along either side of the hall, like the entrances to monks' cells. But, of course, these small rooms weren't cells; they were the "closets of dreams," as they were called in Odessa—tiny rooms, stacked with mattresses and bunk beds, where the opium customers of the Malina paid a high price for a few hours of bliss and solitude.

About halfway down the hall, the blind man turned, automatically, and entered one of the cell-like doors. Zhukov went in after him. They passed a mass of huddled, nodding bodies, each sucking sleepily on one of the pipes provided by the Malina. No one even looked up as Zhukov stepped over the bodies, almost treading on a hand here, an outstretched leg there. Several of the customers were women. They seemed to Zhukov the most pathetic of all, disheveled and listless, helpless. A few had their skirts and dresses pushed up past their waists, naked, exposed to the explorations of anyone who happened to pass through. In one corner, a man was bent low over the waist of one such woman, his trousers pushed down to his ankles. Their sex was silent, passionless, depressing.

The rear of the room was screened by a beaded curtain.

The blind man passed through it like a ghost entering a wall and emerging on the other side, intact. Zhukov, not a tall man compared to many, had to stoop to go in. The beads brushed against his face and hair. The boy was next, nearly tripping into Zhukov's back as he fell over someone's feet in the tangle outside.

"Sit," the blind man said. "You have never come to us before—directly. Something has changed. Tell us."

Zhukov cleared his throat and began. "I have been a trusted associate of your brothers in Moscow for many, many years, on the black market. You can ask them if necessary. They will—"

The blind man interrupted him. "Were that not the case, Comrade Zhukov," he said, "you would already be quite dead. Now, proceed and do not waste our time. You have come to the brotherhood of the Malina for a service. You will have to pay our price for that service, if we choose to perform it. But coming to us in the open like this, while still an officer, in the KGB, can only mean that you are closing the book on that chapter of your life. If you expect us to spirit you out of the country, say so. Get on with it." There was menace in his tone. As he spoke, he motioned to the small boy to pat down Zhukov. The boy stood up, started at Zhukov's neck, placing his small hands inside his shirt collar, and continued until he had reached Zhukov's waist. He stopped at the lumpy bulges.

"Take it," the old man said, his blind eyes still searching sightlessly in the darkness and gloom. He had been wearing a cap of rags and bits of fur, but he now placed that on the low round table in front of him, leaning toward Zhukov on his bent elbows. Suddenly, the boy pulled at Zhukov's shirt and tugged the tail out of his pants. Flat white belly showed through. The boy began stripping off the money belts. One by one, he handed them to the blind man.

Smiling, he said to Zhukov, "I see that you have brought a down payment. That *was* wise. Now, proceed."

"There's more there than you will need," Zhukov answered, angry and a little frightened at this treatment. "Besides, I have a dacha outside Moscow, packed with black-market items, clothes, cameras, wine, video equipment, even a new car in the shed in the back, an American car. Take it all; that should pay for everything."

The blind man laughed, and a sound came out like a gravedigger shoveling dirt on a coffin, raspy and hard. "Don't be an idiot, or naive. You, comrade, are a corrupt policeman, nothing more and nothing less. You must know how these things work. Don't play the innocent with us, nor the man of influence. You are at our mercy. Totally. Before the military transport plane that you took from Moscow to the secret airfield outside Odessa even landed, our people in Moscow were already inside the dacha. Everything you have here is ours now. And that includes your life." Zhukov started to protest. "This is robbery. I never cheated your people, not once. You can't do this to me. I can have you . . ." Then he stopped, enraged, but aware how foolish he was sounding.

"What? What, comrade? You can have us arrested? Here? And how will you explain that?" The laugh again—another shovelful of earth.

"Have it your way," he said, letting his own impatience show. "I must get to America—as soon as possible. Washington or New York; it doesn't matter."

"That's an expensive request," the blind man said. "What is the urgency?"

"Don't tell me you don't know that, too. You're leading me to believe that this organization of yours is all-knowing."

The blind man pulled the child to his side and spoke into his ear. In a moment, the boy was gone. Then the blind man pushed a thin, frail, yellowed hand under his rag hat on the table and produced a small revolver. The gun was aimed directly at Zhukov's heart. His fingernails, tips showing near the trigger, were long, beginning to curl inward on themselves. "If you try to leave now, comrade, you will die instantly. I have no need to see you—I need only listen to your heart. Even now, I hear it beginning to beat much too quickly.

"You have every kopek that I possess in Russia," Zhukov said. "What more can I give you?"

Holding the weapon steady, the blind man held up a single crooked finger.

"More?"

"More," the blind man said.

"How much?"

He held up the finger one more time.

"I assume some zeros go with that," Zhukov said.

"All the zeros that there are." He grinned; several teeth were missing. As Zhukov moved uneasily in his seat, the gun moved with him; the aim remained exactly on his heart, across the low table.

"That's ridiculous. Are you saying that I have to pay *another* million dollars?"

"Dollars or yen," the blind man corrected. "Either will do. You have ten times that in Swiss accounts. We know about those, too. Now, if you wish to leave the country and reach your destination, soon, as you desire, that can be arranged. The price is one million dollars. If you wish to remain here, so be it."

"How can I stay here now? I was watched in Moscow, followed. The GRU—that old pig Zinijakin . . ."

The blind man seemed amused by that reference. "You have less than one minute to make a decision."

Zhukov stood up and pushed against the table. That action merely made the blind man elevate the gun several degrees. But he could sense much movement on the other side of the beaded curtain. Moving it just an inch, he looked out and saw the waitress from the café downstairs, also holding a gun.

"You get me to the United States—within forty-eight hours, that is vital—and you will have the money. My word on it."

"*Your* word. How noble. And worthless. Zhukov, Zhukov, the evil, corrupt policeman, it isn't your word that we will take, but your miserable life. We will be with you every second, and if you even think about betraying us, you will die that much sooner. You know the Malina. Fear us."

"How? How will you do it? Tell me something so I know I'm not walking into my death with you here."

"In less than one hour, a ship, a small merchant vessel, laden with tobacco and processed salt, will sail from the marine terminal. You will be on that ship. Ask no questions. Answer none. The crew is mixed. The captain is Malina. If he suspects anything—anything at all—he has our permission to kill you.

"The destination is the port of Samsun, on the Turkish coast. There the salt will be exchanged for raw opium. Again, no questions will be asked, because the cargo is illegal in both our countries. You will leave the ship at Samsun, dressed as an able-bodied sailor, and behaving like one, too, I might add."

"And then?"

"You stay in Samsun. We will contact you." Just then, the small boy came in carrying a bundle of old, dirty clothes, seaman's clothes. "Put these on," he ordered Zhukov.

"What about patrol boats? We have a sizable fleet in the Black Sea."

"Gunboats at this time of year, that's all. They will cling to the shoreline. The only other vessel you may encounter will be an icebreaker that makes a regular run. The men on board are cold, tired, drunk most of the time. They won't be bothering to search any merchant vessels."

"But what if they do, this one time? I'm more than a mere policeman, as you put it. I'm a very high-ranking KGB official. I will be missed. Recognized, perhaps."

"Never." The blind man was confident.

"How can you be sure?" He was dressing himself in the old clothes as he spoke. Zhukov noticed that the little boy was also helping himself to some clothes. The boy never spoke, but the blind man must have been reading Zhukov's thoughts.

"The boy goes too," he said.

"Why?" Zhukov protested.

"I thought you were worried about being recognized," the blind man said, struggling to his feet, looking slightly stronger and taller this time, but still appearing to favor a sore knee.

"I am, of course," Zhukov said, "but you are telling me it won't be a problem—" Then, suddenly, the blind man, now looking him in the eye, jerked the handle of the gun down across Zhukov's temple and the bridge of his nose. Blood began to pour from his nostrils. The KGB man fell forward, screaming in agony just before he lost consciousness. That's what the blind man wanted. Zhukov's face was a mess now; his own mistress would have a hard time recognizing him.

"Be sure to bandage him good," the blind man said to the small boy. "Then take the green trolley—you know the one—and get off at the marine terminal. There are seven great cranes on the waterfront. Stand with our friend here, hold him up as though he's drunk. Stand under the tallest of the cranes until the captain approaches you. Now be off." Before the boy could leave, searching for the bandages, the blind man kissed him tenderly on the forehead. "Be careful," he said, thinking a blessing to himself, a blessing on this bright, obedient Malina child.

After the little boy left, with Zhukov lying across the table, the blind man reached up into his eyesockets and plucked out both of his eyeballs. They were wax. Then he broke off the long, ugly fingernails, carefully preserving each one. Underneath, his hands were perfectly manicured. Lastly, he stripped off an almost transparent mask of makeup and specially treated rubber resin. His bushy eyebrows stuck to the material of the mask.

As soon as he was finished, the blind man—Marshal Vladik Vladovich Zinijakin—said to the unconscious Zhukov, "So I'm a pig, am I? But we will see which pig gets butchered first, comrade."

THE MORGUE OF THE CITY AND COUNTY OF PHILADELPHIA, 321 UNIVERSITY AVENUE TUESDAY MIDNIGHT

Only a few hours before, Driscoll had been at the Christmas party; now he found himself back at the House of the Dead.

Every time he went to the morgue from now on, Driscoll would always think of meeting Honey there—and of seeing the Meatman. But this time it was a dead prostitute—a .45 in the head—named Arlene. This had to be the woman Tony Bonaventura had gone looking for. She had to be the woman from Presto's real estate office. The .45 told him that much and also told him that somebody had gotten to her before Tony.

He'd looked at her body, filling with fluids now, bloating. But even dead, Arlene's legs looked like the legs of an athlete; only one broad in five hundred had pins that good.

Lida was reading the medical examiner's report, skipping and not bothering to take a breath at the ends of sentences: " 'Oh point one one two residue of some depressant, possibly Quaaludes,' " she read. " 'Signs of recent sexual activity. Vaginal and anal, especially anal. Tissue tears, some bruises, deep penetration, but no indication of forced entry. No significant cuts, contusions or lacerations.' " She stopped and looked up at Driscoll. "No assault, no battery, no rape. Just friendly stuff." Then she smiled sweetly.

"She had to be a whore," Driscoll said. "We need her real name and her street names. She looks clean; she just shaved. Nice clothes in the hotel room." Then he thought about the money they had found in her shoe. "How much money was there?"

"Five hundred bucks and change," Lida said. "Maybe I should moonlight."

Driscoll made an exaggerated motion of turning to look at Lida's behind. "Stick with the day job," he said, turning away so she wouldn't see him laughing.

"Her name really is Arlene," Lida said, suddenly conscious of her rear end. "Arlene Roy, twenty-six years old, three pages of previous arrests, all soliciting or bullshit shoplifting or drugs—just pills. She was really a pill freak."

"You got that fast," he said.

Lida smiled appreciatively. She'd received the call about Arlene's body at the Christmas party and had sobered up immediately. Tonight she felt like a real cop.

"Any connection between her and Presto's real estate place?"

"Not on paper anywhere, but the people there kind of remember her."

"What do you mean, kind of?"

"Tony told them not to talk to us."

"That figures." The next time Driscoll saw Tony—or Marie—he intended to punch one of them right in the mouth, just on general principles."But she did work there?"

"Yes, briefly."

"As?"

"Terri Addario."

"How did she go from the three-page rap sheet to working for Presto?"

"She changed jobs, got off the street," Lida said.

Driscoll's ears actually moved, independent of the rest of his face, as he listened.

"She got hooked up with an outcall message place and never went back on the street. We talked to the other girls there and they said that Arlene made very serious bucks from just one or two steady johns."

"Presto?" he asked.

"They never see any faces, just voices on the phone."

"Who owns the outcall place?"

"How many names in the phonebook?" Lida asked sarcastically. "Joe is on that now, and he already has seven different corporations—none legally connected to the other ones."

"Tell him to stay on that as long as he can."

"It isn't going anywhere."

"It will." Driscoll sounded curt.

"Don't say thanks or anything, Phil."

"I will when it's time," he said.

"Who killed her?"

"Same guy who killed Presto. I'm positive. At first, I thought this guy was in a hurry to get out of town. And I bet he was in the beginning. But he's had a change in plans. He only stays places because he gets paid to kill people. Something tells me this creep has one more big check coming."

Lida went over and glanced at Arlene's body again. She was assessing it. "You an ass man, Phil?" Lida asked, shyly looking at him from the side.

"Depends on the ass." He was expecting an invitation any second.

In her mind Lida was comparing her body with Arlene's.

"You see her legs?" Driscoll asked.

"Muscles, you mean?"

"Not just muscles," he said. "This girl was in training. You don't get legs like that from a Jane Fonda tape. I bet she went to school for it. Maybe she hooked on the side to pick up a little extra money and the little extra got to be too much to walk away from. That make sense to you?"

"Maybe."

"Let Joe do the outcall stuff; you try some dance schools. They would probably only know her by her real name. And be sure to go back a few years to before she hit the pavement."

TWENTY-FOUR

NORTHEAST PHILADELPHIA
WEDNESDAY

Driscoll was in an unmarked car, halfway down the block from the fur store where Vinnie worked. The merchants along the avenue had chipped in and hung their own decorations—flat silver, red and green bells on every traffic pole, cardboard cutouts and crisscrossing green bunting that ran the length of the block. Christmas music was blasting from a loudspeaker somewhere. Salvation Army soldiers were working two of the corners, smiling at women pushing baby strollers past them and nodding toward their fat brass pot. But all Driscoll could see was the fur store.

He kept thinking how much it reminded him of the Presto place down in South Philly, the pool hall where the Meatman had once held court day in and day out, hunched over a big card table, brusquely dealing with the people who lined up to see him, begging favors or waiting for his orders. That had been the hub of the Mafia in Philadelphia, and every career hood who passed through town—and who intended to do any business whatsoever in Philly—had to check in and pay his respects. This place looked like the same setup. Only smaller.

After a stop at the morgue he had stayed up most of the night attempting to force-feed himself with a crash course on the Russian mob, the Malina, as Honey called it. He hoped she was safe with the Fat Man; her father's wake was supposed to take place that night, and he was afraid to even think about what might happen if she appeared. But Honey was always her own worst enemy; he'd given up trying to win arguments with her.

Working the phone the way the old-time cops had showed him, Driscoll had gotten people, cops mostly, as well as a few reporters he trusted and a couple of ex-cops who were working as private eyes, out of bed. He didn't miss contacting an informant, friend, acquaintance, and even a few people he barely knew, all in an effort to come up with some fix, some grasp of what he might be up against.

Much to his surprise, practically everybody had something to add. A security chief for American Express told him that a small, elite crew of Russian emigré con men, operating in New York and Philadelphia, using stolen or counterfeited credit cards, gold cards, had ripped off the company for close to $3 million in the course of less than a year. That was a big-league scam in anybody's game.

It appeared that the various groups, not centered around Families like La Cosa Nostra but around elders and regional clans—Odessa was, by far, the place that was mentioned most often—had begun going corporate shortly after one of the big emigré releases from Russia in 1975. The FBI had been involved right from the start—which might explain the Ed Bellows interest—because there was an automatic assumption that the KGB was sending its men and women in with the real emigrés, especially among the criminal element. But that investigation was so highly classified that none of Driscoll's sources could give him much on it.

It was a different story, however, on the meat-and-potatoes stickups and robberies. The cops in every city he called had been burned: there were over a dozen separate gangs in New York, maybe five hundred members, which meant that they were *already* as big, collectively, at least, as most of the old New York Mafia Families. Only the Gambinos could put more soldiers on the streets. All twelve gangs operated from Brighton Beach, on the ass end of Brooklyn.

A county detective in Los Angeles explained that the Russians were beginning to shoot it out with the Mexicans for control of the reefer trade. They had also made arrests for coke and heroin—sixty-five separate pinches for offenses ranging from murder to arson, in just six months.

By the time he had put the telephone down for the last time and reread his notes, Driscoll was red-eyed and punchy and sick of getting cursed out for waking up people. But at least he had one pattern that seemed to hold for every city where the Malina was hyperactive: a red pushpin. A whacked-out La Cosa Nostra boss. He'd been hearing something else, too. Unlike most of the other small emigré crime groups, which were normally only too happy to pay tribute, street tax, to the local mob padrone for the privilege of doing business in his territory, in exchange for protection, the Malina guys were very reluctant to pay anything. It almost appeared to be a matter of honor with them. In those cities where there had really been tension or open confrontation over these payments of protection money, a red pushpin had inevitably appeared on Driscoll's office map.

Every one of his sources had a different perspective, another puzzle piece to place on the board, but no one had ever before bothered to put it all together. No one had bothered, Driscoll told himself, except one group. And that group *had* to be the Mafia. The *commissione* had been in business too long to ignore a threat like this, once they saw it taking shape. And even as embattled as the traditional Mafia had been the last few years, Driscoll was certain that the *commissione* bosses had to be taking some counter-measures. He wondered if Paul Presto had somehow been part of that secret plan of retaliation. Was that what the body in his basement had been all about? And the guns—where did the M-16s and the .45s fit in?

Now, he *knew* that they would try to kill Honey again. If the Meatman had been right and the threat was coming from this Malina, then the best thing he could do was to try to stop it right here and now.

As Driscoll opened his car door and started walking toward the fur store where Vinnie had worked, his face took on a hard, alert look and his piercing gray eyes went to almost blue.

* * *

Driscoll showed the woman behind the counter his ID and asked to see Vinnie. She had a white, bland face, puffy and soft as a pillow, with brown eyes and a small colorless mouth stitched in. She answered in what he guessed was Russian, then began talking frantically with her hands, pointing toward the back of the store and down at the bulging apron tied around her waist. She kept shaking her head as if to tell him "No, no, no."

There were several stands of fur coats on either side of the narrow shop; he had no idea whether he was looking at real mink or rat pelt, and from what he could see of the back room, over the woman's shoulder, it could have been either. It looked as if she was motioning for him to leave. He decided to see if he could find anyone who spoke English.

Before he had a chance to go around behind the counter, he saw that someone was coming out to meet him. Another woman, but this one was very different. Blond and striking and nearly as tall as Driscoll. "Yes?" Tanya asked him in her accented voice. "Is there some problem, officer?" She had left Butkova's house earlier that morning and stopped in at his fur store after he told her to take anything she wanted, to help herself.

"Following up a missing-person report," Driscoll said. "Kid named Vinnie. Has he been to work in the last few days?"

Tanya asked the other woman a question in Russian. The other woman answered, then quickly left them. "I'm afraid she doesn't speak very much English," Tanya said. "You'll have to forgive her. She tries, and she's a very good seamstress. But this Vinnie"—Tanya turned to glance at a noise in the street, giving Driscoll a nice shot of her fine profile—"we haven't seen him since last week. But she tells me that he's like that, he comes and goes. Not dependable. It's so hard, as you people say, to get good help."

Tina had already told Driscoll that Vinnie never missed a day's work, never even called in sick. "Are you sure we're talking about the same kid?" Driscoll asked. "I was told you could set a clock by this Vinnie. He's the fur cutter—maybe you got two Vinnies in here?"

A small line of sweat was beginning to form on Tanya's

lip. Driscoll could detect her struggling just slightly for control. He decided to push her as far as he could. "I bet Mr. B knows this kid," Driscoll said. "Mr. B around? I have some questions for him, too."

"I don't know who you mean," Tanya answered, hesitating with each word. "There's no one here like that."

"The owner," Driscoll said, tightening up himself. "Get him out here and get some green cards for me to see." He heard some movement on the thin ceiling above his head. "Don't make me call Immigration," he said.

"Of course," Tanya said, producing her green card. The GRU had counterfeited it for her back in Moscow. "But I can't help you with this other person. What was his name again?"

"I think you remember," Driscoll told her, examining the card. It was the first one he had ever even seen and he had no idea if it was authentic. "Everybody's," he told her. "Let's get them out here. Now."

"They don't have them," she protested. "I mean . . . not here. They don't keep them here."

"Where?"

"In a safe. Their sponsor has them."

"Who's the sponsor?"

The voice, harsh and masculine, came from behind him, from the direction of the furs on display. "Mr. Butkova is the sponsor," Boris called out. Driscoll guessed he had been the sound he'd heard moving around upstairs. "He'll be glad to show them to you. My name is Boris. I suppose I'm the Mr. B."

Boris went about three hundred pounds, Driscoll guessed, with forearms the size of his thigh. "May I see your credentials, please?" Boris asked. He handed them over. In a moment, Boris returned them. There was an enormous curved knife sticking out of his pocket. Boris caught him staring at it. "For the pelts," he explained.

"You're the owner?"

"I am."

"You know Vinnie?"

"I do."

"Where is he?"

"We haven't seen him. But, of course, you know that."

Driscoll turned to Tanya. "No Mr. B, right?" His tone was sharp and annoyed.

She smiled at him and pretended that her English was failing her. "I . . . didn't understand . . . please forgive . . . I get so nervous around police." Then she made a gesture of helplessness.

"Me, too," Driscoll said. "You'd better show me that safe now."

"Oh," Boris said, starting to lead Driscoll to the door, "the safe isn't *here,* in the shop. I suppose you'll have to see Mr. Butkova for that."

"Where is he?"

"Out of town," Tanya said from behind the counter, fidgeting.

"Traveling," Boris added. "But you can just check with the Immigration people yourself. Everything's in order here." He fingered the knife blade.

"I bet," Driscoll said. "You do much business here?"

"With the holidays, we're very busy."

"Really." Driscoll stopped in his tracks and positioned himself between Boris and the door. "I've been sitting outside for about an hour and I haven't seen one person come out with a coat. Doesn't that strike you as a little odd?"

"Layaway," Boris said, deciding to play Driscoll's game. "Our coats are very costly. People just pay a little every week."

"You sure all you do in here is sell furs?"

"We repair, too."

"Boris," Driscoll said, "you're *very* good. All the answers. I bet you talk to cops like this all the time. I bet you're an old hand at bullshitting cops."

Boris smiled and made eye contact with Tanya. "In Russia, the police aren't like here. *Very* different. There, you say too much and people never see you again."

"It's a little different here," Driscoll said. "Here, you say too *little* and you'll wish to God that you never saw me. *Capiche?*"

"We *always* cooperate with police," Boris said. "Here, police our friends."

"Gimme a break, okay?" Driscoll had been through this routine plenty of times, but always with the Presto people before. But the feeling was exactly the same, talking to a goon like Boris, who was perfectly prepared to take the fall while the Meatman, or Butkova, or whoever happened to be in charge, remained insulated.

Driscoll decided to try one more thing. "I think you lost something last Friday night," he said, keeping his eye on the curved knife, which, he figured, with all of Boris's weight behind it, could probably gut him like a mackerel.

"Lost? I don't understand." He looked to Tanya for help.

"We don't . . . please say it differently," she asked.

"Emil? . . . Emil Menschikoff . . . a friend of yours? We have him in Lost and Found right now. His gun, too. What's Interpol got on you, Boris? Were you in the same outfit as Emil? Red Army infantry?" Then Driscoll started to laugh. "Who the hell do you guys think you are? You ain't back in Odessa now, pal."

Boris glared at him, his hand on the knife's hilt. Tanya answered for him. "We have no idea who you are talking about. Perhaps . . . Mr. Butkova, when he returns, can be of some help." She tossed her long blond hair and came around from behind the counter. "Please . . . you go now?"

Driscoll sized her up. "Where can I get my hands on Butkova?"

"We told you, he's not here now," Boris said evenly.

"When's he get back?"

"We never know."

"Where does he live?"

"He moves around a lot."

"That's good, too," Driscoll said. "I heard that line about the Meatman once. You Malina guys must take notes."

This time the knife almost came out. Driscoll grabbed for Boris's brawny arm with everything he had and twisted it behind his back, from the elbow. Normally, if he exerted enough pressure that way, he would easily be able to snap a man's arm; but not this time. All he could feel was the muscle rippling under his grasp. The knife clattered to the floor and fell at Driscoll's feet. "If you did the Meatman, Boris," he said, pulling up on the arm as hard as he could, making his huge prisoner grunt, as Tanya stood by looking ready to jump in at any second, "if you did him, or this guy Butkova, you'd better pray to Christ that I get you before the Prestos do, because all I can do is lock you the fuck up. The Prestos got some other ideas." Then he released the arm, picked up the knife—it looked like a small scimitar—and heaved Boris away from him. He pointed his finger right in the big man's face. "This Malina doesn't mean shit to me!" Driscoll screamed. "Your ass is mine!" Then, carefully, making certain not to turn his back to them, he backed out of the store.

He called the Roundhouse, got an automobile registration for Butkova—there was only one on file at the Department of Motor Vehicles in Harrisburg—and asked the dispatcher to find Spanish Joe or Lida. A few minutes later, Joe called back. He was all the way down in South Philly, with Lida, making the arrangements for tonight. Driscoll had wanted them to meet him at the address he had for Butkova, but then he decided that what they were doing was more important. "Go finish what you're doing," he said. "I'll take care of this." If things got spooky, he could always call in the District cops from the neighborhood for backup. But that was exactly what he had told himself that time years before, with Manny. Fuck it, he said to himself. He was pumping now.

BUSTLETON

It turned out the registration was for a business—not a house. He figured this guy probably had a dozen aliases anyway. But whatever he did, he used a fleet of trucks, because that's what the computer in Harrisburg had told him.

The place appeared deserted. It was one of those light industrial compounds that were scattered throughout

Northeast Philadelphia, right on the lip of the rowhouse neighborhoods. Years ago, everybody used to walk to work when the city still had a manufacturing economy; now, places like Butkova's were eyesores, massive, outdated piles of brick and cyclone fence that just attracted vandals and arson.

He could see all the tanker trucks inside—like heating-oil trucks—with fifty-five-gallon drums stacked clear to the roofline. Plenty of skulls and crossbones painted in industrial-safety yellow. A few signs that read "Petroleum product." But the gates were locked with chains and padlocks and the fence was mounted with razor wire, curling all the way around like an ugly silver tapeworm. Driscoll listened for guard dogs but didn't hear any. He opened the trunk of his car and poked around for his sledgehammer. In the old days, when he was a young cop, he had been the designated "sledgeman," the clown who broke down the doors whenever there were people on the other side waiting with guns. It hadn't taken him long to grow up from that, but he still loved the sledge. Driscoll kept it right next to the towel where his gun was wrapped. Given a choice between the two, he had always preferred the sledge. He hauled it out and hefted it up on his shoulder like a Louisville Slugger and went to work.

Five minutes later, he had a door in the rear of the warehouse, at the back of the compound, in splinters. He still had the touch. The only problem was, being out of condition with the hammer, he had damn near separated his shoulders in the process. Leaning the hammer where it was, Driscoll began poking around inside, stepping lightly, moving quickly in the soundless cold.

The ceiling wasn't even visible, too high, like the inside of an airplane hangar. And everywhere he turned, there were more metal slopes of fifty-five-gallon drums. Just for the hell of it, he tapped one. But the damn thing didn't move. No splash, either. It felt as if it had rocks inside. Then he tried tipping it over, but could barely budge it. He looked for some sort of crowbar or prybar to flip off the top, sealed tight.

Before he had a chance to really look, there was this *creck!* that he thought he heard from somewhere above him. It was as if someone had bumped into something and knocked it over, or maybe like a flapping shutter, but a big mother of a shutter. *Creck!* There it was again.

Looking around, getting his bearings in the strange, cavernous building, he saw steps that had to lead to the roof. As he moved that way, he heard it again.

The steps, high, narrow, minus any banister, were unstable under his weight. No support at all; almost like climbing somebody's shaky aluminum ladder. Straight up. He kept on going, uneasily.

The steps took him right to a big skylight like a hatch or attic loft; as Driscoll pushed upward on it, he felt the cold air and caught a sliver of gray, overcast sky.

Leaning on his palms and using his arms as a boost, he squeezed through and kicked his legs loose as soon as he emerged on top. He was high up, easily five stories—and tall stories—with the old mechanical shack for the elevators and hoists right in the center of the roof. Driscoll took a quick survey and saw that there was no railing or guard rope on any of the sides; best to stay well back from the edge.

Using the mechanical shack for cover, he made his way directly to the *creck!*

All the way on the other side, opposite where he had come in, Driscoll heard and saw it simultaneously. It looked like the biggest chicken coop he had ever seen, ten feet high and a good fifty feet long; the doors, spaced at even intervals, were taller than he was. And one of them was banging—downstairs it had made that *creck!* noise—deafeningly in the wind. Driscoll walked over and closed it.

Then, up in the slate-dull sky, diving for him like a bomber, he saw the first one, still a hundred feet up, but coming in fast.

It landed with a loud coo-coo-coo and an angry flutter of wings—right on top of the cage, or coop, or whatever the hell it was, that he had just closed up.

A *pigeon.* A big one—squat and bluish-brown, with a puffed-out chest and a round, compact plume. Ugly, strutting and cooing and dancing back and forth on the ledge above the long, high coop. The small bird eyes were fixing him with a look that Driscoll had never before seen, not this close up. The beak was ivory, stained brown, and curved in like Boris's pelt knife.

Then Driscoll heard the *second* one.

It came down right in front of him, flustering up its tail-feathers like a fan. They were the biggest pigeons that Driscoll had ever seen—twice the size of the scavengers that he was used to on city streets or lurking along telephone wires like so many urban vultures. The first two waited, watchful, standing sentinel.

Suddenly, he heard a deep, penetrating wave descending on him from the sky itself, a rolling, hideous, consuming nightmare of sound. And then he realized exactly why the coop was so large, and the flap door so tall. The entire flock was coming in, homing pigeons soaring down like the sorties from a dozen aircraft carriers.

And Driscoll, the intruder, realized that he was up here in their private world.

He froze motionless as one after another swooped down. Like a feathery cloud suffocating the rooftop, the birds came homing in, littering him with their small, loose feathers and beginning to shriek that eerie coo-coo-coo-coo—so loudly he thought there had to be hundreds of them—that his ears were ringing and his hands nearly shaking. Eyes, beaks, angry flapping tails. With their unerring instinct, wave after wave, perfectly precise flights, descended around him. He'd always thought of them as docile birds, but these big carriers with snaking talons seemed as malevolent as anything that Driscoll had ever encountered.

He didn't have a gun, but even if he had, the noise would only inflame them more. Driscoll knew where the hatch was, but before he could reach it, there would be a gauntlet to run, a cooing crossfire of more birds than Driscoll had ever before seen. Taking baby steps like some frightened kid, he began inching toward the opening that would take him below.

The glassy black eyes never left him.

Driscoll was nearly there when he felt a rocking, vibrating bounce on the tar roof under him; only a split second later, moving in a low, vicious crouch, chugging at him freight-train style, Boris hit the detective with everything he had.

Driscoll saw stars and rolled back, clutching at his rib

cage where the big Russian had hooked a shoulder that seemed to be iron-plated.

Before he really comprehended who or what had slammed into him, propelling him toward the edge of the roof, hard against the steep drop, five stories below, every bird on the roof, the great infuriated flock screaming out its shrill, piercing screech, arose around Driscoll. Shocked to violent life by the Russian's sudden, brutal attack, the birds prepared to repel this invasion of their roosting cote.

Driscoll was on all fours, and he could hardly even see Boris across from him, even though he instantly recognized him, because now the birds were attacking both men, flying low against their heads and faces and exposed bodies, tearing and plucking and ripping at both of them.

The big Russian rose to one knee and batted a large brown carrier away from his temple. Boris's meaty hand seemed to disappear into his belt. When he withdrew it, he slashed at the detective with the razor-sharp pelt knife.

Blocking the powerful knife thrust with his arm, Driscoll recovered and then shocked Boris with a high tackle that bowled him over in a near somersault that took his heels right over his head, a crazy, careening flip of all three hundred pounds.

On top of him, Driscoll began punching any part of the Russian that he could reach, but the rolling had carried them both right to the edge of the roof. Part of the flock, vengeful and anxious for both men to be on the ground, had followed them too, pecking and smashing their wings against hair and flesh.

Boris attempted to use his greater leverage to force Driscoll over the edge, but sprawled on his back, his weight worked against him. Awkwardly, the detective scrambled to his feet, used his arms to shield his face from the persistent birds, and tried in vain to reach behind him to pull out his handcuffs; he'd use them as brass knuckles.

Just then, the Russian bolted upright and lunged at Driscoll, whose back and side had been spun around to face the edge of the roof by the fury of the flock.

Like a dizzy, desperate matador, Driscoll turned at just the right moment, as Boris's thundering momentum carried him past, even as he attempted to reach back and grab the cop's legs and take him with him. But Boris couldn't help himself as he plunged right off the side of the building.

Dazed, but able to see what had happened, Driscoll blinked through the hovering lids and peered over the edge. Five stories below, blood pouring from his head and mouth, Boris was plastered on the ground, a crumpled indentation in the snow. The screeching flock had descended to follow the body.

Still in pain, Driscoll headed for the hatch and safety.

TWENTY-FIVE

SOUTH BROAD STREET,
SOUTH PHILADELPHIA
WEDNESDAY NIGHT

The Prestos always used a legitimate place for their wakes, the Spatino Funeral Home on South Broad Street. Friends and relatives of the Meatman were scheduled to begin arriving at 7:00 p.m. It was already past 6:30, past the time Augie Marranzano was supposed to call.

Driscoll had conducted surveillances at mob wakes before. The floral arrangements came in the shape—depending upon the deceased's interests—of pink cabin cruisers, brown-and-yellow daisy tennis racquets, purple violets sculpted to look like bocce balls or crucifixes, flanked by bleeding red rose hearts. Considering that this was the Meatman's earthly going-away party, Driscoll expected a few meat cleavers, at least. In or out of the mob, wakes were one of life's true tests of character. Usually, in Driscoll's experience, the guy who had given the order for the hit on the deceased liked to show up and stand a respectable distance from the coffin, smacking his chops, looking artificially contrite and waiting to receive the surviving mourners, who were likely to fall over themselves trying to kiss his behind and ensure that they weren't next on his list. A real pro who stood to gain something from the stiff in the box would work a wake like a ward meeting—pumping arms, squeezing elbows, and whispering hushed phrases of condolence, coming up for air only when the priest whipped out his five-decade rosary.

All mob wakes included professional mourners, stacked in the front row wailing on cue. Most of the real people spent their time on the top step of the funeral parlor, outside, sucking in the mean night air, smoking hundred-millimeter cigarettes and flashing Copa Room smiles at all the breathy young things in black silk and dark glasses.

Normally, Honey would have been one of those breathy young things, eating up the attention, while the old folks inside told polite lies about the stiff in the box. Tonight, however, Honey should, if she followed tradition—and he couldn't imagine that she wouldn't—be standing inside, at the foot of the coffin, supported on either side by Uncle Tony, the underboss, and her Aunt Marie, the senior surviving matriarch.

Cops would be there too, trying to look inconspicuous in brown vans and white panel trucks, eyeballing the mourners and snapping long-distance surveillance photos. Not just for the law-enforcement community but for all of South Philly mob wakes were an industry, with the press on hand, red-faced politicians sneaking in side doors, and teary-eyed bimbos standing in lonely ostracism, far removed from the wife and kiddies on this most sacred of family nights.

A little earlier, at the Roundhouse, the phone on Driscoll's desk had rung. "This had better be you, Augie," Driscoll had said.

"At your service."

"Does that mean you got it?"

"I'm *in* it."

"Phone and all."

"Top of the line."

"You're beautiful," Driscoll had said.

Most of the buildings across from the Spatino Funeral Home at Broad and Reed were three-story brownstones. That stretch of Broad Street used to be known as Millionaires' Row, and the old mansions looked it. A few had been chopped up into apartments with stores on the first floor.

Two of them had been torn down to clear space on the corner of the west side of the street for an extra parking lot for Spatino's. Looking across the lot, Whitey could see all the way back to Carlisle Street, one more block west. A clear view.

Whitey loved those stores. At least one floor would probably be unoccupied. Fewer people around. He had boarded the Broad Street subway outside the Academy of Music at Broad and Locust, carrying a black musician's case and affecting his most cerebral, preoccupied look. The southbound train left him off at Broad and Tasker, just two blocks from the funeral home. Many of the musicians and students from the academy lived in South Philly, and a man carrying an instrument case on the subway was a common sight. Whitey hadn't even caught anyone staring at his white hair and waxy skin.

As he walked north on Broad in the block across from the funeral home, he counted two police helicopters twirling overhead and three more from local TV stations; he knew that the Prestos would have their own men stationed on the rooftops as lookouts on both sides of the block.

Whitey made a complete circle of the block twice. He was careful not to even glance over at the steps leading down from Spatino's. Little knots of Presto people had been gathering there all afternoon. On his second pass, he found what he was looking for—a boarded-up, abandoned rowhouse on Carlisle Street, close to an alley and the rear of the Tasty Drink Tavern, a neighborhood bar at Reed and Carlisle.

He stood on the steps of the house, knew instinctively that it was a good angle, and estimated how much elevation he would need for a straightaway shot from two blocks to the west. Glancing up at the vacant windows, he saw, to his relief, that there was no tin covering, just wood. That would be no problem. He decided on the third floor, left front window. That would give him plenty of elevation.

Then he quickly made his way around to the back of the house to break the lock, if there was one. On his way, he passed three policemen, two in plainclothes, and nodded pleasantly to each of them. He was confident that they had no idea of what he looked like. He had already ditched the gun he had used on the two highway patrolmen at the airport; he had broken down the weapon into its component parts and scattered them along a watery mile of the Schuylkill River, dropping each metal piece into the water with a loud plop. While he was there, Whitey stopped to feed a loaf of bread to a hearty flock of Canada geese on the bank of the West River Drive. Whitey loved birds and animals.

It was Honey Presto's trademark to arrive late, but she made an exception for her daddy's wake. The newly ordained Archbishop of Philadelphia, Edmundus B. Mahoney—the B stood for Bible—was waiting on the pavement to greet her in a long black cassock with red sash and buttons, a young altar boy on either side of him. He comforted Honey with a solicitousness befitting her status as the Meatman's daughter. Honey genuflected and kissed his ring, then she lifted her heavy black veil and smiled at the Archbishop.

Driscoll was observing all this from the front cab of the same big yellow Streets Department trash truck he had used for the stakeout outside the numbers bank. More snow had been forecast and plows had been fixed to the front of the trucks, so his cover was golden again. Behind him there were six other trucks lined up, ready to go. They were all legit. Reluctantly, Driscoll had brought his gun with him this time. He hoped to hell he wouldn't have to use it.

Honey was wearing a black veil and a short fur jacket of rare Chinese raccoon—hideous as all hell, Driscoll thought—cut tuxedo-style in the front with strips of mink on the cardigan sleeves and over the buttons. It wasn't appropriate for a wake, but the coat had been her father's favorite and she had put it on thinking of him. She also thought of the Meatman when she daintily put a Walther PPK seven-shot automatic into her purse.

When Driscoll saw the garish fur as Honey walked in with the archbishop, he picked up the walkie-talkie and said, "All yours."

"Sí, amigo." Joe Pepe, Spanish Joe, was inside Spatino's, pretending to be a driver for one of the limos that were beginning to double-park on Broad Street. He was using a lapel mike and an earpiece.

"Lida?" Driscoll then asked, intently.

"Right here, and I'm sweating fucking bullets," she said, bundled up as she was in the long blue habit of the Sister Servants of the Immaculate Heart of Mary. Her mike was in the habit and the earpiece was under her bandeau. She was seated on one of the wooden folding chairs in front of the coffin, trying to maintain her serene smile for the benefit of the other mourners, throwing her voice like a ventriloquist. As far as Driscoll knew, none of the Prestos knew either of them.

"Let me know when he starts the Rosary," Driscoll instructed them over the box. "You probably have a half hour. By the way, did anybody make either one of you?"

"These assholes?" Lida said. "Are you kidding?"

"That's a helluva way for a nun to talk," Driscoll said as he switched off the walkie-talkie.

It took Whitey less than a minute to loosen the three wooden planks, one-by-twelves, that covered the doorway. No lock. Almost too easy. Then he was inside. The wood had given way as if it was used to giving. Whitey knew instantly that somebody had been using the house before him.

The first floor was littered with papers and rags. Then he found the steps; thirteen to the second floor. The treads on five and eleven were missing. At five, he took a misstep and put his foot right through the empty air. By eleven, he was on guard, and on the next step, he crunched something that sounded like broken glass. The air inside the Carlisle Street house reeked of mildew and urine. Somebody, vagrants or junkies, he assumed, had been in there recently. Whitey hoped they wouldn't show up tonight.

He used a small penlight torch with a penetrating beam to scan the litter on the second floor: beer cans and wine bottles and dozens of tiny glass ampules and small clear envelopes fastened with colored tapes. Crack, coke—a shooting gallery, for sure. Whitey didn't like the looks of this place. His bladder was bothering him, too. It was so damn cold. No interior walls. Just one big, open, enormous room. But a room with a view. The third floor was the same. Less dirt and more drug paraphernalia. Whitey sat up there, checking the windows, checking the best angle. Then he felt that burning in his abdomen again. He leaned his musician's case against the wall, walked to the back of the house, to what would have been a rear bedroom, selected a corner, and relieved himself, adding to the overpowering urine stench. Then he returned to his window, the left front. He squinted through a space between the wooden planks and yanked one of them to let in a little more light from the streetlamp outside. He could make out the figures of the mourners on the front steps of Spatino's. The one he was looking for, Honey Presto, the young woman in the funny-looking fur jacket, had just walked in with a clergyman at her side. She *was* still alive.

Kneeling down, Whitey opened his case, an oboe case, and began spreading out its contents on the wooden floor in front of him.

Every few minutes, Driscoll heard from Lida or Spanish Joe, as he checked out the rooftops along Broad Street. From what they were telling him, the wake was absolutely unremarkable, thus far. Honey and her Aunt Marie were running the show—no surprise there—and Uncle Tony was keeping his mouth shut and his eyes fixed on the top of his shoes.

Tonight would be Honey's first public appearance since the bombing. After the attempt on her life at Manny's place, Driscoll had begged her to take a pass on the wake, but Honey, hardhead that she was, hadn't heard a word he said.

The cops had barricades set up to rope off onlookers. They were showing up as if it were the damn Mummers' Parade on New Year's Day. Back when he was in uniform, in Highway Patrol, he had worked this neighborhood and chased some poor bastard, a fleeing felon, as the police termed it, right into the Tasty Drink Tavern.

Two blocks away, back on Carlisle Street, he could see the sigh on the Tasty Drink Tavern, with some of the letters missing, swaying in the wind. Jesus, he thought, the neighborhood had really taken a beating since then. It used to be solid Italian, like a back street in Naples, with old men sitting on marble stoops watching the world go by. Now it was mostly black. The Italians had moved to the suburbs and franchised their drug operations to the blacks. What a shame. It used to be a helluva neighborhood. Even the block next to the Tasty Drink Tavern was boarded up now. He kept looking at the decrepit rowhouses. Once, he'd known everybody who lived in that block. He tried to put faces with addresses.

Nothing doing at the funeral parlor. Just people smoking and talking on the front steps, rubbing their paws together to keep warm like good little endomorphs.

Carlisle Street. Dead houses. A dying block. Boarded-up windows. Two blocks away. Three-story houses. Nice elevation. Nobody there anymore. No obstructions. A clear shot across the parking lot.

Jesus Christ! Driscoll said to himself. A clear shot! Nobody had checked out the empty houses on Carlisle Street. That's where *he* had to be—whoever the hell he was. Driscoll looked again, from the funeral home back to Carlisle Street. Perfect angle of fire.

Suddenly, he turned the key in the steering column of the big truck and started it moving. "Lida," he called into the walkie-talkie, "how the hell does it look?"

"No good, Phil," Lida answered. "This broad Honey never takes a piss. I can't get in there. Too many people around. No go."

"You have to get her in there. Now!"

"How?"

"Call her in. I don't care what you have to do, just get her in there!"

Just then, Spanish Joe's voice cut in. "Phil. Lida. The archbishop's beginning."

"Go, Lida!" Driscoll screamed into the walkie-talkie. "Now! I think I know his location."

Pushing the trash truck's big diesel as hard as he could, Driscoll cut across four lanes of traffic on Broad Street and headed for Carlisle.

The crowning point of any Roman Catholic wake, Irish or Italian, is the communal recitation of the Rosary. All kneel facing the casket, heads bowed, palms pressed together in prayer, minds focused on the Five Sorrowful Mysteries: the Agony in the Garden, the Scourging at the Pillar, the Crowning with Thorns, the Carrying of the Cross, and the Crucifixion.

A caring priest who feels for the knees of the bereaved would end it right there. Only a masochist would insist that people remain kneeling and praying the Five Joyful Mysteries and the Five Glorious Mysteries, too.

Honey had requested all fifteen Mysteries. "I think my father might need them all," was how she explained it to Edmundus Bible Mahoney. He agreed, having known the Meatman, as he had, for the last forty of his fifty-six years. Honey thanked him and requested kneelers for herself and her Aunt Marie.

Right in the middle of a Hail Mary, when they were still at the Scourging at the Pillar, Aunt Marie leaned her gigantic bosom heavily on Honey's slim shoulder and whispered, "I need a smoke."

Only a few of the praying heads turned as the two women arose, genuflected, and made their way toward the Spatino Funeral Home's immaculate ladies' room.

One of the heads that did turn belonged to Lida James, Sister Lida for tonight. Another one belonged to Spanish Joe. They practically ran after Honey and Marie.

Whitey had made the gun himself, rifling the barrel in his father's basement workshop back in Pittsburgh, modifying each piece by hand. He had adopted the single-action firing mechanism from a Heckler & Koch G3 rifle. Roller locks. Concealed hammer. Thumb lever grip. He had nine shells with him. He planned on needing only one.

Sighting through the telescopic lens, with its miniaturized night-vision attachment, Whitey poked the nose of the rifle through the space he had widened between the two wooden boards, and firing imaginary bullets, he pretended to kill every single person standing on the front steps of the Spatino Funeral Home. *Bang! Bang! Bang!*

It was going to be a tough shot. No doubt about that.

But Whitey would make it. His cheek was starting to tingle, the left one.

He had confidence in himself, boundless confidence.

It was nearly 8:00 p.m. Honey Presto had to come out soon.

"I beg your pardon!" Honey shouted as the chunky nun pushed her way into Honey's stall in the ladies' room. Honey's lace panties were down around her ankles; her dress was pushed up, her jacket was around her shoulders. She hadn't even had a chance to light her cigarette yet.

"Be a good girl and I won't break your face," Lida said as she began pulling Honey off the toilet seat; she shoved her hard against the back wall of the stall. But Honey spun away, ducked under Lida's clumsy habit, and lunged for her purse with the Walther PPK in it. Honey was positive this crazy nun had been sent to kill her, and she wasn't going without a fight. But Lida swooped down and got the handbag first. "Gotcha!" she told Honey, pulling out the pistol.

Spanish Joe had waylaid Aunt Marie before she ever had a chance to go into the ladies' room. He was holding her hand, blubbering in Spanish about the *padrone,* the Meatman. Marie just figured at first that he was one of her late brother's Spic strong-arm men. Marie didn't like Spics, especially pushy ones like this guy, but the Meatman had had a soft spot for his men, even Spics.

He had his back turned, so as to block the bathroom door. He was weeping. "The *padrone,*" Joe kept repeating, sobbing and clutching for her.

"Thank you . . . thank you . . ." Marie stammered, trying to get loose. Finally, she gave up and pulled away roughly. Damn that Spic! Now she wouldn't be able to smoke unless she went out to the car. It wouldn't look right if she just stood on the steps outside with the kids. But it would look even worse if she went and sat in the car, acting as though the wake for her dear, departed brother bored the crap out of her, which it did.

Lousy Spics.

Reluctantly, cursing under her breath, Aunt Marie returned to the Rosary. The worst part was that she had to pee really bad, but the stupid Spic was still blubbering at the bathroom door. She'd just have to hold it in.

The service was over, and people had begun to stream down the funeral parlor steps. Driscoll abandoned the truck in the middle of the street in front of the Tasty Drink Tavern and ran the rest of the way, gun in hand.

The Fat Man had come to pay his respects. He had once been Paul's best friend. He pulled up in his brown Checker cab, brown vinyl roof, converted and customized to his specifications—which, in this case, meant *big*—and double-parked at the end of the line. As soon as Manny lumbered down from the front seat of the Checker, the crowd, the cops, the Prestos, the FBI, the visiting hoods, and even the delegation from the Five New York Families all knew who he was—Big Manny. With each unsteady step that the Fat Man took, the crowd tittered. They all remembered—his trials, his being hauled into the courtroom on a mail dolley by the sheriff's deputies. Fat Manny had come to the Meatman's wake. Never before had Manny experienced such adulation.

Whitey vaguely noticed the big yellow trash truck rumbling down toward Carlisle Street, stopping, the driver leaping out and running toward him. But he had Honey Presto in his sights. She was walking slowly down the steps, her face covered by a veil, her fur jacket bunched around her chest.

From his third-floor vantage point, Whitey also noticed that an old brown car had pulled up and an incredibly fat man had gotten out. He seemed to be calling to Honey, trying to get her attention. Honey froze momentarily on the steps and stared at him as he moved up the steps toward her.

That millisecond, that moment suspended in time and space, was all that Whitey needed. He could see it all clearly in the slow motion of his mind. Honey Presto was frozen in his kill zone.

He fired. One round. In the heart. His left cheek was twitching.

She collapsed on the steps of Spatino's, then rolled forward, coming to rest at the feet of the Fat Man. He instantly threw himself across her body, using his great mass to cover every inch of her.

Honey couldn't be dead.

Manny had heard the shots and felt the night air move, as the bullets had found their mark. Yet, as he held Honey close to him, clutching her body so tightly, he could sense some movement. Confused, but elated by the prospect that she might still be alive, the Fat Man tore away her veil and stared uncomprehendingly.

But who was this? Where was Honey? Why was this woman wearing Honey's clothes?

Lida stared up at the Fat Man in tremendous discomfort and pain from the places where the bullets had bruised her through the flak jacket she was wearing. Lida didn't say a word. She didn't have to. The look on Manny's face told her that he understood the switch that had been made.

No possibility of a second shot. Whitey's entire rifle sight was filled with the Fat Man. Suddenly, Whitey saw the Fat Man turning awkwardly in his direction and looking right up at his window on Carlisle Street. He kept pointing to it, screaming, gesturing.

She was dead, wasn't she? She was lying on the steps, her veil pulled back, motionless with this fat man next to her. Whitey adjusted his telescopic lens and tried to peer in on her features on what should have been her death mask. But something was wrong, very wrong. The *face* was wrong. It *wasn't* Presto's daughter. Damn it, what had they done?

All at once the crowd and the police were running in Whitey's direction.

* * *

Driscoll's total concentration, his entire being, was fixed on the man inside 1334 Carlisle Street. He had him now. The front of the house was boarded up tightly. No way out. He'd get him in the rear.

They were after him now, streaming across the parking lot from Broad Street, and that cop in the big yellow truck was coming, too. The keen sense of being the hunted, the excitement, the serene inner certainty that he had killed Honey Presto on the first shot—it was all vanishing now. Something had gone wrong. Killing always gave him an erection, a tremendous hard-on that would remain with him indefinitely. But this time Whitey was reeling from the sick sensation of failure. The erection that had bulged against his tight pants as he had raced down the steps two and three at a time was suddenly turning soft. He charged through the flimsy wooden planks that covered the back door with his shoulder, the oboe case tucked safely under his arm, desperately working against this sudden feeling of impotence. What had happened? Where was the Presto girl?

And then he was outside, in the cold night air.

"Freeze," Driscoll screamed, jumping Whitey from behind and roughly jamming the barrel of his gun into Whitey's right ear. It was the cop from the delicatessen.

Suddenly, voices. Voices everywhere.

"Cops, man!" a young voice shouted out of the darkness of the alley.

"Cops all over," another voice picked up the warning, hysterical. The junkies were back, back to reclaim their vacant house.

They startled both Whitey and Driscoll. Caught them totally unprepared. Both men reacted. Whitey, having recovered in seconds from this crazy cop's getting the drop on him, was just a fraction of a second quicker. He swung the oboe case in an uppercut, smashing Driscoll across the head and face. Suddenly, a tall black junkie bumped into Driscoll and kept on going. The detective cried out in pain.

Whitey looped under Driscoll's gun and was gone.

The corner of 15th and Carlisle was alive with people now. The junkies were running the alleys like rats. The only thing Driscoll could see clearly in the dark was a lurching figure, dressed in black, short, spiky white hair, fleeing. Suddenly, the cop recognized him—not the face, but the profile with his head and neck bending forward from his shoulders like a crane's. It was the creep from Manny's place, the guy in the deli who had refused to leave. *He* was the shooter and was now reeling left on 15th Street, dashing between parked cars. People everywhere. Kids.

Old ladies poking their heads out of second-story windows. Teenagers dancing around and screaming. The junkies still running the alley.

Driscoll couldn't fire. It was too big a risk. He had a line of sight on the white-haired man in black, but there were just too many kids around.

Disgusted, Driscoll depressed the hammer on the .38 and jammed it into his armpit holster.

Then the rest of the cops from Broad Street showed up. Late. Typical. Goddam cops. The white-haired bastard had gotten away. All Driscoll could do was stand there, his scalp bleeding where the oboe case had hit him.

"Phil, yo, Phil . . . over here. In the hearse."

It was Augie. Driving his top-of-the-line hearse. The one with the phone in the front seat. God only knew where he had scrounged that up.

Driscoll walked slowly across Reed Street, amid all the confusion, ignoring the other policemen, and got in. Augie reached over to hold the door open. He looked great—like a professional pall-bearer, all clean and neat in a suit and a black tie.

"Right on time," Driscoll complimented Augie, as the long black hearse sped away.

TWENTY-SIX

THE ROUNDHOUSE
THURSDAY, CHRISTMAS EVE

The Roundhouse at 8th and Race Streets had been built in 1963 when the city decided to clear out skid row. The street bums disappeared, but the feeling of squalor lingered. Driscoll hated the place. Three squat concrete bunkers of circular hallways and dirty cubicles.

Lawlor had been asking to see him, and after the gunplay at Presto's wake, the summons had become a command. As he pulled into the parking lot off 8th Street, skidding on ice that the Streets Department hadn't bothered to clear away, he noticed that not a single parking spot had been shoveled except Commissioner Lawlor's.

Walking in and heading for the elevator, Driscoll passed little plastic models of police cars and paddy wagons, black Marias through the ages, mounted on clear Lucite shelves in display cases. Banners streamed down from the ceiling, urging one and all to support the Police Athletic League.

Driscoll stepped off the elevator outside the commissioner's office and stared at Lawlor's door with its fancy gold lettering. An Internal Affairs captain, whose ears perked up like a guard dog's when he saw Driscoll heading for the commissioner's office, spoke to him. "He's expecting you," the captain said.

The commissioner was off in a corner of his barren office,

conspicuously devoid of mementos despite a forty-year police career, grinding away on a stationary bicycle.

Driscoll wondered if the old man ever broke a sweat. He had never seen Lawlor perspire, yet keeping in shape was the equivalent of a religious tenet with him.

"I heard you had some excitement with the Presto girl," Lawlor began, easing up on his pedaling.

"A little," Driscoll said.

"But you let him get away." Driscoll thought back to the clear shot he had missed.

"It happens sometimes," Driscoll said.

"Not to you, it shouldn't," the commissioner admonished. He was dressed in a T-shirt and gray police department gym shorts. He didn't even look flushed as he alighted from the bike. "Ten miles," he boasted to Driscoll, "not bad—you should try this."

Lawlor began doing knee bends. "Where is she?" he asked.

"She's okay. She's safe."

"Where?"

"She's my responsibility, and if I tell you she's safe, you have to accept that."

Lawlor almost sneered, then turned it into a harmless grimace as he pulled out of the last knee bend.

"Bellows wants to talk to her. What am I supposed to tell him?" he asked.

"You can tell him anything you want to," Driscoll said, trying not to make it sound like a challenge.

Alfred E. Smith Lawlor, Philadelphia's top cop, had the eyes of an executioner and a viselike grip. Right now, those eyes were incinerating Driscoll. Lawlor should have been a priest. He had the hands for it, the voice for it, and even the proper cadence in his walk. Ramrod-stiff and white-haired, with a pair of puffy, thatched snow clouds for eyebrows, he had the bearing of an arrogant Templar. In the church he would have made cardinal. Instead, he had risen to the rank of police commissioner of Philadelphia on merit.

Lawlor released Driscoll's eyes for a moment, then turned to look up at a huge crucifix on the wall over his empty bookcase. The figure of Christ was hanging upon it, the blood from his palms and ankles spilling onto the wooden base. Driscoll felt something ominous about the commissioner's fixation on the icon.

"You overheard a conversation at the morgue—an extremely sensitive conversation. Is that not correct?" Lawlor asked, summoning a disturbing silence in the room as he spoke.

"You've already talked to Ed Bellows, obviously," Driscoll answered. "Why ask me?"

Lawlor was zeroing in on him as he slipped into a pair of long sweats—*Property of Philadelphia PD.* "It's just as well that you heard it." Lawlor gestured up at the crucifix on the wall. "He works in mysterious ways."

The commissioner's voice had suddenly taken on an almost messianic vigor. He spoke to Driscoll as though he were addressing him from some great, inaccessible height, from some towering pulpit. Then, drawing close to the detective's face, his tone suddenly became a near-whisper. "Honey Presto, Phillip—*she's* our problem." When Lawlor was like this, he had a conspiratorial way of convincing people that he was fully prepared to hear their confession.

The only deterrent to Lawlor's entering the priesthood had been the fact that his brother had been born ahead of him. Lawlor had known from the day of his tenth birthday that he had the calling. That day, in the morning, after they had celebrated his birthday, the family drove in their father's big black Buick Roadmaster to a grim, gray-walled minor seminary in Blackwood, New Jersey. On every side, the fields around the seminary were covered with a milky coating of snow. It seemed that the drive would never end. When it finally did, Lawlor was so taken with the place—he had felt such peace inside its high walls—that he cried when it was time to go home. He never forgave his brother. But in his family, the first son was given to God and the second-born went to either the police department or the fire department. It was all very Irish and very traditional, and Lawlor was thirty years old before he questioned any of it. By then, he was married, with one daughter, and a wife who catered to his need for solitude.

Driscoll had to assume that *he* was part of the problem, too, because in Lawlor's mind, despite what he might say, there was no separating him from Honey.

Driscoll was listening. "In that conversation at the morgue you overheard something; it was a reference to 'a man who had been *informed*'—I believe that's how Mr. Bellows put it—and his name is James Xavier Carney. Does the name mean anything to you?"

"Sure," Driscoll said. "He's a big shot in Washington. Like Kissinger. National security adviser." Driscoll shook his head. "What's a guy like that got to do with Paul Presto? Carney would have to be slumming to get down that low."

"Yes, he would," Lawlor said. "Carney happens to be a Man of Loyola. We went to school together. I don't know if you knew that."

Driscoll didn't, but he knew about the Men of Loyola. They were prominent lay Catholics. Very selective. A papist version of the Bohemian Club in San Francisco. The ultimate old-boy network—but Catholic, and as secretive as the College of Cardinals.

Lawlor was sitting on the edge of his desk, almost nose to nose with the detective. "Stay close to Miss Presto," he said. "She trusts you. And whatever we decide to do about her, it stays in this room. Do I make myself clear?"

Driscoll didn't answer. Then, for Honey's sake, he knew he had to. "Do you mean just keep her quiet?"

"Certainly that. At least that." The commissioner knew considerably more about what was going on than Driscoll. With that advantage, he felt omniscient.

Lawlor spent his vacations at Loyola Retreat house in Hastings, Pennsylvania. There he walked the Stations of the Cross outdoors, along a path measured by clumps of evergreen and a thick ground covering of boxwood. Years before, when he was in high school, Lawlor, a strange, morose young man, had helped to carve those fourteen wooden plaques that marked Christ's journey to his crucifixion. When he stood alone in the woods, before the final station, the wind a scourge at his back and the priests in the abbey a constant reminder of his frustrated vocation, Alfred E. Smith Lawlor wept—just as he imagined Christ must have wept. His duty—his vocation—as he saw it was to make the best use of men like Driscoll, regardless of the risks or consequences.

"I'll be watching you, Driscoll. Don't fail me . . . or

Him." He pointed to the wall again, the cross. "If you do betray Him or me, then you're beyond salvation. I—even I—won't be able to fix it this time." Lawlor's eyes narrowed and worked his shaggy eyebrows into a single frosty line. "You are in the middle of something now, and the only way out is through me." He paused. "But I suppose you know that feeling."

"I'll never forget what you did for me," Driscoll said, referring to his affair with Honey and to the pictures that came into Internal Affairs, and to Lawlor's allowing the whole thing to pass—until now. "I've tried to pay you back every day since—"

"Try harder," Lawlor cut him off. He laughed, but only an empty sound came out.

"I won't hurt her," Driscoll said, meaning it. He didn't care if Lawlor liked it or not.

"Did I ask you to hurt anyone?" Lawlor replied blandly. "I don't recall saying that. I know how you feel about Miss Presto. You would *never* let any harm come to her."

Driscoll couldn't wait to get back to Honey, but Lawlor had other ideas. "Before you go," Lawlor said, indicating the crucifix on the wall, "I want you to pray with me."

Driscoll, stunned, disbelieving, remained where he was.

For years, Driscoll had heard stories about the old man—stories that portrayed him as a cross between J. Edgar Hoover and some mad monk of the desert. But none of it had ever really touched him. Now, in a total departure from his normally aloof exterior, Lawlor was creaking open the door on some secret vault and summoning him inside.

"*Pray.* Dammit! Down on your knees, Driscoll. Pray for yourself; pray for your whore . . . *just pray! On your knees!*"

Lawlor dropped to one knee, then the other, gripping the edge of his desk as he did so. After hesitating a moment, Driscoll knelt down beside him, a prop in the old man's fantasy.

"For the greater glory of God, Driscoll; for the greater glory of God."

NOBLE STREET

Manny knew there was something wrong even before he put his key in the lock. He could smell it. Smell the fact that it just wasn't right. He had a gun in the pocket of his greatcoat. It was a solid, hefty revolver, but his fat hand suctioned around it like a man-eating plant devouring an insect.

He was dragging an evergreen behind him, a six-foot Christmas tree. He knew he had to be the only Jew in the world out on a freezing December afternoon paying too goddam much money to a couple of *goyim* crooks selling Christmas trees. But he wanted Honey to have a tree. That was the least he could do for her. She'd looked so sad, so abandoned, the last time he saw her. Thank the good Lord nothing had happened to her at the wake. Maybe now she would come back with him where she belonged.

The jerks with the Christmas trees were half drunk by the time Manny waddled over to the corner where they were warming their hands over a big burning can with cinders inside. He had been the only one there—it was just a couple of blocks from his place on Noble Street. All the gentile rowhouses along the way were glittering with Christmas decorations. Besides the two morons selling the trees—$65 for the damn thing, an obscene profit—he had seen only one other person on the street, a very tall, thin man, dressed in black with crewcut white hair, a crooked face, and motionless brown eyes. There had been something almost shy about him. Manny looked hard at him once, almost sensing a vague kind of recognition, but then, when he looked a second time, the white-haired man had disappeared. The Fat Man was glad for the gun in his pocket. All the strange characters on the street nowadays. Manny looked both ways, cautiously, before he went in.

Marie Bonaventura kept staring at the tiny black-and-white TV screen on her bedroom bureau. It was closed-circuit and it monitored their front steps, part of the street for the width of about three car lengths—that was a little fuzzy—and both entrances to the rear of her rowhouse, the basement door and the garage doors. Several prominent members of the Presto Family had installed similar security devices during the Atlantic City War that followed the great Don Angelo Bruno's assassination on Snyder Avenue. But not the Meatman. He had always ridiculed such admissions of personal terror.

On the regular TV next to the closed-circuit screen, Marie was watching a Christmas special. She was also lapping up a thick eggnog. It was so difficult for her to concentrate on both screens at the same time that she was almost going cross-eyed. About twenty minutes before, during a commercial on the real TV, Marie had almost shot herself, she became so frightened. That was because suddenly, from out of the range of the closed-circuit camera, someone had come running toward her back door. The black-and-white image splashed across the little screen like some disjointed charcoal drawing, much too fast for her to see anything clearly. She uttered the word "shit" and then "thank God," slurring both together when she realized it was just a kid chasing some kind of a ball. The scary thing was that she had the gun that she kept under her pillow, a .22, up and in her hand and ready to use before she could even tell what it was that she would have been shooting at.

That really did it, too. Enough of this being-left-alone stuff.

She picked up the phone and dialed Tony's number. "Come home," she said, "I'm so afraid I can't stay off the toilet. I need somebody here with me. All the time. Besides, we have to get ready for the procession at St. Bibiana's tonight."

"Not possible," Tony replied, afraid to say much on his business phone at the pool hall because he assumed that about twenty-five FBI agents were making notes on the other end.

Marie started bawling into the phone. "You gotta come now," she begged. "Look what almost happened to Honey at the funeral home. Everything's going wrong. Tony, I'm afraid to even leave my house."

"I'll send somebody with the pizza," he said, figuring that that could never be construed as very incriminating. He kept remembering how they nearly nailed John Gotti in New York on some stupid wiretap.

"Hurry," Marie said. "Before somebody else gets shot."

Tony Bonaventura put the phone down, looked over at Joe-Joey straightening his silk breast-pocket handkerchief, and said one word: "Marie."

OREGON AVENUE, SOUTH PHILADELPHIA

Lida James stared at her fingers disapprovingly. The name on the bottle of nail polish had been Vermilion Mist, but her fingers still looked red. Not vermilion, just red as cherry tips. Too red. She made a face. Maybe the nail polish was too much anyway; she could always take it off. Lida loved to make decisions, loved taking action. That's the main reason why she had become a cop—that and the fact that she was a sucker for guys in uniforms.

She unscrewed the top on the bottle of clear nail-polish remover. The smell hit her like cold air through an open window. Lifting the bottle to just a few inches from her nose, she inhaled. Intoxicating, addictive. Then she sniffed a few more times and abruptly screwed the cap back on and pushed the bottle away from her. She thought back to the time that she and Spanish Joe had done a line of coke—Lida had talked him into it—just for the hell of it, just once, to see what it was like. That had scared both of them, made them ashamed. Now here she was, doing the same thing. *Giving in.* Lida wished she had some willpower.

Lida checked her nails again. The Vermilion Mist wasn't *that* bad. Red, but not exactly make-me-gag red. She scrunched up her face one more time. The polish looked pretty good after all. The polish wasn't her problem, her *fingers* were the problem. They were too fat. Nothing else on her was really fat—except her tits, of course. But that was okay. Her fingers, however, were short, pudgy stumps, as far as she was concerned. The color—any color—just brought that out.

God, how she hated her fingers. The rest of her body was fine, better than fine, in fact. Excellent. No stomach; those large, pointed breasts; big, soft, russet-colored nipples; smooth flanks; great legs; black-brown hair that she swept up under her officer's hat, when she was in uniform, but that normally reached to her shoulders; huge eyes, barely brindle-brown, penetrating, but at the same time revealing every thought in her head and every feeling in her heart.

That had always been her problem with guys like Driscoll—there was never any mystery where Lida was concerned. When she liked a guy she let him know it.

Deciding to leave the Vermilion Mist alone, she checked herself in the round mirror in her living room. Not bad at all, not bad considering that the next important birthday she celebrated would be her thirtieth; she touched her stomach, perfectly flat. Finally, Lida dabbed a little extra Coco on her wrists, behind her knees, just below her ears. That was for Driscoll. Just in case, she wanted to be ready. You could never tell with a guy like him. Reluctantly, Lida forced herself to perform the last task she had. Better check, she said to herself.

Lida lived in a one-bedroom apartment with a big living room and a couch that turned into a hideaway bed. For the first time since she had moved in, she had spent the previous night on the couch. As a favor to Driscoll.

She stepped into a skirt, pulled on an old blue uniform shirt that was too frayed to wear to work anymore; no bra, no panties, no shoes. She rubbed her chest above her left breast, where the bullet had bruised her as it flattened against the flak jacket she had worn under Honey Presto's fur. Lida was turning a little black-and-blue. Her shoulder hurt, too, the way the shot had snapped back her whole torso. But that part had been almost easy; her body was tensed, quivering, and her adrenaline had been really gushing because she was expecting to be shot—or at least shot at—as soon as she set foot on the steps outside the funeral home. Driscoll had carefully thought the whole thing through. The hardest part had been getting Honey into the damn nun's habit, unconscious, and then spiriting her out of the ladies' room and into the hearse. Honey had felt like a damn deadweight.

As quietly as she could, Lida opened her bedroom door and looked in. The nun's habit was balled up and tossed in a corner. On the bed, under a sheet, sleeping like a baby, was Honey Presto. That bitch. Safe and sound.

TWENTY-SEVEN

OREGON AVENUE

Driscoll had never even seen the inside of Lida's apartment. The first sensation that hit him when he knocked on her door was the smell of garlic.

"You expecting werewolves?" he asked her as she peeked through the chain lock.

"Downstairs," she answered, slipping the chain out of its plate and letting him in. "You try to live over a hoagie place and see what you smell like."

There was a big sandwich shop and hoagie joint on the first floor; Lida lived three flights up over the store. Driscoll had had no idea the garlic smell would travel that far. He checked the place out; it was nicer than he had expected, more old-fashioned. No leather, no glass, no chrome, two lamps with fringe on the shades caught his eye. So did a rug that looked like Lida had made it herself.

"I rented it furnished," she said, following his eyes. "I ain't that domestic." She was still barefoot, dressed the same as when she had checked on Honey. Her nipples were right *there,* pressing against the Oxford cloth of the police shirt.

"She okay?" Driscoll asked.

"Fine. Taking a nap."

He wanted to tell her what a great job she had done, taking the bullet on the flak jacket, the bullet intended for Honey. But instead he just asked, "Your chest hurt, where . . . you know . . . ?"

Lida smiled. "Wanna see my bruise?"

Driscoll never knew what to say to Lida. "Would you mind going in and waking her?" He stretched his legs and noticed her gun belt and holster on a shelf.

"My pleasure." Lida walked into the bedroom and closed the door behind her. He heard what sounded like a brief, catty argument, then a closet door slamming. Lida returned. "She'll be out in a minute," she said, "but if you think I'm going to let her parade around in my clothes, Phil, you're out of your mind."

"I forgot all about the clothes," he said, feeling like an ass. But he had this little thing that he did with his eyes whenever he got in trouble with a woman. Lida's face softened and she made a small sound of annoyance and defeat.

They were both standing in the living room, and the bedroom door was still slightly open. There was a momentary flash of naked woman, mainly the back of the leg and the buttock, as Honey made a dash for the bathroom. They both looked at her. Honey pretended she didn't notice them.

"I guess this isn't the first time you saw that, is it, Phil?" Lida asked as Honey's naked behind disappeared into the bathroom. This time there was just resignation in her tone, as she sipped from a cup of coffee she had just poured for herself.

"Let's see the bruise," Driscoll said.

Fifteen minutes later, Driscoll and Honey were in Driscoll's car, and he was heading north on Delaware Avenue to pick up Spring Garden Street and then make a right up 5th Street to see if Harry Capri had come up with anything.

"Who was your father buying guns from?" Driscoll asked, passing the three-masted ships at Penn's Landing, nervous because he couldn't see the I-95 overpass above them. It was a perfect setup for a sniper. "I know who he was buying them for," Driscoll said. "Uncle Sam."

Honey shrugged. "I didn't even know he bought guns," she replied. "Is that what this is all about?" She was wearing one of Lida's old uniforms.

"You're the one who's supposed to know that."

"Says who?"

Driscoll believed her, but he knew that no one else would. She really *didn't* know. "Everybody. Why do you think Bellows is so worried? And this guy Carney who Lawlor told me about. Uncle Sam doesn't like to be embarrassed when he gets caught going to the mob for help. They're afraid you'll talk—maybe try to blackmail them, or testify against them if this gun deal ever gets out. And don't forget what happened to the last two guys who almost testified about the mob helping the government."

"You mean John Rosselli and Sam Giancana? Weren't they supposed to assassinate Fidel Castro or somebody, back in the sixties?" she asked, making Driscoll feel old enough to be her father instead of her lover. That was like yesterday to him.

"Unsolved murders," he said, "but everybody in the world knows what happened to them. Rosselli was found in a forty-gallon drum, Momo Giancana had seven slugs in the head."

"My father talked to them. I know that," she said, resting her chin in her hand and looking out across the Delaware River at the murky skyline of Camden, New Jersey. "I know, because I begged him not to. I never wanted to see anybody try to use him, and that's what I told him."

Driscoll respected her point of view, but he couldn't accept it. "The Meatman would never have gone for a one-way street deal," he said. "If Bellows and his people got what they wanted, so did your father."

"Maybe you didn't know him as well as you think you did," she said.

"Don't bet on it."

They made the left onto Spring Garden, passing the new marina nearby and the transfer station where the city's garbage trucks lined up to dump refuse. That was where Driscoll had picked up his trash truck.

Honey lit another cigarette, cracked the car window about an inch, and blew the smoke outside.

"This guy Carney—do you realize who he is?"

"I'm not stupid," Honey said. "My father found out that this whole thing was his idea from the very beginning, but Ed Bellows was the only one he ever talked to. I'm positive of that."

Driscoll turned again at 5th Street, in front of the fire department headquarters. They were less than ten minutes from Harry's place now. He hoped his old friend would know something.

"I really don't see what good this is going to do," Honey said. "I've told you everything I know. My father never mentioned guns to me, or that Russian thing, either, that Malina. But I could tell by the way he talked that he was afraid of it. It's funny—I never knew him to be afraid of anything, ever."

"Harry said he has some pictures. I just want you to look at them. There might just be a face that you know; maybe you don't even realize that you know, but just look at some of them, that's all. And talk to Harry. See what he thinks. It's a helluva lot better than you just sitting around waiting to get shot at again."

Honey closed her eyes, pushed the front of her police cap down over her face and sank into the car seat.

FISHTOWN

He steered the car under the dark shadows of the El tracks at Front and Kensington, practically on top of Harry's store. He parked in the middle, next to one of the pillars, pock-marked concrete, defaced by a blaze of red and blue spray-painted graffiti that read "Cool Earl."

Then Driscoll opened the car door on his side and Honey did the same. "Come on, let's talk to Harry," he said, pointing to the store. The traditional three golden balls were hanging outside the entrance. "The poor man's banker," he told Honey.

Driscoll knocked on the door, because the shade was down, then turned the knob and the door opened. "Harry always keeps this locked," he said. "He uses a buzzer to open the door." The door sqeaked. No lights. No lock.

"Be careful," he warned.

"Harry!" Driscoll called loudly, but there was no answer.

Honey spotted the big blowup of the naked woman over the wall behind the cash register. "That's the most disgusting thing I've ever seen," she snickered, making a face.

He ignored her, then poked around in the corner and aisles of the shop. Honey followed him. There was a small room behind the counter area. Harry had a bathroom back there and a closet that he used as a darkroom for his pictures.

"Stay here," Driscoll ordered. He positioned Honey right in front of the picture on the wall. He passed through the heavy blue drape that separated the back room from the store, stepping carefully, avoiding the high, nearly toppling piles of pawned merchandise that seemed to be sprouting from every square foot of space.

Honey, sensing the danger, searched for something to use as a weapon. She spotted several baseball bats in the inside of a clothes rack, where umbrellas should have been. She grabbed the first one she touched, then followed Driscoll.

Nothing in the bathroom. That was clean. He decided not to turn on any lights.

That left the darkroom. With a sinking feeling, he prayed he'd find nothing in there.

Honey had a light step, but he knew instantly that she had followed him. "I told you to stay back there," he muttered.

"Here." She handed him the bat.

He used it to nudge open the door to the darkroom. A variety of strong, bitterly pungent odors made it seem as though they could taste the air in the closetlike room. This time he had to turn on a light. The bulb burst into a reddish-orange glow. He half expected to find Harry facedown in the tray of chemicals. But all that he saw were pictures—some processed, some still drying on the clothesline that stretched from one wall to the other. Honey was breathing so hard, she sounded like a panting puppy. "Take it easy," he said, then added, "Where the hell is he?"

Grabbing every photo that seemed to be among the ones Harry had been working on, Driscoll stalked into the main shop area. Honey reached for a light switch. He was anxious to see if the gun he had left with Harry was still around. So far, he hadn't seen it.

"I thought you said he knew you were coming back."

"He did," Driscoll answered. "This isn't like Harry."

He spread the newly developed pictures on the counter and stared at them, hoping to see the tall man with the white hair. No luck.

"Take a look," he told Honey. She fingered them, concentrating hard. She separated one from the rest—a photo of an older man. The look was hard; the mottled face suggested a ruddy complexion and a distinctly foreign demeanor. He flipped it over, but there was no name or date. No identification.

"Why did you pick this one out?" he asked Honey.

"I saw him somewhere, but I just can't remember where. But it'll come to me." Then, beginning to play with the tips of her curls, she started walking around the pawnshop, touching things. When she reached the taxidermy wall in the far corner, Honey stopped, stood stiffly, and stared. All manner of moth-eaten stuffed heads and lacquered mounted fish and threadbare animal skins which had been bagged or caught by city hunters had been accepted by Harry Capri in trade. Her throat dry, unable to speak, Honey just pointed and called softly, "Phillip, over here. Please, Phillip. . . ."

Reaching her side, he looked up, saw where she was pointing, and then just sagged, trying to steady himself. There was nothing either of them could say. Driscoll felt Honey recoil in horror and bury her face in his chest.

Suspended from one of the huge, heavy taxidermy hooks, slammed against the wall like some monstrous mounted trophy, was the lifeless body of Harry Capri. His eyes were open. Harry's tongue had already begun to thicken and bloat, protruding from his mouth like a swollen, bluish gag. His arms were tied behind him, and it looked to the cop as though his neck had been broken. Driscoll fought back a violent, all-consuming urge to tear everything else off the wall; the crazy urge to give Harry some small measure of dignity in death. But it was too late.

Shaking his head helplessly, not even sure how he could

get Harry down, Driscoll wanted to say something to Honey and turned to find that she was gone. He called to her, but no sound came back. In an instant, his reflexes switching to automatic, Driscoll knew that they were not alone. One last time he called her name. Ducking his head low, he began moving in the direction where he had last seen her.

He was in a crouch when he heard the first shuffle of feet. One person, moving heavily, quickly. But he couldn't see a thing—the pawnshop was like the musty, crowded backstage of a theater, jam-packed with strange props and useless objects, a lifetime's collection of other people's treasures and tragedies. Inching along the floor, Driscoll passed, one after the other, displays of drums, a nine-foot-tall wall of used household appliances, one and a half motorcycles, a forest of old lamps, most of them minus their shades, and a tall shaky stand of headboards and footboards from a generation of discarded beds. They were arranged in ascending sizes with the tallest running away from him. He had the feeling that all he would have to do was breathe on them and the entire structure would come crashing down.

Flattening himself on the floor, he looked under the bed stands, his nose parallel with the dusty casters on the legs of some of the bedboards. Then he saw them. Boots. A man's boots. They were moving awkwardly—as if the man who belonged to the boots was under pressure, staggering.

In his mind's eye, Driscoll could see it all. The guy had picked Honey up and was probably holding her, maybe around the middle, just off the ground. He had to be using his other hand to gag her. And knowing Honey, she would most likely be biting the hell out of his fingers and kicking. Even if he had a gun, he wouldn't be able to use it.

Driscoll raised himself from the floor to shoulder height and charged into the row of headboards as hard as he could. The headboards went sputtering forward like a row of oversized dominoes, fanning out in all directions on the tile floor of the pawnshop.

Driscoll practically sailed over the top, aiming for the unfamiliar figure on the other side. Then, suddenly, in a surge of recognition, Driscoll realized that this was the same man who had come after him in Paul Presto's basement that first night—the night it had all began. Honey was exactly where he had imagined she would be—several inches in the air off the floor, with a rough arm gripping her waist. The girl was flailing away, kicking like some small, hobbled animal, but her captor managed to hold on to the blue serge jacket of her borrowed uniform.

Driscoll was in midair for less than a second. He landed with a hard, painful, jarring thud. As he did so, he grabbed for the guy's leg and caught it. He was so close to flipping him off balance that he could feel the muscles in the other man's leg tighten as he gripped it, Honey's assailant almost toppling over backward and Honey going with him.

Driscoll could see Honey squirming down, past his waist, and almost breaking free as she spun around and aimed a beautiful kick right at his balls, but he was just too strong for her and just a fraction of a second too quick for Driscoll.

Slipping and falling again on the headboard, reaching out, Honey's captor backed away from Driscoll, slipped out of the leg hold, and renewed his grip on the screaming, hysterical young girl. Just then, he brought out a shiny silver gun—Driscoll knew it was a .45 automatic by its shape and size, another .45—and pointed it at the side of Honey's head.

Triumphant, grinning fiendishly, he backed out of the door of Harry Capri's pawnshop, dragging Honey Presto with him, taunting the detective, daring Driscoll to give him the opportunity to use the big gun.

As soon as he was out the door, Phillip Driscoll was on his feet, running madly after Honey and the man who had taken her hostage.

TWENTY-EIGHT

GIRARD ESTATE, CHURCH OF ST. BIBIANA

Every Christmas Eve for the last century, rain or snow, without fail, despite a thermometer that sometimes plunged below zero, the people of South Philadelphia, the faithful of the Meatman's neighborhood, had marched in the procession of the Living Nativity of St. Bibiana's. While he had been alive, Paul Presto had been the *padrone,* the Caesar of the procession, financing it, providing security, renting animals from camels to cows, and once even offering the procession his own daughter, Honoria, in the role of Blessed Virgin. This year, the procession went on as scheduled, with the Meatman's spirit, an all-seeing, all-knowing shade, hovering above it.

There was no greater honor in the environs of South Philadelphia than to be selected to play one of the Nativity roles—wise men, shepherds, Roman centurions, innkeeper, angel, baby Jesus, Mary, Joseph.

The procession began at 9th Street and Washington Avenue, serpentining its way through the narrow byways of South Philadelphia, finally reaching its climax back at St. Bibiana's, where a magnificent stable had been erected in the churchyard, larger by far than a Broadway stage. There was a small orchestra in a heated enclosure, bleachers for the faithful, bales of hay for the animals, a raised platform for the archbishop, and a large cleared area for the ever-present television trucks and minicams that appeared each year to cover this quintessential South Philadelphia celebration of the season. Never once had there been any violence or rowdyism or public intoxication associated with the event, since it was well known in the neighborhood that Presto Family button men provided security as backups to the large contingent of cops on duty.

Right on schedule the procession had begun at twilight, with hundreds of the Meatman's grateful subjects walking side by side, lighted candles in hand, reverently treading the freezing, snow-cleared streets. A motorcycle with sidecar led the procession, clearing traffic and onlookers. Immediately behind the first contingent, in the van of the spectacle, sat the Blessed Virgin Mary, in costume, astride a live donkey, cradling the bundled-up baby Jesus, the three-month-old grandson of one of the Presto Family's *capi.* This year, Joe-Joey's oldest daughter, Lisa, played the part of the Virgin. Walking beside her, leading the donkey, was a twenty-one-year-old St. Joseph, a linebacker from Villanova University, whose family of sheet-metal contractors had donated the scaffolding for the stage this year.

Bringing up the rear were the open cars of dignitaries, including the parish's 1959 Cadillac Fleetwood with a beaming Archbishop Edmundus Bible Mahoney in the backseat. He waved benignly to the crowd, like a South Philly pontiff. The slow procession was rounded out by a shaky group of elderly, red-cheeked Italian musicians, providing musical accompaniment on mandolins. A phalanx of parishioners, dressed as Roman legionnaires, marched parallel to the procession on each side, resplendent in shiny breastplates of silver, deep maroon kilts, high leather boots, and plumed helmets. Each carried a pointed spear, doubled as a parade marshal, and personified the historical accuracy of the parade in that a decree went forth from Caesar Augustus "that a census of the whole world should be taken . . ." Every member of the Presto Family not on duty elsewhere was on hand. When she was a little girl, the Meatman had carried Honey in his arms through this cold night every Christmas Eve with blankets snuggled around her.

FISHTOWN

Driscoll had a big, fat, dirty-looking Pontiac Catalina in his sights as he dashed off the pavement outside Harry's place and ran toward his own car. He'd seen Honey's head disappear inside the front seat with a hairy arm, crooked at the elbow, around her neck. He blazed away from the curb before his car door was even shut. He floored the gas pedal, fishtailed wildly on the frozen, glazed asphalt directly beneath the superstructure of the overhead El, and took off after the Catalina. For about a block and a half, he followed the man in front of him, crisscrossing thick concrete El columns and support pillars and very narrowly missing a long, articulated Septa bus discharging passengers near Front and Girard. Just then the Catalina made a sharp left, spinning out on two wheels as it swerved to avoid hitting a station wagon stopped for a red light. Driscoll was bouncing around in his own seat, gunning his LTD, trying desperately to control it on the congested city streets as he watched his speedometer pass sixty-five miles an hour.

Less than a car length behind the Pontiac, he screeched to a near stop, then he too ran the light and took a pitching, headlong left to maintain the desperate pace.

They were heading east toward the Delaware River, breaking eighty now, when the Pontiac hung the one left that Driscoll didn't anticipate—it went crashing and bumping across a long, wide vacant lot where houses had once stood. It took Driscoll too long to react, and the Pontiac managed to stretch its two-block lead a little farther as it took a hard diagonal turn onto Delaware Avenue, racing south, with the river on the left and the stark, deserted skeleton of industrial Philadelphia on the right.

All the while, Driscoll was screaming an "Assist officer" call into the dashboard radio, trying to raise any cop who could hear him.

The waterfront flashed by, transformed into a surreal landscape of bizarre shapes, splashes of light reflected off the river and brilliant chains of neon that stayed in Driscoll's eyes and blinded him, once his peripheral vision picked them up.

Opposite Society Hill, almost at Penn's Landing, tracks for the tourist trolleys intersected the wide, curving highway and formed a lane of their own. Straddling the tracks, Driscoll closed in fast on the tail of the Pontiac. Then he gave his Ford everything it had and slammed in hard to the right rear quadrant of his quarry.

But the Pontiac never eased up, and the hard tap he administered, while it jarred every bone in his own body, did no appreciable damage to the car in front of him.

Three or four blue-and-whites had closed in behind him, lights flashing, shrill sirens pulsating.

Ahead of him, Driscoll could see the window coming down on the driver's side of the Pontiac. An arm snaked out past the rearview mirror, and what he was sure was the mouth of a .45 pointed directly at him. Veering sharply to the right, Driscoll attempted some evasive action.

Suddenly, there was an explosion of sound and color and the big pistol's projectile smashed into his windshield, shattering glass, whizzing past his head, and burying itself somewhere in his backseat. He heard more discharges and saw more flashes, but none of the other bullets found their mark. That first shot had done real damage. Now he was driving blind, because the bullet's penetration of the windshield had sent out a circumference of jagged glass cracks and circular splashes like a grotesque spider's web. All he could see was the perfectly round hole the big bullet had made—yet he was still doing eighty. There was nothing he could do except stand up on his heels in the driver's seat, pressing the steering wheel against his pelvis as he leaned forward and punched savagely at the weakened windshield. When he withdrew his hand, it was bloody, especially his knuckles, but he had knocked out enough glass, smashed it right down onto the hood of the car, to give him a small window of visibility that his own life depended upon.

No longer thinking, merely reacting, he used both feet now, one on the gas, one on the brake, as he tried to keep up with the Pontiac, but it was just too far out in front. Other drivers were swerving all along Delaware Avenue to avoid crashes.

Suddenly there was a blinding blur on his left as a dark, unmarked sedan—a *third* car—came barreling out of nowhere, leap-frogged Driscoll's car by veering around it, and closed in on Honey's captor in the Pontiac. Driscoll didn't recognize the maneuver or the car, but whoever was behind the wheel was damn effective.

Another right; it put all three of them on a big straight-away, and over his shoulder, Driscoll recognized the brightly lit facade of the Mummers' Museum jet by. Now they were on Washington Avenue, pushing hard toward the innards of South Philadelphia, three abreast.

Driscoll clutched the steering wheel, and the exertion forced blood from where he had cut himself on the windshield. At one point, he had the eerie sensation of actually flying, of hydroplaning on the wet road inches above the street surface, a distant dimension of speed and motion. He kept on going.

For the first time, he checked his rearview mirror and realized that the handful of blue-and-white flashers had now multiplied into an unbroken convoy zigzagging crazily in his wake.

Crash! . . . *Crash!* Pain gouged the center of Driscoll's brain and he felt as if some gaping, flesh-torn cavity had been scooped out of his skull.

Driscoll's neck whiplashed and his chest almost impaled itself on the steering column. It took him several extra heartbeats to realize that his heaving chest was still in one piece and his eyes still sighted, even though he was positive his head had been ripped free from his body and deposited somewhere in the trunk. He shook his eyes clear and looked around him.

Everything was perfectly still now. His automobile was as dead on the road as a harpooned fish in the water. But on both sides of him and in front of him, the rest of the world appeared to be in motion—in a crazy, speeded-up, cinematic motion with men and women and children running and screaming and pounding against the sides of his car. But Driscoll's strained movements were those of a man in quicksand.

He had no idea of how many seconds passed before it came to him. The Pontiac he had been pursuing had slowed or stopped entirely as it banked to avoid a big news van that had been parked directly in the center of Washington

Avenue with thick black cables tethering its front and rear like synthetic umbilical cords. He hadn't even noticed the news truck, because all he could see through his smashed clearance in the windshield was the Pontiac.

But the bloated white-on-white Catalina was crumpled now and accordioned against a wall somewhere—Driscoll still didn't have his bearings—and the front of his own car had been sucked up and pulled within the rear of the Pontiac. The intercepting car that had been beside him for so many blocks had miraculously avoided the crash.

But now there were so many people around, dressed in the most outlandish costumes he had ever seen, and before Driscoll knew what was happening, rough hands were reaching in to pull him free of his car, past the steering wheel, and out onto the street, then he felt himself being rolled farther and farther from the car, pulled and dragged by people who were hitting him and beating him and screaming out obscenities even as they were saving his life.

Once free of the LTD, his head cleared and he came to himself. They had rocketed along Washington Avenue and had slammed right into the Living Nativity of St. Bibiana's, and the people who had rescued him from his car were berating him, bellowing at him in English and Italian that he had tried to kill everybody in the procession. As he looked back, all along the street there was carnage—bleeding, twisted, broken bodies sprawled where they had fallen as the Pontiac hit.

He couldn't answer because he couldn't talk. But suddenly, the voices of his accusers were drowned out as the car behind him exploded, blasted the blackness out of the night with a fireball of gasoline and metal and glass.

They were still tearing at his clothes and abusing him as Driscoll fought to his feet and looked in vain for Honey Presto and the kidnapper. Then he realized where they were. They were just across the street from St. Bibiana's churchyard, where the huge Nativity stable and stage rose out of the night like an electrified billboard of color and light. Abandoned in the middle of the street, with its headlights on and its doors open, was the intercepting car that had avoided the collision, and running away from that car, a moving force with such height and weight and speed that he appeared to menace everything in his path, was Ed Bellows. He was running right toward St. Bibiana's itself, past the outdoor stage, in front of the bleachers, carving his way through the stunned orchestra members, who were running for cover, tipping over their chairs and throwing their instruments aside. Limping from a twisted knee that he had suffered in the crash, Phillip Driscoll fell in behind Bellows. He couldn't see Honey or her captor, but he was sure that he and Bellows were after the same thing. From several blocks in the distance, he could see the shape of one ambulance, then several, approaching fast.

Blue-and-whites closed in around them, with cops jumping out of cars and ordering anyone in motion to halt, as Driscoll reached the steps of the church.

The scene within was chaotic. First Honey and the man with the gun had come bursting in, followed by Bellows and several cops and Presto soldiers, all with their guns drawn.

The head of the procession had reached the main altar of the church at the same moment that the cars had come crashing through the rear of the line of march. The impact of what had happened had traveled from marcher to marcher like an electrical current. Sitting in the front pew, with Joe-Joey between them, were Tony and Marie Bonaventura. The camels were grunting frightened camel noises and the rest of the animals were beginning to break free from their handlers. Almost in unison, Tony and Joe-Joey pulled out weapons as Marie dropped to the floor of her pew. St. Bibiana's was high and deep, like a pocket cathedral, with a catwalk balcony and choir loft extending around the entire interior of the church. Driscoll saw Bellows's broad back disappear near the steps that led the catwalk, and Driscoll followed him. Suddenly he saw Honey, looking terrified and disheveled in the police uniform, but standing free in the loft, alone. He looked, but didn't see any sign of the killer.

Driscoll ran up the catwalk to the balcony. As soon as she saw him, Honey ran for Driscoll and threw her arms around him. Bellows had his gun out too and held it loosely at his side. The man who had grabbed Honey was nowhere in sight.

"Where is he?" Driscoll screamed at Bellows, fully prepared to repel the man he had been pursuing should he suddenly come hurtling out of the darkness like one of the apparitions from St. Bibiana's cloister of ghosts.

Before Bellows could answer, Driscoll grabbed the gun at the Strike Force chief's side, pulled it away from him, then turned on Bellows and stuck it in the black man's Adam's apple, just below his bearded chin.

The detective cocked the trigger on Bellows's own .38. "You'd better tell me right now what's going on, Ed," he said.

Bellows was moving his neck back and forth, trying to free his Adam's apple. He cleared his throat and swallowed before answering. Even arched back as he was, bent from the waist near the railing of the balcony, with Driscoll determinedly pressing in with the gun, Bellows still had a head on the cop.

Bellows's eyes seemed to bulge. He knew Driscoll, and he knew that Driscoll wouldn't hesitate to kill him, if it came to that.

"Cut it out, Driscoll," Bellows said, in a tight, constricted voice. "The guy you want is probably getting away." Driscoll dug the gun in farther.

"Where the hell did you come from?" he asked Bellows.

"Pawnshop," Bellows grunted. "Followed you . . . gotta get the girl. That's all."

Driscoll refused to back off on the pressure. "I saw what happened when the *Spetsnaz* grabbed your girlfriend," Bellows continued hoarsely.

"That was *you* back on Delaware Avenue?" Driscoll asked, and he let up enough on the gun for Bellows to nod his head.

"What's a *Spetsnaz?*" Driscoll demanded.

The black man was reluctant to answer, then he looked at the point of the gun again, managed to raise his palm level with the weapon, and hesitantly nudged it away from his face. The detective allowed him to do it. "*Spetsnaz* are like our Green Berets, Driscoll, only better—commandos, the elite of the elite."

"Russian?"

"Russian. You'd better believe it. Who the hell do you think the guy was who was in pieces in the Meatman's basement? We know all about him."

"What about the Malina?" Driscoll asked excitedly. "I thought they were behind this?"

The black man looked almost relieved as he answered, "That's a good guess, too, Driscoll. But the *Spetsnaz* are GRU—that's their military intelligence, and nobody knows where the GRU begins and the Malina ends." Bellows pointed a big paw at Honey, who had said nothing as she listened intently. "This girl's daddy didn't know it, but he walked right into a war between this GRU and KGB. But it wasn't his fault. He was trying to help—"

The next thing Driscoll and Honey saw was gurgling blood pouring from Ed Bellows's mouth as a huge tipped spearpoint suddenly protruded right through the Strike Force chief's chest. A fountain of the crimson liquid pouring from a severed artery began to bathe both of them in Bellows's blood.

Bellows died with his mouth open, strangling on words he was fighting to get out as he fell forward on top of Driscoll, collapsing around his shoulders and clutching the cop's sides in a fruitless effort to keep his own life from slipping away. As he fell, Bellows knocked the gun out of Driscoll's hand, and the gun fell to the church floor below, banging loudly. Driscoll pushed Bellows away from him with the heavy spear tip, crimson and wet. The black man's great weight and size pulled him backward over the balcony railing and he tumbled downward into the pew behind Joe-Joey, Tony, and Marie. Then Driscoll realized what had happened.

One of the parishioners, who was dressed as a Roman legionnaire, was hollering and pointing to a running figure. It was the same man, rangy and muscular, who had taken Honey hostage. As he ran he turned from side to side, looking frantically for an escape. The other Roman legionnaires started to pursue him, along with the Presto soldiers. He had evidently seized one of the spears and hurled it, javelin-like, with amazing strength, and with such accuracy that it had homed right in on Bellows's back. Instant death. The Roman legionnaire from whom he had wrested the spear was still on the church floor, injured, and shouting the alarm.

"Phillip, that's him!" Honey screamed, gesturing. "That's

the man! He's Russian, too! That's what he kept saying in the car. Talking crazy, all in Russian."

But Driscoll had to ignore Honey as he spotted his adversary sprinting toward the rear of the church. A towering candelabrum, its branched tapers in flame, came clattering to the floor as the running figure tripped over the footed base.

Bounding back down the catwak as quickly as he could, the detective hurtled the steps two and three at a time, determined to catch Bellows's killer. The man surged forward with powerful, wide strides, bowling over anyone who blocked his path. But Driscoll knew he had to get him.

He could feel people closing in behind him, and as he turned a corner, bolting forward and almost losing his balance, he spotted Joe-Joey, gun in hand, outdistancing the other pursuers. But then he realized that the Presto soldier had not joined in this chase at all, but was jumping over pews, tottering precariously on the back of each one, and rushing toward a hysterically shrieking young girl, dressed in the costume of the Virgin Mary. Joe-Joey, fearful for his daughter, had chosen to fight his own battle.

They were outside the church now, Driscoll bumping into two, three, five people, shouldering them out of his way, eyes set, never allowing the killer to get too far ahead.

A crowd had gathered behind him, cresting outward in a human torrent to get a better look at the chase.

Slipping, tripping, barely managing to keep his feet, Driscoll stayed with him. Except for his blackjack, he was unarmed. Bellows's gun lay next to his body on the church floor.

The running man bolted across a street, dodging one car, then another. Driscoll dodged them too, barely escaping being run down.

He was headed for the 9th Street Market, for the closed produce stalls and butcher shops. Driscoll saw him careen off Washington Avenue and head down 9th. Either he was tiring, or Driscoll was catching up. The distance separating them was down to a few feet now.

There was a butcher's market in the middle of the block, fronted by a plate-glass window. The killer lowered his head, squared his shoulders, and took it with dizzying momentum, glass shattering everywhere. But Driscoll was on top of him, slapping the cold .45 away from him across the sidewalk.

Inside the stores, between the darkened aisles, he saw the man suddenly turn, then reach up to an overhead rack of cleavers, knives, and saws. Without even bothering to look up, the Russian selected a weapon.

All at once he was coming at Driscoll with something heavy and sharp, a meat cleaver. Driscoll warded off the first blow, his feet two-stepping in a tight spiral. Then he gave the man an uppercut, cracking his jaw, but hardly stunning him. Dancing, he lunged to one side, then the other, feinting, testing Driscoll's reflexes.

Swinging wildly with the meat cleaver, he chunked off sections of butcher block, splintered wood, and came within an inch of Driscoll's ear. Then they were rolling together on the floor, under stalls and tables in the sawdust.

The cop was trying to reach around behind him to get his hand on the jack in his back pocket to defend himself. But the killer was pushing his head backward into the floor, smashing Driscoll's face with a muscular, gnarled hand as he held the cleaver over his head with the other.

Driscoll could scarcely see. He was dizzy, close to blacking out, the Russian straddling him.

The two were no match at all in strength. Driscoll could never begin to pound away at this guy, punch for punch. But it wasn't strength now, it was will, and Phillip Driscoll was one stubborn son of a bitch.

Reaching back fifteen years, back to his days as a young cop, back even before Harry Capri, before the Silver Bullets, before Honey, Driscoll used his right hand for one last, desperate thrust, bringing the round, blunt head of the blackjack digging into his opponent's left temple. The jack connected with the skull with a deadly, liquid-sounding squish.

Driscoll hadn't jacked many people in his career, but he knew when and how to do it. Jacking was being a cop the old-fashioned way—beating your adversary senseless before he had a chance to beat you senseless. And Phillip Driscoll was good at it.

The Malina man staggered momentarily, then slumped and fell off Driscoll's midsection. The heavy meat cleaver clanged to the floor.

TWENTY-NINE

ODESSA
FRIDAY, CHRISTMAS DAY

The vast, cobwebbed room had been sunken like some dingy shaft that descended straight into hell. It was at least one hundred yards below the structures of the surface. Directly above the room, above sea level, on the central boulevard, Primorsky Prospect, sat the vaulted, domed State Opera House of Odessa. There, stone nymphs and pudgy angels, carved over a century before, clung to the walls of the old Opera House, frolicking in a state of suspended lifelessness—but somehow eerily more real than the weary people who passed by on the street in front of them. Never once had these sculpted cherubs dreamed that far below them, the elders of the Malina had been meeting to settle disputes, to right wrongs, and to pass the sentence of death ever since Odessa's ancient days as a Roman encampment.

The room where the elders gathered, at no set interval, had functioned as the Malina's command center during the Great Patriotic War against the Germans—World War II, to those outside Russia. Over the years very little in the room had changed. Torches still provided most of the illumination, supplemented by ornate candelabra, pillaged from the homes of the wealthy too long ago for anyone living to remember.

A mist of smoke hung near the ceiling of the room, like

a constant reminder that the Malina was a creature of foggy mornings and misty twilights.

Every man in the room had committed murder—at least.

The early Christians had built these catacombs beneath Odessa to escape persecution. Over the centuries, the face and religion of the persecutors had frequently changed, but the mentality of bloodlust had known no abatement. For a price, in those catacombs, which they controlled as completely as Lucifer reigned over the Fires of Hell, the generations of the Malina had always provided safety to those who sought it from them.

The Malina had positioned its disciples—its *children,* more precisely, since it had always raised foundlings and orphans and had, historically, discovered its best recruits from among the ranks of these homeless—in virtually every level of Russian life, including the state, the church, and the military. No one, in all the endless horizons of the Soviet Union, was unaware of the power, the influence, and the diabolical vengeance of the Malina.

Over all the centuries, many Russian rulers had attempted to put an end to the Malina, just as police forces and politicians would seemingly battle forever against the Western institution known as the Mafia. But in both places, the rulers and the politicians—and even the Pope in Rome, who knew full well the reach of the Malina—understood that in the end, the Malina, like the Mafia, would continue to exist just as long as men harbored greed and avarice and jealousy in their hearts.

Anything that the Soviet state could not provide—from protection to medicine to consumer goods—the Malina could, and did, for a price. That was the way of the world, and also of the Malina. The price might be money, services, loyalty, a safe house, a secret skill in rare supply; even an introduction to a friend in high office.

In America, through men like Butkova—primarily through his vision and discipline—the Malina took root. There, it zealously studied the police, the capitalist industries, the federal government in Washington, so similar to the Kremlin power bloc; and the Malina especially studied the competition—the burgeoning ethnic Mafias of the

United States. Above all, it studied the masters, like Meatman Presto.

Once it had become strong enough, and was convinced that it could wage a war against the older American crime cartels and survive, the Malina struck.

In America, Butkova had secured yet another beachhead for the Malina. Now, the Council of Elders was considering his latest request.

Over the centuries, the composition of the council had never varied—twelve advisers who served at the pleasure of the Headman, the wisest, the most respected, the most feared among them. His word was final, his decision more binding than any law on earth. At all times, under any circumstances, his edict carried the power of life and death.

The meeting began with the traditional breaking of the bread, passing the loaf from one to the other, the tasting of salt, and the sipping of the strong, bitter wine from a chalice that was known as the Cup of the Twelve.

Their comrade and brother, Nikolai Butkova, was anxious to begin consolidating his power in America. Many, many lives would be taken. In fact, Butkova was requesting nothing less than permission to continue the virtual extermination of the hierarchy of the American Mafia that was already under way.

Out of deference to his brothers in Odessa, he had sent word from America about his ambitious plans. The council's decision would be final, provided, of course, that it could somehow control Butkova.

Debate had raged ever since the request had been made—bitter and contentious. The Headman already knew what his decision must be, but he would patiently solicit advice from every other elder present. He had served as the Headman for almost twenty-five years. He had been proclaimed by all as the bravest man of the Malina. Orphaned after the first war against the Germans, he had been raised by the Malina as one of their own. They had placed him in the military and had watched as his career flourished.

He had been listening for hours. The last elder had just had his final say. Now it was time for the Headman to explain his position, defend his decision.

He arose stiffly to address them. His arthritic knees bothered him in the damp, subterranean chamber. Over his uniform he wore a heavy scarlet cloak. Still, the cold cut through his old bones like a Tartar's scythe at harvest time. Harrumphing loudly, Marshal Vladik Valadovich Zinijakin, General of all the Soviet Armies, Headman of the Malina, began to speak to his brothers on the Council of the Elders.

ATLANTIC CITY EXPRESSWAY, SOUTH JERSEY CHRISTMAS DAY, BEFORE DAWN

Driscoll knew what broken ribs felt like. He'd had them before—once in college, twice on the police force. They weren't broken now, but almost, too sore to touch. Still, he felt strong, alive, energized by the fight he had just won and by the knowledge he had picked up from Bellows. At least now he had some idea why the feds were so vitally interested in the Meatman. GRU, Soviet Military Intelligence; that's what Bellows had said.

The three-lane blacktop cut through the New Jersey Pine Barrens like a sooty ribbon of asphalt, intersecting campgrounds, pine forests so dense they were almost impenetrable, and hick towns where the phony log-cabin bars were all called "Package Goods."

Casino Row, laden with glitz and glitter, would have been a hard left, but Driscoll angled onto an exit well before the cutoffs for the Casino City—an exit that would take him right and south, parallel to the Irish and Italian Rivieras of the South Jersey seashore. In the middle of the winter, on Christmas Day, before sunup, there was no more forsaken spot on the face of the earth. That's exactly what he wanted. Honey on ice—for her safety, and for his. He was buying time.

There was practically no traffic, just an occasional local car that had hopped onto the expressway to cut from point A to point B quickly, motoring from one sprawling bedroom development to the next. Normally, the big double-decker Golden Nugget or Resorts International Casino buses would be creeping up on his exhaust, practically inhaling his car into their grilles, like famished dragons. As it was, though, all he spotted was a couple of stretch limos, hauling high-rollers, blinding him with their high-beams as they nudged around his left to pass, imperious.

She was sitting pressed against the window on the passenger's side. Quiet. Pensive. The heater in the LTD worked erratically, and he could see her breath. She wasn't looking at him and did not speak, just smoked, blowing the smoke out the window she'd cracked open.

"I was in your room," he said. "Nice stuffed animals."

Honey was hardly expecting that, but reviewing everything he had related to her she knew it had to be the night he had found the body in the freezer, the night her father had been murdered.

"You *broke* into our home, Driscoll."

"Served its purpose." She'd seen him in action, fighting, savagely swinging a blackjack, threatening to kill Bellows just before he was killed. It had scared her.

"You aren't going to get hurt," he said, wanting to reach out to her but keeping his hands on the wheel. "I won't let anything happen to you."

"You don't have to say that. I can take it. I was raised in this life. What did you call me—the Godfather's daughter. Don't worry, Driscoll. I'm tough, just like my old man."

"I know you are," Driscoll told her. "Tough, I mean. You go through a thing like this and come out of it. You don't have to explain yourself to anyone."

For several long moments, the only sound was the howling wind, wet now with the pungent smell of ocean merely a short distance away.

Honey was cold, tired, disoriented. She wanted all this to go away, to get back to her life—back to any semblance of the life she had known.

"Are we going where I think we're going?" she asked.

Their destination had to be her father's place in Stone Harbor, twenty miles down the coast from Atlantic City. Deserted now. Closed up for the fierce shore winter. Isolated. Maybe it would be a good place to run away to. Maybe . . .

"When we hit town, you'll have to give me the directions. I don't know the address, but I did see a picture." He smiled knowingly, warmly.

For some reason, Honey thought that sounded almost intimate. As if Driscoll knew something he wasn't supposed to know. Something about her. She turned around in the seat, folded one knee under her, and smoothed out Lida's oversized police uniform coat. It had to be a size 14—big girl. At least it was warm, like a cape. Under it she wore black jeans and one of Lida's old flannel shirts. That had been the warmest, softest thing she could find. And under that, nothing. She'd washed her bra and panties just before Driscoll had yelled for her to get a move on. Honey couldn't believe the way she had been living for the past week—on the run, irregular meals, no clothes, catching sleep when she could, nodding off, afraid that somebody was trying to kill her—convinced that they were—but fueled by nothing except the hunger for revenge. Now she was sitting here with Driscoll, listening to him talk about her like some curiosity he had researched. About her life, her possessions, her private things.

"What picture?" she demanded. "Don't tell me you have surveillance photos of my father's house at the shore. We *never* use that place for business. He'd never allow it."

"Aerial and telescopic. Of course we have surveillance pictures," he answered. "What d'you think we are?"

They were on Ocean Drive now, crossing a small toll bridge, unmanned, naturally, heading through Avalon, then into Stone Harbor. The sea air smelled acridly of decaying fish and shell creatures oozing sticky death, mulching for millions of years on the ocean floor. To be a shore person you had to love that smell. Driscoll wasn't and he didn't.

On their left, the Atlantic pitched and rolled toward an India-ink horizon, immensely restless, forbidding, agitated. They drove past a water tower, protected dunes, a cluster of padlocked shops that wouldn't emerge from their cocoons for months; past traffic lights that had been turned off, along pavements where only the occasional windborne flotsam detracted from the sterile, relentless cleanliness.

"It must be hell living down here in the winter," he said. "It's like the elephants' graveyard—great place to die." He wanted to take that back as soon as he had uttered the words. Honey looked sleepy, but wary. She had heard too much talk of dying.

"You still haven't told me *what* picture you saw. *Burglar!*" Loosening up now.

"Just one of my many accomplishments in the line of duty."

"Some duty." Honey wanted to know everything he knew about her.

"Picture . . . let me see now. . . . Oh, yes, I believe you were posing in front of the house on the beach, very coy; you were standing on something, one hip elevated a little above the other. Nice bikini; cheesecake almost. I would say—"

"My God! I don't believe you saw that. How dare you? That was none of your business." A blush burned through her dusky complexion.

"Police business."

"Like hell."

"Hey, it was a nice picture. Tasteful."

"Fat, you mean."

"Fat?"

"I looked so *fat* in that picture. I told my father to *burn* it. I *hate* that picture. You had no business looking through my things."

"Very vain." He sounded teasing.

"Take a right at the next corner," she told him, "then a left. We're in the dead end. On the beach."

Very high-rent, he thought. "Where else? Beachfront. Crime pays." Nothing here cost under one big one.

"Am I supposed to say I'm sorry because my father happened to be a very successful businessman?"

He gave her a look that told her to get off it.

"Will the heat be on here? Telephone?"

"The heat, barely; just enough to keep the pipes from freezing. Phone, maybe."

"Anybody come down here in the winter?"

"Never."

"Uncle Tony, Aunt Marie?"

"Not at all."

"That sounds fine. I'm running out of places to stash you."

The more she thought about it, the more Honey had to admit to herself that it actually *did* sound pretty good. Once again, Driscoll was making her feel very safe. And that wasn't so bad. His gray hair was really handsome—it gave him such a look of authority. Command. She loved that in men. But his eyes gave him away. They looked so vital, so ready. The night her father had been killed, Driscoll had looked strange—*haunted.* That was it—so *preoccupied.* Not now. Now, tonight, today, Christmas Day, he appeared ten years younger. Not like some seedy cop anymore, but a real person. He even had his devilish sense of humor back. Honey could tell. That hair was so cute. She could go for a guy like this—again, in spite of herself.

The Meatman's seashore house looked much too California for New Jersey—high and sweeping and dramatic. Big Sur. It commanded a gorgeous stretch of beach with no neighbors on either side. Presto had purchased three lots and built in the middle. Nobody visible. Not even a car.

He parked, took the door key from Honey, and checked out the first floor. Her eyes were riveted on him from the car. The house smelled as musty as a dock; he could hear the silence. Driscoll started up the steps.

The remainder of the house was clean, too.

Outside, he opened the doors to the double garage, off to the left. Then he slid back into the seat beside Honey and squeezed his car through the narrow bay door. He tried a light. The electricity was still on. Then he broke into an appreciative grin as he saw that another car was already in the garage. He could make a switch now, if the battery wasn't dead.

Honey, standing beside him, brushed against the car, maneuvering between the two automobiles. She looked so small, so girlish.

"That yours?" Driscoll asked, pointing to the two-seat Mercedes convertible, cream-colored, buffed and polished.

Stored for the winter, but shiny enough to have just been driven off the showroom floor.

"Present from an admirer?" he continued. Vanity license plates on the Mercedes spelled out her name, HONEY.

"What's that supposed to mean? My father bought that for me. It's my *summer* car." She looked slightly embarrassed. It sounded strange now, saying it to Driscoll. "He kept it down here for me . . . to use . . . oh, why do I keep trying to justify myself to you? He spoiled me rotten, is that what you want me to say? If that's what you think, you're right. I *am* a princess. Big deal."

THIRTY

SAMSUN, TURKEY, ON THE BLACK SEA

Mikhail Zhukov had not fully regained consciousness until he was aboard ship and several miles out to sea. He awoke on a metal bunk, slung between two rusty bulkheads and supported at the four corners by strong chains. It was little more than a hammock with a thin, sour-smelling mattress of rags and foam.

Moving cautiously, he sat up on the bunk and tried to make sure that he could still stand. His legs were as wobbly as noodles. The floor was filthy and slippery with water that seemed to leak from everywhere. There was a single light in his cabin on a pull chain, just above the sink and toilet. Fearfully, Zhukov stared at himself in the mirror above the sink. The image that came back at him was one he had a little trouble recognizing at first. Heavy gauze bandages, blotted brown with dried blood, covered his right temple and extended back around his head, turban-style. His cheek and nose were puffy on that side, as well, and a blackish-purple mouse crawled out from beneath his right eye. The beating that had been administered to him had been quick and thorough, the work of an expert.

Two days out of port, heading south by east, they encountered the Soviet icebreaker he had been warned about. It was armed with a small Gatling gun and a missile battery.

But after only the most cursory unfurling of signal flags, the dull gray icebreaker allowed his tanker ship to proceed. Ice floes banged against the side of the ship, rocking everything inside and creating a more or less permanent sense of disequilibrium. He knew he would never get used to it.

Meals were delivered to him by the young boy who had been in the café in Odessa. Throughout the entire voyage, no words were spoken to Zhukov, and save for the Malina child, he saw no one except an occasional sailor sleepily tending to his chores. Once the KGB man ventured out to his cabin and went up on deck, in the black winter fog from which the sea had taken its name. But by then a storm had come up and a fierce hail drove him back below deck almost immediately. Little marine life could survive in the Black Sea—no animal or plant life below a depth of three hundred feet. The water itself was dead, without enough oxygen to keep anything alive. This chemical imbalance seemed to deaden everything connected with the voyage—sounds were muted, the cries of birds never heard; the lapping of the cold water against the hull of the ship became the eerie sound of water buffeting a casket.

Twelve miles north of Samsun, the fresh river waters of the Danube, the Dniester, and the Dnieper began to flow into the sea, diluting the salt content of the black waves and bringing with them the saving warmth that allowed the ports along the northern Turkish coast to remain in operation throughout the year.

Once landfall was made, the Russian felt as though he had stepped back in time. Samsun was a low-lying village of dusty minaret towers, lofty and slender, scattered in a landscape of ancient hovels, cafés, and the foreboding ruins of a brown brick wall that had once encircled the entire town. There was some industry on the waterfront, with occasional soaring cranes and cargo unloaders and a single Western-style hotel for the visiting sailors who refused to partake of northern Turkish hospitality.

The Malina captain—who Zhukov had never once met during the coarse of the voyage—accompanied him with the child to a waiting car, a beat-up Mercedes that had been converted into a taxi. Coughing smoke and fumes, the old car took them along winding, narrow streets, over dusty byways and cobblestone lanes, to the oldest section of the town, where the two of them, KGB man and Malina boy, retired to a single spacious room above a private residence. They waited there for a day with nothing to drink but goat's milk and nothing to eat except black bread and boiled beets, until sunrise the next morning. Following its own mysterious schedule, the Mercedes arrived at precisely 5:00 a.m., parked, and waited.

After shaking him awake with small, strong hands, the Malina child handed Mikhail Zhukov a different bundle of clothes this time—the well-cut shirt and suit of a Turkish businessman—and motioned for him to get dressed. Dutifully, the boy also changed his bandages, bathed his forehead with a balm, and acted, always in silence, like a perfect little valet.

But for one significant detail, this whole Malina excursion would have been almost ordinary, but that detail would forever remain in the KGB man's mind. Unfailingly, the rough, unkempt men he encountered on the voyage, and later in Samsun, were as heavily armed as any soldiers he had ever seen. Indeed, most of the Turks wore crossed bandoliers, bristling with bullets. To avoid attracting attention, they wrapped their bodies at all times in cloaks. But beneath those cloaks, their personal firepower was formidable.

From his years as an antismuggling policeman in the KGB, Zhukov had developed a tremendous respect for the Malina's capabilities, especially for its business acumen. His transactions with it had always been from afar, and then strictly on black-market deals that concerned both him and it. Never had he seen the Malina manifest itself as the private army that now held him under virtual house arrest. It was far from being a mere cartel of clever smugglers; Zhukov now understood the paramilitary capabilities and the international scope of this clandestine conspiracy.

That morning, the old Mercedes took them to a clearing several miles outside the ruins of the city walls. Then the armed driver pointed to a shady spot near a stand of dead trees and ordered both of them to wait.

Inspecting the terrain, as he always did, Zhukov knew at once that the hard, packed ground, with its slightly sloping shoulders and absence of any significant foliage or forest area, was an illegal airstrip—a smugglers' airstrip used in the opium trade. In the distance, on three sides, bluish hills arose around them in the cold dawn. The airstrip was secluded, yet readily accessible to any pilot familiar with its location.

No more than ten minutes had passed when Zhukov heard the low drone of a small, prop-driven aircraft. Cupping his hands above his eyebrows, the KGB man squinted into the morning sun and saw what he guessed was a two-engine American-made Cessna airplane begin its descent.

STONE HARBOR

He was rummaging around in the kitchen, in the freezer, looking for something to eat. Two frozen dinners, both Stouffer's Lean Cuisine, one frozen pizza, thick as a hubcap, that seemed sacrilegious in the home of Paul Presto, some coffee and tea in canisters and one case of red wine in the pantry. Where was the turkey with all the trimmings? At least they wouldn't go thirsty.

Driscoll could hear Honey running the shower. He had to take it on faith that she was leveling with him now. Considering who Presto was, he certainly should have known who was likely to take him out. This Russian mob, this Malina, was as good a suspect as any. Organized-crime specialists had been building a case for years that the American Mafia was vulnerable—not just to the Sicilians, who had already moved into the United States in a big way, but to all the other incipient ethnic Mafias as well. The more he thought about it, the more Driscoll could see that this did tie in perfectly with his map of red pushpins. There was one mental stumbling block, however. How could any outfit, even something as complex and deadly as the Malina, be so ballsy that it would attempt to take over the mob? Yet that had seemed to be the case, which meant that every cop in the country now had a very large problem. If the Mafia couldn't hold its own against the Malina, then who could?

As he listened to the water from the shower beating against the tile wall in Honey's bathroom, he reviewed the hit on the numbers bank. Definitely a Malina job. Interpol had confirmed that. Then he remembered what Bellows had said just before he was killed. He had said that the man who had tried to kidnap Honey was GRU, military intelligence, a *Spetsnaz*. But Bellows didn't even know where the Malina began and the GRU ended, he had said. That must be some kind of network they had back in the old country. Bellows had also tied that connection in with the body in Presto's basement freezer.

Enter Bellows and Carney. Bellows was the gopher, the muscle; Carney was the brains. Carney must have had a deal going with the Russians, and for some reason, he had needed the Meatman's help. Bellows had set that up with the promise of immunity for Presto and Honey, should that time ever come. Bellows worked for Carney. The Meatman had become an eager subcontractor. Honey had confirmed that. Lawlor was probably working for Carney, too. At least, he was a fan. So that put all those guys on one side with the Russians on the other.

Then, suddenly, the Meatman got hit—by the guy with the white hair. Somebody had to be paying him, but who? The feds had gone to too much trouble to recruit Presto in the first place. While it wasn't entirely inconceivable that they would kill their own subcontractor, it was highly unlikely. Especially in view of the fact that their deal had not yet been consummated.

That left the Malina. That was Presto's choice. But something about that *still* bothered Driscoll. The whole key was the bastard with the white hair. Find out who signed his check and it would all begin to unravel.

But why was Honey in jeopardy? Bellows might have locked her up somewhere to keep her quiet, but Driscoll had known him well enough to believe that he would have stopped short of killing a woman like her. Yet there was no question that someone wanted her out of the way.

The Malina? Driscoll liked that even less. Why bother?

Honey wasn't a *capo,* but she was the heiress. That must be bothering the hell out of somebody.

And the guns? He kept coming back to those guns.

A .45 had been used on the highway patrolmen; on Arlene. There was a .45 in the basement—the gun in the frozen hand. Then there were the rifles in Presto's bedroom closet, loaded with full clips. And as long as Driscoll lived, he would never forget the damage caused by the M-16s that had been used in the assault on Presto's numbers bank.

"Do you know you're talking to yourself?" Honey called to him from the shower. "You're really getting loud. I heard you all the way in here." She was drying her hair, toweling that glistening mop of dark brown curls and enjoying the sensation of finally being clean and dry and warm.

Driscoll had lived alone for so long that he had gotten in the habit of talking out loud to himself; there was never anyone with him for it to bother. He just shook his head and didn't bother to explain. She was moving around in there, and he could see her bare back as the white towel caressed her olive skin, moving toward her hips. He'd almost forgotten how much fun it was to see Honey naked, but it all came back to him now. He wished that they were somewhere else, far away, all by themselves, with only each other to enjoy, and no Malina or murders to worry about. He almost wished that the Meatman were still alive, that god was in his heaven and all was right in his world.

Honey opened the door and came toward him, trailing a sheet that encircled her like a toga. She could have been a beckoning figure from an alabaster vase that an excited archaeologist had just unearthed. There was a timelessness to Honey, a wantonness that transcended the ages. She brushed past him, and their hips touched. Her cupid's face became pixieish and daring. Despite the fact that they were hiding out, that she had almost been killed, not once but twice, Honey was almost relaxed.

"This turn you on?" She flashed her thigh through the folds of the sheet and giggled. This was really the old Honey now—the Honey he had fallen for, hard, oblivious to danger or anything else.

Driscoll knew what he wanted, and Honey was telling him that she wanted it, too. But something—everything—

was holding him back. Maybe five years had been too long, or maybe it had all been wrong from the start. If this was some kind of contest, he didn't want to win it. Not now, anyway.

She was practically dancing around him, playful, teasing, taunting; wanting him to help her forget everything too. "Come on, Phillip," she said, surprising him. "Remember . . . It wasn't *that* long ago. I haven't changed that much, have I?"

This wasn't right and he knew it. He could feel himself responding to Honey instantly, but he wasn't just asking for trouble, he was begging to get his head blown off. Hers, too. "I'd better check outside again," he said.

Honey couldn't believe what she was seeing. Big, tough Phillip Driscoll, supercop, was acting shy. She wouldn't have been stunned to hear him say, "Ah, shucks," but Honey had a way of taking care of that. A triumphant smile brightened her face. Honey adored the shy ones.

When Driscoll returned from his cold, wet reconnaissance, he saw two glasses of wine poured and waiting on a low table near the fireplace. It had looked perfectly deserted outside, safe. Then he had the strangest urge: Should he call Lawlor? Was that worth a try? What about Carney? He appeared to be running this show, and Driscoll knew that the time had arrived to take this to the top.

"Oh, I meant to tell you something," Honey called to him from the kitchen. "You remember those pictures you showed me back at Harry's place? I think I remember where I saw him—the one I picked out." She came out of the kitchen, swept past him, still in the sheet, and began sipping from a glass of red wine as she handed him the other glass.

"It's Christmas morning," he said. "Isn't it a little early for this?"

"You'd make a lousy Italian. This stuff is mother's milk." She drained her glass.

He couldn't remember the last time he had eaten. He stared at the wine, sparkling and mellow, with moisture beading on the outside of the glass, and imagined how good it would taste. Just one.

Honey jumped up and grabbed for his wine. "Oh, my God, Phillip," she exclaimed. "I'm so sorry. I forgot . . . I don't know how I could forget. It's just that so much has happened. I'll make tea. I'm sorry." She looked ashamed of herself.

He pushed the wine away from him, regarding it like a draft of hemlock. "What do you have to be sorry for?" he asked casually. "You aren't the drunk, I am. Remember?"

Honey started making tea. "What about the picture?" he asked. "You were just about to tell me."

"Oh, I'm not even sure," she said, the uncertainty evident in her tone. "But I'm almost positive that I saw him on Rittenhouse Square one day, when I was there for the Flower Show. The reason I remember is because he was there talking to somebody I knew, but now I can't remember who he was talking to, either."

"How could you remember a thing like that after all this time?" he asked. "That had to be last spring. And then not remember who the people were?"

"He just had the kind of a face you don't forget," Honey answered, "but maybe it wasn't even him. I'm not absolutely sure."

"What did they talk about?"

"Who knows, Phillip? I was there to buy flowers." She looked at him as though he were crazy. "Maybe they were there to buy flowers, too."

"Was it like a casual encounter, or did they seem to know each other?" He was shifting into his interrogation mode now.

"What's with the third degree? Do I look like a detective?"

"If you saw him again, would you remember him?"

"I remembered him this time, didn't I?"

He started to say something else, but Honey was getting impatient. "Enough, already. I'll see if I can fix us anything to eat. And take it easy, okay? I'm the one they're after."

ISTANBUL

"Are you certain the boy is to accompany me?" Zhukov asked a Buddha-shaped Turkish policeman who was sweating through his olive-drab uniform. At first, Zhukov had been taken aback when he realized that the Malina, with the help of the Turkish black market, Kara Borsa, had compromised enough Turkish customs agents and border patrolmen to facilitate his flight from Samsun to Istanbul. But his amazement soon gave way to resignation, because it was now clear to him that the Malina could do anything. The Cessna, a four-seater with three occupants, himself, the boy-child, and the pilot, had put down on a private estate in a suburb of Istanbul called Pera, where most of the foreigners lived. This landing field was on the European side of the Bosporus Straits, across the Golden Horn from the old city. But he was in the old city now, in Stamboul, a triangular island within the storied capital city of the Byzantine Empire, separated from the rest of the metropolis by a series of filthy, polluted interlocking canals and high stone walls, built at the behest of some long-forgotten sultan.

At the estate where the Cessna landed—a Malina safe house, Zhukov decided with professional certainty—he had seen no one except for the ever-present guards, outfitted in this instance in the casual clothes of Westernized Turkey. From the estate another car and driver had taken him to a small inn in the central district of Stamboul. That had been less than an a hour ago. Shortly afterward, the policeman he was now addressing had shown up.

"My Russian is hopeless," the policeman said in a guttural accent. Then he immediately switched to English, in which he was more fluent; he assumed that the KGB man would be, as well. "My instructions are very precise," he continued, as he handed Zhukov an expensive-looking leather valise that smelled of well-tanned cowhide. "Here you will find all the necessary papers, visas and passports included. You will be traveling as a Hungarian businessman, and the child is your son. When your plane lands in the United States, someone will meet you. You have no say in the matter, sir. Orders are orders."

The child stood by silently, listening to the conversation. Zhukov had no idea whether or not he understood English. "These arrangements aren't at all satisfactory," he protested. "This child with his dreadful silence makes me nervous. I suppose you have no idea the fortune that this little trip is costing me. I'm a policeman like yourself. I'm sure we can come to some understanding."

The Turk had been dealing with smugglers on the border for most of his career. He was the father of six children; he had a mistress in Pera and a taste for night life. Never once had the Kara Borsa failed to see to his needs. This Russian was not getting through to him. "If you're a policeman like *me,*" the Turk said, "then you understand the seriousness of the people with whom we do business." At this point, he placed a fat hand on his white holster, a flashy Sam Browne affair, and loosened the flap that covered the revolver's grip. "Don't make me kill you. That would cost me a great deal of money. They're holding half of my fee until you are airborne again." He closed the flap again. "Now be a good fellow and move along. If I kill you and lose that money, be assured, comrade KGB man, the death will be painful." Then the Turk removed his uniform cap and brushed back his hair, revealing the glistening moisture between the curls.

When Zhukov looked over at the boy, he was already packed for what the Russian hoped would be the last leg of the journey. "As you wish," he said.

STONE HARBOR

Honey wanted him again, and nothing else mattered—where Phillip Driscoll was concerned, nothing else ever did. "Was the tea all right?" she asked. He didn't answer. "Are you still hungry?"

Driscoll was famished, but Honey's skills had never extended to the kitchen. "It's tough when you can't call room service," he said sarcastically.

She looked hurt, but not really hurt. Honey had been raised as a princess, and cooking had always been done by her aunt or her father or one of the housekeepers. "Forget it," he said. "I'll fix something." But when he turned around, she wasn't there. "Jesus," he called out, "it was only a joke."

Honey was in her bedroom making herself cry. He hated that and she was so good at it. After a few moments, he found her with her face buried in the pillows and the sheet still around her.

"Cut it out," he said gently. Honey was hot to the touch. He raised one shoulder, then the other, and turned her around to face him on the bed. She stopped him from saying anything else with her mouth, her tongue, and her hands. Part of what they had had together was passion, but most of it had been nothing more than understanding. They were both players, and neither was quite sure what the next day would bring. It had always been enough that they had each other. When he looked at Honey, he was looking at some strange reflection of himself, but in her he was turned inside out. All feeling, emotion, and fiery animation.

She let the sheet fall, and he touched her breast for the first time since they had had that last night together. He had to fight hard against flashing back to what had happened the following morning when he had awakened to find her gone. Surgically removed from his life.

He smelled her hair, tasted it, felt the silkiness. Then he began to move against her body—almost kissing her, but again holding back.

Immediately sensing his hesitancy, Honey closed her eyes, reached out toward his face, and drew it close to hers again, as she maneuvered herself beneath him on the bed. Honey arched her back slightly as he kissed her nipple. He could feel every heartbeat—even the little catch in her breathing that told him that she was racing to meet him.

"What's wrong?" she asked. "If you don't want to, we don't have to. You can sleep. We're both tired. I'll watch."

"It isn't safe," he answered. "It's never going to be

safe." He closed his eyes and let his cheeks absorb the moisture and the softness of her skin.

"That's not it," Honey said. "What's wrong?"

"You," he answered.

This time Honey pulled away, almost pushed him off her and threw herself back on the bed. "Before, I used to think I was too good for you. That's the truth. Now you make me feel that I'm not good enough."

Neither of them spoke again for the next few moments, and Driscoll started to move away from the bed. She stopped him with a firm hand on his arm. He was almost at the door.

"Just tell me." She was pleading. "Why won't you make love to me?"

He looked right at her, all pretense gone. "Why did you leave me?"

She didn't know what to say.

"Tell me the truth this time," he said.

Honey had been thinking of that last night, too, and of all the other nights afterward when she had picked up the phone or taken pen in hand, wanting so desperately to contact him.

"I was afraid," Honey said sadly, searching his questioning eyes, trying not to show what she had *really* been terrified of five years before. She was holding on to him, trusting him completely. He could feel the fire between her legs, her readiness. As he responded this time, first tracing the delicate bone structure of her cheeks and chin, his hands again drifted to her breasts, and finally her thighs. A fine angel down covered every inch of her body, a downy filament that was yielding to his touch.

Then, knowing that the past no longer mattered, Phillip Driscoll took Honey into his strong, powerful arms, his cop's arms, arms just like the Meatman's, arms that she knew could protect her against anything. They kissed again, longer this time, a kiss of reconciliation.

He didn't speak but just picked her up and carried her back to the bed, where all of the memories could be behind them, all the bitterness. As he lifted her like a bride across the threshold, the naked, soft flesh of her buttocks and thighs were resting against his muscular forearms. Still kissing, her tongue sought the space between his teeth.

Then Honey was on the bed, or maybe next to it, she couldn't tell. He was in a hurry, but not in a hurry, too—all at the same time. They *had* to do it now, before another heartbeat passed.

Moist, full, Honey couldn't wait a moment longer. Reaching down, she took Driscoll in her damp, flushed hand and guided him, rising, opening, taking him inside of her. She'd begged God to let it be like before, like that last night, but this time it was even better. She could feel Phillip coming in a great wave.

She pulled away, excited, calling his name; then she searched for him again, wanting him to go on and on, even as he exploded against her, inside her, filling her with pressure and pleasure and contentment. Finally, she dozed off with his head on her breast; her hand still held him, refusing to ever let him go again.

The pain was unbearable. Driscoll felt as though his testicles were being squeezed to mush. Someone had him by the balls. He was trying to shake himself awake. Then, he doubled up in pain.

"Tony, this is so *cute,*" Marie Bonaventura's husky voice called out in an obscene singsong. "We caught Driscoll the cop layin' pipe to dear little Honey. But now we got him by the short hair; now we got both of them."

He couldn't see Honey, but Driscoll could hear her breathing; it sounded like someone had put his hand over her mouth. Honey was coughing, gagging. The last thing he could remember was falling asleep with her.

Marie had her hand under the sheet Driscoll and Honey had used to cover themselves. She had been squeezing him with all her strength; she let up just a little. He was trying hard not to scream. Suddenly, Marie yanked back the sheet. He was exposed to cold air. Marie's mouth never seemed to close.

"Not so bad, huh, Tony? This Driscoll, he's a big one." She was leering at his genitals. "He your stud, Honey? This cop, he's hung good. But then, you never were anything but a little *puttana*. So this is how my brother, the Meatman, taught you how to do it. But I got news for you, little girl. This lousy cop, this Irish shit, he won't be no good to you no more, because me and Tony, we gonna cut his balls right off. Maybe the rest, too. Then you have a eunuch instead of a stud."

She laughed again. An oppressive climate of evil emanated from Marie like some persistent foul odor.

Driscoll couldn't see Tony, but he could feel the cold gun barrel against the back of his head. Marie was taking perverse delight in manipulating his testicles. Her long fingernails had stopped digging in; she was merely holding him now. "How you like that, Driscoll? That feel as good as little Honey?"

He had always known that he would die someday. He fully expected it to be at gunpoint, but he had never dreamed that he would be bare-ass naked when the time came, staring up at the grinning red lips of Marie Bonaventura. Suddenly, she twisted and squeezed him again.

He struggled up to his elbow. As he moved, straightening himself into a sitting position, he could feel the gun barrel moving with him, against him. Then he looked around. Tony had Honey in a hammerlock. There was adhesive tape across her mouth, and the crook of Tony's arm was jammed against her windpipe. She was arched back against the underboss. Her toes barely reached the floor. He was practically choking her.

In his other hand, Tony held the gun that was pointed at the back of Driscoll's brain. As usual, Marie was doing all the talking.

Tony's eyes, leering and hungry, kept devouring Honey's naked body, roaming from her breasts to her dark pubic hair. Marie noticed.

"You see enough, Tony? How 'bout we get back to business. You ain't here to drill her, Tony. You're here to get rid of her. Him, too." She yanked at Driscoll's testicles again.

Driscoll had been stupid, sloppy; a dumb-ass—it was just like the time with the Fat Man. And the worst part of it was that he couldn't even blame this lapse of professionalism on the Silver Bullets. This time all he'd had to do was catch Honey's scent and it had started all over again.

Now he was paying for it.

"You know, you're a lot of trouble, Driscoll," Marie said. "Tony here, he almost got you. But no, you gotta have the goddam luck of the Irish. You made him miss, damn you, but not *this* time. Not you and not that slut."

She sat down heavily on the bed next to him, releasing her grip just a little. As she did so, she reached into her pocket and withdrew a small pistol. Then she pointed it at him. Behind him he could still hear Honey struggling, putting up a fight.

They were going to kill him. That was the only choice they had. This was business, and they planned to come out ahead. But he hated like hell dying curious. "Let me guess," Driscoll said, putting the pieces together as they came to him. "That night I went to see Honey at Manny's place, Tony followed me. I guess he figured that Honey and I were cooking something up . . . figured that just maybe Honey even knew what the hell was *really* going on. So Tony, being the bright boy that he is, decides to kill me quick while he has the chance, just in case Honey had already told me too much."

He couldn't see Tony from his position on the bed. But Marie's face was telegraphing a message to him. He was right—about most of it, anyway.

"As soon as the Meatman gets it," Driscoll continued, "you two assholes see the chance of a lifetime to really move uptown. All you have to do is kill Honey, get the money, eliminate the heiress, and throw the whole fucking Family into chaos. Honey might as well have had a bull's-eye on her back."

Through all the mascara and eyeshadow, past the blue tint that encrusted her eyelids, Driscoll could see that Marie's eyes were becoming tinier and tinier—two pin-points struggling to connect themselves. Once that connection was made—and Marie's mind was made up—he and Honey would die. In the Presto Family, this had to be the natural order of things. They and the police already knew that he and Honey had once been lovers. Call him a bad cop, a corrupt cop. The evidence was certainly there. He had a feeling that himself, Alfred E. Smith Lawlor, wouldn't break his neck trying to solve a murder like that. Tony and Marie might actually be doing the police department a favor. And Honey? With the Meatman dead, she was helpless.

He had to hand it to these two slobs. Their timing was absolutely impeccable. Even from the point of view of the feds, he and Honey probably both knew too much to stay alive.

"Wrong, Driscoll," Tony cut in gruffly. "You ain't so smart as you think you are. You made one mistake. The best part was—"

"Shut your mouth, Tony. Enough."

Like a Pavlovian puppy, Tony, reacting to the stimulus of his mistress's voice, gagged himself in midsyllable.

"Let's go," Marie commanded.

Tony and Honey went first, Tony more or less dragging her with his arm still at her throat. Then Driscoll, Marie marching behind them with a gun in the small of his back. As Driscoll passed her, she gave his bare buttock a hard slap. "Not bad, Driscoll, not bad at all."

The house was freezing. Being naked didn't help. Honey had stopped even trying to free herself. It appeared that they were headed for the garage, but Driscoll couldn't be sure. Midway through the living room—dark, quiet, funereal—he heard what he knew was the cock of the hammer of a gun. The sound came from behind him. Marie. It looked like she'd be doing it herself. She wouldn't miss, like Tony.

"Far enough," Marie barked. "Kneel down, Driscoll. Tony, put her down over there."

Driscoll did as he was told. The fibers of the carpet on the floor of the living room felt prickly against his knees. For the first time since the night before, the pain in his ribs was really bothering him. About ten feet away, on the other side of the room, he could see Honey's eyes searching desperately for him, for a way out, for *something.* She looked afraid. Defeated.

Driscoll could see Tony tying Honey's arms behind her, while Marie gripped his own wrists. He was on his knees, and she was trying to make the cord or whatever the hell she was using hurt as much as possible.

Honey was wiggling a little—certainly distracting Tony every time she moved. And Marie, busy as she was, was reading his mind.

"You need some help over there, Tony?"

Driscoll could see what was happening. Honey was trying to inch her way toward him across the darkened floor, attempting to reach him, to be near him one last time.

It was now or never.

It began with him leaning backward, threatening to press himself against Marie's big bosom. Then, suddenly, like a cat, Driscoll flipped himself to once side and barreled into Marie, still on his knees. She fell, face forward, injuring her mouth.

His shoulder caught her knees, and she toppled face forward on top of him. Because his hands were still half-tied, he couldn't reach out for the gun. It landed on the carpet between them.

Smashing Honey on the floor in front of him, prepared to use her naked body as a shield, Tony had opened fire the instant that Driscoll had begun his backward collapse. He counted . . . one . . . two . . . three bullets.

Tony's aim was lousy, and he was firing in the dark. Driscoll scooted from one piece of furniture to another, running low, almost crawling, and made it into the kitchen.

"Kill her, Tony," he heard Marie gurgle through bruised, bleeding lips—Driscoll had really whacked her. *"Kill her now!"*

He freed his hands. He needed a weapon . . . had to save Honey . . . Marie's gun was still on the floor . . . he could lunge for it . . . hope that Tony's aim would still be off . . .

Boom!

Boom!

Boom!

That was *another* gun. Heavy. A big weapon. A real cannon. That wasn't Tony's gun.

Hurling himself out of his hiding place, between the kitchen and the dining room, heading straight for Honey, all Driscoll could hear was Marie screaming, wailing, over and over and over, "Tony . . . Tony . . . Tony . . . you all right? Tony, they shot you . . .

All he could see was a group of men, looming dark shadows in the doorway, entering the house, filling the room. Then someone clubbed him with the butt end of a gun.

One of them was reaching out toward Honey, draping an overcoat around her shoulders, clumsily helping her cover herself. At the same moment, he saw someone direct a vicious kick against Tony's rib cage. The underboss was now sprawled on the floor, blood pooling under his chest.

Honey was sobbing, clinging to the man who had offered her the coat, but she kept calling out to Driscoll plaintively, "Oh, Phillip, *Phillip!*"

Then Driscoll heard a sound that he had heard only once before in his life. Once before, at the morgue.

Bing . . . Bing . . . Bing . . .

Milton Littlejohn, Presto's mouthpiece, was tapping his duck's-head cane against the hardwood floor that separated the living room and kitchen.

Somebody hit Driscoll again, and he passed out.

Driscoll came out of it before he could see; his eyes were caked shut by drying blood. The pain in the back of his head, sharp and stubborn, remained fixed there like a nail that had been driven into his skull.

Something liquid and a little cold—maybe water from a damp cloth?—was gradually bringing him out of it as it moistened the congealed mess that had kept his eyelids stuck to his cheeks. Slowly, he blinked his way through the cloying goo, hoping he would be able to see once he finally had his eyes open.

"You took a nice shot, Phil," a vaguely familiar voice said. It wasn't anyone he knew; or did he? *Who?* Still, he recognized it, didn't he?

"You see me okay, or what? Your eyeballs ain't moving around like they should. I seen this before; you got a concussion. That's what you got. Take it easy. Just sit up. That's blood on your face; no big deal. You know me now, right? It's okay."

It *wasn't* okay. Honey was gone, and someone was using

a hammer to drive the spike in the back of his head in a little deeper. A pair of hands were helping him sit up now. But it hurt too much to open his eyes.

"I don't know who busted up your head back there, Driscoll," the voice said, confused itself this time. "But no hard feelings. We all seen Honey was in trouble and just dove in. That stuff happens, you know."

Who the hell was talking to him like this?

"Where's Honey?" Driscoll asked again, groggily.

"Safe now." The voice sounded very concerned.

"Who are you? What happened? Where is she?"

Driscoll could focus his right eye well enough now to see the person talking to him. The left eye was still blurry—the pain in the back of his head was coming from the left side, too.

"Joe-Joey?" Driscoll said, surprising himself. "How the hell did you get here?"

Joe-Joey used a balled-up wet cloth to smear more of the dried blood away from Driscoll's left eye. That helped. He could almost see normally now.

"The Family got a little nervous about Honey. Littlejohn came with us to bring her home." There was considerably more to it, but Joe-Joey figured that that was enough in the way of explanations.

Driscoll grabbed a fistful of Joe-Joey's suit coat, forgetting his pain, banishing it, intent on learning exactly what had happened to Honey. "Who has her?" Driscoll rasped through the pain and confusion he was still feeling.

Joe-Joey yanked Driscoll's clenched fingers away from his coat. "We'll take care of her, Driscoll. Bet on it. You can take your help and shove it. You damn near got her killed already."

Driscoll fought to get to his feet, but he was still so dizzy that Joe-Joey had to help him. He started to thank him, then hesitated. It seemed so strange, needing a Presto soldier's assistance just to keep his balance.

THIRTY-ONE

THE PALATA, THE KREMLIN

Marshal Zinijakin had always rejected as nonsense and superstition any theories of reincarnation. Fortune-telling gypsies who worked for the Malina could gull their customers with better tricks than that. Yet he had a certain preternatural sense that he might very well have lived as a warrior under the old czars in some previous existence.

Zinijakin was in the Palata, the secret inner heart of the entire Kremlin. Within it lay the Armorer's Chamber, the underground vault that contained the Soviet state's—the Russian state's—most priceless treasures.

He had let himself in, after the tourists had gone for the day, by pushing open heavy iron gates decorated by four fierce czarist eagles. In most ways Zinijakin regretted living in the modern age. How could a man, a warrior, pledge his life and honor to an icon like the hammer and sickle? To a plain red flag? It must have been so much easier to identify with these fierce eagles, claws bared, ready to tear the heart from any enemy of the Motherland. And how Zinijakin did love the good rich earth of Mother Russia.

Within this room, the marshal would always perform the same ritual. First, removing a small key from his pocket, he opened a bulky square chest that scholars had estimated was at least three hundred years old.

He lifted the lid. It creaked on ornate hinges that had been fashioned by some nameless craftsman who had never dreamed it would one day occupy the highest place of honor in the Kremlin's vast treasure coffers.

The chest contained a velvet bag, similar to that used by diamond merchants, but several times larger. There was usually an involuntary tremble in Zinijakin's left hand, but he stilled it long enough to reach into the brown velvet sack and grasp the heavy weight of an ancient crown, known as the Cap of Monomakh.

Struck ages before civilization had even agreed on the proper design of the crown, the golden Cap was domed in the Tartar fashion and appeared to be as functional as a helmet. Its decoration, however, indicated its tremendous value. The peak was crowned with a cross of gold in the Byzantine motif with the vertical bar intersecting the horizontal and a third bar lying across the base of the cross diagonally. Each corner of the cross was set off by an enormous pearl. The body of the dome was composed of eight symmetrical rectangles, each clustered with rubies, emeralds, and lesser jewels. A soft, cushiony garland of dark sable was wound around the base of the Cap, buffering the head that wore the gold and its two solid pounds of precious gems.

The Cap of Monomakh symbolized the rule of the old czars from horizon to horizon, from the setting of the sun to the rising of the sun. If a man could wear the Cap and live, then he had earned God's favor. For a usurper to seize it would have been a blasphemy too base to contemplate. More than anything else in the Kremlin's treasure rooms, the Cap embodied the living tradition of imperial Russia—Zinijakin's Russia.

Once he was absolutely sure that no one was likely to intrude upon him in the Palata, Zinijakin would remove the crown and spend long moments, blissful moments, trying to interpret the intricate carvings of scrolls and mystical designs painstakingly worked into the gold and promising the wearer every manifestation of good fortune and wisdom. The passage of time had obilterated the specific meaning of each sign, and even in the time of the czars the Cap had been recognized as the relic of some long-forgotten empire.

The Cap had first been seized by the rulers of the Kremlin fortress in the twelfth century. Before that, the Emperor of Byzantium had worn it. Once, according to legend, the Cap of Monomakh had even adorned the furrowed brow of Caesar Augustus.

In its venerable presence, Zinijakin never failed to absorb a surge of power, perhaps the charged molecules of telekinetic energy. Whatever, the effect was profound on the aged marshal, renewing him and blessing him with a tangible sense of physical well-being. He considered its medicinal properties far superior to anything in science. He knew that the czars before him had similarly drawn strength from it.

As the Headman of the Malina's Council of Elders, he believed that the Cap of Monomakh belonged to him by divine right. Zinijakin would have given his life to make it so. But that was not the sacred mission of the Malina. The Malina's destiny was to endure for all time, safeguarding the Brotherhood—and Russia, the Russia of the czars—against time itself.

Dreaming enchantedly of how the Cap would feel crowning his own head, Zinijakin settled into a throne in a nook of the Armorer's Chamber and cast his eyes along the dark corridor before him. After a few reflective moments had passed, he heard his aide approach. His aid was Malina, too, but a career army man like himself. No one else knew where he was. Reverently, he put the Cap back where it belonged, struggling to control the tremor in his hand again.

"The message has been delivered," his aide reported. "No break in the human chain."

The Malina had used a system of personal couriers for important communications since ancient days. Once a message was set in motion, it would pass from mouth to mouth, from courier to courier, life to life, nonstop, until its destination had been reached. No obstacles—national frontiers, oceans, mountains, continents—could deter it. The Malina's human chain could never be broken.

"That is very good. And the other?"

Reaching into a military-type attaché case, the aide handed him a sheaf of papers, cables from abroad. "Four ships. Four messages," he said to Zinijakin. "The captains are standing by, offshore, waiting for your instructions."

"Excellent," the marshal said, harrumphing his way into

a loose cough. "I'll be with the Chairman. But before I go, another communication for the human chain."

The aide listened carefully. Zinijakin repeated his message twice. It was his instructions for Tanya, cryptic and brief, and an answer—the Council of Elders' final decision for Nikolai Butkova. Even with the miracle of air travel, the marshal calculated that it would take the better part of two days to reach Tanya, but reach her it would. The Malina's human chain never failed.

HASTINGS, PENNSYLVANIA LOYOLA RETREAT HOUSE, SATURDAY, THE DAY AFTER CHRISTMAS

Carney had intended for Ed Bellows to conclude this final phase of his negotiations, but with Bellows dead, he had no choice but to go himself.

Carney had been airborne for an hour as his Marine helicopter pilot kept searching the wintery Pennsylvania farmscape—brown-and-green terrain from the air, dissected by plowed fields that led to his old retreat house in rustic Chester County. As a youth, the Jesuits had marched him here several times each year, disciplining him and instilling in him their narrow, inflexible vision of heaven, hell, and eternity. The older he got, the more nostalgic he became for that simple time.

One of the first friends he had ever made during those school-boy pilgrimages was Alfred E. Smith Lawlor. Their careers had paralleled one another's, and that friendship had endured—more cerebral than emotional, and not even remotely sexual, which Carney had always regretted, because Alfred had looked like a youthful Hercules in his boyhood, but unmistakably genuine. Despite all of his political bloodletting in Washington, and regardless of all he had learned of men's crass motives and their grasping, unsteady egos, Carney had never lost faith in or respect for his friend Alfred. Now he would have to ask Alfred to put it all on the line again.

"This it it," Carney said to his pilot, tapping him lightly on the shoulder—what a fine muscular shoulder. A very pretty boy, too. Much too young-looking for the uniform and the cold air of Marine professionalism. Carney had always adored men in uniform. As he found himself staring at the boy and wanting to touch him again, Carney forced himself to look away. He recognized the familiar gothic towers of the retreat house as the chopper put down, its long rotors twirling, on the wide lawn of the abbey. Wasn't Alfred going to be surprised!

It was a tradition and an unalterable constant in his life that every year, in the week between Christmas and New Year's, Alfred E. Smith Lawlor would seclude himself in the Loyola Retreat House and immerse himself in prayer, fasting, and scrupulous examination of conscience. It was his annual exercise whereby he justified himself and his life to his God. Not to anyone else's God, but only to his own.

During his week of reflection each Christmastide, rape, riot, or murder could take place in Philadelphia, and Alfred E. Smith Lawlor wouldn't care. This was his private time. He used it to recharge his batteries for the year ahead. He had never said as much, but most of the men who served under him knew that it would be suicidal, at least professionally, to disturb him during his week of recollection.

Police officers, eager to move up the ladder to the next rung of command, also learned quickly that it couldn't hurt their chances for promotion to spend all or part of that week with Lawlor at Loyola.

This year, about twenty men had elected to stand a seventy-two-hour shift of sacred duty in the rural tundra of Hastings. They talked among themselves in small groups, gossiping mostly about Roundhouse politics. Occasionally they swapped stories about conquests of women. Maybe once during those seventy-two hours they would stop to meditate or to pray. But always, they were tuned in to himself, Alfred E. Smith Lawlor, taking their lead from him, walking the Stations of the Crucifixion when he did; keeping silence during his hours of silence, and industriously attempting to ingratiate themselves with the indomitable police commissioner of Philadelphia.

Captain Biaggio Marinari, Phillip Driscoll's boss in Homicide, had taken the retreat this year, hoping for the best. He was returning from the underground crypts, where a memorial service had been held, to his small, sparsely furnished room, admiring the striking Renaissance reproductions that lined the corridor, when he heard the helicopter outside. Marinari had never lived like a monk before. He had gone to public school, not Catholic, and this entire experience had been enlightening for him, and unnerving.

Marinari knew enough to keep out of the way of superiors from his years at the Roundhouse. He had followed the same policy while on retreat. That's why he was surprised to see the retreat master approaching him.

"Captain, may I have a word with you?" the retreat master inquired.

"Of course, Father," Biaggio answered.

"I hate to bother you with this, but there's a gentleman here—he arrived by helicopter, no less—who claims to be an old friend of Commissioner Lawlor's. I wonder, could you talk to this man and see what he wants? Try to find out if he really is what he claims to be. Would you mind doing that before I disturb the commissioner?"

Biaggio's face seemed to ask "Why me?" The observant retreat master caught the cautious cop's hesitancy. "I ask you, Captain, because the commissioner has spoken so highly of you."

Biaggio beamed. Proud. Happy to serve Lawlor. The retreat master was lying, of course. Marinari happened to be the first cop he had spotted outside the chapel. But it was only a white lie—he could confess it. God would forgive him.

* * *

"You aren't Commissioner Lawlor," Carney greeted Captain Marinari, not bothering to buffer the dollop of acid in his voice. "I have no desire to see you, whoever you are. Run along now and fetch me Alfred Lawlor, and tell him that James Xavier Carney has come calling."

Marinari left at once, wondering just who the hell this abrasive old man thought he was.

He found Commissioner Lawlor kneeling stiffly and reverently on a prie-dieu in the chapel. Except for Lawlor, the small church was empty. Taking a deep, fearful breath, Marinari approached him.

FAIRMOUNT, NORTH PHILADELPHIA

Zhukov and the boy, who was sleeping now, although Zhukov would have sworn that he slept with one eye open, had been told to take a flat at a rooming house in Fairmount, an old mixed neighborhood in Philadelphia that had once been heavily Russian and Ukrainian. Now, the landlady had informed him, it was called the Art Museum Area because of its proximity to the venerable Philadelphia Museum of Art. The landlady was a rotund little American with a puckering, persistent smile that fought through haggard features and wispy, unkept hair, so white that it could have been alabaster. She told Zhukov, in her cheery, busy-body way, that she had lived in the neighborhood before the Ukrainians started to come in the late 1950s. "All Polacks and Irish then," she said, chattering away. "*You* people, you can't talk right, but thank God, you're better than the niggers, at least. I always got along fine with my Ukie neighbors. Anybody's welcome, that's what I say, so long as they're white."

Zhukov didn't tell the landlady that he wasn't Ukrainian—just as well for her to think that he was. She inquired about his wife. He stammered in the best English that he could muster that he was a widower. "Same here," she said, as she finally left Zhukov and the boy alone.

Everything had gone well at Kennedy Airport in New York. A woman who looked more matronly than Malina had met them at the overseas terminal and easily escorted them through customs. The forged documents that he had received back in Turkey were as good as any that he had ever seen. After customs, the woman took Zhukov and the boy to her car, making sure that he caught a quick glimpse of her gun, and then drove them down the New Jersey Turnpike to Philadelphia. She didn't speak to him once during the whole journey. But for the very first time, Zhukov detected something very different in the child. He was animated, eager almost, clearly anticipating the end of the long trek.

He had showered and changed and eaten a little when he heard a knock on the door. He recognized the landlady's cough, then her voice. An envelope had been left for him, she said, excited to be giving him news.

He had been expecting no envelope, but he opened the door hesitantly. This was the very first event that had taken place throughout his long, exhausting trip that had not been fully communicated to him by the Malina as something that he should watch out for.

Thoroughly examining the large gray envelope, turning it over with anxious hands, he worked a sharp letter opener into the sealed fold at the top.

A photo. Nothing else. But what a photo! It was a picture of Tanya. Her lips were parted slightly, her tongue caressing perfect teeth. Her blond hair shimmered against an azure-blue skyline. She was dressed in winter garb. Behind her there appeared to be a building with a religious motif of some sort—perhaps a shrine. In the photo, Tanya was holding a newspaper just beneath her breast. The headline announced the triumphant return of the President of the United States from his Christmas Summit at Geneva, his pivotal meeting with the Soviet Chairman.

Performing a quick mental calculation, Zhukov counted back the days, remembering everything that had happened in Russia before his fateful encounter with the Malina in

Odessa. He moved the fingers on his hand, adding up to five.

It *had* to be! Tanya had to be holding *today's* newspaper. This was the signal he had been praying for. She had gotten away and would make contact with him after all.

The newspaper was telling him that she was ready to see him immediately!

Zhukov screamed for the landlady; in a moment she appeared. "What is it?" she demanded, annoyed. "It's so late to be hollering like this. What is it with you people?"

"Today's newspaper." Zhukov shook her shoulders roughly. "I must see it!"

"The cat," she protested. "I use it for the cat. What newspaper? You want to read now?"

Rushing past her, Zhukov ran downstairs toward the shed he had noticed at the rear of her first floor, screaming all the while, "The paper, I must see it!"

Then he spied the creature, a fat tabby, black-and-white, just about to settle into the litter box. With Tanya's photo still clutched in his sweating palm, Zhukov dropped to his hands and knees and began tearing through the litter box until he had located the front page that corresponded to the one Tanya was holding. Cat urine and feces clung to the paper, and by now, to his own hands. It *was* today's date—December 26! But what else was she telling him? He kept rereading and scanning the story about the President. But as far as he knew, that didn't affect him. What else?

Zhukov looked at the photo again. A gloved hand. Tanya's slender, tapered hand, *could* have been pointing to another story on the bottom of the *Philadelphia Inquirer's* page fold. Or her hand could simply have been resting that way.

But he knew his Tanya; every gesture had always been calculated. She *was* pointing to another smaller headline. Through the cat pee and filth, he stared at it: *Loyola's Shrine of the Holy Grail Attracts Season Crowds.*

Shrine? What shrine? He read the story. Loyola House? What could this be?

"Look what you've done to my kitchen!" the landlady yelled at him as she puffed her way in after him. "Where's my cat?"

"I'll clean it up," Zhukov said testily. "But *please,* you

must tell me of this shrine . . . here in the newspaper . . . what is it? Where is it? How can I get there?''

Sniffing at the stink, she examined the newspaper story as Zhukov glowered at her threateningly. He was growing impatient with this silly old woman and was more anxious than ever now to make good on his defection and rendezvous with Tanya. ''This place,'' he shouted, forcing the Russian words out of his mind and the English words to the forefront, ''what *is* this place? I must know!''

The landlady's hand rummaged around in the wide pocket of her housecoat. She withdrew small metal-rimmed glasses and used them to read the stained newspaper page. ''So, what's all the fuss?'' she asked. ''This is the Shrine of the Holy Grail. People visit there during the Christmas holidays. Our priests run buses out there from my own parish. It's way out in the country somewhere. Don't get all excited. You Ukrainians get all hot and bothered for no reason at all.''

Zhukov looked at the date on the newspaper again—today's date—then turned on the landlady, his eyes flashing with anger and annoyance. Unconsciously, he was again becoming the KGB interrogator. ''And this pilgrimage,'' he demanded. ''The buses . . . when do they leave?''

The landlady was used to strange boarders, waking at odd hours, making unusual requests, but never had she taken in anyone who so intimidated her. She was used to putting up a brazen front. That was how she got by. But all of a sudden, she felt very uneasy; she was afraid not to answer this man.

''I'll find out for you. Don't get excited,'' she said nervously. Then she crossed the kitchen to a wall calendar and traced out the last week of the month with her fingertips. ''Good Lord,'' she said, relieved, ''I wrote this on here myself from the church bulletin. The pilgrimage is tomorrow. Aren't you the lucky one, if you wanta go.'' She smiled faintly, hoping this would please him. ''I'm already signed up for a seat on the bus myself.''

Oblivious to his prosaic surroundings, Zhukov drew himself up to his full height and paced momentarily in the kitchen, his arms crossed behind him. ''Very good,'' he said commandingly, still eyeing the landlady. ''These buses.

Can you take me to them?'' *Tanya was so close now.* He was practically losing control, the vein in his neck engorged to twice its size.

''Tomorrow is Sunday,'' she said, her voice sounding a little more buoyant as she carefully instructed him. ''Our buses leave from the rectory at eight A.M. sharp. I'll ask Father to find room for you two.''

''Two?'' Zhukov asked, not understanding.

''Why, sure,'' the landlady said. ''I'm sure this little sweetheart will be going with you,'' she said, as the boy-child wandered into the room, rubbing his eyes and looking almost doll-like in his pajamas. She hugged him against her, rumpling his beautiful hair.

Now, even Zhukov recognized the tension in the room—the tension his arrogance and impatience had caused. Seeing the boy brought him back to where he was, what he was doing.

''We've come so far,'' he said. ''We're so tired. My command of English .. you'll have to bear with me . . . I become so angry with myself when I can't find the right words.''

Finally, the woman smiled, her skepticism and momentary alarm fading. ''It's a good thing you were referred to me,'' she said, ''if you want to go to see this shrine.''

Zhukov nodded his head.

''Seems like an awful long way to come, though, all the way from the old country just to visit a shrine.'' Her natural suspicion was evident.

Zhukov was thinking fast. He noticed the boy again. ''The child,'' he said, counting on her sympathy and pity, ''he is not well . . . the shrine . . . we pray for a cure.''

''Oh, the poor little thing.'' She touched his hair again.

''Off to bed now,'' he said, turning to the boy. ''We have to get up early.''

But before he left the kitchen, the little boy suddenly took the picture of Tanya out of Zhukov's hand and studied it. Then he smiled, looking for the very first time like a normal, happy little boy. The KGB man followed him back up to their room.

BUSTLETON

Tanya awakened with Nikolai Butkova's thigh lying heavily across hers. She tried to wiggle away without disturbing him, but as she moved, his eyes opened and the long, blue-black serpent tattooed on his arm rippled.

"Where are you going?" he asked, a little sleepy and still sore from the place on his back where the fire had burned him.

"It's time, darling."

"Are you absolutely positive that your KGB lover will come to the shrine at Loyola House?"

"I know him. He'll come. He loves me," Tanya said coldly. Naked, she slipped into one of the furs from Butkova's store. Holding it to her breasts, she said, "I'm very worried about the policeman, this Driscoll who came to the store. I think he must be the one who killed Boris. He was asking about the boy, Vinnie. I see him every place I go. I even see him with Presto's daughter." She was thinking out loud, but she did value Butkova's opinion on matters like this.

"Who care about one American policeman? We buy him off; we kill him. What does it matter? Very soon, nothing else matters." Butkova was staring up at the ceiling thinking about Odessa, about the Headman.

"Have you heard from him?" he ask Tanya.

Before they had fallen asleep, they had been talking about the request Butkova had made to the Headman to kill all of the American Mafia leaders, or at least as many as he could. Many months before, Whitey's client had given him the idea. Tanya knew that by "him," Butkova was referring to the Headman.

"No," she said. "Nothing yet."

"Just the same," Butkova growled, "what must be done must be done. I'm sure that once he thinks about it, the Headman will agree with me."

"Should you act without his specific permission?" she asked, crossing to the bed and peering down at the great bear of a man whom she had once loved very much. She wanted him to throttle his ambition for once.

"He's getting very, very old," Butkova said of the Headman. "Maybe, these days, he needs a push."

Tanya didn't say anything, but started getting dressed.

THIRTY-TWO

SATURDAY NIGHT

Honey Presto had just finished reading a bedtime story to Joe-Joey's youngest child, a little girl. Gently, she lifted the tiny head from her lap and carried the child to her crib. Not making a sound, she backed out of the bedroom.

"You're going to be a very good mother," Joe-Joey's wife said, startling Honey.

"I hope I live that long," Honey replied wistfully.

The older woman, struck by the sadness in Honey's voice, put her arms around her. Joe-Joey had brought her to his own house after the trouble at the shore.

"You should get some rest," Honey told her, suddenly aware of just how soon Donna's new baby would be born. "How long now?"

"Maybe a month."

Honey looked at her with a strange envy, a hunger for children, that she had never felt before. Was seeing Driscoll again doing this to her?

They walked into the kitchen, and Joe-Joey's wife fixed coffee for Honey. She sipped at it, made a face, then added four sugar cubes.

"Watch the sweets," Donna said.

Honey reached for a bun. Then the butter. "Honey, you haven't stopped eating since you got here," Donna said, not meaning to scold her. "Pretty soon you'll be bigger than I am."

They laughed. Honey relented on the butter. "I get nervous, I eat," she said. "I feel guilty, I eat. I guess I better watch it. I'll look like Manny."

"Oh, *that* man," Donna said, sounding exasperated. "The *size* of him. And years ago he used to be so cute. You wouldn't remember that, Honey, you were too little. But Manny was quite a man in his time. Always big, of course, but a big *handsome* man. He and your daddy—what a pair."

"What happened, Donna? With Manny, I mean?"

"Nobody ever said." Donna was no longer looking directly at Honey.

"Donna, I never knew my mother, but you did. What was she like?"

Joe-Joey's wife had never met a woman as cruel, as selfish, as Teresa, Honey's mother. But she couldn't tell Honey that. "Teresa was beautiful, like you," Donna said, desperate to change the conversation.

"I know that," Honey said. "I've seen all her wedding pictures, but I mean, what was she *really* like? When she died, I was so . . ."

"Let the dead sleep, Honey. God bless your mother and your father. No more talk about this." Donna gave her back the butter. "It's too dry without that. Eat! *Mangia!*"

A few minutes later, Honey asked, "Where's Joe-Joey?"

"Don't worry. Plenty of men outside, they'll take care of everything. I heard Joe-Joey tell them."

Honey, college-educated, assertive, sophisticated, couldn't believe the change that had taken place in her life so suddenly in such a short time. Her father had kept her at a safe distance from so much of his world, but here she was sitting in Donna's kitchen, bodyguards outside, being told that *the men* would take care of the important matters, hiding out, yet somehow feeling so *comfortable,* so much a part of it all. It was as if she could step right into her role as a Presto Family woman without ever looking back. The fit was perfect.

"Did Joe-Joey say anything about Driscoll, the cop I was with?"

Donna gave her a motherly look. "Honey, I know all about that Driscoll character. I remember how mad your father was."

"But did he say anything?"

"No." She was lying, and Honey could see it.

"Donna . . . please . . . I know he was hurt. Is he all right?"

"Fine. A bump on the head. Joe-Joey stayed there with him till he came around. You got nothing to worry about." Donna had been spreading icing on a big cake. She put down the knife, licked her fingers. "Stay away from him, Honey. *Please.*"

"I still love him."

"You don't know *who* you love; not now. You're too upset. Wait until this business is all over. Then, we see."

"That's what I'm afraid of—it might never be over."

Donna knew better than that. "Joe-Joey told you about the sit-down, didn't he?"

"On the way up from the shore."

"Littlejohn—and God knows I don't like that man—he called the men in the other cities and said that we have to do something about these Russians. This time—and I may never say this again—*this* time, I think Littlejohn might be right. It has to be settled once and for all."

"I know." Honey had been thinking about the meeting.

"Joe-Joey's there now, making sure that everything goes okay. Everybody there will be our people. And you know how careful Joe-Joey is. Nothing's gonna happen. You'll see."

Another thought had been troubling Honey. Donna was the only one she could mention it to. "What happens now, Donna? Tony's dead. And Marie . . ." She let that remain unsaid. "Littlejohn's nothing but a lawyer—and he's an *American.* He isn't one of *us.* You know how the men are. They need a leader.

"What are you saying, Honey?" Donna sat down across from the young girl. "It's all yours now. The Family. Whatever you say should happen, happens."

Honey had been thinking about this ever since her father died. "Donna, it *has* to be Joe-Joey," she said. "He's the only one who can control them. I *know* my father would want that."

"No!" Donna shouted, edging away from Honey. "Not Joe-Joey! Look what happened to your own father! We need

him too much—his real family needs him too much.'' All she could see was the fire at Paul Presto's house, the flames that had killed the Meatman.

Donna didn't know what to do, how to react. This wasn't what she wanted. But what if Joe-Joey *did* want it? How could she not support him, help him?

''Donna, just think about it . . . please. Don't say you won't help me.''

The older woman just looked at her. The baby was moving again.

''Antonio Coia is supposed to be coming to this meeting—he was like my grandfather. He loved the Meatman. I'll ask him, talk to him about it. See what he thinks. If he says yes, then that has to be the way—don't you see?''

Donna did not want to live to see her husband hurt, ever; not even for the sake of the children. That would be more than she could stand. ''Can you promise me that no harm will come to him, Honey? Can you do that any more than you could for your own father?''

''Nobody can do that,'' Honey said. ''Not anymore.''

''What about the lawyer, Littlejohn? Did you discuss this with him?''

''Of course not. Why should I?'' Honey thought that was a very strange question to be coming from Donna.

''Don't you think he'll have *something* to say about this?''

Honey was beginning to feel nervous; the sweat was dampening her underarms. ''He worked for my father, that was all. He isn't one of us.'' Suddenly, Honey felt as though she were talking about Phillip Driscoll—she remembered her father saying the same things about him, only more forcefully.

''If Littlejohn gets too pushy, we get rid of him, replace him, that's all. He can't hurt us.''

''I worry about that one,'' Donna said. ''He has bad eyes. Maybe you should talk to Don Antonio about him, too.''

''Whatever you say,'' Honey answered, pleasantly surprised about how close she suddenly felt to Donna, a woman, a friend of the family she had known since she was a little girl, but the kind of friend, older, mature, whom she had always taken for granted.

"Let me sleep on it," Donna said. "But I don't know why you even bother to ask me. Joe-Joey's the one who has to say yes."

Joe-Joey's wife started to cry to herself as Honey moved closer to her and kissed her the way she had always wanted to be able to kiss her own mother.

WILLOWS HILLS, PENNSYLVANIA, OVERLOOKING THE SCHUYLKILL EXPRESSWAY

Whitey was in the driver's seat of a four-wheel-drive jeep, bouncing and jostling over some of the roughest terrain he had encountered since his army days as a Ranger. But it felt good to be out in the woods again, under the stars, on the hunt. As soon as he saw the iced-over river they had told him to expect, Whitey shifted the jeep into neutral and killed his headlights. Another cold night, another wait. But at least the money promised to be good.

The moonlight and the stars gave him a good glimpse of the restaurant complex, about a mile away. His isolated hiding place was almost level with it; then the Schuylkill Valley took a dramatic descent toward the expressway below, under construction now, with a line of cars crawling along slowly.

A bracing wet wind began to tear at Whitey's back. Just then he heard the sound of another vehicle approaching his location as it crunched through the dry forest bed. He watched as it pulled up alongside his jeep and turned off its headlights.

Whitey got out and walked toward it, sensing more anticipation than he had experienced since the night he killed the Meatman.

NOBLE STREET

Still annoyed, Manny turned off the videocassette player. He had replayed Paul's tape a dozen times, searching for some message, some sign that was for his attention alone. But there was nothing—just the final goodbye to Honoria and the warning about the Malina. The tape had been for Honey exclusively. But so much had been left unsaid between Paul and himself. The simple fact that Paul had still felt comfortable sending Honey to him after all these years told the Fat Man that Paul had been on the verge of healing the schism between them. Could it be, Manny asked himself, that Paul had even been ready to forgive him just before he was murdered? But why had he said nothing?

Manny was still sitting, staring at the blank screen, when he heard a footstep behind him. "Driscoll!" he shouted in surprise. "What are you doing here? I thought you were with Honoria." Manny was suddenly very afraid.

"Tell me about it," Driscoll barked, moving toward the Fat Man, transfixing him with eyes that spoke of contempt. Driscoll's fist was curled around a blackjack. He hadn't seen Honey since Joe-Joey had come charging in at the shore house. And he hadn't heard from her either. That made him *very* nervous.

At this point he wasn't sure where Honey would go for help or for her own safety. She had watched them kill her Uncle Tony and drag her Aunt Marie away screaming. Honey had to know that she would never see Marie again.

He didn't even want to think about what that must be doing to her—first her father's murder, then the realization that her own aunt and uncle had tried to kill her. Honey was running out of options, running out of family. That's why he gambled that she might have gone back to Fat Manny, although Driscoll was damned if he could see the attraction between those two.

He had used the fire escape to come in through the deck and the bedroom where he and Honey had almost been killed—Driscoll had retraced Tony's own steps. Then he had merely checked doors and rooms from one loft floor to the other in Manny's warehouse building until he had located the Fat Man.

Manny was starting in again, protesting that he hadn't seen Honey.

"What're you talking about? Your people told me that Honoria was safe; that she was in your custody following the wake. What're you saying now?"

"I'm telling you she's *gone.* Marie and Tony tried to kill her down at the shore. That's where we were hiding. And that's the second time they went after her. Don't worry about those two anymore—Joe-Joey and Littlejohn took care of them. But there's not a trace of Honey. I thought she might have come here with you."

Manny wouldn't answer. Driscoll was beginning to think it was a mistake to have come here. Then he spied the empty black cassette box on top of the VCR. "Is that the tape Presto left?" Driscoll asked.

Manny still wouldn't speak, but his eyes, guilty and nervous, gave him away. They both walked in the direction of the tape. Driscoll easily beat him to it. He pushed the tape in the slot and touched the play button.

The Fat Man didn't even seem alarmed. "I'm sure Honoria has already told you everything that's on it. No clues. No hidden code. Just a warning and a farewell. Quite worthless, really."

"Worthless?"

"It doesn't begin to tell us who killed Paul, or why. And it won't help us to find Honoria. But go on, see for yourself."

The tape started. After a few minutes, after the Malina part, Driscoll got up and turned it off. "Hell, why didn't he give us more to go on?"

"I'm sure he did," Manny said, surprising Driscoll, "and I can only think of one possible explanation. I've been struggling with this ever since I saw it the first time. There has to be something—another tape, maybe. Some kind of message. I'm positive. Something for *me.* From Paul to *me.* I knew Paul like a brother. He would have done that."

"Don't overestimate yourself."

"I'm not, but I *knew* him. He wasn't a man to leave unfinished business behind him."

''What business are you talking about?''

''With *me,*'' Manny said. ''Paul only said goodbye to Honoria. He didn't deal with *me* at all. And that wasn't Paul. Even from the grave he would have found a way to tell me what he had to say.''

''About what?'' Driscoll asked.

Abruptly, the Fat Man's mood changed. ''None of your goddam business, Driscoll,'' he shouted. ''She isn't here, and even if she was, I wouldn't tell you. You took her away from me once and almost got her killed.''

''If you lie to me, Fat Man,'' Driscoll said, jamming his blackjack against Manny's windpipe, ''I'm gonna hang your balls over one of those telephone wires outside. You're nothing but a fucking disease. I don't know what you're up to with her or why the hell she can't see through you, but I can.''

''Get out!'' Manny screamed. *''Out of my house!''* Then, moving more quickly than Driscoll had ever thought he could, Manny sprang to his feet and tried to push him out of the room. Manny was awkward but powerful, and he momentarily pinned Driscoll against the door. But the cop easily broke away and knocked the Fat Man on his ass. Then he straddled him with his knee to Manny's throat.

''What about that second tape?'' Driscoll pressed. ''You said there had to be reasons for it. Besides this feud between you and the Meatman, why else would there be a second tape?''

Driscoll's knee was planted firmly against Manny's neck, and his answer came out in hissing spasms of speech. ''The Family . . . Paul . . . no successor . . . has to be more,'' he gasped.

He was trying to squirm away, but Driscoll jammed the blackjack handle into his ribs. ''Where? Where's the second tape? Who has it?''

Manny was turning blue. He shook his head. Driscoll jacked him one more time. Manny didn't know. Driscoll was convinced. But the tape had to be somewhere. *Where?* All at once, the cop was reading the Meatman's mind.

THIRTY-THREE

WILLOWS HILLS, OVERLOOKING THE SCHUYLKILL EXPRESSWAY

A cold crosswind had blown up from the Schuylkill River. Whitey opened the door of the car that had come through the woods and sat down in the front seat, next to the driver—-Milton Littlejohn, the man he immediately recognized as his client. Littlejohn smiled at Whitey and switched on the dome light between the front and rear seats. In the back sat a man almost as tall as Whitey, but much heavier, and older. His face was deep-eyed, with the shatterproof resilience of iron.

"I would like you to meet Mr. Butkova," his client said to Whitey.

Whitey just looked at the man in the backseat. Then Butkova said, "What is your plan?"

Whitey was reluctant to say anything, but Littlejohn's facial expression seemed to be urging him to tell this man something. "Dynamite," Whitey answered. "Very simple. I rig up the explosion where you tell me the targets will be gathered, detonate it from somewhere between here and the restaurant on the hill, then I lie in wait to see if anybody escapes, and if anyone does, I shoot him. I may not get all of them—somebody always gets away—but I should get enough of them."

Several seconds went by while Butkova digested that information. Then he spoke, not to Whitey but to the lawyer. "My friend that is a very reckless plan. If someone happens to kill you, then we have nothing. You're a proud man." He switched his focus to Whitey this time. "And the danger in your plan comes from pride."

Whitey was visibly bristling, as Butkova continued. "Just to be safe, I should have some of my men here in reserve, as backups, nothing more. Then if there is a problem, if, as you say, somebody gets away, then we can shoot them all."

"I work alone," Whitey said, an inflexible stiffness in his voice. "You paid me for Presto. I can walk away now. Get somebody else." Then he put his hand on the door handle of the car and opened it.

"Oh, please, reconsider," Littlejohn said coaxingly. "I'm sure we can work this out. What you have to understand, my good friend, is that ultimately in this daring endeavor, we are all working for Mr. Butkova. We're both older than you—cautious. Indulge age."

"Experience," Butkova cut in. "What is your name? Whitey? Whitey, you think you have killed a few men . . ."

Whitey sneered.

Butkova went on, "Maybe more than a few, but you haven't killed as many as I have. Do it your way." Butkova leaned forward and tapped a thick finger on Whitey's shoulder. "All I'm telling you—and I am *telling,* not asking—is that just in case, my men will be here, in place, around the lake to cut off any avenues of escape. Other than that, do it your way."

Whitey sighed and fingered the door handle again. "Maybe you'd better tell me a little more about what's going on here," he said to Littlejohn. "I was just expecting you to bring someone who could get me the supplies I need, the dynamite, the detonator."

"You will have as much as you need," Butkova said gruffly.

"Some time ago," Littlejohn said," after I learned—I should say after I stumbled upon—some very sensitive intelligence concerning Paul Presto and his activities, I approached Mr. Butkova with a proposition that was mutually beneficial. He agreed, and you, Whitey, became the executor of our decision. Now we're merely asking you to keep working for us."

Whitey thought about it, but he didn't answer for a long time. Then he said, "He has his own men. Let them do it."

"Son," Littlejohn replied, "you're a specialist. Very skilled. We need men like you. Think about it."

"How much more if I kill them all?" Whitey asked.

His client started to protest. "I thought we'd already agreed on a fee."

"One million dollars," Butkova said. "My personal guarantee."

Whitey produced a small slip of paper from his pocket and handed it back to Butkova. "This is what I need. Have it here tomorrow. Ten A.M., no later. Leave it in the trunk of a car with the keys in the ignition. Then park the car and walk away. I'll take care of the rest."

Butkova read the list and cleared his throat. "Done," he said.

Without another word, Whitey slid out of the seat and disappeared into the darkness of the night.

"What do you think?" Littlejohn asked Butkova.

"Wonderful, if it works," Butkova answered. "This Whitey is a valuable asset, but if he becomes a problem, the only course is clear. You agree?"

"Utterly," Littlejohn responded, without hesitation. Then he started the car and drove away.

FLETCHER STREET

This time, Phillip Driscoll didn't care how much noise he made. He was going back inside the Meatman's house, back to the scene of the assassination. Moving slowly and deliberately, nursing his bruised ribs and the assortment of other cuts and contusions that he had collected since the night the Meatman had been hit, Driscoll climbed right up onto the porch at 2117 Fletcher Street.

The door had been repaired, and the vestibule was boarded up; all the police sawhorses and yellow-tape barriers had been removed. Fletcher Street appeared quiet, almost contented in its post-Christmas lull.

When he couldn't figure out how to get around the padlock, around the damaged entrance, the detective just probed until he found a loose board, ripped at it with all his might, and tore it down. Then he squeezed into the house. He had a big flashlight with him this time, which he used freely. He didn't give a damn who knew what he was doing or who saw him. Driscoll had come to retrieve the second videotape that the Meatman had made, and so much of his soul and determination had been invested thus far that nothing short of a bullet in the brain was about to stop him.

He went right to the basement steps and pulled the door open. Dark again down there, but he knew what he was doing and where he was going. By now, he was used to these steps in the darkness, and the big six-battery flashlight that he held in his hand like a club provided as much illumination as he needed.

As soon as he opened the walk-in box, the vapor from Driscoll's breath began materializing in a series of small, foggy puffs.

He played the beam of the flashlight on one shelf after another, once again seeing all the neatly wrapped cuts of meat and fowl, caressed by their cream-colored freezer paper. Eerily, that first night came back to him in a rush of adrenaline and memory—the holdup at the Presto numbers bank; Spanish Joe informing him that the Meatman had been hit; his sudden, all-consuming concern for Honey's welfare; his clandestine exploration of the Meatman's house; finally, his confrontation with Honey at the morgue. Just like the very first time that he had encountered Honey Presto, five years before, when he had first fallen in love with her, he knew that after tonight nothing would ever be quite the same for him again. After that quick check in the box, Driscoll headed for the freezer.

The beam from the flashlight stopped as the unyielding

angle of light picked up the top shelf where he had discovered the body parts and the .45. From where he stood in the entrance to the freezer, it looked clean up there this time. Probably Bellows, Driscoll thought to himself. At some point, the dead Strike Force chief had probably had the same idea as Driscoll, and he must have come down here to see what he could find. It would have been just like Bellows to remove anything that he thought might give them a clue.

Stretching on tiptoe again, just like the first time, Driscoll stood on the bottom shelf and raised himself high enough to check the uppermost storage space. It was just as he had surmised—Bellows and the Strike Force had removed what was left of the corpse. If there had been any other guns in there, they had probably taken them, too.

Driscoll just hoped that the Strike Force scavengers had overlooked the videotape. Nothing but pure instinct told him that it had to be here.

It was bitterly cold in the freezer, but the detective didn't care. Attempting not to give in to the pain from his ribs, he slipped off his overcoat and even removed his gloves, then went to work.

Systematically moving from one shelf to the next, Driscoll used one of the Meatman's own boning knives to slice open package after package. He had propped open the vacuum-sealed door, and now the warmer air from the walk-in box was beginning to pour in and commence the long process of defrosting the meat. Only a few moments had passed when his bones began to ache as his fingertips went numb. Stopping for a moment, Driscoll held up his hands and examined them. His own bottled-up energy was making them shake, and his fingers were turning blue. Banishing any thought of abandoning his search, he went at it again with the boning knife.

Twenty minutes later, just as he was tapping the flashlight to bring the frozen batteries back to life, Driscoll picked up an ordinary-looking package that felt much lighter than the others. But it didn't look anything like the square shape of a videocassette box. Could he be wrong, after all? For a while there, he could almost have believed that Paul Presto's presence was somehow there with him willfully prompting Driscoll to go on, not to give up until his search was completed. But now the detective's doubts were beginning to surface.

With a single, swift motion of the knife, he split the wrapper on the box that had raised his interest. Inside, the tip of the blade caught on something that felt like cloth, a material that wouldn't give.

An apron—a white butcher's apron.

He tore the apron away. Driscoll couldn't believe his luck. The apron had been wrapped around a black plastic case that contained a videocassette. Popping open the case, he inspected the tape. Somehow it looked different. Not like the one that he had just seen with Manny. Bearing down with the flashlight, he searched for some mark, some identification. Then he saw it. Pasted to the back of the tape box was a small tag with the letters "DUP" penciled in.

This was it. This was the duplicate that the Meatman had kept for no other reason than that he was a compulsive saver. This was the duplicate of the tape he had left for Manny—the *second* tape that Manny suspected did exist. But if this was the duplicate of that second tape, and if Manny had never seen the original, as he claimed, then that could only mean one thing—the person whom the Meatman had trusted to give the tape to Manny had failed to do so and had betrayed Presto. And that could only be *one* man.

Suddenly, just as that first night in Presto's house, Driscoll heard a noise above him—someone walking, more than one pair of feet; one light, the other heavy. The menacing sound moved closer and closer, shuffling in the darkness.

He stuck the tape inside his shirt and looked for a place to hide.

The door at the top of the cellar steps creaked open. Driscoll reached for one of Presto's sharp knives. He held it at his side, ready to jab it up and in through a deadly arc.

The first figure coming down the steps was smaller than he expected—so small it could almost have been a woman. Someone larger was right behind. He saw two guns, held police-style with the right hand gripping the pistol and their left hand supporting it. Pros. Maybe Presto people—or the Malina.

His back pressed against the wall, Driscoll was prepared

to come up hard with the knife, as hard as he could, cutting off the first figure.

He lunged, kicking hard as he did so. The first one went down, but the second man caught the knife in midair before Driscoll had a chance to do any damage. Now he would have to fight them on their terms. Twisting free, the detective brought the knife blade up once again.

Just then, a bright flashlight was shining in his face, the blinding rays penetrating his eyes as painfully as lasers.

"Phil! What the hell are you doing down here? Put that knife away!"

It was Spanish Joe. Lida was still on the floor, trying to pull her skirt down over her knees. She was rubbing her ankle where Driscoll had kicked her.

"Oh, Jesus," he said. "I'm sorry, Lida."

"Thanks a lot, Phil." She stood up and started brushing herself off. "You're a goddam maniac, in case you don't know it."

"How did you know I was here?"

"We didn't," Joe said, examining Driscoll's knife. "*You* were supposed to be a burglar. The neighbors called the cops. And soon as the District found out that it was Presto's house, they got in touch with Organized Crime." He smiled. "And that's yours truly."

"I'm sorry. . . . Are you okay, Lida?"

"Fine. But tell me, what the hell are you doing down here?"

He left the tape box in his shirt and put his coat back on. "Just thought I should look around again, that's all." Nobody was going to know about the second Presto tape until Driscoll had had a chance to look at it.

"That's *not* all," Lida said excitedly. She pushed a piece of paper in his hand. "Look at this. Lucky guess on the dancing schools."

"What?" He shone the flashlight on the paper.

"Arlene. Remember?"

Driscoll had been so intent on locating the tape that he had almost forgotten about Arlene and the rest of the investigation.

"Phil, you can't believe the pressure we're getting from

Captain Marinari on this stuff. They're going ape-shit over those two highway patrolmen," Spanish Joe said.

"Yeah," Lida butted in, "and you got the little shit convinced that the same guy killed Presto and the cops."

Driscoll did remember that.

"Where the hell have you been, Phil?" Spanish Joe asked. "Lawlor practically has an APB out on you."

"They think you must've been killed, too," Lida said.

"Marinari said that you'd better be dead, because that's the only fucking excuse he's gonna take. Phil, do you realize how long it's been since you checked in with anybody?"

Suddenly, it all hit him. Driscoll hadn't bothered to let anybody know what he was up to. The last time he'd even talked to Lida was back at the morgue, days ago. In Stone Harbor, with Honey, he'd lost all track of time.

"Goddammit, Phil," Spanish Joe said, "just call somebody. Let them know you're alive. Get Marinari off our asses, and Lawlor."

Driscoll told himself that he had to do that, but he wasn't up to offering any explanations, not even to these two. "What about Arlene?" he asked. "What do you have on her?"

Lida handed him what looked like a student transcript. He started to read it. "What's this, Lida?"

"I'll translate. See the name at the top?"

It read "Arlene T. Roy."

"Pennsylvania Academy of Ballet Arts. She lasted a semester and a half, then dropped out. Four months later she took the first pinch for hooking."

"It says right here she was on a partial scholarship."

"Right. Look at the sponsoring agency."

"This is some law firm—that was just a tax writeoff for them."

"Ah," she said, "but *whose* law firm?" Lida was moistening her dry lips.

"Milton Littlejohn's," Joe said from behind them, his thick accent mispronouncing the "j" in Littlejohn's name. "We asked how they worked, and they told us that the partner requesting the scholarship money had to interview the prospective student and introduce her all around."

"Who requested this?"

"Littlejohn." Driscoll *knew* that the lawyer had been the one who hit him at the shore house—even though he hadn't been able to see, he remembered the cane.

"Arlene was his, all the way," Lida said, "and I bet that sooner or later, we could trace the outcall service back to him, too."

"He set up the Meatman," Driscoll said, his voice as brittle as one of the knives on the butcher's block. "That's what I had to have had wrong—Tony told me I had one thing wrong—down at the shore. I never put Littlejohn into it."

"We got every cop in the city looking for him," Joe said. "And for Honey."

Just the mention of her name left Driscoll feeling helpless. "I don't know where she is," he said. The one thing he had to do was protect her. But she was out there somewhere, away from him, exposed. Driscoll's eyes began to change color.

"Lawlor," Lida began, "he says he has to see you—about the matter you two discussed. That's what he said. We're supposed to make sure you go."

"Where is he?"

"The retreat house."

"Loyola?" Driscoll knew that this meant Carney was calling the shots now.

"It's a long ride. We'd better get going."

"If we don't find Honey, Littlejohn's going to kill her. He must be with that white-haired son of a bitch."

"Maybe Lawlor knows something," Lida suggested. "Just get it over with, Phil. We'll find Honey. Captain Marinari called us—he said Lawlor was acting like he was going nuts."

"I know exactly how he feels," Driscoll said coldly. "Let's move."

THIRTY-FOUR

LOYOLA RETREAT HOUSE AND SHRINE OF THE SACRED RELIC OF THE HOLY GRAIL SUNDAY

Through the tinted windows of the tour bus, Zhukov saw that the grounds were dotted with pastures, barns, cattle pens, and several outbuildings that allowed the religious order that ran the place to maintain total self-sufficiency. There was even a slaughterhouse, as well as a large commissary that sold religious articles and souvenirs to pilgrims from the nearby cities and suburbs. In the daylight, Zhukov assumed that the sizable parking lot would be filled with tour buses. There was a shrine on the grounds that drew crowds, summer and winter.

The woods were thick and the floor of the forest was still covered by vagrant patches of snow and ice from the previous week's blizzard. The main house, the abbey, could have been a Bavarian castle. It was shielded by tall pines, above which rose decorated battlements. The house was over a century old and impossible to reproduce using modern methods and materials. Ruins of an even earlier chapel sat on the edge of the forest line. The monks who had taken over the operation of the estate and retreat offered three-day or week-long periods of prayer and reflection; a full complement of nuns and seminarians were in permanent residence, and they performed all the necessary kitchen and household chores.

Zhukov was concentrating on the long, low, disconcertingly contemporary-looking dormitories that had been attached to the flanks of the abbey less than ten years before.

If Tanya was telling him—via the photo—that she intended to meet him here, then she had been able to make contact with Carney and expedite his deal with the American. But he knew there was bound to be trouble, because the whole gun-selling scheme had been turned into turmoil by his black-market accomplice in the United States—Nikolai Butkova. Somehow, Zhukov had to convince the Americans that he had played no part in the betrayal. Only Butkova and his cutthroats.

As the crowded Greyhound tour bus pulled into the parking lot, Mikhail Zhukov turned in his window seat to check on the little boy at his side. The child was on his feet before the lurching vehicle had even come to a complete stop. Getting to his own feet, Zhukov took him by the hand.

A dozen other buses were lined up, discharging passengers, as Zhukov and the child exited their bus. Zhukov's small black eyes kept trolling the horde of pilgrims, searching for Tanya. There were school groups, neighborhood parishes like the people on his bus, and several out-of-state tour coaches. The shrine and massive, modernistic church which housed it were located midway between the old walled retreat house and the gray-brown curtain of trees and shrubs. The air was noticeably colder and damper. Whether in Russia or America, the taste and scent of snow in the air was unmistakable. Zhukov glanced up at the troubled clouds. Soon the flakes would begin.

A few feet from the bus, he felt the fat hand of his landlady prodding him from behind. Still tugging the little boy along with him, the KGB man followed where the landlady took him, still pretending to be interested in touching the relic of the Grail—the relic amounted to an impossibly old-looking swatch of cloth, just a large patch of fabric, really, mounted and encased in vacuum-sealed glass. According to stories that had been handed down from generation of monks to generation, the fabric supposedly came from the sack that had once held the Grail, following the Last Supper.

Ordinarily, Zhukov would have scoffed at such pious nonsense—at least, he considered it nonsense—but here, in the presence of this multitude of faithful, at this American version of Lourdes, he had to admit to himself that the spell cast by this *thing,* this relic, was capable of producing one of two reactions: instant conversion or a humbled amazement at the power of mass delusion.

The vast, tentlike "church" consisted of an outdoor superstructure covered at all times by a canvas roof, with matching canvas walls that were left rolled up. The place could hold at least five hundred of the faithful. There were no pews, as such, just row after row of wooden folding chairs, with irregular aisles cut through at intervals. The rear area of the structure was an open-air bazaar of souvenir stalls and ethnic food carts. Fires had been lighted in several rusty trash cans to provide some heat for the merchants.

There was an altar-in-the-round at the front of the church, decorated wtih contemporary stained-glass panels and assorted icons. A long, slow line stretched from front to rear; he would have to wait in this line to kiss the relic. Still searching, but failing to see any signs of Tanya, Zhukov fell into line behind his landlady, the child at his side. He was still hopeful; the place looked exactly like the building in the background of the photo Tanya had sent him.

WILLOW HILLS

The car, with the supplies he needed in neat bundles in the trunk, had been left, right on time, at the prescribed place. Whitey had taken the key from the ignition, opened the trunk, and gotten right to work. It was just a matter of connecting a series of wires to his detonator and securing the explosives with tape and just enough epoxy. Because he wished to travel light, he had selected a small UZI machine gun as his weapon. No range, but enough velocity and speed to lay down a wall of lead, if necessary. Nobody would escape. He wasn't even concerned about that. Donning a photographer's vest, with plenty of oversized pockets, Whitey shoved the material inside the sturdy pouches and prepared to move out. Over that he wore a long white deliveryman's duster—the white was disconcerting to him; he would have preferred his usual black. But since he was posing as a linen supply deliveryman—with his client's help, of course—he had to look the part. A black knit cap was pulled down as far as it would go over his hair and most of his forehead. He was wearing gloves, but his fingers were still tingling.

He knew where he was going, because his client had given him very detailed instructions. As he crossed the hard, grassy lawn where Antonio Coia's helicopter would land in less than twelve hours, Whitey kept looking behind him to make sure that none of Butkova's men had tried to follow him. Actually, he had not detected any signs of them at all, not even in the woods where he had spent a cold, miserable night sleeping in a tree near Mill Creek. Just the same, however, he knew they were out there. Whitey didn't want any slipups this time. His missing the Presto girl was still a tormented memory. So was the clumsy attack on her at the Fat Man's house. But at least the two fools who had attempted that assassination were no longer around to interfere with him. His client had assured Whitey of that, the client insisting that he had been in the very room when they had been taken care of.

The restaurant wasn't open for business yet, but there were plenty of busboys and kitchen help and other deliverymen noisily unloading trucks, clanging dishes, inspecting food shipments, and cursing at the bitterly cold weather. There were several Presto soldiers present, too, eyeing everyone, including Whitey, suspiciously. But because linen supply had traditionally been one of the Meatman's thriving enterprises, they assumed that anyone working for the supply house had long since been checked out. The security men just glanced at Whitey's unusual height and allowed their eyes to shift to his strange face, then quickly looked away. Whitey was used to that, used to making them pay—just like the Meatman.

Then he saw what he was looking for. It was the downstairs lounge, actually a spacious, ornate private dining room, heavy on gold and brocade, used exclusively by executive board groups, fraternal organizations, and unusual gatherings like the one called by the Presto Family, which required tight security and a privacy that bordered on secrecy. Going down the double staircase that opened into a large service-bar area, Whitey went to work, dragging a heavy laundry sack after him.

As soon as he was sure that he was alone, he made a quick study of the room and its surroundings. Where? He'd have only one chance. Where?

The bar, the kitchen, the tables and chairs, even the alcove for the wine racks were all too visible. *Where?*

Just then, someone walked in from the unloading dock in the rear, behind the lower kitchen. Whitey pretended to be taking inventory of the bar linens and extra napkins and tablecloths. He ducked his head down behind the glasses.

It was one of the waiters arriving early for work. He looked appraisingly at Whitey. "Do I know you?" he asked, not the least bit put off by Whitey's face. The restaurant wasn't connected with the Prestos at all; they had chosen a legitimate place on purpose. Whitey had expected complications like this.

Trying to seem obliging, Whitey just shrugged. "I'm a fill-in today."

"I hope you get a union button," the waiter said. "We don't want no damn scab weekend men."

"In the truck," Whitey told him. "I can go get it if you want to see it."

"Let's see it," the waiter said, feeling good that he was giving such a hard time to a man a head taller than he.

"I'm with the guys upstairs," Whitey said, not moving from behind the bar. "Joe-Joey and them, you know."

A sick look spread across the waiter's face. "Excuse me," he said, gathering up his things and looking for a way out. "Hey, I'm really sorry I said anything. Okay? You don't have to tell anybody about this right?"

"Forget it," Whitey said, amused at how frightened everybody was of the Presto mob. "Just close that door over there, okay? I got a shitload of inventory to do here."

"You got it."

After the waiter left, Whitey locked the door and resumed his search. *Where?*

Leaning against the bar rail, Whitey crossed his arms over his narrow chest and happened to look up.

It was a dropped ceiling.

There were panels inserted between crisscrossing metal runners. Everything was flocked with gold and set off by rows of dim brass track lights.

Whitey poked his head through one of the panels and felt around in the top. There were clumps of twisted electrical wires and sticky insulation rubble from the ceiling material. The clearance was a good six inches—more than he would need. The design of the room was ideal for the percussion charge that he wanted to use. With any luck he would kill most of the people in the room.

Smiling his disjointed, lopsided smile, Whitey opened his coat, unzipped his photographer's vest, and began assembling the bomb. He needed to stand on top of one of the tables to position it where he wanted inside the ceiling. He selected the very center of the room.

As soon as he was finished, he replaced the ceiling panel, made certain that he hadn't left anything behind, and put his coat and vest back on. He turned around just once to look at the now-peaceful dining room before he let himself out. He could picture the room bursting into flame and fire and death—just like Meatman Presto's front porch. Whitey's left cheek began to twitch. It was almost time.

LOYOLA RETREAT HOUSE

Phillip Driscoll had Lida and Spanish Joe drop him off near the crowds at the shrine, then decided to go the rest of the way on foot. Everybody turned around to look at cars, but worshipers on foot were so common, it seemed they were invisible.

He had never been to the abbey or retreat house before, but he imagined that whatever was going to happen would have to take place in the most secluded part of the complex. Lawlor was a man who didn't like an audience. Driscoll figured he'd look around a little and maybe catch him off-guard.

As soon as he was inside the main building, he fell in line with a group of older men who appeared to be following a priest from one large room to another. Head down and hands folded loosely in front of him, Driscoll followed his group right to the threshold of their destination, then peeled off by himself.

First Driscoll saw Biaggio Marinari, then he spotted Lawlor. He had the impression that Lawlor had sent Marinari somewhere. Neither man saw him. Somehow, he was counting on them to lead him to the truth behind the guns as well as Presto's murder. But probably Carney was the only man who could really do that. It annoyed Driscoll no end that Lawlor knew so much more than he had admitted. Driscoll just prayed that somehow, Lida or Spanish Joe or somebody would locate Honey before she did something foolish. But he knew he wasn't wasting his time. Carney had *all* the answers.

The passageways of the retreat house all connected; they radiated out from the central hub like the spokes of a wheel, quiet, gloomy, poorly lighted. Lawlor was well out in front of him, walking quickly toward a staircase that descended to the crypt level. Lawlor disappeared down the steps. Driscoll waited a full minute, then followed him.

THE SHRINE AND RELIC OF THE HOLY GRAIL

Tanya was wearing a heavy veil and sunglasses when she saw them. The sight of the little boy caused her face to blush and her heart to begin pounding inside her chest; there was no way she could fight back that first welling rush of tears. Composing herself, she broke into the long line of worshipers, just three people away from the relic altar, and pushed in front of Zhukov. There were a few titters and dirty looks, but most people assumed that they were merely a family that had finally found one another.

At first, Zhukov had no idea who she even was—he wasn't expecting anything like this. Then Tanya turned, daintily pulled aside the fold of her veil, and kissed Mikhail on the lips, never removing the sunglasses. As she did so, her hand reached down and pulled the little boy-child to her side. He buried his head against her flank and began to cry, gently, like a lost boy found. Zhukov was speechless. Tanya pulled the two of them out of line, and they followed her.

WILLOWS HILLS

Butkova was impressed by the modest, well-hidden campsite that Whitey had improvised. It reminded him of his own soldiering days, back during the Malina's secret war against Stalin. He had just sent Tanya on her way, to the shrine, to make contact with Mikhail Zhukov.

Now he was positioning his men all around the acreage above the palisades. He intended to keep his word—he would give Whitey his chance to kill the Italian bosses first. But if anything went wrong, then Butkova's men would begin advancing down the gently sloping hillsides like a vengeful army, their M-16s blasting. One way or the other, Butkova would win.

He was curious to see what this great Mafia sit-down, as the Italian-Americans called it, was all about. Most of them were great men, outlaws and businessmen alike. Butkova didn't care what Whitey's client had told him, he was going down for a look.

THE ABBEY

How handsome he looks, she thought, as she was seized by a sudden flight of inspiration. So confident; so sure of himself. The haunted look that had perpetually masked his deep-set eyes in Moscow had disappeared.

Braless, Tanya was dressed in a long skirt and a high-necked black cashmere sweater. Her boots were calf-length. Butkova had cautioned her to be sure to take a gun; she'd hidden it in the deep pocket of a hooded raincoat.

The prospect of seeing her lover after their enforced absence—even a lover whom she delighted in abusing—thrilled her. Every muscle was taut; her nipples, bare against the caress of the cashmere, tingled, hard as pink rocks. She had received her orders from Zinijakin, by way of the human chain, and was prepared to carry them out. Once her task had been completed, she would notify the Malina in the same way, courier-to-courier, from her lips to the Headman.

Just once more, she had to have Mikhail. For both their sakes. Promising that they would soon be introduced to Carney, she had sent him with the boy—Zhukov had protested, firing questions at her, especially about the child, *her* child, but she hadn't responded—to a study on the first floor and told him to leave the boy there for the time being. He would wait for her, she knew—the precious child had already been waiting for her, and she for him, for so long.

She hoped that Mikhail would be able to find the study and return. He was very nervous, almost disoriented. She knew that he suspected a problem, a trap, perhaps, and that was the last thing she could deal with today. Too much was depending on this. But she understood Zhukov and his obsessive need for her better than anyone else. They could communicate from trust on only one level. And for the next hour she had to have his complete trust.

Glancing about her, once, twice, and a third time, she crossed into a big room of the abbey and hid behind a tall china cabinet. She loosened the belt on her raincoat and reached under her skirt through a slit, cut daringly high on her thigh, and quickly removed her panties—black silk, then Tanya dropped the panties on the floor and leaned back against the wall and waited. Soon she was comfortable, warm, so she removed her coat, threw it across an antique divan, and sat down next to it. She moved the slit in her skirt around until it was directly below her navel. Then she hiked her skirt up and waited. Outside, the last of the lights were extinguished.

Five minutes passed, then ten.

Suddenly, she heard Zhukov's voice, speaking in Russian. He was calling her.

More seconds elapsed, suspending her in a limbo of anticipation.

Then he was there, smiling that doleful, preserved half-smile that she had seen so many times before. The black silk panties were clutched tightly in his trembling hand.

She was on the verge of replying. The words had formed on her lips, when he threw himself at her, embracing her waist, burying his face in the waiting wetness that beckoned him.

WILLOWS HILLS, NEAR THE RESTAURANT

From the vantage point that he had selected in a maintenance shed, Whitey checked the UZI on his lap. It wouldn't be long now. He was staring at a window in the ground-floor room of the restaurant where he had placed the bomb. His client, Milton Littlejohn, had told him that his raising the window would be the signal. Exactly sixty seconds later, he was to detonate the bomb. By then, Littlejohn would be clear of the room. If anyone did escape, that's what the machine gun was for.

Then Whitey saw Butkova, moving quickly toward the restaurant. Right where he shouldn't have been. Whitey was furious.

THE CRYPT LEVEL OF THE ABBEY

When he realized that Lawlor was meeting someone, Driscoll slammed himself against one of the curved indented alcoves beside a peeling alabaster pilaster outside the crypt entrance. In the cop's mind, the commissioner had become the key—ever since that night at the Christmas party when Bellows appeared to be reporting to the commissioner. Lawlor had to know far more about all this than he had led Driscoll to believe.

Just as Driscoll saw the commissioner make contact, a well-dressed, commanding figure came walking purposefully out of the inner darkness of the main chamber. The detective wasn't certain, because he had never seen James Xavier Carney in person, but he was willing to bet that this had to be Carney.

They were at the far end of a long passageway and began

to converse. The wall curved just enough for Driscoll to remain hidden from them. Because of the eerie acoustics of the crypt area, he could hear almost everything they were saying; the vibrations of their voices echoed, carrying along the surface of the walls. They were apparently setting up some sort of meeting, but someone was yet to arrive. Just then, Lawlor pointed toward the main chamber of the crypt and said, "I'll go and get him and bring him down here. Wait for us inside."

Carney, if it indeed was Carney, answered, "Presently, Alfred, but first I must get the bait."

"I almost forgot about that," Lawlor said. Then the two men moved off together as Driscoll dropped down behind an exquisitely carved high-backed bench.

As soon as he was sure that he was alone, Driscoll quickly abandoned his hiding place and made his way into the main chamber. He saw that he was in a subterranean cemetery with galleries and recesses for tombs like the coffin-sized shelves of a mausoleum. The large, gloomy vault was dominated by four stone coffins, sarcophagi, positioned in the four corners of the room. Driscoll approached the first one. He noticed that the stone receptacles were shaped like small houses with curving roofs. Each marble coffin bore religious figures, carved in relief on all four sides, as well as on the lid. He read the small brass plate that identified the occupant of the first sarcophagus—it must have been one of the early priors of the abbey. As he moved from one to the other, his clothes picked up the dust and cobwebs that clung to each tomb. The musty odor of decay pervaded the whole place, and soon Driscoll found himself almost gagging in this stale air and oppressive dampness rising from the soft strata of earth just beneath his feet. Wherever he touched the wall, a film of crumbling clay remained on his fingers.

The entire crypt had the dilapidated, moldering atmosphere of a dying place. Above his head, however, the beams supporting the ceiling were stout, close together, massive as tree limbs, crisscrossing at right angles in an ornamental pattern of perfect squares. He knew from his inspection of the outside that all around him were Pennsylvania granite walls, reinforced by tons of rich black earth. For all its appearance of rot and decomposition, the timeless architecture of the crypt rendered it utterly quiet, private, and probably indestructible—a shelter to withstand the centuries.

At the head of the room there was a small, tablelike altar on a platform about a foot high. On each side of the altar was an uncomfortable-looking chair, the sort used in liturgical services. They were wooden thrones, upholstered in heavy velvet, where the celebrant of a mass would sit during moments of quiet reflection while the congregation prayed in vocal unison. Both chairs were almost completely obscured in shadows.

In the open space between the sarcophagi, Driscoll briefly walked around a catafalque, a raised bier, covered with a black cloth. It was really just a frame, hollow underneath, on four shaky legs—a facsimile of a coffin used in religious services when the body of the deceased was not present. The catafalque was facing not the head of the altar, but the back or entrance to the crypt. Driscoll knew from his altar-boy days that a priest or monk was being buried, because in requiem masses for the dead, a priest who had died never faced the altar.

He nudged the black cloth draped over the catafalque. It reached to the floor. His foot went all the way in. Suddenly, that gave him an idea.

Tall, freestanding candle standards had been placed alongside the catafalque to create the illusion of an aisle running down the crypt. Either one of the old monks had just been buried or he was about to be buried. Everything in the crypt was set up for the celebration of a very private requiem mass for a priest. Because the candles were lit, Driscoll had just enough light to be able to see all this. Something was about to take place in the crypt—something that involved Carney and Lawlor and the third person whom Lawlor had gone for—and Driscoll wasn't about to miss it.

He surveyed the chamber one last time, trying to imagine where everyone would be positioned and determine the best vantage point to see it all. He was about to conceal himself when he realized that there was something wrong with the left front sarcophagus—the one farthest from him. Everything in the room was perfectly symmetrical save this tomb. It bothered him so much he took the time to investigate.

He was practically on top of the massive marble burial

structure, his clothes picking up more dusty cobwebs, when he leaned the palm of his right hand, his full weight behind it, on the curved lid of the sarcophagus he was examining. Without any warning, the lid began to slide, and Driscoll went with it.

That's what it was! That's what was wrong. This lid had been ajar all along, just slightly, but enough for it to be out of alignment with the others. Their lids were firmly attached to the bases.

How come this one wasn't sealed? The sarcophagi had probably been down here for over a hundred years. Why the hell tamper with one of them?

Driscoll was dying to look inside this tomb to see why it had been disturbed, but he heard voices echoing behind him, pealing along the same curved wall where he had concealed himself before.

Too late now. All the cop could do was strain and shove and push the lid back in place as best he could, the way he had found it—slightly off-center.

He heard Lawlor's voice, louder and more distinct now. He hurried over to the wobbly catafalque in the center of the room, dropped to his knees, then rolled over and under the black pall, into the cramped space beneath the phony coffin.

Listening intently, the detective lay flat on the stone floor, the rough, hard surface damp against his cheek. Then he inched his fingers out and curled his fingertips around the edge of the black drape, pulling it aside just enough to see what was going on.

Driscoll had expected Lawlor to come in first, but the crazy acoustics down here must have played tricks on his ears, because the first person to enter was not Lawlor, but the guy he thought was Carney. This time he was carrying a small satchel, like a Gladstone bag. He moved briskly past the catafalque where Driscoll was hiding, mounted the altar platform, seated himself on the chair at the left, and eased back into the shadows. Driscoll had to maneuver like a contortionist in the narrow space to turn over and follow Carney's movements. Once he had seated himself on the altar, nothing was visible except the toes of his shoes.

Driscoll bent himself in half in order to swivel around and

face the other way. Peeking out from beneath the pall, he did see Lawlor this time. The commissioner was preceded by a man Driscoll had never seen before. After those two there was a third figure, a woman, and a fourth, a small boy.

Driscoll kept staring, trying to place the woman's face in the dim light. He had seen her before. Then it hit him—she was the woman from the fur store, the Russian woman, Tanya, she had called herself.

What was Lawlor doing with these people? Driscoll watched and listened, trying not to even breathe.

"That's far enough," Lawlor said to the man whom Driscoll hadn't recognized, as he approached the catafalque and stood next to it. His feet were only inches from Driscoll's face; the detective was afraid to move a muscle. As the man had come into the crypt, Driscoll had noticed that he was slightly built, wearing glasses, with a neatly trimmed beard. From his hiding place, Driscoll couldn't see where Lawlor, the woman, and the boy had gone, but he heard footsteps and had the feeling that they might have left.

At that instant, the four unsteady legs of the phony coffin, with the black pall draped over it, shook noticeably, as Mikhail Zhukov slouched his weight against the contraption. Beneath it, all Driscoll could do was close his eyes and hope for the best.

"Good day," a voice, cultured and articulate, boomed at Zhukov from somewhere to the immediate left of the raised altar before him. "I hope your trip was a pleasant one." Now the KGB man could pinpoint where the voice was coming from—there was a chair up on the platform to the side of the altar, obscured by the dark shadows. Zhukov stood there, uneasily shifting his weight from foot to foot, leaning nervously on this odd structure in the center of the room. At first he had thought it was a coffin, but it was much too light, too flimsy. He felt like a subject being addressed by a monarch magisterially speaking down to him.

"And to whom am I speaking?" Zhukov demanded.

"James Xavier Carney," replied the voice authoritatively.

"How do I know?"

"Does it matter?"

"The money matters. I have been given promise of a payment."

Driscoll watched as the bag that Carney had been carrying came hurtling through the air from the elevated blackness of the altar, directly toward Zhukov and the wobbly bier. As Driscoll steeled himself for the impact, the KGB man reached up both hands above his head and snared the bag in midair. He immediately opened it and began fingering crisp packs of American currency, each secured by a paper wrapper.

"Don't bother to count it," Carney said. "That's your down payment—five hundred thousand dollars, our agreement."

"And the rest?" Zhukov asked. "Our deal was for five million."

"Zurich," Carney said. "A numbered account under the code name we agreed on. After you have given me the information we seek, you will be free to go and pick up the remainder of the payment, or you can accept our offer of protection. Your decision entirely."

The light from the candles flickered unevenly between the altar and the Russian. "How do I know the money's in Zurich?"

"How do I know you aren't tricking me?" Carney retorted.

"A standoff then?"

"Quite."

"I must think about this."

"Don't think too long, my friend," Carney advised. "You are getting the best of the bargain. Either way, you're walking out of here with a half a million dollars and your freedom."

"Why am I meeting you here? In such a place?"

"Dies Irae," Carney answered. "The day of wrath. These days I find myself quite preoccupied with personal security and thoughts of the hereafter. I'm sure you are aware of my close brush with assassination. Your countrymen, I believe."

"We play a dangerous game," Zhukov said, without a hint of emotion.

"You must admit this place is secure."

". . . as a tomb," the Russian replied.

Carney forced a laugh. "And what about our offer of protection? Will you be availing yourself of that?"

"I am quite capable of protecting myself," Zhukov answered. "Your secret services are no better than ours. I'll take my chances."

"As you wish—but Zurich can be a very unwholesome environment."

"Shall we begin?" Zhukov was anxious.

"I believe *you* might begin," Carney said languidly, "by telling me exactly how it came to pass that I was double-crossed on the delivery, in full, of the weapons that I arranged to purchase from you."

Without even trying to sound intimidating, Carney's almost too understated manner was beginning to remind Zhukov of every KGB interrogation he had ever conducted. It felt oppressive and terrifying, being on the receiving end, as he now found himself, but he was beginning to see some small leverage. "I have enough of the money so that we can begin, although, as you say, it's a mere down payment. Perhaps I'll take a page from your book, Mr. Carney, and give you a down payment on the information."

There was a long pause. He knew that Carney was calculating his response. The guns that the Americans had left behind in Vietnam in their captured war arsenal had become an object of increasing embarrassment over the years. Zhukov had determined to capitalize on this embarrassment. The Americans would pay dearly, he knew, to get the guns back and to keep them from falling into the hands of terrorists or unfriendly governments that could easily turn around and use the same weapons against the Americans themselves, or their friends. At that point, acute embarrassment would become hopeless humiliation.

Zhukov was protesting in accented English that Driscoll could just about hear.

"I double-crossed no one," he said heatedly to Carney. "I am the one who has been double-crossed."

"Explain yourself," Carney demanded.

"In 1977 I was a special envoy to Vietnam. They were holding seventeen hundred American servicemen in prison camps then. The KGB wanted to buy them, hold them for ransom, as it were. But the Vietnamese refused. They were already doing that themselves. Instead, they offered me—as an individual, rather than as a representative of my government—the guns. But I had to turn them down, because I could not come up with enough money. I considered going to you Americans back then, for financing. I agonized about it for months. In the end, I was too frightened to risk it.

"The Vietnamese are starved for hard currency, especially foreign currency. They can grow one cash crop—opium. Nothing else is suitable for export. The Manila offered to distribute the opium for them on a worldwide basis. When the North Vietnamese protested that they could not begin to meet the Malina's price, the Malina suggested a barter arrangement. They would take the guns—eight hundred thousand M-16s, I believe, seven hundred thousand .45s, and tanks, jet fighters still in packing crates, uniforms, computers, plus other items—in exchange for marketing the opium. The Malina offered to split profits with the North Vietnamese on a per-kilo basis, fifty-fifty, after the first five hundred million dollars."

"How do you come to know all this?" the voice asked.

"Do you have any idea how many Vietnamese I bribed to get as far as I did? They remained in my service—and my debt. If the guns ever left Da Nang, I was to be notified."

"Very professional," the voice said approvingly.

"Thank you."

"But the North Vietnamese never accepted the Malina's offer?" Carney asked, sounding as though he already knew the answer.

"Of course not," Zhukov answered quickly. "The Malina they could never hope to control. The North Vietnamese were simply afraid to do business with them. For several years, as black-market arms became more and more in demand and more expensive in international circles—secret wars, I think you Americans call them, like your secret wars in Central America—the Vietnam booty just sat there waiting for a purchaser.

"Many arms merchants approached the North Vietnamese. Your American Sam Cummings of Interarms got further than most; he almost made a deal for the whole lot, but at the last moment, the North Vietnamese backed out again. They were content to just sit on the arms. They had no use for them and took perverse pleasure in denying them to all who asked.

"As you know, I was the official responsible for dealing with all black-market activities in the Soviet Union. I was *very* good at my job, comrade; so good, in fact, that the Malina suggested I make money with them—as a kind of silent partner. That's quite common in my country. I believe you have a name for it here . . ."

"Corruption," the voice said.

"I was never Malina; they select you for induction into their brotherhood, you do not select them. But I did work with them—most profitably. I was never able to reach the top of their organization, but I did do business with important middle-level people. After a few years, I mentioned the Vietnam guns to them again. I suggested they finance me, then I would have come up with some excuse to return to Vietnam.

"Instead, they turned down my proposition. But then it suddenly came to me that I didn't need anyone at all—merely a source of supply and a means of distributing the guns on my own. I bribed the North Vietnamese lieutenant colonel who actually sat on the guns—with the help of a black-market merchant in Singapore—and began smuggling out as many weapons as I could in small lots, in oil drums. Ingenious.

"That took care of my supply problem. And as to my distribution . . ."

"That was where this Butkova chap came in," Carney added thoughtfully.

"Exactly. I thought we had an understanding, but this man cannot be trusted. He decided to begin doing as he pleased with the guns—selling even to the Mafia. I told him that you have first right of refusal for *all* the weapons. But Butkova is a greedy, impatient man, I have discovered to my regret. He treated the weapons as though they belonged to him!"

"Effectively eliminating you," the voice said with an edge of amusement.

"As you Americans call it, a double-cross."

"You said the guns were at sea now," the voice continued. "How do you know that?"

"You contracted on behalf of your government for all the guns from Vietnam that I could deliver," Zhukov explained. "It wasn't safe for either of us to deal directly. So you chose your man Paul Presto as an intermediary and I used my best black-market contact here in Philadelphia—Butkova."

"At least we agree on that much," Carney said patronizingly.

Zhukov was sweating heavily. Tanya had assured him that everything was going to be fine now, because she had made contact with Carney and had received a guarantee from him that Zhukov could safely defect to the United States, bringing with him his invaluable information about the location of the weapons he had managed to smuggle out of Vietnam, the weapons that Butkova didn't yet have control of. But Zhukov had expected a much warmer welcome from the man Carney.

"*All* of the guns were to be delivered to *me!*" Carney thundered, angry and frustrated. "Yet we found that the weapons were being sold indiscriminately to the highest bidders *anywhere!* Our own gangsters were buying them, for God's sake!" Carney hissed. "That's *really* how we found out about Presto. It was damn lucky for us that he agreed to help us."

"I cannot be held responsible for that problem," Zhukov explained nervously. "Butkova cheated and betrayed me, too. He was never supposed to allow the guns to leave his warehouses. They were to be kept there for eventual delivery to you, Carney." Zhukov wiped the sweat from his forehead, desperate to convince this Carney. "Some of those weapons even turned up in *Russia!*" he said, straining not to scream. "Do you have any idea the problem that caused for me? I am KGB, Carney. Those guns could have cost me my life. This Butkova is an enemy to both of us. Accuse *him* of a double-cross, not me. I risked my life coming here. You must protect me!"

Images—from newsreels, from the past, from all things that had happened to him since the night of Paul Presto's assassination—were suddenly swirling through Driscoll's mind as he absorbed what he was hearing. The Meatman *had* been running guns for the government. Vietnam guns, of course! He could remember the disorderly retreat from Saigon, the famous shot of the helicopter swooping low to rescue the last man from the roof of the U.S. embassy in 1975. It had sickened Driscoll the first time he had ever seen that. And Butkova! Those heavy 55-gallon drums that Driscoll had tried to pry open the day of his fight with Boris. There had to be guns in there too. More military hardware than anyone could imagine—enough to equip a dozen secret armies. No wonder Carney was so adamant. They were using our own guns from Vietnam—the ones we had abandoned in disgrace, in abject retreat. It was all that Driscoll could do to keep himself from jumping out from under the pall and strangling this Russian traitor and Carney, too.

Then Driscoll understood what Milton Littlejohn must have done. He must have known about the dealings that Presto had with Carney, working as his middleman to get the guns away from the Malina, and he must have gone to Butkova and set up the Presto murder plot. That was the only possible explanation. Littlejohn had added Presto to the list of dead mob bosses—probably with an assurance of money and power from Butkova.

Driscoll had heard enough. He had to find Littlejohn and Honey. He almost bolted from his hiding place under the catafalque. Then Carney's probing tone stopped him. He listened again.

"Where do you suppose the guns are now?" Carney asked, almost as if he were a cat toying with a mouse. "I mean the ones that you assume you still control."

This was what Zhukov had been waiting for. "At sea," he answered. "On board ships that are owned by an associate of mine in Singapore. They are safe. Butkova can't possibly get to them. If you keep up your end of our bargain—five million and my freedom—I will give you the locations of the ships and see that you get *all* of the weapons this time."

"I'm afraid that you have lost your bargaining position,

my friend," Carney said. "World events have moved too quickly for you."

Zhukov was stammering. "What can this mean? . . . The ships, I know where they are . . . the captains are loyal to me, alone."

For the first time, Carney stood on the altar platform, crossed to the center, and looked directly at the terror in the Russian's eyes. "I believe that you are acquainted with Marshal Zinijakin, are you not?"

That name—just the mention of it—convinced Mikhail Zhukov that he was a lost man. "I am," he said quietly, the defeat already evident in his voice.

Carney was enjoying this, manipulating his pawns. "I'm afraid that *he* now controls the ships and their cargo, my good man," Carney said. "And you, comrade, are left with nothing to trade."

"That's impossible," Zhukov protested again, but feebly. "How could Zinijakin possibly know? The GRU?"

"I don't believe that he's acting as the GRU in this case," Carney said. "I believe that the Malina—Zinijakin is the Headman, you know—enters into it." Carney hesitated long enough to really make the Russian squirm. "But, dear boy, I suppose you didn't know . . ."

"Zinijakin . . . the GRU . . . the *Malina?* It can't be!" Zhukov said, feeling that a death sentence had been delivered to him, here in this infernal dungeon.

"Oh, it's quite true. If we want the guns, the marshal says that we deal with the Malina now. Not Butkova. The marshal seems to have a problem with that rogue, too. Of course, it's immaterial to me, either way. As long as I get the guns."

"You *can't* trust Zinijakin!" the KGB man screamed. "You are a fool, Carney. He is worse than any of them!"

"Be that as it may," Carney said, leaning on his elbow on the altar, "Zinijakin's terms were firm. His man told our man at the Christmas Summit. It seems that you have become an enormous embarrassment to them, too. Therefore, you fall under the category of rubbish to be disposed of."

"How dare you?"

"I'm afraid you're the fool," Carney said. "You were

dealing with the Malina all along—as far back as your first contact with this Butkova.'' Carney laughed evilly. ''You merely did them a favor by getting the guns from that North Vietnamese lieutenant colonel. You saved them a great deal of money, in fact. And those precious ships of yours, old man, they were Malina ships. Zinijakin has everything now, even Tanya.''

''Tanya?'' Zhukov refused to believe it. ''She loves me!''

''Correction,'' Carney said. ''She loves the Malina and her son—who do you think that little boy is who came with you? Up until now, the old marshal has been holding him as a kind of ransom to make sure that she contacted my people and did as she was told.''

''But what about me?'' Zhukov protested. ''I've been helping you Americans get back your arsenal from Vietnam. You need those guns for your Contra friends in Nicaragua.''

''And so we shall have them,'' Carney retorted. ''But Zinijakin's terms are firm. He has the guns now, so I must negotiate with him directly. As a sign of our good faith, he has requested that we eliminate a rather vexing problem for them.''

Zhukov knew that Carney meant him.

''We received a message at the Christmas Summit, as I told you. They did it on a staff level. Told us exactly what would have to be done. And you, Comrade Zhukov, or I should say your life, must be our down payment. As soon as I found out, I contacted your lovely Tanya, had a darling boy pilot me here in a helicopter, and this very meeting was arranged. Farewell, Comrade Zhukov,'' Carney said. ''Our conversation has been stimulating. So sorry, old chap.'' There was only cold resignation in Carney's voice.

Desperate, Mikhail Zhukov turned this way and that, thrashing as he ran from side to side in the burial chamber, searching for a way to escape. The crypt, he feared, was about to become his tomb.

Suddenly a gunshot rang out from the rear of the crypt, and Mikhail Zhukov's body slumped heavily against the thin legs of the bier, partially collapsing it. Driscoll was driven from his place of concealment. He sprang to his feet. He looked behind him and saw Lawlor, standing stiffly, the smoking revolver still in his hands, in the standard over-and-under police grip.

Straightening himself up, Driscoll heard Lawlor begin to say, "It's done, Jim, praise be to God. Now, we can . . ." Then the commissioner abruptly stopped and stared open-mouthed at the detective.

Lawlor was watching him, but all that Driscoll could see was the gun. The two policemen stood frozen, facing each other.

"My God, Alfred, this must be the young man you told me about," Carney began, his composure still intact, despite the murder that had just been committed a few feet away from him. "Don't be alarmed, Driscoll," Carney said with forced familiarity. "This is a Christlike thing your commissioner just did—ridding the world of that man. *Judicium Dei,* the judgment of God; *Latae Sententiae,* sentence imposed." With that, Carney strode down from the altar, walked past Driscoll, carefully stepped over the crumpled body of Zhukov, and approached Lawlor, whose gun was still up and in the firing position.

"That'll be enough, Alfred," Carney said, as he pointed the gun toward the floor with a gingerly flourish, guiding Lawlor's arms in the direction he wanted. "I had hoped that Ed Bellows would take care of this unpleasantness for me, but that's quite impossible now. Alfred, you have my eternal gratitude and the President's."

Finally, Lawlor spoke, addressing Driscoll. "You've been hiding here—heard the whole thing—saw it?"

Driscoll didn't answer as he watched the last wisps of smoke drift from Lawlor's weapon.

"Of course he's been here, Alfred," Carney said. "Concealed under the catafalque." Carney looked at Driscoll approvingly. "You're a very capable young man, infiltrating our sanctuary like this."

"I'll take care of Driscoll," Lawlor said gruffly.

Just then, Tanya came rushing into the crypt. As soon as she saw Zhukov's prone form, she let out a gasp of alarm. Then the expression on her face underwent an instantaneous transformtion from remorse to relief. She turned to Carney. "I'll inform the Headman that his wishes have been carried out." It was only then that Tanya realized that Driscoll was there, too. They eyed each other warily.

"Alfred tells me that you've been working on this case since the beginning," Carney said. "You know more about this Whitey than anybody."

"Whitey?" Driscoll was incredulous. "The man with the white hair. You *know* about him?"

Carney reached down and picked up the bag containing the money and handed it to Tanya. "I believe this is the expression of our good faith that your Headman requires," he said.

Tanya took the bag.

Carney faced Driscoll. "More about Whitey, as you call him, in a few moments. First things first, Alfred . . ."

"Driscoll, I'll need a hand here," Lawlor ordered. Then Lawlor reached down, put his hands under Zhukov's armpits, and began to hoist him up. "Get his ankles. Be quick about it."

Driscoll wasn't even sure why, but he did as Lawlor commanded. The Russian was heavier than he looked. He kept expecting Carney to come over and help them haul the body, but the man from Washington merely stood off to the side, disdainful of their exertions. He wasn't one to get his hands dirty. Then, surprisingly, Tanya pushed ahead of them, with Lawlor walking backwards, gripping Zhukov's corpse by the shoulders.

Tanya began pushing and pulling at the lid of the fourth sarcophagus. Bellowing over Tanya's grunts, Lawlor said, "Get that damn lid for us, Driscoll."

No sooner did Driscoll drop Zhukov's ankles to work on the lid than Tanya moved right in and picked him up. In a few moments, with the lid pushed aside enough to accommodate Zhuykov's body, the three of them deposited Zhukov's corpse into the waiting tomb. Lawlor pushed the curved marble lid back in place himself.

When the body had been removed, Carney came over to them. "I do hope the old abbot won't mind some company in there," he said jauntily.

Driscoll still wanted to know about Whitey. "That white-haired psycho who Littlejohn paid to take out Presto and his daughter—what do you guys know about him?"

"Tanya, here," Carney said, leading the woman over to Driscoll, "has some rather alarming news for all of us, and it concerns this Whitey."

Driscoll looked at her as she began. "The man you've been looking for," she said to Driscoll. "Butkova. He did conspire with Littlejohn to kill Paul Presto. He told me so. But there's more."

"What?"

Carney cut in. "This Butkova—he's something of a maverick, causing problems for everyone. The bastard tried to have me assassinated, in my own limousine, no less, and now . . ."

Tanya was excited, agitated, lapsing into Russian phrases. "Our Headman wants this Butkova stopped, now. He's an ambitious, grasping man, uncontrollable, utterly without restraint. Now he makes war on your Mafia and forces the Malina into it with him.

"Our Headman forbids this. He told Carney so; he told me so. Butkova must be stopped. But even now, he and this hired killer, Whitey, are planning to murder all of them—all the Mafia bosses, even the Presto girl—at the restaurant in Willows Hills."

"How do you know all this?" Driscoll demanded, looking skeptical. The detective was afraid to trust anybody anymore at this point.

"Lovers tell secrets," she said. "Once I did love Nikolai . . . Butkova . . . very much." She thought of her little boy—*their* son, although Butkova had no idea the child even existed. "Butkova believes we are still lovers. The Headman ordered me to make him think this, to get close to him, learn his plans. I know everything now. And the Headman wants this massacre not to take place. He wants no war with this Mafia, with the Americans."

"Too damn bad," Lawlor growled. "I'd love to see somebody get them all at once."

Driscoll was thinking about Honey. "Whitey," he said. "Where is he?"

"At the restaurant," she said. "Stalking them. He's with Nikolai. They planned it together." She was almost shrieking.

"This Whitey is a killing machine," Carney said. "We know. We trained him." Carney's voice had risen to a shrill intensity. "But unfortunately, we lost him a long time ago." He turned to Tanya. "Like Butkova, he went into business for himself."

Driscoll had never before met anyone whose blood ran as cold as Carney's.

"Do you know what she's talking about?" Carney asked Driscoll. "Is there a restaurant like she's describing?"

"I know exactly where it is," Driscoll answered, anxious to get away from them as quickly as he could. Picturing the place on the high palisades above the river, he had a vision of Honey Presto dying there.

"I have men on their way there now," Lawlor said. "I hope we won't be too late."

Driscoll was already pushing past them. Tanya grabbed his arm. "I must come, too," Tanya said. "The boy, also."

Driscoll edged her away from him.

"Do what she says, young man," Carney ordered, in a tone that would accept no contradiction. "We have quite a good deal of business to do with these people now, if we are to satisfy this Zinijakin."

Driscoll looked disgusted, but he kept his mouth shut.

"Take my helicopter," Carney said. "Just point the pilot where you will—where you want him to take you. You'll be there in minutes, and for God's sake, Driscoll, I want this Whitey stopped. Understand?"

Tanya and Driscoll ran out of the crypt together. The little boy, sad-eyed and frightened-looking, was waiting for her just outside the main chamber.

The screaming rotors of the helicopters dinned in Driscoll's ears like metallic thunder. He lifted Tanya's little son up to the pilot's waiting arms and then spun around to get her, but she was racing away from him, screaming over her shoulder, "Carney . . . I must tell him one more thing . . . I have one more message from the Headman, I won't be a moment. Wait for me . . . wait, Driscoll." Then she was gone.

The detective climbed up next to the pilot and said, "She's got two minutes."

When the crypt was completely empty and Zhukov's body disposed of, Carney felt a sense of relief such as he had never known before. Elation, almost. He left the main house of the abbey for the first time since he arrived at Loyola House.

The chill afternoon air made him feel light-headed, intoxicated. The muscles in his legs had stiffened in the damp crypt. Using them, stretching them, he tingled from thigh to ankle. He found himself walking toward the ruins of the old church near the tree line. Suddenly, he had a compelling desire, a longing, to visit the ruins. He gathered more strength with every step.

Then he saw them. An explosive revelation was unfolding.

Pigeons. A flapping, cooing flock of gray-blue pigeons. They soared overhead at his every footstep, animating the dull sky with their racket.

Carney was almost at the ruins. High stone pillars; a few walls with gaping, colossal openings—space for windows. Suddenly a dove executed a graceful dive and flew through one of them, piercing the air.

He stood in the center of the gutted house of worship and peered up at the sky. Like some violent fit seizing him, Carney felt remorse.

This was it.

This place was his dream! Had he finally found salvation? Release from the evil grip of the recurring nightmare?

Had he banished the terror?

The moment held the promise of enchantment. Carney had conquered his dream. A calm, gentle beam of tranquility seemed to be enveloping him.

He heard someone approaching. He hoped it would be Alfred. He could tell him about the dream. Alfred would appreciate such a titanic struggle.

Then Carney saw the hooded figure.

Man or woman? He couldn't tell. The hood was up over the head and a cape billowed out from the slender body.

Once his own body had been that slender. Healthy. Vibrant.

Without hesitating, the hooded figure slowly raised a black, shiny revolver and pointed it at Jim Carney's head. *Would he see his own face?*

It was Tanya. At first, she didn't say a word—just held the gun on him.

"Why?" Carney stammered, attempting at that moment to understand death itself.

"The Headman will share the guns with no one," Tanya said. "Not even for a price. They belong to the Malina now."

The hooded specter took aim, advanced a step closer, and fired once, sending a bullet directly into James Xavier Carney's heart. At that moment, Tanya said, "Carney, know the Malina. Fear it."

The last thing Carney ever saw was the face under the hood—Tanya's face. It was not his own. Carney's nightmare had been vanquished.

Tanya leaned down, fired a second round into Carney's brain, and then began running as quickly as she could in the direction of the waiting helicopter.

THIRTY-FIVE

WEST RIVER DRIVE, PHILADELPHIA SUNDAY NIGHT

Even though it was cold and damp outside, with more snow forecast, Honey Presto asked the driver to turn on the air conditioner. Suddenly she was very warm, flushed. They were riding in the back of her father's big baby-blue Lincoln Town Car, just Honey and Joe-Joey in the back, with a driver and a bodyguard in the front seat. There was a crash car in front of them just in case anybody tried to intercept them, and a chase car behind them, which would double as transportation for Honey and Joe-Joey should they have to abandon the Lincoln for any reason. There were six men in each of the other two cars, armed, handpicked by Joe-Joey, trustworthy. He was carrying a gun himself.

It was a long ride from South Philadelphia to the restaurant in Willows Hills, and Honey had maintained an uncomfortable silence. She was thinking about a lot of things—about the way it used to be riding in the backseat with her father; about the sit-down she was en route to; about what had happened down at the shore with her aunt and uncle. But most of all, she was thinking about Phillip Driscoll.

"Will Antonio Coia be here?" she asked Joe-Joey. "Are you sure we can talk to him?"

"I heard from his son, myself," Joe-Joey answered. "The

old man wants to get this straightened out. He'll show." There was so much that had to be done now, stepping in for her father as she knew she would have to do.

"Are you *sure* he was all right?" she asked Joe-Joey.

"You mean Driscoll?" He was glad she was acting more like herself. "Yeah, he was fine. Just a knock on the head, that's all. I just had to lie to him a little."

"Lie? Why?" She turned to face Joe-Joey.

"Well, just about the knock on the head," he answered, settling back into the soft leather seat, just the way her father used to do. "What I mean is, I *did* see who konked him. Littlejohn did it. But I'm sure it was an accident. Geez, Honey, we come busting in there like the cavalry to get Tony and Marie after Littlejohn told us they were after you, and we figured that you better be the only one standing. So Littlejohn, as soon as he sees Driscoll—I don't know, maybe he didn't even recognize him—he hauls off and wallops him with that cane he has. But that guy's tough."

"Why would he do that? Hit him, I mean? I don't understand." Honey was upset now, and Joe-Joey wanted to keep her calm to face her father's old rivals on the *commissione.* Suddenly, Honey was mentally reviewing everything that had happened between her and the lawyer since the moment of her father's death.

Joe-Joey was still talking, but she heard only part of what he was saying. *Why had Littlejohn hit Phillip?* "Tell me *exactly* what Littlejohn said about this meeting." She turned to the Presto soldier, the new Family boss. Joe-Joey was a little taken aback.

"Littlejohn called the *capis* and the main soldiers together," he began, "and explained that the Meatman had been real suspicious of Tony and Marie. He said he was acting with your best interests at heart, and he asked us to keep an eye on those two."

"That had to be right around the same time that they tried to kill Phillip and me at Manny's place," Honey said, attempting to reconstruct what must have happened.

"I guess." Tony shrugged. "We didn't know anything about that."

"Then he told you about this sit-down?"

"Not exactly. He said this sit-down had been in the works

ever since your father . . ." He could never actually bring himself to say that the Meatman was dead, most of all, not to Honey. "Well . . . you know . . . your father . . . anyway, he claimed that this was the best thing to do. So he called the Coia boys and put out the word. We figured you had to know all about it too, Honey. That was the way Littlejohn made it sound." Now Joe-Joey was beginning to feel too warm.

Slowly, Honey shook her head. "Joe-Joey, Littlejohn never said a word to *me*. I thought this sit-down was something that you and Tony and Marie and the men had agreed to."

The new boss made an exaggerated gesture with his hands, a gesture of extreme annoyance. She had often seen her father do the same thing. "Littlejohn asked them to convene this emergency sit-down. That's exactly how he put it—to decide how to fight back, or *whether* to fight back," he added.

Honey looked at him as though she couldn't believe what she was hearing. "What do you mean—whether to fight back?"

Joe-Joey looked disturbed himself. "I know just what you mean," he said. "I didn't like that, either. Not after your daddy. What they done to him. But Littlejohn says the bosses are all businessmen, which they are, and if they figure it's worth their while to cut a deal with these Russian bastards, that's what they'll do. Maybe not give them everything they want, but most of it. You'd better get prepared for that, Honey," Joe-Joey cautioned. "These guys have their pride and they love to fight. But the thing they love most of all is to count their money."

A mile went by, then another. Honey asked, "Much farther?"

"A good ways yet. This place is out in the 'burbs."

"I haven't seen Don Antonio since I was a little kid," Honey said. "I hope he remembers me."

"He could forget?" Joe-Joey had always admired Honey from afar, always in a chaste, almost fatherly way. But he knew that once a man saw Honey Presto, he didn't forget.

A mental image of the boss of bosses flashed through Joe-Joey's mind. It was too much to hope that he might actually be in the same room with a man of such reputation and respect. "I guess Don Antonio is the most worried about the Russians because he has the most to lose," Joe-Joey said.

"Why do they always have to come themselves?" Honey asked. "To these sit-downs? They could send representatives."

"First," Joe-Joey said, "that isn't their way. Not the old ones, anyway. And when you're talkin' about the *commissione,* you're talkin' about the *real* old ones. They don't trust each other, to start with. So they gotta look somebody in the eye to make sure they're tellin' the truth. And second, Honey, these Russians really got them scared."

"Probably," Honey said. "I guess it can't hurt to see what they have to say."

"Step on it, Vito," Joe-Joey yelled to the driver.

ABOVE THE SCHUYLKILL RIVER, BEARING SOUTH BY SOUTHWEST

Don Antonio Coia was terrified of flying. Still, he took his customized chopper everywhere—a four-seat commuter with a wet bar and icebox built into the console behind the pilot. The pilot had been a combat veteran in the United States Air Force. Coia was trusting the man with his life. He never got used to that. In flight, the seating arrangements never varied. Coia was on the left, with his oldest son on the right; behind them sat two bodyguards, each armed with an automatic rifle. Coia's youngest son always handled the security on the ground—a perimeter of more bodyguards, enough firepower to repel any attack; even a nurse and a team of paramedics. In their world, Coia had to be protected as ferociously as the President of the United States. Presidents could get changed every four years—

Coia's term of office was for life. And there was only one way to make a change there.

Wrapped around his fists as tightly as a rope was a thick brown-beaded rosary that had been blessed by the Pope himself and handed to Don Antonio at a private—a truly private—audience. He figured that as long as he had the Pope's rosary beads he would never die in a helicopter crash. Still, the old Don sweated through every second of every flight, his eyes closed most of the time. His sons had insisted on using the helicopter for this trip—he knew they were taking precautions for an eventual quick getaway.

"When?" he asked his oldest son, straining to be heard above the loud rotors.

"Two, three minutes, no more, Pop," the son said. "Everybody else is there already—just waiting for us. In and out; you'll be home in your own bed by the time the news is on." Don Antonio was a man of constant habits—by eleven o'clock, every night, he had to be falling asleep in his own bed, in his own home.

"These Prestos better not be long-winded," the Don said, caressing the beads. "I hope what they got to say we don't already know."

"You can always cancel," the son said, since that was precisely what he had advised.

"We keep our word."

"I can see the restaurant now," the son told his father. "They got the flares out in the parking lot, waving us down."

"Your baby brother's a good boy," Don Antonio said with parental pride, as he pictured his youngest son, age fifty-one, screaming orders in the parking lot down on the ground. He had always believed that children were a comfort in old age.

WILLOWS HILLS, NEAR THE RESTAURANT

Butkova and Whitey were arguing loudly in the maintenance shed, behind the old converted carriage house where the restaurant kept its small fleet of limos.

"You aren't even supposed to be here," Whitey said angrily. "You're only going to get in the way." As it was, they were risking that they might be heard.

Butkova wasn't used to this, although he did prize a man with spirit. "Where did you acquire your vile manners?" Butkova asked, amused.

"In the army, Rangers," Whitey answered, tired of the conversation already.

"This Littlejohn, does he pay you enough?"

"Enough."

"You work for me, you get more, much more."

"Where does that leave Littlejohn?"

"He came to me," Butkova said. "I would have had to kill the Meatman eventually, and he offered to let you solve our problem. To me, the guns were incidental, just surplus from the Vietnam War, but the Americans were willing to pay dearly for them. I plan to do what this Meatman has done—create a Family, rule the cities from the underworld, have *my* own thing as they have *their* own thing, their Cosa Nostra." He was waiting for some reaction from Whitey. But there would be none.

"I never went in for empire-building, myself," Whitey said. "I just contract out."

"To me—exclusively," Butkova said. Then he tried to pat Whitey on the back, but the tall killer pulled away.

"My skin," he stammered, "in the cold, on a day like this, something happens to it. I can't . . . can't stand to be touched. That's all."

Butkova had seen men like this before, in Siberia, men who had been too long in the eternal cold of the Arctic. "You let a woman warm you," he advised. "Maybe the cold never goes away, my friend, but maybe you can escape it for a little while. A woman . . ."

Whitey went back to checking his charges. "Your men must stay clear. Otherwise they might suspect something. This is the only way I can be sure of killing them all together."

"As you say. My *men* stay back—but not Butkova. I must see this gathering of the old ones, this *commissione.* I must. It is what I came to America for—to take what is theirs and make it my own."

Whitey's left cheek was twitching so badly now that he didn't even try to hide it. "When this goes," he said, pointing to the toggle controls in front of him, "it should take care of everyone in the room."

"What about Littlejohn? He has to get out, doesn't he?"

Whitey smiled that lopsided smile. "Does he?"

Butkova's eyebrows raised a full inch. "I see," he said, grinning.

"I thought you just said you could pay me more?"

"And so I can," Butkova bellowed. "Whitey, we understand each other—you should have been a Russian, my friend!"

For one of the few times in his life, Whitey laughed. "I am," he said. "Born and raised, in Pittsburgh, PA. Nice little Russian neighborhood there—Russian Hill. But we never knew any Russians there like *you.*"

Nikolai Butkova almost forgot himself and tried to hug Whitey again; then he caught himself and backed away, still trying to smother his laughter.

IN THE AIR ABOVE THE SCHUYLKILL

Driscoll could see the lights below, outlining the expressway and the bright skyline of the city beyond; auto headlights seemed to merge into single, brilliant pinpoints of white glow. Floodlights positioned on the underbelly of the chopper played on the expressway palisades until the rough, rectangular shape of their destination came into view.

He was surprised to see dying flares being extinguished in the parking lot as he craned his neck and head out into the cold air to get a better look.

The pilot, young, his face red-burned from exposure to the wind, screamed right into Driscoll's ear. Tanya and her son were behind them, the child whimpering, his mother comforting him.

"We got some company down there, already," the pilot said. " 'Nother chopper, looks like. Might be crowded, buddy. You call it."

"I gotta get down there," Driscoll said. "That mountain won't be there in a few minutes."

"Down we go," the pilot hollered. "I'll get you in as close as I can. You might have to jump."

"That will be fine," Tanya cut in, pushing past Driscoll, leaning near the pilot, sweeping her blond hair away from her forehead, as she looked with concern back toward her son. "We can jump."

WILLOWS HILLS, THE RESTAURANT

For their sit-down at Willows Hills, the Prestos had deliberately selected a site with limited accessibility. There was only one way in and out—through a winding driveway that rose on a steep incline, opening into the large parking lot where Antonio Coia's helicopter had landed. The restaurant itself occupied just the corner of several acres. It was located on the flattened top of sheer palisades, perhaps a hundred feet high. At the base of the palisades, the Schuylkill Expressway hugged the limestone and rock, fanning out for six lanes in a series of hairpin curves. On the other side of the expressway, the earth again stopped abruptly, falling away to the frigid, icy waters of the river below. It was like the precipice at the edge of the world that ancient mariners had so dreaded. From the parking lot of the restaurant, the Prestos could look down on the expressway below and the river from a height as commanding as a battlement. On three sides, the area was secure—no side roads, no back roads, no secondary entrances or exits, and only one way down, grappling hand over hand along the face of the rugged hill. Densely wooded parkland lapped the very edge of the restaurant complex. It was there Whitey had hidden.

Inside the restaurant, the large private dining room they were using had been cleared and a podium placed at the head table. The room was well secluded from the rest of the restaurant, which was upstairs. The last time Honey had seen most of these men she had been a child. Tonight she wasn't sure whether to genuflect or behave like a granddaughter at a family party. She was worrying about this when Don Antonio Coia, tottering on his short, bowed legs, not much taller than Honey, approached, kissed her on both cheeks, and said, "I loved your father, too. His murder strikes at my heart." Then, like a gallant old despot, he kissed her hand.

That was the signal for the serious segment of the sit-down to begin. As the hosts, the Prestos had assumed a low-key diffidence—they had been served last; older *commissione* members had been honored with the seats closest to Don Antonio; every toast had been offered in Italian.

Littlejohn was at the podium. Just as he cleared his throat, Coia interrupted and spoke for the gathered bosses. "The Presto Family has called this emergency meeting of the *commissione,*" he said gruffly. "I agree that some strategy is needed. No longer can we idly accept the threat from this Russian thing, this Malina, this barbarity that took Paul Presto from our midst."

Overwhelmed, Honey took a seat near the window, as Littlejohn began, "Acting on behalf of the Presto Family, with Miss Honoria's permission, I would offer the following options for your consideration . . . ."

The old men of the *commissione* sat stiffly, listening intently, but making certain that their stolid faces and hard eyes gave nothing away. Coia's two sons were the most watchful. Others picked their teeth thoughtfully.

For a moment, Honey's concentration was interrupted. She was thinking about her father and about Phillip. Then she glanced out of the window and saw *him*—the same face that Phillip's murdered friend, Harry Capri, had selected from among his files of photographs. What had Harry been trying to tell them, and what in God's name was this man doing here?

Littlejohn was lecturing on, like a lawyer, parsing thoughts as precisely as a Talmudic scholar. He caught Honey peering at him out of the corner of his eye. Coia's eldest son also caught the look on Honey's face. *"Hold on!"* he screamed, bolting upright and knocking dishes and silverware to the floor.

There were twelve of them seated around four large square tables that had been pushed together to form a single great island. Coia and his sons sat at the head of the table—they had moved their chairs aside to make room for Littlejohn. Honey and Joe-Joey were opposite them at the other end of the table. The other members of the *commissione* and their retainers faced each other on either side like a board of directors. Because Honey was the youngest person there, by far, and had been included only by virtue of her position as the Meatman's heiress, she hadn't said a word up until this point. Neither had Joe-Joey.

The wide table was still set with food from the remnants of the enormous meal that had been served, and starched white tablecloths reached almost to the floor.

The moment Coia's son was on his feet, a waiter darted in front of him and bent down to retrieve one of the plates that had fallen. The sudden movement unnerved him and he grabbed the waiter by the scruff of the neck, pulled him to his feet, almost choking him in the process, then threw him crashing into the bar several feet from the table. At that, the other waiters and busboys began cowering and backing their way out of the room.

Opposite the bar, along the side of the restaurant that overlooked the river, curved bay windows that looked from a distance as though they had been bunkered right into the earth, chiseled out of the rock, reflected the beams of headlights, thousands of them, from the superhighway beyond.

It was outside one of those windows that Honey Presto had glimpsed Nikolai Butkova's heavy features, silhouetted in the dying light. At that instant, her olive complexion had washed almost white. She'd halfway risen out of her chair and stifled a cry. Because Coia's son had been studying her with such rapacious intensity, he knew immediately that something had frightened her.

Suddenly, Don Antonio was on his feet, too, beside his son. Then the rest of the Coia men. On all four sides, the room's walls were paneled and the wooden planking covered by large Renaissance-style paintings, except for the three bay windows. Everyone's eyes were on the walls, the floor, the ceiling. On the steps that led upstairs, some of Coia's men had already moved to cover the service door in the back. They didn't even know what they were looking for, but they anticipated trouble nonetheless.

Honey watched in horror as one after another, the bosses and their bodyguards pulled weapons from waists or shoulders or ankle holsters. The room was like an armed camp, the participants of the meeting ready for a war, despite the ostentatious formality of their attire and the civility of their behavior up until now.

Furiously, Littlejohn tapped his cane, vainly begging the group to come to order. His efforts were wasted, as the room slowly dissolved into chaos.

Before Honey even realized it, Joe-Joey was getting her to her feet and protectively backing her away from any line of fire through the windows. In minutes, several Presto soldiers took up positions around the perimeter of the room, poised to repel any actions by the Coias or the other bosses.

The image in the window that had first attracted Honey's attention was gone now. Littlejohn saw that everyone's attention was focused in that direction. *Something was going wrong.* His signal to Whitey would be the opening of one of those windows. After that, he would only have a minute to escape from the restaurant himself before Whitey detonated the charges. He'd have to do it now, Littlejohn told himself.

"Did something over here frighten Miss Honoria?" Littlejohn asked, as he headed for the windows, moving as quickly as he could on his bad leg, using the cane for support. *Now—he'd have to open it now.*

Littlejohn's hand was on the window, but Joe-Joey placed a strong arm around his waist and dragged him back to the center of the crowded room. Littlejohn eyed him, terrified.

"Grab that waiter," Joe-Joey barked to one of his men.

The waiter was brought before him. "What's outside there?" he demanded.

After hesitating, his mouth so dry from fear that he almost couldn't speak, the waiter stammered, "Nothing. It just runs off to the cliff. Over to the side there's a garage and some maintenance buildings, that's all. Nothing's out there except the expressway."

They released the waiter.

"Is this a setup or what?" Coia's eldest son screamed.

"We're gonna find out," Joe-Joey told him, slamming Littlejohn down into a chair. Then he asked Honey, "What's wrong? What did you see?"

This time Honey moved to the window and peered across the snowy grass into the twilight as it merged with a faraway horizon. She thought she saw a figure running off into the distance toward the woods beyond the restaurant, but she couldn't be sure. She did know one thing, however. She'd never forget that face.

Turning on her heel, Honey marched back to the big table where Littlejohn was sitting with Joe-Joey hovering over him. The lawyer looked calmer now—Honey assumed he was collecting his thoughts, confident that he could talk his way out of anything.

She had the same small, beaded purse with her that she had been carrying the night of her father's murder. She put the purse down on the table, clicked it opened, and withdrew a small photograph. Nikolai Butkova.

Very carefully, she watched Littlejohn for his reaction, but the lawyer was a master of restraint, betraying no emotion at all.

Joe-Joey seized the picture, looked at it once, then threw it down on the table.

"What's with the picture?" Coia's other son asked suspiciously.

Honey didn't back down from him. "I think Mr. Littlejohn has to tell us that," she said, her voice suddenly turning harsh.

Littlejohn began shaking his head, muttering to himself. Joe-Joey poked him in the shoulder viciously, and the lawyer quieted down.

"A man died making sure that we got to see this picture," Honey began. "He was a friend of Driscoll's." She addressed the Coias and the other bosses. "You don't know Driscoll. My Family does. He's a cop." They started to protest, but she ignored them and went on, "Nobody knew it, but I took this picture with me from Harry Capri's place. He was the man who died. I took it because I was sure I knew that face from somewhere. But I couldn't place it. I was just too upset over everything that had happened."

Joe-Joey started to interrupt, but she stilled him. "Now I remember," Honey announced, walking directly over to Littlejohn and facing him. "I saw this man with *you.*" Honey threw the photograph at Littlejohn. "It was the Flower Show at Rittenhouse Square. Crowded. Jammed with people. Very open, very public. A great place to meet someone and pretend you were bumping into him by accident. You didn't see me that day, Mr. Littlejohn. I almost went up to you and spoke to you, but I couldn't get over to where you were fast enough. You left as soon as you had finished talking to that man. But it was him, all right, and I just saw him outside this window a few minutes ago. I'm positive. And all I know is that Harry Capri died trying to tell his friend Driscoll that this man had something to do with my father's murder. Now, you'd better tell me."

Littlejohn didn't open his mouth. He kept watching the window.

Joe-Joey eased himself between Honey and the lawyer.

"That's the Russian bastard I tried to burn out up in Brighton Beach," Joe-Joey told Honey. "You said you saw him with *him?*" He pointed to Butkova's photo.

"What *did* you do?" Honey shrieked at Littlejohn. "Did *you* have my father killed?"

Butkova had made his way around to the sheer side of the palisades where the restaurant crowned the steep hills above the expressway. In the darkness he had believed that he could observe them undetected—this great sit-down of the Mafia bosses. He had to see this gathering once, before they all died. He knew that he could hear little, but at least he could watch them. It would be like seeing the Headman's Council of Elders of the Malina—witnessing an ancient senate in session. Butkova had to see it.

At first, Littlejohn had seemed to be conducting some sort of after-dinner discussion, with the others listening attentively. Then, abruptly, the meeting had broken up with everyone gathering around the Presto girl, who had begun screaming and pointing in his direction at the window. She had seen his face, recognized him. He knew it.

The room quickly became a confused bedlam of swirling forms, raised weapons, and tables and chairs being knocked over. The last thing he had seen was Littlejohn being pulled away from the window.

Somehow, the Prestos had found out about the plan.

He had to let Whitey know. Butkova began to stumble through the darkness.

•

Driscoll ran up the driveway toward the restaurant, slipping, almost falling. It had been impossible for Carney's helicopter to land in the restaurant parking lot because of the Coia craft already there. So the pilot had put them down as close as he could, positioning his cyclic pitch stick as steadily as he could as the big twin-rotor helicopter lunged sideways with vibrating dizziness. Driscoll had plunged out first, followed by Tanya and her son. Then the pilot had risen in a vertical arc, kicking up papers and debris, before disappearing into the winter sky. A miniature tornado had descended on them, almost bowling over Tanya and the boy.

"That kid could get killed out here," Driscoll screamed behind him, toward Tanya.

"He'll be safe with me," she bellowed back. The chopper's noise finally died in the distance. "The boy must come. He has to meet his father."

Driscoll gave up on her as he encountered the first swarm of Presto men surrounding him from the barricaded parking-lot entrance. Suddenly, several guns were pointed at the cop.

Driscoll knew the first man, and the recognition was instant and mutual.

"What the hell is this, Driscoll? A raid?" he shouted.

Without waiting to answer, the detective flipped his badge out so that it was visible over the lapel of his coat and grabbed the Presto soldier's weapon out of his hand. Then he pushed past him and turned around to see what had happened to Tanya and the kid, but both of them were gone.

For one long moment, Driscoll stood there alone, against half a dozen of Joe-Joey's men. No one had put his gun away yet. He took one step forward and heard a trigger being cocked.

"In about two seconds that restaurant's gonna blow up and everybody with it," Driscoll said to the hood he had recognized. "You can come with me or you can get shot." The detective pointed his weapon at the man's forehead. *"Move!"*

They let him pass, and he took off at a run.

With everyone still crowded around him in the restaurant, Littlejohn appeared to be gasping for air. Joe-Joey had several of his men beside him now. He reached for one of the kitchen knives that had been dropped to the floor by the escaping staff.

Joe-Joey spread Littlejohn's outstretched palm on a ruined tablecloth, then stunned and frightened Honey and his own people by arcing the blade down with a vicious thrust and pinning the hand to the tabletop, penetrating flesh and bone. A thick, ugly rivulet of blood trailed away from Littlejohn's hand. A few of the Coia soldiers even remained to watch. One of them whispered loudly, "He's just like the fuckin' Meatman." There was genuine awe in his voice. Joe-Joey paid no attention to it.

"Talk!" Joe-Joey screamed at the lawyer. "You're gonna die anyway."

The old man, still clutching the duck's-head cane with his free hand, looked to Honey Presto for help, for mercy. He found none as his screams of agony and pain filled the private dining room.

"Why?" Honey hissed. "The Meatman was so good to you . . . so good to all of us."

Littlejohn was coughing badly now, gagging on his own phlegm. 'Honoria," he implored. "I beg you . . . have pity . . . my hand . . . the pain . . . please, Miss Honoria." Littlejohn shrieked again, his suffering acute.

She was numb, angry. Rage had transformed Honey into a person she did not know. Just reacting, not even thinking, Honey leaned over and grabbed the hilt of the knife, but instead of pulling it out, instead of freeing Littlejohn's bloody, contorted hand, she merely twisted the blade cruelly. Littlejohn began weeping and gagging as he spoke. Honey Presto, the Meatman's daughter, refused to release the knife hilt.

"The money . . . I did it for the money . . ." Littlejohn stammered. "Your father was planning to get rid of me; he'd come to distrust me. I couldn't let that happen."

"You traitor!" she screamed, attempting to strangle the old man. This time, Joe-Joey gently pulled her away.

"Butkova?" Joe-Joey demanded. "You went to him. Why?"

"The guns." Littlejohn was on his knees, holding on to the side of the table, tipping it. The blood pouring from the hideous gash in his hand had worked itself all the way up his forearm. "I learned about this Malina through the gun-running your father did for Carney and Bellows. I even helped him buy some of the weapons—then we found out about Butkova. Your father was trying to lure him into a trap, kill him, be done with the Malina once and for all. But they found out about it and sent a man—a *Spetsnaz*—to kill your father. But even the *Spetsnaz* was no match for him. That was the body in the freezer." He looked to her again, pleadingly. "Miss Honoria . . . on your father's soul . . . take this knife out of my hand." The lawyer's wailing bore witness to the ugly torture he was enduring.

"Go on," Honey answered coldly. "Then what?"

"I sought out this Butkova . . . convinced him . . ." He tried to avoid Honey's relentless gaze. "Convinced him that Paul Presto . . . and you . . . had to die, that he could kill all the old leaders of the Mafia if he followed my plan. When we took control of what was left of the Families together . . . everything would be ours . . . just the two of us. But somehow, your aunt and uncle found out and demanded that I cut them in. . . . Honoria, *they* were the ones who really wanted you dead . . . more than *I* . . . at my very first opportunity, I had Joe-Joey and his men come with me to the shore house and *kill* them. I swear, Miss Honoria, somehow I would have seen that no harm came to you, *believe* me . . ."

"Liar!" Joe-Joey said. "You planned to kill Honey all along—you and the Russians and Butkova."

"No!" Littlejohn protested. "No! . . . Honoria . . . it was Tony and Marie. I know my life is over now . . . Butkova insisted that you be killed . . . he wanted no trace of the Presto line . . . but, don't you see? . . . That was how I could have saved you . . . Marie told me before she died . . . she told me about you . . . that would have saved you . . . ."

Honey was suddenly very unsure of herself. What was Littlejohn talking about? What had Marie told him about her? What secret? "You can't be lying now," she said. "Because you are going to die. Now, tell me what my aunt knew. Tell me!"

But Honey's last words were drowned out by the blast of a gun as Joe-Joey yanked Littlejohn back and fired a single round into his heart. There was a dire look of concern and relief on his face.

"Why did you do that?" Honey implored. "Why? Joe-Joey, why didn't you let him talk?"

"We heard all we need to know," the new boss said, looking at the open-mouthed faces in the sea of Presto and Coia soldiers. "Now the Meatman has been avenged."

"Joe-Joey?" Honey still couldn't understand why he had silenced the old lawyer.

"Butkova! We have to find him!" Joe-Joey ran out to look for the Russian, and Honey knew that it would do no good to try to stop him.

Using his infrared field glasses, Whitey had seen enough to give him an idea of what was going on—he had seen the

Presto men pulling Littlejohn away from the window, the commotion inside the room, Butkova attempting to make his way through the darkness and over the unfamiliar ground after someone had apparently recognized him. His plan was beginning to unravel.

Too many men had been crowded near the steps that led up from the downstairs meeting room to the main level of the restaurant—the Prestos had rented the entire place for the evening, so there was no one anywhere in the building or on the grounds except Family associates and restaurant staff. But as soon as Joe-Joey had shot Littlejohn, the sit-down room had begun emptying in a sloppy, rushed evacuation, so Joe-Joey knew that it would be almost impossible to bull his way through the crowd at the staircase.

He had to get out and get his hands on that Russian, Butkova. There was no time to lose. Honey was a worry, too. Littlejohn had set up this meeting—which meant that it had to be a trap. They had to get out of there as fast as they could.

Sure that something awful was about to happen, Joe-Joey searched the room for another way out. Then he remembered the service entrance at the rear that opened onto the rocky, treacherous ground near the slope that plunged down toward the expressway. There was a narrow driveway back there, too, and the maintenance sheds. He could escape the confusion and the crowd that way, get some of his men to watch Honey, then go looking for Butkova. But he realized that other people had the same idea. A small throng was surging toward that door also.

The Coias and the Prestos were beginning to scream at each other now, with big, beefy men pushing and shoving and trampling anyone near them in their panic. There were curses and threats and too many unholstered weapons.

"Stay right next to me," Joe-Joey told Honey as he grabbed the metal handle of a wheeled dessert cart, angled it around in front of him, and began using it like a battering ram to clear a path toward the lower-level service door, off a smaller room behind the bar. As he drove the cart ahead of him, cakes and pies and gooey desserts squashed on the floor, but Joe-Joey and Honey pushed through. His wedge was working; he banged into backs and sides and hips, anyone in his path. A few turned to stare at him, screaming, angry, but Joe-Joey just kept going until he was close enough to the doorway to shove Honey out into the darkness. Joe-Joey followed her, cutting in front of an enormously fat Coia capo who had attempted to used his bulk to block out Joe-Joey. But the smaller Joe-Joey was much too fast for him, and he made it out onto the cold surface of the driveway to find Honey waiting for him, just a few yards away.

"Over here," Honey called to him. "I'm over here. *Joe-Joey!*"

He turned, and had started in that direction when suddenly a belching bubble of fire and flame and death blinded him. The new boss of the Prestos was rocketed into the air and thrown forward by the concussion of the blast. Within seconds of actually being airborne, Joe-Joey landed on his ankle with a painful thud.

Whitey had waited to see if Butkova had gotten clear—but he could delay no longer.

It was like that first night at Presto's house; the snow had swirled itself into a thick coating of frosty white. Shivering, Whitey gave in to the left-cheek twitch completely and flipped the three small control switches on his lap. One after the other. The sound of the dynamite echoed across the still valley.

Before he even reached the front of the restaurant, a swarm of men pushed out the door and bolted past Driscoll. There were so many of them he had to pull up and wait. The Presto soldiers, who he had encountered back at the parking-lot driveway, had been chasing after him, but they too found themselves trying to move against an irresistible force of escaping beef and muscle.

What was going on? What about Honey? He hadn't even had a chance to look for her when the explosion from Whitey's detonation jetted from the back of the restaurant to the front, hurling the men on the threshold of the building, as well as Driscoll and those standing near him, across the parking lot with tremendous force.

A small grassy lawn in front of the structure was now covered with bodies of those who had failed to escape in time. One man's clothes were on fire, and he was rolling in crazy circles of pain trying to extinguish himself; one of the Presto men who had been farthest from the explosion threw his coat around the burning victim, trying to smother the flames.

The force of the blast had been confined to the back of the building, some basement-level meeting room. Now the fire was funneling upward and outward, devouring everything in its path. Anyone who had been trapped in the meeting room itself had to be dead by now.

People were rushing past Driscoll, bumping into one another, confused, desperate. The fire was burning all along the upper story of the restaurant now and was threatening to jump to the tall bare trees that surrounded the parking lot.

Somewhere Driscoll heard sirens. Fire engines? Police? Were Lawlor's men finally showing up?

A phalanx of bodyguards was shoving its way through the parking lot outside the restaurant and cutting a path through the milling, escaping figures toward the Coia helicopter. The chopper was still on the ground, its outline illuminated by the rough circle of burning flares that had guided it down. Suddenly the screeching rotor came to life, and Driscoll realized that the craft was preparing to take off.

Driscoll looked back at the phalanx, and there was Don Antonio Coia himself, shielded on all sides by his men, coughing from the smoke, bewildered and frightened, but still very much alive.

The Coias were no more than twenty yards from the helicopter when one of the last of the tall power lines still standing overhead outside the restaurant suddenly snapped from the intense heat. As it fell, sizzling and sputtering, like an enormous Fourth of July sparkler, the live electrical wire made contact with the whirling rotors of the helicopter, encircling the metal blades like a tentacle. Instantly, the airship became a fireball, and Driscoll found himself still on the icy ground of the parking lot, caught between the blazing restaurant in front of him and the helicopter behind him. The flames hadn't reached him yet, but he knew he had to move quickly.

Shielding his eyes against this new inferno, the detective looked around and noticed that the phalanx had scattered—every man for himself. Old man Coia and his two sons, on their hands and knees, their clothing blackened and singed, were crawling away from the burning chopper. The sons were tugging at their father like children pulling a sled. The boss of bosses was moving as slowly as a capsized turtle, but he was moving.

Then he heard it—his own name. She was calling him.

"Phillip, Phillip!"

Running in the darkness, falling snow clinging to her thick, curly hair, Honey Presto was repeating his name over and over again, her arms reaching out to him. In the tumult and disorder of the massacre, they had somehow found each other.

He saw Joe-Joey behind her, limping, dragging an obviously injured ankle. They were both alive. He couldn't believe it. He could see them clearly now, coming along the curving driveway beside the restaurant. The flame-filled sky seemed as bright as daylight. Struggling to his feet, not even sure if he had been injured by the blast, Driscoll ran toward her.

She kept approaching him, as if in a dream—gliding, seeming to move inches above the surface of the ground, the acute intensity of her need for him propelling her. The flames were casting her face in a reddish, fiery glow.

But Honey was dangerously close to the flaming restaurant. Before the explosion, it had been a huge, rambling, two-story country inn; the lower-level room where the sit-down had taken place had been a modern addition. Now Driscoll eyed what was left of the upper stories nervously—the whole wall, both stories, and the roof on top of it could come crashing down any second; because of all the kitchen supplies stored in the restaurant, additional blasts were still possible.

The sirens were closing in on the complex now, growing louder. Driscoll screamed for Honey to be careful, to give the burning building a wide berth. "Honey . . . be careful . . . the fire . . ."

But the girl didn't seem to hear him. She was answering him, yet ignoring his warnings. "Phillip!" he heard her call to him. "We're all right, both of us. Joe-Joey got out in time too. Oh, Phillip!" She was reaching for him again, her arms extended, ten feet away, no more. Even in the cold, Honey's face shone from the terrific heat of the blaze. Joe-Joey was waving to him, too.

Then, like the appearance of a nightmarish apparition in his dream, Driscoll watched, horrified, as Joe-Joey suddenly fell to the ground behind her. But Honey didn't turn around; she didn't realize what was taking place—who was rapidly closing in on her. The only sight she could see was Phillip Driscoll.

Whitey had clubbed Joe-Joey from behind with the butt of his gun. After the initial explosion he had watched to see which ones had escaped from his ambush. As soon as he had seen Joe-Joey shove the Presto girl to safety, Whitey had leaped into action, abandoning his shed hiding place and following after the girl and the new Presto boss. But both had moved so quickly, despite the man's injury, that it had been all that Whitey could do to catch up with them, racing across the acreage behind the restaurant and finally catching up with them as they turned the corner of the burning building, where the Presto girl was desperately searching for someone. Who?

No sooner had Whitey blind-sided Joe-Joey, knocking him down with effortless brutality, than he spied the man Honey was looking for. Whitey kept staring, trying to discern that face, that thick muscular body in the darkness. Then a tongue of flame erupted so high in the sky that it appeared to lick the stars, and Whitey recognized Driscoll's face in the eerie, incendiary illumination.

Driscoll. The same cop he had confronted in the Fat Man's place. Whitey had promised himself that he would always remember that face.

The cop had immediately realized what was happening. He lunged, leaping the last few feet, in an attempt to pull Honey away from Whitey, who was so close that he could practically touch her now.

But the cop was still too far away; the blistering heat created by the inferno of the restaurant was too much for him. Whitey, so much taller, his strides so much longer, got to the girl first. He yanked her from behind, snapped her head backward, and looped a thick arm around her neck. Whitey's elbow and forearm crushed her breasts against her chest. Honey never even had a chance to turn around and look back at him. With his other hand, Whitey placed the muzzle of his gun against her right temple, the metal point digging painfully into her soft skin. For a moment, all three of them were motionless. Then Whitey very slowly began easing Honey backward, while walking backward himself. Unflinching, Driscoll stood his ground. Honey's terror-struck expression was calling to him.

Whitey could have killed the cop here and now. He had seen him with the Presto girl before, and now, the way that she kept calling out to him, Whitey could see that there was something very powerful between them.

Driscoll didn't move.

Whitey suddenly sensed the tremendous power he held over these two. It would be so simple to snap the girl's neck and kill this cop—but a compelling feeling of his own superiority stopped him. Whitey was really enjoying this—watching this damp cop squirm, helpless. Driscoll's impotence in this situation was beginning to bring Whitey's own tumescence to life. The girl struggling against him helped, too. How he wished that he could have somehow taken the girl long before—taken her and used her. Whitey would have enjoyed that.

A crazy, desperate thought came into his head. Maybe he still could. If he could just get Honey away with him. There might still be time to have her.

Just then, through the smoke and flame, Whitey realized that Driscoll was coming for him.

* * *

Nikolai Butkova stood, gaunt, tired, and battered, in the clearing in which he had first met Whitey. His men of the Malina were scattered—dispersed in the trees and darkness of the woods, fleeing themselves now, from the police who had arrived as well as from the Coia and Presto soldiers.

Some of the old ones, the *commissione* members, had been killed. But not enough. Not Antonio Coia—Butkova had seen the old man's sons rescue him and hustle him away through the shooting and the fire.

Whitey's plan had been brilliant—it had *almost* worked. But in the end, the bosses had escaped, survived. Butkova would have to fight another day.

How had it all gone so wrong?

Suddenly, he heard rustling, movement in the trees behind him. Gun in hand, Butkova turned to his face his attacker.

"Tanya!" he exclaimed upon seeing the woman. "What are you doing here? It isn't safe."

Then, he saw the little boy—a handsome boy who had a very unsettling effect on Butkova—peeking out from behind his mother's skirts. "This child," he said. "Why do you bring him here? I thought you were taking care of Zhukov and Carney."

Tanya too seemed exhausted. But at long last, her time had finally come.

"I took care of both of them, Nikolai," she said, approaching him. Smoke from the fire drifted up to them, enveloping them like a malevolent mist. "You should be very pleased."

"I . . . I am, Tanya . . . but the little boy . . . where did he come from?"

Now, free of the skirts, the child was standing on his own two legs, a little apart from his mother. "Look at him, Nikolai. Look closely. Who do you see, in his eyes? Hard eyes for such a beautiful child, wouldn't you say?"

Butkova touched the boy's cheek, tilted his small face up so he could look. "You, Tanya," he answered. "I see that this child must be your son. God bless him."

Drawing the boy to her side, she kissed him and stroked his hair. "Who else? The father, perhaps?"

As Butkova came close again, the boy bristled. "Don't be afraid of your own father," Tanya cautioned him.

"Father?"

"Say hello to your son," she said, "and goodbye."

"What? . . . I thought he was Zhukov's."

"Zhukov could father no children," she said savagely. "Most of the time he was impotent. Not really a man at all—not like you, Nikolai."

He smiled—a strange, accepting sort of look. "How could he be mine? When?"

"After our first time together. *Surely* you remember. I didn't see you for more than a year after that. He is why—I was having *our* baby, Nikolai."

"But Zhukov?"

"He came later."

"The child . . . ?" He went to take his hand, but the boy pulled back. "Who cared for him?"

"He is a Malina child, Nikolai. You know what that means."

He began shaking his head, "No . . . no . . . don't tell me that you have given them my only son."

"It's true."

"What now?"

"I have a message from the Headman, the one you were so concerned about. The human chain did not fail."

"Yes?" Butkova asked expectantly.

"A few minutes ago I told you to say hello and goodbye to your son."

"I just thought you meant to keep him for yourself."

"Oh, I do, indeed. The child will always be mine—I am his mother."

Now, as he saw the look on her face, Butkova understood.

"Greetings from the Headman and the Council of Elders," Tanya began, carefully repeating each word of the ancient, immutable Malina sentence of death. Obediently, Nikolai Butkova, the fierce warrior of Siberia, bowed his head.

"Because you have violated the ancient convenant, the Brotherhood of the Catacombs, the Order of the Sacred Cup of the Twelve, because you have done all this, Nikolai, because you, ambitious and selfish, have acted without even waiting for the decision of the elders, of the Headman, the sentence must be death."

"Why?" His eyes were pleading for some explanation, even as he reached into his coat pocket for his own gun. But the little boy spotted the almost imperceptible movement of his father's arm and screamed to his mother. She fired first.

"Know the Malina. Fear it," Tanya said.

The boy began to cry. "Don't," Tanya said gently, trying to take the fear out of the child. She turned his small face away from the dead body of his father. "That man *was* your father—but the great Headman is the father of us all, and you know that he loves you."

The little boy wrinkled his nose and put his face in her skirts again. "All this is *yours* now," she said. *"Ours."*

The boy looked as though he didn't quite understand.

"Now, the Headman says that *we* rule the Malina in America for him—until you are old enough to rule it on your own. Until that time, I will help you. By then, living here, you will be a thorough American—a *Yankee.*" Tanya laughed as she mispronounced the word.

"For now, the Malina remains secret—no more war on this Mafia. We will fight it again and conquer it. But the time is not yet right. Like the tiger in the grass we bide our time, patiently, waiting until the Headman calls us. The human chain will advise us."

"Mommy," he started to say, then, changing his mind, he said, "Mommy, I'm so sleepy. Can we go home now?"

"Of course, darling," Tanya said. Then she bundled him up in her arms and carried him to her waiting car. Tanya knew it would be there; she had made the arrangements the night before. The girl Svetlana, the dancer from Butkova's club, was behind the wheel. Tanya settled the boy in the rear seat under a blanket, then slid in beside Svetlana; as she did so she made sure that her hand brushed against the dancer's large, soft breast. Putting the gun on the dashboard, Tanya leaned over and kissed the dancer on her lips. Svetlana smiled to herself, the comely smile of a woman who knows that she is loved. Then Tanya squeezed her hand.

Driscoll knew, too. He understood now; recognized Whitey from that time at Manny's. And the cop hated himself for not taking him out then and there, for not linking the description of the killer called in by the highway patrolmen, just before they died, with the strange sullen white-haired creep he had encountered that night on Noble Street. So much killing could have been avoided.

He watched helplessly as Whitey inched Honey backward, closer and closer to the burning restaurant. He saw her struggling to free herself, trying to escape from this killer's iron grip—looking to him, to Driscoll, to her lover, for rescue—and as focused as he was on what was taking place, suddenly all that Driscoll could think of was how sloppy he had been that night. Sloppy. Again! Just like with Manny. He should have put two and two together; *sloppy*. And this time Honey might have to pay with her life.

Driscoll saw that Honey was holding her body taut against Whitey's. He was dragging her on her heels, on the backs of her heels. Where? Close to the fire, but even Whitey wasn't crazy enough to try to go back in there. There would be no escape. Where was he taking her?

The cop moved out slowly, his hands trembling. But it wasn't fear—it was a rage such as he had never known. He wanted to kill Whitey—kill him as quickly as he could.

The gun that he had taken from the Presto hood had been knocked out of his hand when the restaurant had first exploded. The cop was unarmed. But he was almost on top of Joe-Joey's unconscious body. Without ever taking his eyes off Whitey and Honey, who were moving steadily closer to the flame-engulfed walls, already beginning to totter and pitch in the artificial wind that the blaze was creating, Driscoll lightly dropped to one knee and took the gun out of the small brown leather holster that he remembered from past encounters that Joe-Joey always kept strapped to his left ankle. The gun was there. As Whitey watched his every movement, Driscoll began closing in on the killer.

Whitey *did* have an escape route in mind. He guessed that he would never be able to get back to his jeep, still concealed in the woods. The cops would be all over there, maybe the Prestos, too. But there was a way. And Whitey knew that he was the only one skilled enough to possibly attempt it. The cliff. That was the only way. Whitey knew that none of them, not even Driscoll, would ever be able to climb down after him. The wall of rock was too sheer, too treacherous. But Whitey knew that he could do it. He had free-climbed down steeper mountains than that before. Then they would never be able to follow him. Once he was down, on the expressway at the base of the cliff, he would commandeer a car and get away. It was risky; it would require a long, cold, quick descent down the face of the cliff—but Whitey had enough confidence in himself to know that he could do it. Then he would really get away—to the sea, the warmth of a beach, to the sun. Escape. Just as he had planned to do after he had killed the Meatman. Finally he could escape this damnable cold.

But first Whitey had to take care of this girl once and for all. He was going to kill her now, at last; destroy the daughter as he had destroyed the father. It would represent another contract fulfilled. And the very thought of it excited him, aroused him as no woman every could. Whitey was beginning to feel it even now; he sensed his erection, huge, hardening against Honey Presto's small back as he clutched her to him, pressing powerfully against her spine. She was whimpering, digging her fingernails into his flesh.

Whitey was almost there. Almost at the beginning of the steep cliff face. He just had to make his way past the final obstacle, the rear wall of the restaurant, what remained of it, burning into the black night. By this time, the structure had been incinerated into little more than a skeleton of what it was.

Break her neck and throw her into the flames—then escape. It was going to be so easy. Whitey knew that Driscoll had picked up Joe-Joey's gun, but it didn't matter, not as long as he had the girl as a hostage. No cop, especially not this one, would ever risk taking a shot like that and killing the hostage by accident. Whitey held Honey in front of his own body, a living shield. No marksman could execute such a shot.

Whitey tightened his choke hold; he was nearly ready.

Driscoll could never make that shot. It was no use even trying. It was dark to begin with, and the flames from the fire were distorting his vision. There had to be another way—another way to save Honey. But there *was* no other way.

Whitey was just a few yards from him. Honey struggled to call out to him. "Phillip!" She sounded so afraid—it was almost as though she were saying goodbye. Whitey pulled her head back again, but she managed to pantomime something to Driscoll. *What was she saying?*

Whitey was heading for the cliff, and Driscoll knew it. He also realized that he wouldn't be taking Honey with him. That meant he had to kill her now.

They were on the side of the restaurant where the first explosion had taken place—most of a stone wall was all that remained, the rest consumed in a hideous, superheated blanket of solid red-orange flames. The wooden interior of the building, gutted, turned into scorched kindling for the firestorm, breathed out the hoarse fire jets of a giant blowtorch. The thick smoke had become a deadly, choking fog. Even the air the cop sucked in was singed by heat, tasting of embers.

Driscoll sensed that this was the moment. Whitey was going to kill Honey and shove her into those flames just before he vanished over the palisade wall.

He had to risk it—had to try a desperate shot. Driscoll raised the gun, aimed his sights on Whitey's head—bobbing, weaving, allowing him practically no target at all—and started to squeeze the trigger.

The gun fired. Driscoll *was* a lousy shot—the bullet whizzed harmlessly into the night, missing them both. But, as it did so, Honey screamed an anguished, penetrating wail. Momentarily, Whitey loosened his grasp.

Driscoll looked up, in the direction of the remaining rear wall of the big building. The whole thing was coming down, crashing toward Honey and her captor with a sickening sound of timber beams and granite falling.

Whitey had never expected the cop to shoot. Driscoll had missed, of course, but he had gambled, and that was an unnerving contradiction to Whitey. Driscoll had put everything on the line to get him. What else was this determined cop capable of? He'd have to kill him immediately before he tried something else unexpected. Whitey aimed, allowing Honey to squirm away—she was struggling so much that she was ruining his concentration.

She ran in the direction of the cop. No matter. He could easily kill them both from here. Whitey's left cheek was twitching more uncontrollably than ever. But at least the fire at his back was warming him, calming him.

Honey had just managed to clear the spot on the ground where the collapsing restaurant wall hit, landing around her and the white-haired killer, as Whitey's bullet sailed over her head. She looked back, sure that he wouldn't miss again, afraid that the bullet might have hit Driscoll.

But he was no longer there. Whitey had disappeared under the flames and rubble of the fallen wall. There would be no more bullets. The flames had immolated him.

All at once, Driscoll was holding her, kissing her neck, lifting her into his strong arms, carrying Honey to safety.

Whitey died almost instantly. The weight of the wall, the fire, the insatiable flames ignited his clothing, his white hair, his flesh and bones; at the last, in that final, all-knowing, desperately clear moment before death, in that fleeting, evaporating flash of eternity, Whitey was no longer cold. Completely enflamed, beyond pain, past the threshold of feeling itself, Whitey finally knew warmth.

EPILOGUE

LENIN'S HALL OF HEROES, THE KREMLIN THURSDAY NIGHT, NEW YEAR'S EVE

A simple handwritten note from the Chairman of the Politburo and General Secretary of the Communist Party had requested Zinijakin's presence at a diplomatic gala in Lenin's Hall of Heroes—the football-field-sized multipurpose auditorium that hosted most of the larger public gatherings. The event was a New Year's Eve party to which most of the embassy community in Moscow had been invited. Obsessed with flaunting his knowledge of all things Western, the Chairman had even commissioned one of the huge cakes to be decorated with a miniature replica of the descending ball on Times Square—accurate to the last detail and powered by tiny transistors.

The party would continue until well past midnight. Zinijakin had hours to kill, waiting for the nod and the quick wave of the hand that he knew would eventually come from the Chairman and for the arrival of the last link in the Malina's human chain. He would not know for certain—for dead certain—about developments in the United States until the courier contacted him. In fact, Zinijakin did not even know who this Malina messenger would be, because the process had been started on the Philadelphia end. He was the brotherhood's Headman with a term of office that would last until the day of his death, but there were still mysteries in the international organization that continued to escape even him. Chief among them was the identity and extent of the Malina's American network. That had been Butkova's responsibility.

He looked up at the wall clock. Still hours to go.

STONE HARBOR

Trying not to make a sound, Driscoll closed the bedroom door. It was the same bedroom where he and Honey had made love, in her father's summer home. On tiptoe, he walked into the living room, where he had already started a fire. She was still asleep.

Driscoll reached inside his topcoat pocket and took out the second tape that he had taken from Paul Presto's basement hiding place. He had waited until now to look at it. Manny had refused to actually tell him what the trouble had been between Paul Presto and himself, but an idea had already formed in the detective's mind.

Adjusting the VCR, Driscoll placed the tape in the rectangular mouth of the device, twisted the volume button down so low that it would be audible only to him, then tapped the play button. He'd been waiting for this a long time. Just Driscoll and the Meatman.

Then he heard that familiar voice, very low this time but sounding more relaxed and, if it was possible, more lifelike than on the first tape. Presto wasn't actually directing his remarks to the detective, but somehow Driscoll *knew* he was.

"Manny, my old friend," Presto began. "We wasted a lifetime in bitterness. I knew what my Teresa was and so did you, but Honey is the one we must protect. She can never know. . . ."

For the next twenty minutes, Paul Presto, speaking directly to Manny Goldberg, revealed a long-kept secret of Honoria Maria Presto's birth.

"She seduced you to hurt me—I know that now," Presto's voice said to Manny, the man he thought was listening. "You were a handsome man then; she always flaunted you to me. Anything to make me jealous."

Driscoll was imagining the way Manny looked now—he could hardly believe what he was hearing. But there was no denying what Presto was saying.

"I couldn't give Teresa children, Manny. Maybe today it would be different . . . with the doctors, the medicine . . . but in our time you didn't even speak of such things, not even a man and wife." Driscoll could see the Meatman's hard eyes filling with an unutterable sadness.

"She never forgave me . . . refused to try to understand . . . all she knew was that it was *my* fault. It was never the same after that. We stayed together, but I'm not even sure why. Maybe . . . I don't know . . . I just kept hoping . . ."

Now the detective could finally understand. Without realizing why, Honey had always been drawn to her real father—to Manny. He listened as Presto continued; he'd checked over his shoulder a few times to make sure that Honey hadn't come out. But there wasn't a sound.

"I know it only happened once. I was away. Teresa said that you two had been betraying me behind my back for years—but I knew that was a lie. You were like my brother. I always believed you, Manny, never her. But my pride was hurt. My wife and my best friend . . ." Presto's voice trailed off. Then, as he visibly composed himself on the screen, he resumed. Driscoll was sure that never before had the Meatman revealed this much of himself.

"I let you hold your daughter—once, at the christening," Presto said. "And I told you and Teresa that if anyone ever found out, both of you would die. And I meant that—then. I was crazy with hurt; crazy with pain . . . when I lost my temper, anything was possible."

Now the detective knew why the two men had gone for so many years refusing to see each other.

"But just before she died," Presto said, "Teresa told my sister, Marie, the truth. It was just to hurt me. I found out about that, and I knew from that day on that Honey's life would never be safe, because Marie and Tony knew that she wasn't my blood. But I didn't know what to do, who to turn to. You had been my brains for so many years—but I cut you outta my life. So I found this Littlejohn and tried to use him the way I used you. But you know it wasn't the same. I never really trusted him—not like you, Manny."

Driscoll thought about Manny again, about his size. He must have eaten to forget; eaten to try to escape the guilt. He'd turned himself into the Fat Man.

"I held my grudge for a long time. I never wanted her to go near you. Told her never to see you. But I know she did. She loved you, Manny. Just like me.

"I almost told her the truth myself when she started with that cop, Driscoll. I was so mad at her. She hurt me and I woulda hurt her—just the way I tried to hurt you for so many years. But I'd learned my lesson. I held my tongue.

"You remember that, Manny—that was the only time I went to you since the day she was christened. And you remember why. I wanted you to kill Driscoll for me. To take care of it, because he was tryin' to ruin the life of the little girl we both loved.

"But you said no; that wasn't the way. Then Honoria would hate me forever, never forgive me. You said let the cop live—use the pictures we had and frame him. Make him so worried about tryin' to stay a cop that he would have to forget Honoria. And we did that—and she never went near him again, because I did tell her that if that didn't work, then I *would* have to . . ."

Presto stopped again, and Driscoll pondered the implications of what he was saying. It was hard to believe, but he had Manny and Honey to thank for even being alive. Presto *would* have killed him.

Presto was almost finishing up as he explained his slowly growing distrust of Littlejohn, and the need for the Family to find a new adviser. "That has to be you, Manny," Presto said. "Guide your daughter—*our* daughter. She needs you now more than ever, now that I'm gone. . . . And forgive me, Manny; I forgave you a long time ago.

"And I have a confession to make," Presto's voice declared. "The sadness of my Honoria's birth, the heartache, was more than I could bear alone. A long time ago, I confided it to a man who was like my son—to Joe-Joey. And I made him swear on the life of his children that he would never allow the secret to be revealed. He's a good man, Manny. Make him the boss after me. I know Honey will agree. . . ."

"She already has, Meatman," Driscoll said. "She's more your child than you even realized."

"Joe-Joey understands," Presto's voice said, "about his family and about our Family. He's the one."

Then, with a chilling certitude, Phillip Driscoll knew that Paul Presto was speaking directly to him, even as he was addressing Manny from the tape.

"That cop, Driscoll," the Meatman said, "he ain't so bad. You watch him and Honoria. You'll know what's best for them, because you love her. So will the cop. He loves her, too. I could see it. And Manny, when you see that cop—" But Meatman Presto never completed that thought, as the screen suddenly went blank.

What was he about to say? What?

"Maybe he was trying to tell you that he wouldn't have killed you after all," Honey Presto said, taking Driscoll completely by surprise. She must have heard the tape playing or awoken suddenly, because she was there with him now, in her nightgown, staring longingly at the TV screen. "He loved me too much to do that."

"You were there, heard it?" Driscoll asked, ashamed of himself for not taking better precautions to avoid Honey's finding out. But he had just been so damn anxious to see the second tape, hear what the Meatman had to say.

"Most of it," Honey answered. "The important part." She wasn't talking to Driscoll now, but to the blank screen where her father's image had so effortlessly dominated the big room.

"Did you know?"

"I always had a funny feeling whenever I was around Manny . . . like he cared for me more than my own mother. I never guessed because I never wanted to. . . . Does that make any sense?"

Driscoll nodded. He crossed the room and put his arms around her.

"I think I knew for sure when Aunt Marie and Tony . . ." She couldn't finish. "It was right in this house . . . they tried to kill us . . ."

He didn't know how to answer her.

"The tape . . . can I have it?" Honey gently freed herself from Driscoll's warm embrace and took the black box out of the VCR. "Manny has to see this. He has a right." She looked a little melancholy, but also more at peace than Driscoll had ever seen her.

Just behind the detective, the hungry flames were crackling in the hearth. "Manny will believe you," he said. "Tell him everything your father wanted him to hear. But let me take care of this." As he said that, Driscoll removed the tape from her grip, walked over to the fire, and threw it into the flames.

A brief look of alarm darkened Honey's face. She momentarily made an effort to retrieve it. He caught her by the wrist and pulled her away from the hearth. Placing his finger to her lips, Driscoll refused to allow her to speak.

"You're Honey Presto," the big detective said with finality. "You're the Meatman's daughter." She searched his eyes, ready to protest, but then Honey realized they had flickered from their steady gray to a burning almost-blue. Honey stroked his face, and he caressed hers, then she held his hand and Driscoll followed the Meatman's daughter into her bedroom.

LENIN'S HALL OF HEROES, THE KREMLIN

Marshal Zinijakin was sipping his third snifter of cognac when he looked up at the massive chandelier directly above his head. It was beginning to spin, orbiting in fascinating elliptical patterns that kept widening their arc. He shook his head, set the cognac down on a serving table next to him, and looked at the chandelier again. This time it was perfectly still. He harrumphed loudly and vowed to touch no more of the potent liquor until he had settled things with the Chairman.

He was rehearsing in his mind exactly what he would say. It wouldn't be long now. The party had extended well into the morning, almost until dawn, securing the Chairman's coup among the embassy crowd, but keeping the old marshal up well past his bedtime. Zinijakin was weary indeed, but the Chairman would never let him get away without some sort of explanation concerning Zhukov and the Americans—*and where was that infernal Malina courier from the human chain?* He should have received Tanya's confirmation by now. Without that, he would really be running a big risk if he dared tell anything. *Where was the damn courier?*

If all else failed, he could blame everything on the Malina. Zinijakin laughed out loud when he thought about that, a deep, roaring laugh.

"Is something funny, Marshal Zinijakin?" The delicate feminine voice startled him.

It was the American ambassador's wife. He hardly knew her. She was a striking woman of middle years and aristocratic bearing. Zinijakin was surprised that she was singling him out amid all the glittering celebrities of Moscow for this idle banter.

"I suppose I'm just remembering old war stories," Zinijakin replied in passably good English.

"Oh, really. That reminds me of a marvelous old story that I've heard. It concerns the price of raspberries in Odessa. Very expenseive, you know, but someone always finds a way to pay the price. . . . Good evening, Marshal Zinijakin, or should I say good morning?" Smiling coquettishly, the ambassador's wife returned to her husband's side. Just before she left, she added, "Tanya begs to assure the Headman that the will of the council has been carried out."

Zinijakin looked after her in amazement. Here he was, in his seventy-fifth year, Marshal of all the Soviet Armies, the Headman of the Council of Elders in Odessa, and still the Malina had the capacity to cause him wonderment and awe.

The Malina was forever, like the Cap of Monomakh.

The human chain had not been broken. That was the message he had been waiting for, delivered by the most unlikely courier he had ever encountered. Incredible. Nikolai Butkova had been stopped. Now Tanya and her son would secure America for the Malina—until it was time to unleash the full fury of the brotherhood.

This time, emboldened by the guarantee of success that had just been passed across the world from Tanya's lips to his ears, Marshal Zinijakin was the one who confidently sought out the Chairman.